BLUE MESA

A Fable with No Morals
by Tom Wilmot

ISBN 978-0-578-03519-2
MMIX

Printed in the United States of America.
Wax Moose Press – Denver, Colorado

For My Dad –

It takes a lot to laugh
It takes a train to cry.

Forward

The great American curmudgeon H. L. Mecken wrote the following around 90 years ago:

"[Aspiring authors] are unanimously commonplace, unanimously stupid. Free education has cursed them with aspirations beyond their congenital capacities ... they lack the primary requisite of the imaginative author; the capacity to see the human comedy afresh, to discover new significances in man's eternal struggle with his fate. ... material prosperity and popular education have made it a sort of national disease."

I imagine he'd be dying of apoplexy in the age of blogging, social networking and Twittering. It's a curious thing however in that since the time he wrote this poison bon mot, the requisite assumption regarding education has fallen by the wayside to a large extent.

What lives on, for good or ill, is the need to document and/or record things from a personal perspective. Blue Mesa is a deliberate attempt not to do that.

Having labored away at other works much deeper in thought and fraught with meaning, I came to a point where I wanted to work on something that required me to remove myself as much as possible from the equation. Comedy, combined with magical realism seemed as fine a method of reduction of the personal as anything else I could come up with.

Additionally, it allowed me to cheaply dodge a few of Mencken's complaints regarding most dilettante writers. It still may be stupid (stupidity, aside from such things as sticking one's tongue in a light socket being a judgment call) but fortunately, it's not commonplace. (Not that originality is all it's cracked up to be.) It's also up to the reader's judgment as to whether or not I've viewed the "human comedy afresh"; that again being something that's not necessarily guaranteed.

What's left is a thing based upon the premise that regardless of anything else, the true dichotomy within us all (at least us Americans) is the conflict between the need to declare our individuality and our desire to be part of the whole. This continual bounce back and forth is something that gives us both strengths and weaknesses and at the end of the day tends to leave us where we were when we woke up that morning, but having had a good share of internal adventures along the way.

The best thing about the "continual bounce" is that we discover the contradictions in our own nature nearly every day. Given time, a rapidly diminishing commodity, we can learn a few things about our own nature in the mere act of living.

Writers tend to want to broadcast these revelations.

I think it's impossible to completely avoid infusing writing with one's personal revelations on how life works, but you can at least bury them deep enough within the story that the reader can come to their own conclusions regarding the message of the tale. Hopefully, it's the respect that the author owes the audience. A number of transitory issues weave themselves into and out of this story; the downside of contemporary novels tend to be the proliferation of contemporary issues that a number of years later seem as archaic as bodkins and buttonhooks; but they reflect constants in the human condition regarding how we define and express ourselves within the context of societal flux.

Gee whiz, that was a bit more pontificatory than I'd really wanted to be.

Breaking it back down to basics, if this forward serves any purpose, it would be to explain WHY I wrote this book. Primarily, it was written to give the reader a chance to look at his or herself through a funhouse mirror – to find the shared meaning they have with each character in the book. Just as characters tend to reflect aspects of the writer, hopefully, these same characters will reflect aspects of the reader – tipped sideways and wearing funny hats, but still relevant to the person reading about them.

Or it could just be about the laughs.

Tom Wilmot - July 7, 2009

Acknowledgements

I'd like to start off by thanking Flo Cameron. While she wasn't part of the feedback team for this book, she's been quite encouraging over the years, a great ear to bounce ideas off of and a real gem of a pal when it comes to being supportive. Additionally, she's got a wickedly funny novel that just needs some shaping and elbow grease before it takes the world by storm. If you've enjoyed Blue Mesa and are reading this strictly because you're wondering if I have any other jokes to tuck in here, send me emails instead at tomwilmot@earthlink.net with the subject line "Hey Flo! Finish your damned book!" and I will forward them on.

If anyone derserves as much credit in actually seeing this novel metamorphose into something more than a collection of notes, it would be the Sage of Saint Cloud Street, Ted Mabus. He read chapters as I cranked them out, consistently berated me for not infusing more muscle into the prose, discussed meter, pace, scan and arc endlessly and wielded red pens like scalpels – deftly, surely and with as little blood loss as possible. His own prose is something to envy and aspire to. Hopefully, the project he's involved in currently will see the light of day before too much longer – it's buffalo meat, friends. Lean and lacking fat, but incredibly rich and savory.

Both of the above mentioned people can actually refer to themselves as "professional writers" and their insights into publishing, agents, book sales and marketing convinced me I would never get a legitimate press to handle this novel. As a result, it hung around in draft form forever and a day.

Herein enters the Canadian bureaucrat and the Wet Coast musician.

If you are fortunate in life, at some point you will meet a person who is too self-effacing to grasp how terrific they are. Oscar Jacobs, the brilliant Canerdian is just such a fellow. Aside from a mystifying love of the Doors and a penchant for groan inducing puns, I have met few folks in life who are both stunningly deep thinkers and effervescent optimists. Oscar is one such person. If I was "targeting a demographic", I'd have to say, he's the audience I was gunning for. The shorthand here is, after the first draft had been sitting around for a year or so, I sent a manuscript off to him and his positive feedback was the stimulus for rolling up my sleeves and saying, "okay, let's try her again".

Then we come to Paul Ellis, a truly magical song crafter. The fact that he creates stunning gems in both the so-called "new age" venue (handy tip – go on to CDBABY.com and order a copy of "PAUL ELLIS: The Sacred Ordinary" as well as "POP ARCHEOLOGY TRANSMISSION: It Is What It Is") and re-vamped popcraft. Paul is a living testament to that old saw, "true genius doesn't always get it's due". Here's a fellow that is creating some of the most luxurious and sonically rich sound knocking around the world today and he has to have a real day-job. While his electronic stuff is handled by a German or Dutch (sorry Paul, you know, I really AM brain damaged) label, the pop stuff is self published and distributed through outfits like CDBaby and Not Lame. His enthusiasm for the second draft was the impetus for the third go round and final polish.

To all of you, thank you so much. Support is one thing, but even if I were working on re-painting a bathroom, friends like these make any endeavor a marvelous adventure.

Table of Contents

Chapter One -

In which we come to Mesa Azul and Coyote drops a bug in the Doc's ear.

There is a place at the foot of the Sangre di Cristo range where they've spilled out below the Colorado border that things cannot figure out exactly what they are supposed to be. The mountains butt heads with a desert and while no one was looking a number of mesas sneaked in and a river runs through it all.

Color and light run rampant here. Imagine a world created by tossing colored glass into the air and calling the variations of light and hue that occur while in flight the life and landscape of this world and you might have an idea. The mountains feel a need to be sharper and bluer than any other alpine heights, the mesas must be much stripier; ribboned and festooned with bold strokes of dusty yellow and red, while clouds billow and tumble in towering castles like hope rising and then exploding in the pure blue. Water chuckles loudly at the sheer exuberance of it all.

Thanks to this contrariness, nothing behaves like it would in the more orderly parts of the world. Due to the confusion of the land and the water and the sky, the rest of the world has ignored it. It sits, as it always has, grudgingly allowing a few measures of the passage of time on this old planet but for the most part embracing its' unique spirit and its' singularity of being while the stars wheel overhead and the cosmos lives and dies around it.

For millennia upon millennia, people have left their mark in passing. The river here has existed since the mountains originally blasted their way through the crust of the earth and has cut a deep canyon for itself through the sandstone and shale. The walls of this gorge are decorated with ancient cliff houses, overgrown swallows nests of an unknown people who came and went, leaving only these stone houses in rock walls. Up in the high meadow that the river trickles out of, there is a tumbled down hut, little but footings and a doorframe now; but hung over the lintel is a carved sign that says "El fantasma de pierna". Some shepherd's enigmatic leftover from a bygone age.

Whereas humanity has taken over the rest of the planet; at least those regions hospitable enough to support human endeavor, in this place, mankind cannot adapt the world to meet its' needs. Instead, the few souls who have set

1

down roots are not unlike reeds before a rushing wind. They learn to bend.

It's not a hard place to forge an existence; the environment is soft and welcoming, but it is quirky. The weather, for example, is capricious in the extreme. Seventy miles to the south, in Santa Fe, it is June and people sit in the sun, basking in the Plaza, yet in this little anomalous world, John Elkfoot stands on his front porch, shaking with cold and curls around a cup of coffee that billows enough steam to obscure his face.

John is a man perfectly suited for this world. A Seneca Indian, whose family still holds passports from the Five Nations, he has forsaken the ancestral land of the east for the Southwest. Four hundred and sixty feet below his front porch, there is a pueblo of the last remnant of the Shantis people. The government bureaucracy of John and the Shantis has classified them both as Native Americans, although they are as similar as the Irish and the Portuguese. He lives among aliens and is the happiest of people. He is a man who's found his niche. He's also a man who's found a guest waiting on his doorstep when he stepped out today.

"What the hell do you want?" was John's greeting.

Coyote smiled. "Come on, John," he said, "is that any way to treat a god?"

"You're not a god," was John's response. "At best, you're a spirit. And not one that I believe in anyway."

"Now, now. I can see right into that obstinate little head of yours. Let's just say you're ambivalent."

"Whatever. I'm having a good month. Go bother someone else."

Coyote put on the best crestfallen face he could come up with. "I'm really hurt John. I was just in the neighborhood and thought I'd look you up."

"You look like a dyspeptic baby. Do 'gods' like coffee?"

Coyote enjoyed John immensely. Of all the human beings he'd encountered over the millennia, John's bland acceptance of Coyote being something supernatural and yet as commonplace as a flake of shale or a robin's egg was unique. Not long after the Miracle of the Bridges, Coyote asked John why he'd never questioned Coyote's reality.

"If I questioned your reality," John replied, "I'd have to question my own." John reached over and flicked the tip of Coyote's nose with a finger. "You flinched," John sat back and shrugged, "you're real. Question resolved. Next."

That sort of behavior delighted Coyote no end. For the most part, people tended to treat him with either reverence or fear. John gave him acknowledgement as a thing that exists, as a sentient being. No more, no less. John was also the first human being who ever lectured him on his behavior. The novelty was exhilarating.

"So," Coyote said, settling at the kitchen table, "fill me in on what momentous events have transpired during my absence."

John smiled wryly at his guest. "See, this is what I don't get. Aren't gods supposed to be omnipotent and shit? Shouldn't you be telling me the secret stuff that goes on in the world? Can't you see everything?"

"Nope," Coyote said complacently. "I see what's in front of me." He pointed at his eyes. "Binary vision. Got depth perception but not much peripheral. That's supposed to be the mark of a predator, isn't it?"

"I guess," John replied. "For a supreme being, you don't seem to have the tools of the trade, do you?"

"I get by," Coyote said as he turned into a formless mist and then dispersed into the atmosphere. "Neat trick, huh?"

The town of Mesa Azul sits near the Shantis pueblo in the shadow of the high butte that is its' namesake. The few accidental tourists that have passed through invariably refer to it as almost picaresque. Every building except for the La Fonda hotel and the hardware store is made of adobe and fronted with either a wooden sidewalk or a hard stamped dirt path edged with river rock. There is a single blacktop lane that's considered the main drag and all roads branching off from it are dirt. Everyone has adobe walls around their homes to protect their summer gardens from the mule deer that venture down in search of sweet corn in mid summer. Due to the town's proximity to Huernafano Creek, there is an abundance of cottonwood.

The Azulians, as they like to call themselves, are a mixed bag of people. Founded by a couple of persecuted Hermanos de Penitante in the 1700's, Mesa Azul became a salvation of sorts for the lost adventurer. Various Latinos, gold seekers, speculators and homesteaders who ventured into the broad American west without maps in the previous centuries stumbled across the place and found themselves too weary to leave. The populace is known throughout the county for their lack of a sense of direction. Strangers asking for directions to Taos or Santa Fe usually get a response of, "if I knew where I was, I'd leave".

Discounting the pervading sense of not feeling like they're where they ought to be, Azulians are a remarkable content people. The possibility of ever being rich has never existed there, but at the same time, no one lacks for the necessities. Every now and again, items of curiosity appear in their midst and become a sort of communal property.

In the midst of the Cold War, representatives from NORAD showed up in their town to install a satellite tracking station. The benefits to the town when these soldiers arrived were manifold. Mesa Azul suddenly became part of the power grid. One tech-grade soldier who'd formed an unrequited attachment to

Myrna Lopez secretly diverted an electrical line into her home as a token of affection and from that single, romantic gesture the entire community soon had unbilled electricity.

The tracking station was a dismal failure. For some reason the microwave dish wouldn't stay on target, but drifted its signal about the cosmos. Military engineers pulled their hair out for months; geologists and meteorologists came and studied the environment in order to determine what sorts of anomalies existed there which prevented the dish from doing as it was told but with no success. In the end, no explanation, no theory or conjecture could explain why this was happening. Shoulder shrugging became the SOP response to the conundrum.

This little military contingent stayed for a decade, struggling against an unknown force to get their damned dish to behave. When the first television relay satellites were launched in 1967, the tracking station discovered its' raison d'ete. It locked onto those satellites and wouldn't let go. Peruvian football and Japanese game shows having no military applications, the army threw up its' collective hands in disgust and departed. The citizens of Mesa Azul commandeered the stations moments after the last deuce and a half disappeared down the blacktop and within weeks the community was enjoying satellite broadcasts.

The residents of this corner of Huernafano County have adapted to self-reliance over time. Quirkily independent, they also have had to develop a communal sense in order to survive, much to dismay of the state and federal government. Anything that is cost prohibitive for an individual to own or operate becomes a collective endeavor. The Valley Clarion is a perfect example.

Sometime in the latter part of the nineteenth century a printing press arrived in Mesa Azul. How it got there no one remembers and whom it belonged to, no one cared. It sat in the back of the hardware store covered by a tarp until 1963, when Terri Hodel, daughter of John Hodel, owner of Hodel's hardware uncovered it. The minute she threw back the tarp, the desire for a newspaper swept through the town.

It took a bit of puzzling out how to work the large flat-bed press, how to lock type down and build a page, but they did it and the Valley Clarion was born.

The Clarion never had a publisher or an editorial policy. Basically, anyone who felt like putting a paper together would print it. It was a good supplemental income to anyone who needed it. For example, Ralph Armejo put out one week's edition when he needed a new propane heater for his house. He roamed all over town selling ad space for his edition of the paper, made up some news stories and started running the press. An unspoken agreement amongst the townspeople set the price of any edition of the Clarion at two bits and everyone felt obligated to buy a copy. Ten cents of every sale was put back into the publishing coffers to pay for paper and ink.

Usually, the Clarion was dull as dishwater. Sybil Greenway needed a new motor for her washing machine once and put out an edition that detailed her lifelong correspondence with her cousin in Fort Collins, Colorado. Jerry Moss' bulldog edition that raised money for a new carburetor was a two-page screed on the trouble raccoons had caused him. Ralph's heater edition was a sensation and had far reaching repercussions.

Ralph had an inventive and relevant imagination. His edition of the Clarion ran twenty pages and painted Huernafano County as a hotbed of violence, intrigue and sedition. Among his more creative ideas was the notion that a rogue contingent of Weathermen, SDS and SLA members had resurfaced from ten years underground, taken over Shantis Pueblo and were preparing a new revolution in reaction to the election of Ronald Regan.

The Shantis, in particular the Pep Boys, were very taken with this conceit and quickly made flags of the various contingents mentioned in the article which were soon seen flying proudly from the Pueblo walls. A nervous BIA agent noticed them and flew down the valley to Santa Fe, screeching to a halt in front of the local FBI office. Within twelve hours, a battalion of FBI, ATC and Justice vehicles had surrounded the Pueblo, loudspeakers demanding the surrender of all federal fugitives. Doctor Pepper, the Shantis' wizened and venerable shaman eventually limped out from behind the barricades and calmed things down.

The repercussions of that event were an elevation of the stature of the Pep Boys among their own people, a severe lecture to Ralph by a Justice department attorney on the responsibilities of the Fifth Estate and another embarrassment to the Bureau of Indian Affairs.

The Shantis went through BIA agents like other people go through socks. Thanks to the obscurity of the region they'd lived in for the past several hundred years, they'd gone unnoticed by that benevolent agency long after every other indigenous culture had been hogtied into submission with red tape and kindly incompetence.

During the Great Society years, the Bureau of Indian Affairs suddenly discovered Shantis Pueblo. A BIA representative was informed that the Census department noticed there was a clump of indigenous people in northern New Mexico that existed without the help of the federal government and the Bureau had better rectify the situation post haste. The result was the dispatch of a tan Dodge sedan driven by a wan beanpole with a comb-over, a pocket protector and a sheaf of papers.

The Shantis are an easygoing tribe. They tend to take what is given in stride and not puzzle a lot over the motives. Having a government agent arrive with concerns over their access to health care, government commodities and education caused no great outcry and his queries into their needs were met with a hearty, "sure, why not?" rather than the usual rhetoric of oppression encountered elsewhere by BIA agents in the early 70's.

Negotiations for government largesse were speedily dealt with. The only sticking point seemed to be on the matter of education. Government policy for remote enclaves of indigenous people was to send a teacher to the reservation. The problem was, the pueblo wasn't a reservation. It had existed long before the United States came into being and had gone unnoticed, unclaimed and untreatied during the entire course of westward expansion. The Shantis didn't want to build a schoolhouse. They didn't want to have a schoolhouse built on their pueblo and they didn't want the responsibility of looking after the welfare of a teacher.

The resolution to the entire matter was a school bus. A nice, big Bluebird school bus was given to the Shantis so they could ferry their offspring to the Taos Pueblo school twenty-five miles away. The Shantis loved their new bus. They loved it so much that they painted it a bright blue immediately in order to make it look more like a blue bird. When their BIA agent saw what they'd done, he blew a gasket.

"You can't do that!" he cried in horror.

"Why not?" Bob's Big Boy wondered. "It's a Bluebird bus. Says so right on the side. Makes sense to me that it ought to be blue."

"Because yellow has been proven to be the most visible color to the human eye in the spectrum. A yellow bus is obviously a school bus. Drivers will be cautious around it and your children will be safe."

Bob's Big Boy pointed at the iridescent monster in front of the agent, so vivid it made the eyes water. "Are you telling me that people aren't going to see that?"

The majority of bureaucrats working for the B.I.A. at that time tended to view their clients as an aggregate rather than as individuals, which was a shame, since Bob's Big Boy was a celebration of individualism. Appropriately, he was a hair's breadth short of seven feet tall and broad enough to block the sun from lesser people. He liked to cut his own hair, which meant that his bangs were well kept, the top a mass of uneven spikes and the back resembled something the mice had gotten to. Painfully happy and optimistic, the lines on Bob's Big Boy's face had worn themselves into a permanent grin even when he was asleep. He also liked straw cowboy hats and denim jackets that he'd get his friend Reddi Kilowatt to paint Calvin and Hobbes characters all over with Dutch Boy exterior latex.

Bob's Big Boy discovered he was a natural born wheel jockey. The first time he climbed into the driver's seat of the Blue Bus, he suddenly wondered what he'd done with the first thirty years of his life. He quickly became addicted to manhandling his azure chariot all over northern New Mexico. He filled his hours between dropping the Shantis' children off at the Taos Pueblo School in the early dawn and picking them up again in the evening with a shuttle service from Mesa Azul to anywhere anyone wanted to go.

Naturally, the BIA became upset with this misuse of the bus. As soon as word reached the agency that the requisitioned school bus was being used for non educational purposes, the wan beanpole with the comb-over and pocket protector leaped in his dun Dodge sedan and rolled his way over the hills to straighten things out.

"You can't do that!" he cried in horror.

"Why not?" Bob's Big Boy wondered. "It's a bus. It exists to take people places. I'm a bus driver. If you wanted something to sit still in front of a school, you should have given us a rock."

Arriving back at BIA headquarters in Albuquerque, the wan beanpole asked for a transfer to a different office.

This place and these people, the unpredictability of it all; drew Coyote back again and again like a magnet. For thousands of years he could range over a land that accepted him and acknowledged his being. Then reason and logic began its' inexorable approach into these vast spaces and the people that dwelled there. Coyote soon found himself questioning his own existence. But never at Blue Mesa. His power had never flagged there.

Coyote drifted as particles about John as his host cleaned the kitchen, checked his pantry and then headed down to his offices. John clanked musically as he worked. Like the natives of the Huernafano valley, John unconsciously had developed a slightly eccentric appearance over the years. More as a gesture of his affection for the 1960's of his childhood and the musicians that filled the airways when he was young and easily influenced than as a nod towards his heritage, john grew his hair waist length. Or so it would appear when he was relaxing. When he was physically involved in something, he tended to wrap it into a sloppy bun at the back of his neck and secure it in place with an elastic cord. It gave him the appearance of a tall, thin schoolmarm who probably sewed costumes for her dozen or so cats in her spare time. John also liked to wear at least half a dozen bracelets on each wrist, three or four necklaces, including one with I-Ching coins strung on it and ankle bells over his left boot. Coyote loved the theatricality of his friend as well as his constant musicality. He also liked John's straightforward refusal to believe that anything Coyote did was extraordinary. Even as a disembodied voice, John reacted to him as if he was an urchin tugging at his coattail for attention.

"Aren't you curious as to where I've been?"

"Not really," John said distractedly as he fired up his banks of computers. Coyote loved John's computers. Every so often he'd slip inside them, bask in the warmth of the CPU's, race with the electrons through the circuitry and bounce like a pinball among the silicon chips.

As the processors finished their booting up sequences and the monitor sprang to life, instead of John's corporate wallpaper that said "Blue Mesa CGI", Coyote's face materialized on the screen.

"Hey look, John" Coyote's voice came out of the speakers, "I'm a ghost in the machine!"

"Knock it off," John said irritably. "I've got a lot of stuff on my plate today."

"Anyway," Coyote went on blithely, while moving pixels around on the screen, "I've been over to Sedona. You ever been to Sedona?"

"Er, yeah," John said, turning off the monitor that Coyote was messing with and flipping on a flat screen. "South of Flagstaff, isn't it? I think Walter Matthau and Jack Lemmon had homes there."

Coyote had yet to figure out how to navigate John's network. He was an intuitive creature and technology was beyond him. He exited the box through the fan grid. He decided to enter a small stuffed toy monkey that sat on John's desk. He strolled among the coffee cups and paper clips, coming to rest on a CD burner.

"How old is some of the coffee in these cups?" he wondered. "You could be breeding something."

"Yeah," John acknowledged. "You should leave. I'd feel terrible if I accidentally infected you with something."

"Well," Coyote ignored the surly comment; "I had a great time in Sedona. All sorts of crystal gazers and flakes reside there nowadays."

"So I hear. You should go back. Sounds like you found your niche."

"No," Coyote went on. "They're too new-agey for me. I listen to their babble for a while and it gives me a headache. They're very suggestible though. I had everyone on mountaintops in white robes waiting for the Harmonic Convergence at the Summer Solstice."

"Sounds great."

"You're distracted," Coyote observed. "You ought to count your blessings that I'm a benevolent spirit. Some other gods might take offence."

John spun around in his chair and shook his finger at the little plush monkey. "You're a pain in the ass! In case you haven't noticed, I'm trying to work here." He picked the toy up and held it close to his face, peering into the button eyes that stared out blankly. "If you need to socialize, go see Doc Pepper. He'd love your company."

Coyote cocked the monkey's head. It's little hand waved back at John in perfect mimicry. "The Doc doesn't talk, he chants. He throws pollen all over the place and burns sage. It's entertaining for about a half a second. You and I can have a dialogue. We connect."

"Seriously, buddy," John said, setting the toy down, "I've got a ton of work to do and then a guy's flying in from Seattle this afternoon. It's kind of important."

Coyote had drained the novelty from the toy and resumed the form John was familiar with. "Okay. Yeah," he oozed understanding and contrition. "I understand. I shouldn't have dropped in unannounced. Want to do dinner tonight?"

"Sorry," John shook his head while peering at lines of code flitting past his screen. "No can do. This guy flying in is going to be around for a couple of days."

Coyote began rapidly materializing and dematerializing inches from John's face. "Really? It does sound like a big deal."

"Cut it out," John's level of irritation was rising. "That's really distracting."

"Isn't it?" Coyote said. "I was hoping it would be. How about this weekend?" Coyote touched the screen and an ASCII figure froze, with all the number strings behind it rapidly colliding together into a tangled black ball. John swatted at Coyote's hand and the code began streaming past his vision again.

"Sure," John agreed testily. "Come by Saturday night. We'll toss some pollen around or something. Now, don't catch your tail in the door on your way out."

Doctor Pepper was already tossing pollen into the air. It hung like a golden veil in the air, defining the beams of light that came in through the window of his home. Blue smoke from a smoldering branch of sage coiled in serpentine patterns among the drifting particles. In alcoves along the adobe walls, ogres and maidens, gods and spirits, carved from cottonwood root and painted with Sears best exterior latex house paint in riotous color and adorned with fantastic headdresses stared blankly out at the old shaman as he leadenly performed a ritual that hadn't yielded results in years.

A medicine man bereft of his medicine is like a horse that can't place or a boxer who leads with his chin. The comic value of the enterprise is sapped by the sadness of the thing. Poor Doc went through the motions of appealing to the wind and the water and the earth while his heart bled. Beneath the chants and incantations, he pleaded for some response from the ether, some sign that

9

he was in fact a true seer and not a fraud.

Until he'd gone to the 12th Annual Inter-tribal Pow-wow in Denver four years previously, the Doctor had never questioned his spiritual abilities. He'd had his first vision in 1934 when he was ten years old and since then spent the rest of his life with one foot on the Hanging Road. Granted, it was a pretty mundane vision, but a vision nonetheless.

His father, Old Tobacco, had a desire to see Kansas City. He couldn't say exactly why he wanted to see it, but one morning he woke up and said, "I want to see Kansas City," and the boy and his mother merely nodded obediently, gathered up what they felt were necessities for the trip and followed the patriarch out the door and down the road.

Twelve weeks later, after a journey of some effort, much confusion and a lot of backtracking, they found themselves on the outskirts of Kansas City. Standing with their back to the Missouri River, the nomadic family took in the skyline. The Doc's mother stated blandly, "here we are."

"Yup."

"Was there anything in particular you wanted to see?" she asked tremulously. Travel tends to play havoc with family bonds and the relationship between her and her husband had grown increasingly frail over that past few weeks.

"Don't think so."

"Oh," she said. "Well, what do you want to do now?"

"Go home."

At that the boy and his father turned on their heels and started in the direction from whence they'd come, while their mother and helpmate stood looking to the east with tears welling in her eyes. The Doctor, then known as Ashianti, looked over his shoulder at his mother standing still and then tapped his father on the arm. Old Tobacco looked back and sighed. Women were a burden. They seemed to be nothing but needs waiting to be met.

"We're going this way," he informed her.

"We need to find a market first," she informed her husband. He speculated out loud on the fate of the food they'd bought previously.

"We ate it."

"All of it?"

They had indeed devoured everything at hand and so they entered the suburbs of Kansas City, in search of fodder. As they walked along, the Doctor noticed a fat man in a brown serge suit come out of a little white bungalow and walk towards the detached garage. Suddenly, as clear as day, he knew exactly what was about to occur. He informed his parents that the fat man would emerge from the garage backing a brown Model T out of it. As he came down the driveway, he would hit the mailbox nearby. They all stopped to watch and see. The events came to pass just as little Ashianti had foretold. His parents informed him that the gods had touched him and he would be the Shantis' spiritual leader from that time on.

That instance of his life, so clear, so pure and untainted by doubt played through his mind over and over again as he continued his supplications to the heavens. Coyote heard both, the incessant chanting and the internal agony of the shaman as he left John's house high on Blue Mesa. The first was annoying, but the second held some appeal.

"Poor old Doc," he mused to himself as he dissolved into particles and drifted down towards the Pueblo. "You've waited a long time for a message. I ought to give you one."

Faith untainted by reason or skepticism was Coyote's favorite conduit. Back in the day when men huddled in the wilderness, grasping at anything to explain the vastness of the cosmos and their own insignificance in relation to it, their thoughts flowed to Coyote and his brethren like sweet fragrance on a zephyr. It was a savory bouquet and Coyote missed it. The sour breath of empiricism was to bitter for him and it poisoned the atmosphere constantly.

"Yes," Coyote rumbled happily to himself, "this dear old mystic deserves a balm. Besides," he crinkled himself into the simulacrum of a smile, "it ought to be fun."

When the cornflower pollen he'd scattered into the air began to form an arabesque, Doctor Pepper held his breath and felt his heart began to lift. Finally, he'd broken through to the netherworld.

Up from the earthen floor rose the yellow and black powders, swirling into serpentine bands that intertwined with the deep blue figures already hovering. The dusty, smoke riddled bars of light streaming in the window began to break into pools of iridescent light that captured and framed the intricate figures roiling in the air. Tiny sparks, like static off of a cat, flashed along the edges of the sage smoke as it turned in the light. Finally, the large, filigreed oval in front of the shaman flattened, a pool of pure darkness appeared like the pupil of a cosmic eye and time froze.

The Doc was mesmerized. While physically capable of movement, the situation was such that he felt paralyzed, waiting in an eternal moment, trapped in amber and breathlessly awaiting whatever the denouement would be. The hairs on his arms rose as a voice surrounded him, emanating from every point of the compass and softly declared, "someone's coming".

Chapter Two -

Of motion and stasis and a conspiracy theorist's worst
fears are confirmed.

Ted Marquis couldn't shake an image out of his head. He sat in his corporate jet, 20,000 feet over the Rocky Mountains and played a snippet of film over and over in his internal projector. Early on in the movie "2001" an ape grabs the jawbone of a tapir and uses it as an offensive weapon. Ted muttered to himself, "that's where it started".

Ted was lost in technology. Surrounded by it. He sometimes felt as if he was being sucked into quicksand made of binary pairs; nulls and ones swirling about him, overwhelming, dragging him in. Technology had made him rich and for a while, it even made him happy. Those days were long ago though. Back when his company existed in a small warehouse in Phoenix and his staff consisted of his best friend, Marty Evans and two kids from the university at Tempe who were more than happy to just hang around, go on donut and pizza runs and watch the magic evolve.

In spite of the esoteric and the discipline of the work they were involved in, Ted thought of it as magic too. The wonder of writing a series of algorithms, a string of code and passing it into a set of transistors, resistors and circuits, then having a result from all that obtuse irrelevance appear as green letters on a dark gray screen was, in the end, nothing but magic.

Like human existence itself, it had become more complex and yet even more magical as time and understanding went on. Going from a teenage wunderkind in a garage to the head of a corporation that was responsible for three fourths of the world's ability to compute, network, and really nothing less than communicate, had left him inspired and terrified by what he'd set in motion.

It seemed like humanity at large shared his mixed emotions. A few years ago, the revolution in computers had gripped the world in a fever; it was the threshold of a golden age. Then, in a matter of months, a Ludditic reaction had set in, destroying companies, fortunes and reputations. Now, his industry wallowed in torpor, waiting for the next magic incantation that would revitalize it. Ted was in search of that key.

Ted had built his empire not only on his own abilities but also with a keen analytical sense of the abilities of others. His core product was built around a concept that wasn't his, but that he'd bought for a song. He'd heard recently of a new conceit for compression of data that had piqued his interest and might just be the touchstone the industry was looking for.

In the meantime, he had his moment of peace. In the air, he was away from boardrooms and cell phones, reporters and analysts. Travel was his only refuge from the world he'd created and he longed for his lost youth of inspired reflection. If he'd known what the course of his life would turn into back when he was happily juggling binary groups as a callow youth, he'd have stopped tinkering with the magic box and learned to carve toy trains instead.

The person Ted was going to see had stood on the same threshold years before and chosen a different path. John Elkfoot recognized early on in his life that he had a gift for the abstract as well as an understanding of how to apply it. He'd come up with a theorem on particle mapping in a three dimensional space when he was seventeen years old. After a number of years at MIT, then the Rand Corporation and finally at a "black box" military installation, he'd walked away. Not only had he walked away, he'd nearly disappeared from the face of the earth.

He might have stayed hidden if it hadn't been for the insatiable curiosity of Ted Marquis. John had formed Blue Mesa CGI to create computer landscapes, creatures and special effects for his brother's production company in Hollywood. Before long, the two of them came up with a syndicated television show called "Warriors of the Whirlwind" which was juvenile, silly and a runaway success. Packed to the gunnels with monsters, wizards, pneumatic women and brawny heroes, it struck a nerve with every Dungeons and Dragons geek around the world. To produce the necessary animations and effects in a cost effective manner, John had created new methods of spline modeling, motion capture and most importantly, information compression. His compression technology allowed him to send digital video to Hollywood via satellite in a matter of seconds, rather than the hours it took under the current compression standards.

It turned out that Ted was as addicted to the series as any of the seventeen year old target demographic that tuned in weekly and during a junket to Los Angeles, asked for and received a VIP tour of the Hollywood facilities a few months back. Seeing the speed with which data was compressed, uploaded and then downloaded again left him in a cold sweat. He'd just seen the next revolution in communications, if he could get his hands on it.

"Your phone's out again," John said to Angel Ramirez as he walked into the

Marguerita Bay Club.

Angel flashed a grin at John while wreathed in vapors swirling up from his griddle. "I know. State inspectors called this morning. I got bored listening to their beefs after a little while and left it hanging. Nice to know they finally hung up. I got customers to serve."

John took in the two other patrons in the joint. Rodent-like Barry Moss was sitting at the counter and the tiny fiery poblana Irene Naha had commandeered one of the checkered oil-cloth tables. Judging by the photographs she was busily dissecting, she and Rick Arnold had broken up again. "Yeah," John commented to Angel, "deep in your lunch hour rush, I see."

"I tell you, it's been crazy." Angel shrugged fatalistically. "I forgot that Huerno High had its graduation yesterday and when I showed up this morning there was four pickups in front of the place. Ten customers and I got caught short handed."

"Brutal," John commiserated. John wearily recognized that he'd have to do quite a bit of commiserating. Barry was giving him a sidelong glance trying to catch his eye without being obvious while Irene announced that she and Rick were through.

"Sorry to hear that, Irene." John held up one finger to Barry in the universal, "give me a minute, okay?" gesture, ordered a Dos Equis from Angel and sat down next to Irene.

There are people in this world who are doomed to be the listeners. No matter what superficial pose or verbal protestations they may make, the rest of the world penetrates all the facades they throw up and wait for them to pull up a chair. John was one of those unfortunate creatures. Rarely did he have to ask a question; more so his mere appearance signaled to the penitent that the confession booth was open. Irene began her litany of sorrows.

"Rick just won't be serious. He won't plan or focus on anything other than partying with his friends."

"It's a common failing, hun." John was grateful for Angel's timely arrival with his beer. Angel set it down and tried to run interference for John. "He's an asshole, Irene. Ask anyone."

"What do you know about it?" she huffed indignantly.

"Plenty," Angel replied and sat down. "Remember when Rick got his realty license and went to work for Johnny Gee? Well, my cousin Marie was working as the receptionist there and..."

John recognized two things. First, his presence at the table had just been made irrelevant and secondly, it would be a while before he could place his order with Angel. As he got up from the table and wandered over to where Barry sat at the counter grinning furtively from behind a weedy mustache and yellow tinted aviator glasses in his direction, he internally debated the merits of driving the fifty miles down the valley to Las Delicious bakery to pick up two dozen of the tamales he had a craving for.

"You're taking a big risk drinking out of the bottle," was Barry's opening salvo to John. Barry was a man of theories; a man who saw that the world as a mere illusion created by nefarious hidden ghouls to keep the populace at ease. Behind the everyday placidity of life lurked shadow governments and diabolical cabals that controlled most of humanity like puppet masters and he was one of the enlightened few that managed to pierce the veil. It was a hard knowledge to carry and the burden afflicted the man with constantly shifting eyes, quick, darting movements and a sense of high vibration that ran through his entire being. For John, the hardest part about having a conversation with Barry wasn't keeping a straight face but trying to hold on to the players. One day it might be the CIA and the next it would be either the Trilateral Commission or the Skull and Bones Club.

Barry took a pencil out of his pocket and pointed to John's bottle. He tapped the label where the recycling information was printed. "See there," he said, "you don't think they really recycle these bottles, do you?"

"Sure," John said, "why not?"

"They got a different agenda, man." Barry went on to explain how the real government of the US had started Project Genesis over a decade ago. "They can get a DNA sample off of the saliva you leave on the bottle top, pick your fingerprints off the bottle and enter you in the database."

"Oookay," John said, bemused. "And the point of that would be?"

"To eventually replace you with your clone."

"Ah, gotcha chief." John rolled the bottle around in his fingers and wondered if it was worth asking up a follow up question such as why would a cloned John Elkfoot be of any benefit to a government, shadow or not. The largest problem with most of Barry's theories was that they didn't go anywhere. At some point, the fabric of logic unraveled and you wondered why you'd invested the energy to listen in the first place.

Oddly enough, Barry had a large fan base for his conjecture. He earned his living off of his self-published book "Shadowlands", which laid out a schema of world domination by an unholy alliance of aliens and the Freemasons; as well as his trillium net; a wire mesh that fit comfortably inside any hat and prevented microwave probes from reading ones thoughts. His brother Jerry was his sales agent and traveled to gun shows throughout the southwest, while Barry hunkered down in their trailer waiting on the apocalypse.

The Moss brothers had arrived in Mesa Azul twenty years earlier. Barry had studied USGS maps for four years previously and decided that between the atmospheric anomalies and the high content of iron ore in the mesas, it was the safest place in the nation to live "under the radar". Even so, he'd constructed a large copper cage that their trailer sat inside of, to disrupt any stray probes that might get through. He lived completely off the grid and on clear still nights the thump of his generators could be heard up and down the valley.

Barry now started up on his continuing plea for John to remove his transmission dish from the top of Blue Mesa. "You're drawing undue attention to us."

"Gotta make a living, Barry," was John's response.

"Walking on the razor's edge, man." Barry crumpled up the paper cup he'd brought with him to savor his own beer with and stuffed it into the pocket of his army surplus field jacket. He'd burn it once he got home. "One of these days, that thing is gonna bring a squadron of black helicopters down on us."

"That makes no sense at all, Barry." John pointed out the window at the abandoned government radar station down the road, while at the same time castigating himself for once again being suckered into a debate.

"That's passive," Barry patiently explained. "It's a receptor only. You can't triangulate from a one way signal." Barry then went on to explain the nature of compressed waves. John was always impressed with the depths of Barry's knowledge while simultaneously appalled at how he applied it. Conversations with Barry always left John feeling like he was teetering on the edge of an ant lion's trap. The bait was a conceit Barry might throw out and before you knew it, you were sliding down into the pit where the vicious rending jaws of paranoia waited to tear you asunder.

"You should come by the compound some night," Barry said as he swiveled away from the counter. "I could really open your eyes."

Bob's Big Boy's eyes were as open as a morning sky. Ever since the Blue Bus had granted him access to the world outside of Shantis Pueblo, he'd been anxious to exploit it. Deep in the recesses of his obsidian pupils there glittered gold.

Beyond their little corner of the world, the Shantis were a rare and precious thing. Bob's Big Boy knew enough about commodities to recognize rare things tend to have a high market value and he was in a lather to find the right angle to market his people. In his view it was unfortunate that they'd been undiscovered for so long. Thanks to never having had their land taken away from them and in exchange for a new and much less desirable tract of land, the Shantis didn't exist on a reservation; therefore they couldn't take advantage of Federal laws allowing gaming on Indian land. He'd traveled to the 12th Annual Inter-tribal Pow-wow in Denver a few years earlier to attend a series of seminars including "Indian Gaming - Treading the Fine Line", which examined issues regarding how narrow an interpretation of "Indian Land" the courts would allow. After talking to a number of Native attorneys, Bob's Big Boy conceded that Shantis land was merely privately owned land, nothing more and nothing less.

It broke his heart to see the revenues tribes in Taos, Camel Rock and Obisbo were raking in, still he felt certain there were other avenues to be explored. Anglos, especially well-to-do guilty Anglos, had an appetite for Indian crafts and spirituality and he was busily examining what might be done there.

The fly in the ointment was the lack of craft and deep spirituality in Shantis tradition. Shantis', throughout their oral history seemed to have had a relatively easy time of things. Back in the mists of another age they'd stumbled on to a remarkably fertile corner of the world. Crops grew with little effort, water was never an issue and game was abundant. The result was a very bare bones spiritual life, consisting mainly of two festivals which merely thanked whatever powers there were for seeing them through the winter and then later for the usual bountiful harvest. These ceremonies involved no elaborate costumes or dances, no representations of the gods. Usually everyone got together, burned some ceremonial corn, watched the smoke rise into the ether, said, "thank you," and then went home for dinner.

They wanted for nothing so they never left the valley once they'd settled in. No raiding parties or rival tribes ever ventured in so the concept of trade remained unknown to the Shantis. Bob's Big Boy found the lack of motivation in his forbearers nearly criminal.

Shantis were just as uninspired when it came to the decorative arts. Silver and turquoise were unknown in their little valley. Jewelry tended to be colored corn kernels; dried, drilled and run onto strings as necklaces and bracelets. Earthenware pots were unadorned terra cotta in utilitarian shapes. No one even owned a loom until Bob's Big Boy bought one at the Pow-wow. Mrs. Butterworth had volunteered to learn how to use it. She'd actually become pretty proficient and had recently turned out a number of Gray Mountain rugs Bob's Big Boy had tried to sell at the Indian Market in Santa Fe until an attorney from the Gray Mountain tribe slapped him with a trademark infringement suit.

"Branding," Bob's Big Boy muttered to himself as he walked down the blacktop to Mesa Azul. "I got to get something that says 'Shantis' to the buying public." How he envied tribes with a rich iconography. If he couldn't inherit one, he was damned sure going to create one. Well, he wasn't, but he was on his way to see someone that could.

Camille Ryland-Bowles was the closest thing to a famous individual in Huernafano County. Now well into her seventies, she'd made a career for herself as the icon of an icon; to wit, she was one of Georgia O'Keefe's last confidantes. She painted large canvases of vaginal Calla lilies as an "homage" to her mentor and found a ready market among empowered women. She'd set up residence in Mesa Azul due to the need to be associated with New Mexico in the public's eye and property around Ghost Ranch, Santa Fe and Taos was prohibitively expensive. Warmly greeted by the little town on her arrival, she quickly isolated herself due to a personal deficiency in small talk. Instead of discussions about either the weather or how people are feeling, Ms. Ryland-Bowles tended to toss opening salvos such as, "how do we free art from the constraints of bourgeois self-referentialism?" People would abruptly recall leaving the cat on fire and walk away feeling as if they'd been spun around quickly while being hit with a very soft mallet.

To actually seek out conversation with such a person demonstrated the depth of Bob's Big Boy's commitment to the welfare of his people. Knocking on her door unleashed a maelstrom of stimulus; a tiny woman with quick, bird-like movements flitting about him as he felt overwhelmed by strong odors of turpentine, linseed oil, patchouli and Gauloise smoke, while being peppered with a hundred rhetorical questions involving esthetics, social responsibility, gender assumptions among indigenous people and other esoteric matters far beyond Bob's Big Boy's experience. Grimly, the resilient Indian held on until his hostess finally settled down enough to ask why he'd called on her.

After explaining his dilemma, he was both surprised and delighted to see her face light up at the challenge at hand. "I see your problem," she said, tapping a bejeweled finger against her chin. "As a necessity for human survival, art is a confrontation of man with the illusion of the world, and a way of subduing this illusion through a symbolic representation."

"Yeah," Bob's Big Boy agreed. "Now, the way I see it, if you can come up with something like Kokopelli, you know, simple but recognizable. Something that people go apeshit for..."

Camilla shook her head and grasped Bob's Big Boy's hand. She peered at him with an intensity that could melt plastic. "Don't you see? In this day and age contemporary art does not speak any more of this illusion, it does not try to subdue this illusion any more. It plays with its own history, and this is a weak strategy. Art exhausts itself in a game that does not commit to anything and in which there are no more rules."

"Uh, okay," Bob's Big Boy nodded his head in tentative understanding. "Now, I don't wanna tell you your job, but I've looked at a lot of what sells at the Indian market and stuff and it seems Anglos really go for that sort of geometric stuff. You know, all angles and things?"

Ms. Ryland-Bowles began pacing across the room. "Exactly! You need simulation, not representation!" She paused in front of a bookcase and began running her finger across the spines. "I have something here by Jean Baudrillard that speaks to the exact point you're trying to make. Let me see..."

Bob's Big Boy had a sinking feeling. The sun was creeping towards its' apex and he felt the urge to get back out into the world. Camilla pulled a slim book from the shelf and began leafing through the pages. "Well," Bob's Big Boy said, starting to rise from the couch, "I think you've got a good handle on the project..."

"Now, don't rush off," Camilla said distractedly, still leafing through the lavender covered volume. "I really think you'll find this edifying. Baudrillard has a comment in here about tribal and folk modes of socialization being almost completely assimilated by the post-modernist."

"Sure," Bob's Big Boy said while inching towards the door. "It's a big problem. Keeps me awake at night and shit."

Camilla flapped her hand in either a signal for Bob's Big Boy to sit down again or in goodbye as he had deftly extricated himself from her home. While he hurried back up the road, he could hear her going on blithely about the necessity for symbolism to be diagrammatic. He thought he might hunt down Reddy Kilowatt. That guy was always doodling on napkins. Maybe he could come up with something.

Any country that sits above five thousand feet tends to have light that's a little different than most people are used to. Humidity is a product of the lowlands. Mesa Azul sits high on the spine of the country and has a polished light that almost magnifies things. There is no atmospheric haze to blur one's perceptions. Watching the populace of this territory however, one becomes aware that just because you can see clearly doesn't mean your perception is all that great.

When the sun has traveled to the apex of its' arc, the world turns into objects carting around an intense dark blobs. People appear to be walking over tiny pits of oblivion that they could disappear into at any moment. Shadows hang as straight as a judge's ruling and their eyes disappear. Unless of course, they're wearing brimmed or billed caps, in which case their entire face is a void. Coyote liked to think of it as the hour of anonymity.

Thanks in large part to the influences of the culture that founded the town; it is a time of lethargy. Industry slows and moments are taken to think about what the morning has wrought and the possibilities of the afternoon. Sofas and daybeds are well used and ceilings are studied. It is also the time when Coyote travels from home to home, listening to the voices no one wants the rest of the world to hear.

While Coyote can eavesdrop on thoughts at any time, he preferred to listen in when people aren't talking or dreaming. Eavesdropping when people are engaged was the same as listening to chatter at a cocktail party, voices mingle and it's unclear what is of value and what is merely social noise. During this time of reclusion, the reception is mighty clear. As he moved through the town and the pueblo, he found little to prick his ears up about. Most people were spending their time mulling over little events or snippets of information they'd garnered in the first half of the day. Angel Ramirez, for example was casually wondering whom he could bet with on the date of Irene Naha's reconciliation with Rick Arnold. Those two were like a set of magnets, constantly flipping polarities. Bob's Big Boy was wondering if a set of Shantis' Tarot cards would be a marketable item. Camilla Ryland-Bowles was mentally trying to break down the vaginal folds of a Calla lily into something more primitive. Barry Moss was thinking about the hidden Masonic symbols he'd seen at Denver International Airport during a recent fly through and why an airport needed so many underground tunnels.

The only two folks in all of Huernafano County not taking their ease were Doctor Pepper and John Elkfoot. The Doc was still reeling under his revelatory gift from the morning and John was driving over the crest of the mountains to the east to pick up his motion actor, who'd called to say his truck broke down and needed a lift to Blue Mesa for the afternoon's work.

It dawned on Coyote that John's studio sat empty at the moment. It would be an interesting opportunity to learn more about John's magic boxes. He hoped they were all on.

John, in the meantime, was enjoying his respite from the day's activities. As he drove up the washboard, boulder-ridden track that snaked its' way over Madre di Cristo, he realized he'd been too involved in his work recently. The whole point of walking away from his previous existence had been to insure he had the time to get out in the world and enjoy life a little. He'd been so wrapped up in creating imaginary worlds, he'd lost track of the one he existed in.

It was quite a world to be in today, as well. Thanks to the axle banging condition of the track he was on, John had plenty of time to savor the cosmos and paintbrush that grew in profusion on the lower slopes, the bands of blue spruce and loden that delineated the midline and the mixed growth of Ponderosa, cedar and quaking aspen that ringed the high alpine meadows near the crest. Up among the lichen encrusted and sun-dappled granite boulders, John slowed to a crawl, watching pikas lazily gather early summer grasses while ground squirrels flashed across the open spaces in search of seed heads and marmots lolled about the rocks like fat burghers. At the crest of the pass, there was a small, snow-fed lake, looking for all the world like a piece of sky caught in the jagged teeth of this mountain. He turned off the engine of his jeep and sat there for a little while, listening to the gentle passage of wind, warmed by the heat of the rocks and rising in thermals towards the faint mares tails gliding in the jet stream miles overhead. A red-legged hawk circled easily inside those upflows, rising into the blue.

"The world is something we fritter away," he thought to himself. He felt for a moment as if he had only now come alive, as if he was experiencing this for the first time. Getting out of his ride, the crunch of gravel under his feet sounded too crisp, too precise for reality. Mingled with that was the ticking of his engine cooling down and even the rustle of grass as a snake passed through it. He wondered if he could hear the heartbeat of the marmot that warily sat erect a few feet away; paws folded in front of his chest as if in supplication. The world went on with its' work as John hung in stasis and part of him reached out to feel the heartbeat of the universe.

Gods are not immune to hubris. Or whatever Coyote might be, he tended to be misled by his own sense of infallibility. He found himself lost in the magic box. Like a Boy Scout troop without a compass, he kept returning to the same points in his exploration.

"This is ridiculous," Coyote muttered, "I know mechanics." To a certain extent, this was true. Since the dawn of time, Coyote found himself drawn to the constructs of man. What Coyote failed to take into consideration was a vast gulf in perceptions. Coyote couldn't make connections between disciplines. There was a differential logic to Coyote's processes. Where a human being could understand on some level how the mechanics of a computer were merely a physical means by which electronic signals acted in concordance to the programming, Coyote kept looking for an organic stimulus. To Coyote, the computer seemed very much an organic being. It pulsed, it moved, it generated warmth. It only lacked that essence, the ineffable thing that defined an organism.

In a simpler construct, say an internal combustion engine, Coyote could process the mechanics of the thing. Coyote could even understand how power was transferred from the engine to the transmission and onto the drive train. All the connections between one process and the next were obvious. You could see, feel and examine them. In here, Coyote was in a wasteland.

Then an incessant ringing interrupted his meditations.

Steve Abrams was a man firmly in the center of his universe. It wasn't often that he got to pull out the cell phones, the day runners or the personal data manager; but when he did, it was akin to watching Barishnikov dance. Normally the director of regional sales for ByteStream Information Systems; today he was acting as point man for the top dog, the lead wheel, the big Kahuna, Ted Marquis himself.

Ten years ago he'd been hired out of the Seattle office and almost tingled to be at the core of one of most dynamic corporations in world. At that time, he'd been fresh out of college, the vellum of his MBA still seemingly damp from the calligraphy ink. Ever since he'd met with the recruiter on campus, he'd rushed back to his dorm and began laying out his career path. His strategy differed from the vice president of Marketing and Sales however and he'd been sent out to a "soft" territory, where he'd languished ever since.

His life in New Mexico hadn't been anything close to what he'd envisioned life should be for a guy who lived for the deal. He'd felt like a Fuller Brush man. This was an exceedingly low-tech environment. If Los Alamos and White Sands hadn't been part of his territory, he might have resigned after a couple of years, but fortunately, he'd pulled off some impressive government contracts with those agencies.

The government facilities knew how to treat a guy like him as well. Once he'd networked his way inside the system, he got the plush presentation rooms, the respect and peerage a real hard charger deserved. The rest of the state was a wash. He'd cooled his heels in some of the dingiest little vestibules on earth, waiting to lick boot on some low level bureaucrat drunk on his own middling power. Still, he made the numbers roll in.

Now was the moment to collect on the dues he'd paid. He'd pulled together an impressive reception and itinerary for Mr. Marquis and would be attached to the guy's hip for the next couple of days. Steve's personal drive and charisma was bound to impress the man and he was already speculating on where in the SeaTac area he'd buy a home.

The bitch kitty on the deal had been arranging transportation from Albuquerque to this spit-ball fly speck called Mesa Azul. It didn't even appear on most maps. Zia Chauffeur Services told him that a limo or town car was out of the question. The single blacktop that ran in and out of the joint was so narrow their insurance wouldn't cover a limo. New Mexico drivers were insane. Given the amount of open space in the state, no one felt that speeds in excess of ninety miles an hour were unwarranted. Four point speeding tickets were considered a mark of residency. There was no slow lane in this world.

Fortunately, he'd arranged with Black Mountain Air Tours to have a Bell Ranger helicopter fly them up there. Steve sat in his leased Jaguar and stared across the tarmac at the bird they brought in. Sweet. Lean and angular, it looked liked it was speeding along even when sitting still. The glass canopy had tinted polarized windshields. Even the paint scheme worked for him; a deep ebony like the finish on a Mercedes.

Between the closed concourse Mr. Marquis' jet would be pulling up to and the helicopter that would ferry them onward, he'd arranged for the State's premier caterer to set up a canopied tent and serve lunch. He'd had his personal assistant work her connections up the ByteStream network until she'd managed to wrangle an in with Mr. Marquis' assistant in order to learn his preferred menus. Steve knew that attention to these sorts of details separated the men from the boys in this league.

Speaking of details, he gave himself one more once over. His feather cut hair was laying perfect, corporate short but styled with an élan that said he was no nine-to-fiver. Gray, nail-head silk Verasé suit, conservative in cut except for those tiny touches and fitting that announced to the world you couldn't pull this sucker off for less than three grand. He'd upped the ante with a Contesse Mara tie and hand-last Bally shoes as well. The single item he was most proud of however, was his pocket square. Of an exact matching material and fabric as his tie, he'd had a miniscule exquisitely embroidered skull sewn in to the top corner. You had to be within three feet of him to notice it, but when you did, it said predator.

Steve could actually feel his confidence drain out of him the moment he clapped eyes on his CEO. Ted Marquis looked like an IT guy heading for his quarterly review. Tall, with a head of hair that consisted of a series of cowlicks looking for direction, Ted favored tan Dockers and navy blazers with only an approximate grasp of his body shape. If he turned around really fast, there was a good chance his clothes would still be facing in the original direction. He had a laptop bag hanging over his shoulder and carried his own garment bag.

Steve swallowed hard and greeted his fate. "Mister Marquis? Steve Abrams, regional sales."

Ted looked him up and down. "Hi. Looks like I pay you well."

Sweat began to pool under Steve's arms as his mind tried to parse the statement. Was this a criticism or a compliment? The delivery was as bland and unaffected as the face he was trying to read.

"Heh, yeah," Steve fumbled. The old adage of clothes making the man wanted desperately to burst from his mouth but one glance at his boss' wardrobe convinced him it would be impolitic.

"I've arranged for a luncheon before we continue on to Mesa Azul," was the safest thing he could say.

Ted looked around the closed concourse and then saw the open doorway with the Jaguar parked just outside it.

"That's okay," Ted evenly replied, "I had a couple candy bars on the plane. That your car?" he looked at Steve who imperceptibly nodded. Ted whistled.

Steve snapped his fingers and Carl Lumley, a summer intern in his office trotted up. "Carl, take Mister Marquis' bags, will you?"

Ted shied back just a bit. "Naw, I'm used to carrying this stuff." Steve could feel the lakes of perspiration growing. He started to dismiss Carl, but the intern seemed reticent to leave. "Is there a problem, Carl?" Steve said officiously.

"No," Carl said. He started to turn and then blurted out, "Mister Marquis, can I ask you a question about Torrent?"

Steve froze. Torrent was ByteStream's latest operating system. It had recently been rolled out after months of delays and tons of budget overruns. Massively hyped, it was fantastically flawed and the press backlash was horrific. Steve himself refused to try and market the product. As far as he was concerned, his customers could hang in there with the old Cascade operating system until the bugs were worked out. He could only imagine what was going through Ted's mind. Any references to Torrent had to be akin to saying to a new mother, "My, what an ugly baby."

Surprisingly, Steve saw the top dog smile. "Sure," Ted said, "I probably can't answer it, but fire away."

Carl had gotten an early Beta version of Torrent and was thrilled by the principle of the system. As he'd taken apps apart and pried into the core kernels, he'd discovered what he felt was a fatal flaw in the OS. He quickly summarized what he'd found and asked the Big Kahuna's opinion on it.

Steve ground his teeth. Everything was going wrong. Marquis' focus should have been on him, not some geek intern he'd brought along strictly as a spear-carrier. Ted and the kid were hip deep in nerd city and Steve was quickly turning into excess baggage. He tried desperately the right the situation.

"Mister Marquis, if you don't want to take a luncheon, maybe we should just head over to the chopper."

"Chopper?" Ted asked. He looked querulously at Steve. "You mean a heli-copter?"

Steve explained that no limousine service was willing to drive them that distance. "Is that a problem, sir?"

"Heck no," Ted grinned. "I've never ridden in a helicopter. I've meant to, but it never came up." Steve felt the tension in his shoulders begin to flee. Fate was finally swinging around to his side. Just as he started to breathe again, he heard Ted say, "What about you, Carl? Ever been in a helicopter?"

Steve couldn't win for losing. He was quickly being demoted to chauffer and tour guide. Where he'd once assumed he'd have at least eight hours of face time with the most powerful man on the planet, he now got to listen in as two computer lab rats chattered at each other. Things got worse when they reached the helicopter. Their pilot, looking for all the world like covert operations guy in a black flight suit informed them that he was unsure if he could get them to Mesa Azul. Due to anomalies of terrain and atmosphere in the region, the Global Positioning System didn't work there. Aerial mapping and distance satellite mapping hadn't ever been able to take any images they would work for them and the best flight references he could get his hands on were U.S. Geodetic Survey elevation maps from the 1940's.

Cursing a blue streak internally, Steve collected himself and dialed Sharon, his office girl from his cell phone. "Sharon, look up Blue Mesa CGI and give me the number." As he punched the number in, he thought to himself, "the way my luck's running, the place will have burned down."

Coyote was a pretty fair mimic when he wanted to be. Even so, he felt it would be best to act as John's assistant when he answered the phone. Whoever was on the other end was rapidly falling apart, even though he tried to keep a cool façade going. Micro-tremors in the human voice cut through Coyote like a hot knife through butter. The only voice he'd heard recently that was wired this tight would be poor old Barry Moss.

Serendipity is a wonderful thing. There were few occasions in Coyote's long life where everything fell into place as neatly as this was. He looked out the door of John's studio at the nice, flat expanse that was the top of Blue Mesa. Off, down the valley, the copper cage of Barry's compound twinkled in the sunlight. Coyote smiled broadly for the second time that day.

"Sure," he told the angst-ridden voice on the other end of the phone, "The whole north end of the mesa is as clear as you could want. Tell your pilot to fly up the Rio Grande until he gets to the confluence where the Huernafano creek pours into it. Just a couple miles up the canyon and you'll see a copper caged RV. Straight north of that is Blue Mesa. Just fly over the RV and you can't miss us."

Chapter Three -

The Big Kahuna arrives while Barry heads for the hills and Coyote tosses the joint.

In addition to the strategic value of the place, Barry enjoyed life in Mesa Azul. There was a singular serenity to the area that was like slipping his psyche into a warm bath. While not allowing such feelings to sap his natural vigilance, sometimes looking out his windows for anything unusual become more of an exercise in appreciation. Time worked little miracles day by day. As he looked down the valley, he was mentally assessing the changes in light and texture from the day before. His trailer sat on the gently sloping crest of ground in the south end of town. Aside from John's place atop the mesa, he commanded the highest ground of Huernafano valley. The ground sloped back towards the creek from there and then fell away into a small canyon. Cottonwood lined the stream, while dark firs found tenuous footholds on the canyon walls. The broad leaves of the cottonwood trees would sometimes catch reflections from the creek and appear to glow with an internal light. This phenomenon danced like fairy beams among the trees.

These constantly changing surprises caused Barry's near constant state of anxiety to slip a notch every now and again. When it did, he would secretly question his worldview. It would be nice; he thought more often than he realized, to shed himself of the covert agencies, shadow governments and cabals that populated his thought processes. His brother Jerry never seemed to let these revelations upset his life. Jerry was out there, rolling all over the southwest, calling in daily with requests for more brochures and books and telling Barry about the pretty women of San Antonio or the terrific back ribs to be had in Kansas City.

The trouble was, Barry had gone too deep and couldn't ever come back. Maybe if he hadn't ever written and published what he knew about them, the system would let him slide. The southwest was land that called out to the wanderlust in everyone. Its sheer expansiveness beckoned to him. The skyline glowed with promise and all he could do was look at the horizon with hungry eyes.

He'd consciously chosen to be a martyr to liberty however, and if he ever stuck his nose out where the rest of the world lived, those he'd exposed would swarm over him and the real nightmare would begin.

He wasn't worried for himself, but for the few fellow resistance fighters he knew. They had a nicely hidden network and it was slowly growing. As long as they weren't penetrated, they could gradually expand until the day came when they would drive the aliens from their land. It was his duty to keep from being caught. They had ways to make a man surrender everything, with or without his complicity.

Barry felt himself virtually shrink as that thought skittered like a mad rat through the dark recesses of his mind. Deep in the folds of his cortex he hid the visions of gray, blank faces adorned with huge compound eyes. Splintered imagery flashed momentarily against the backs of his quivering eyelids. He could feel their thought projections probing relentlessly and he thanked whatever fates there may be for his discovery of the masking properties of his trillium net.

They were out there, the alien horde and their coterie of human lap dogs. He could sense them scouring the earth for him. He had such a frail protection, this anomaly on the earth; this valley of the innocents and his wits. The thought of his fellow Azulians caused a smile to dance across his face. Well, Barry thought to himself, if he had to hide, at least he'd found a pretty bolt hole. He watched the light on the leaves and felt himself relax.

Ted was soaring, literally and metaphorically. As he looked out the cockpit windows, watching the shadow of their helicopter race over the landscape, he felt his heart run with it. He felt as if he'd just emerged from a cocoon and on still drying wings caught a fresh wind. He'd shed something in the last hour; worry, drudgery; who knew? He could feel he was becoming something he'd never been before and was happy.

Maybe it was escaping the dampness and claustrophobic atmosphere of Seattle or maybe it was just being away from the meetings and constant pressure to perform for the stockholders, the department heads, the news media. Maybe it was the diamond sky, the green river and blue canyon walls. Maybe it was the enthusiasm of the kid Carl, who was happily jabbering about his discoveries in the object handling properties of the new operating system. Ted remembered when the process of development was as big a narcotic for him. He caught a contact high off the buzz this kid projected.

Their pilot was the epitome of cool as well. The guy flew like the helicopter was an extension of his being. There didn't seem to be a request Ted threw out that the guy didn't easily fulfill. When they first began following the Rio Grande north, it quickly dropped into a canyon it cut for itself. Ted had wondered what it would be like to fly in the canyon. Their pilot looked over and smiled, nodded in recognition and threw them into a stomach tingling dive. Moments later they had been swallowed by the rock walls, racing with their reflection above the churning water of the rapids. Ted shook with adrenaline.

Steve was in purgatory. He'd been in helicopters before but never for more than fifteen minutes at a time and never with a pilot at the controls who needed to compensate for his manhood so badly. If he wanted thrills, he would have gone to Six Flags and bought a ticket for the Wild Mouse. If that wasn't bad enough, he had to choke down his anxiety and nausea and pretend that he was enjoying this. He stared fixedly at the floor in front of him. Even catching a glance peripherally out the window at the blurred and shaking landscape would be enough to send him over the top. Now they were flying in the goddamned earth, for Christ's sake. He could see the shadow of the canyon falling over them.

Steve had an epiphany during their flight as well. He realized, after listening to the big Kahuna gibber with his new-found friend and then squeal with delight at the reckless abandon of their pilot, that he'd spent the last ten years of his life working for an idiot. It was pure serendipity that this guy had become the richest man on earth. What this boob knew about business, power and the art of the deal could fill a tooth. Somehow, he'd just fell in with excellent handlers. There couldn't be any other explanation.

"You know what would be great?" he heard Ted say to the pilot and his toes curled inside his hand-last Bally shoes. The knob-jockey pilot turned his helmeted head with the smoked visor toward his boss. Steve momentarily felt as though an automaton was flying the craft.

"If you could fly this thing underneath that bridge up ahead." Steve risked looking forward where, sure enough, there stood a steel expansion bridge over Rio Grande canyon.

"No problemo," their moronic pilot replied and Steve felt them dip a little further toward the river. The copter shook violently for a moment and he heard through the blood pounding in his ears, "there's a little wind down here, sir. It might get kind of rough."

Steve vowed to himself that if he got out of this in one piece, his life was going to change. Before he was done, he was going to eat Ted Marquis for lunch.

Rick Arnold was having a late lunch at the Marguerita Bay Club. It had been a rough week for him. Frankly, it had been a long rough patch. He was still firmly convinced that he was sitting on some of the most valuable land in the southwest down here, but convincing anyone else of that seemed to be impossible. Mesa Azul itself may not have been much to look at, but the countryside surrounding it certainly was. This should be a vacation paradise but you would have thought you were trying to sell prospective investors swampland in Mississippi the way they reacted to it.

He'd first come up here by accident five years ago and the second he saw the panorama spread out before him as he dropped down from Chingaria Pass, he could hear cash registers ringing in his ears. It was like coming into Aspen, Colorado before the millionaires and movie stars discovered it, or Santa Fe before the millionaires and movie stars discovered it. He was positive that those places had been just as pokey, just as inconvenient to get to as Mesa Azul was. The only difference was that those places found the money, the vision and the cachet. Or maybe those places didn't have as nutty a populace as this county did.

Rick's speculation was interrupted by an outburst from Angel. "Jesus," Angel yelped, "the Mayor almost got hit by a truck." Rick looked out the broad plate glass that fronted the Club in time to see Buckeye scurrying around the corner.

"We really need some speed limit signs posted," Angel went on.

"Yeah," Rick concurred, "or a better mayor. Either one works for me."

Angel walked over and picked up the plastic basket that once held Rick's lunch. "You want another beer, amigo?"

Rick declined, as much as he'd like one. Another possible client was coming in to look at a thirty-acre parcel that bordered on the Shantis property. It really was picaresque, with barely a two percent grade from end to end and a view that took in both Blue Mesa and the pueblos. It would be perfect for a resort area. It even had an aquifer that would supply them with well water that had been filtered underground through thirty miles of bedrock. If you drilled to the water table, it came out in a geyser, running at sixty PSI naturally. You could run a sprinkler system for a golf course with that sort of pressure.

"You still upset about Irene?" Angel inquired.

Rick smirked just a touch. He just knew that Angel had the worst characteristic on earth for a bartender. Rick was certain the man was an incorrigible gossip. Anything he said to Angel would probably make it around town fifteen minutes after he left. Hell, he'd bet a sawbuck that anything he related might beat him out the door. Rick was one of those folks who assigned his own worst characteristics to everyone else on the planet. Angel might be nosy but he was a quiet as a priest in confession. Not that you'd ever convince Rick of that.

"Things are cool again with Irene, cholo." He looked up at Angel and gave him his most sincere smile. "You know, she needs a little more attention than I can give her sometimes." What she really needed, Rick thought to himself, was some therapy. While there was a lot to recommend her as a girl friend, she had so many self-esteem issues that no matter what he did, she always felt like he was snubbing her. They had been off and on again so many times in two years that he couldn't even remember half the reasons they broke up. If there was anything he knew about the gulf between men and women, it was that men always assumed the girl they met would be exactly the same from that point on, whereas women assumed men could be molded and shaped into everything they desired.

With Irene, he constantly existed in a state of contradictory goals. They'd met in a nightclub in Santa Fe and she dug older men who still knew how to have a good time, who were spontaneous and on the move all the time. Of course, as soon as they started running around together, this turned into a problem. Then she couldn't understand why he wouldn't grow up and become responsible. Naturally, the second he decided to really knuckle down and focus on his career, she accused him of becoming a stick in the mud. If she didn't have such a cute figure and if every other decent looking woman within one hundred and fifty miles didn't think he was sort of smarmy, he'd have walked away a long time ago. Still, he was taken by the amount of energy, sexual chemistry and enthusiasm that radiated off someone not even five feet tall and with a curiously adorable bean-shaped torso. The fact that she favored thong underwear and obscenely short skirts tended to draw him back repeatedly as well.

Well, his latest attempt at being free spirited had backfired on him so he was once more putting his nose to the grindstone. A few months back, he'd run into a guy down at Clearwater Ranch Resort who owned title to half the land in the county. The guy was a complete trust-fund loser who had no idea what he had. Rick had cosied up to him and wound up with an exclusive contract to rep the fellow's property. Now Rick was calling in favors and networking with his old Fraternity brothers from the University of Chicago. While he could bust up the property into small four-acre parcels, it would take forever to move them at that rate and he was hungry to retire young enough that he could enjoy life. He had everyone he knew beating the bushes for the big developer, the guy with dreams who could turn Huernafano County into the vacation destination of northern New Mexico.

He'd had a couple of nibbles but nothing had panned out yet. Today, a couple of speculators from Lake Forest were coming in to take a look around. Rick did his Willy Loman incantation and popped a breath mint into his mouth. You never knew what the day was going to bring.

Terror. He was instantly in an absolute, stark screaming nightmare. Barry's worse fear was hurling up the canyon at him. When he first heard that chilling staccato booming up the cliff walls, he shook his head thinking he was imagining it. He'd played this scenario out in his head so many times that it seemed unreal. Now it was a daydream that had taken on a bit more substance than usual. One look out his smoked glass window at the gorge drove all delusions out of his mind, however. There it came, black and menacing, like some primordial insect, skimming low over the river and below the sightline of the canyon rim.

"Smart," Barry thought to himself. "Swing well below radar."

Fortunately, Barry had drilled himself over the years. The question was, were the Spooks on to him or was this merely the first wave of colonization? Was the company moving in or was he the hard target? How they behaved in the next few moments would tell him a lot. He didn't want to have to fire his compound just yet. He'd sit tight and watch what they were up to.

He backed slowly away from the window towards the kitchen. He'd positioned the RV originally so that he could have a clear view of the only two access routes in and out of Mesa Azul. He could back up without losing his line of sight for an instant. Twelve steps and the kitchen cupboards were right behind him. He flipped open the door to the cupboard on the right side of the sink and slid his hand in to hit the switch hidden on the inside facing wall. A counterweighted trap door swung up from the linoleum of the kitchen and he moved fast, dropping underneath the RV. He hit the release under the trailer and the door closed behind him. He'd planted a mess of redbark willow to screen him under the trailer, as well as the access hatch to an escape tunnel he'd dug at night over the course of three years. Even his brother Jerry didn't know about this. It ran from the trailer to a small cut in the rock six hundred yards away from the trailer that he'd screened with sagebrush. The tunnel itself was made of culvert piping that he'd bought at more than twenty different home improvement stores throughout the state. The tunnel had a downward slope that would carry him on a little wheeled cart away from his compound in absolute secrecy in less than a minute.

Looking out from the screen of the sagebrush, he could just make out the helicopter. It swept past him and then, to his horror, slowed. It hovered over the compound for a moment. Barry cursed himself. He should have hit the panic button and fired the place before he escaped. All his records, all the evidence he'd collected and collated over the years was just sitting there; waiting for the company guys to seize. Once they knew how much he'd pieced together in his life, there would be no safe place on earth. He'd be the most wanted human being on the face of the planet.

Unbelievably, it didn't land. After hanging over his place for several inexorable beats, it continued up the valley, heading for Blue Mesa.

Grabbing his emergency kit, Barry scrambled through the sage and into a natural washout that he could follow up the slope of the riverbed. The canyon walls fell rapidly from that point and splintered off into coulees on either side. Barry moved up into one of the coulee branches, keeping in a crouch so that nothing below his eyes was visible. He watched as the chopper settled at the far end of Blue Mesa in a swirling haze of dust. He couldn't believe that his finely tuned senses had never picked up on John Elkfoot being a company man. Well, he knew now.

Barry decided he'd best lay low for a day or three and watch what went on. Further down Huernafano Creek he'd constructed a safe house for himself inside one of the abandoned cliff houses. Unless a body knew what to look for, it appeared to be another ancient kiva tucked in the rock face. Secreted inside hidden passages were two weeks worth of self-heating MRE's and bottled water. Barry had hidden away a pair of night vision goggles, a sniper scope with a compound lens capable of twelve times magnification and a directional listening cone. All these items were neatly packed in front of thirty-seven pounds of C4 plastic explosive.

Coyote couldn't have been more pleased with Barry's reaction to his little prank. It had been sometime since the influence he exerted had the amount of impact it did today. Happily, Coyote drifted up into the atmosphere and looked down on Mesa Azul. He allowed his consciousness to balloon outwards to embrace the entire valley. All these marvelous people were going about the business of living and letting Coyote in without question. He'd been away too long.

Coyote was never one to think about the long-range impact of what he did. He was an essence from the time when humanity first came upon his shores. For millennium upon millennium, changes on the topography of the planet occurred faster than the behavior of people. Those original invaders, chasing the eohippus and mastodons, accepted the existence of beings such as Coyote without question. It had only been in the past century and a half, a blink of an eyelid in Coyote's frame of reference that logic had impeded belief and acceptance. It was nice to be dealing with people who appreciated the innate mystery of existence again.

What Coyote lacked was an understanding of human psychology. Coyote was an action/reaction sort of being. The possibility that any interference he might toss into an individual's life might be misinterpreted was beyond his grasp. Coyote instilled notions or created scenarios for the same reason that a kid might trap some bees in a jar, shake them up and then let them loose. It was the resulting behavior that interested him.

There was no malicious intent at all in Coyote as he floated down to Barry's compound, found a narrow gap in the weather-stripping of the door that he could filter his being through and congeal into a solid being again inside the RV. Once inside, Coyote looked around.

While it wasn't as entertaining as John's abode, there were a number of things to pique Coyote's interest. Coyote spent quite a bit of time puzzling out the booby traps that were wired all over the place. He found it curious someone would be willing to destroy everything they possessed merely to make sure no one else could possess it. That seemed to be the principle behind every trip wire, pressure plate and electronic eye Coyote found. It was frustrating. The only way Coyote could inspect the locked cabinets, the wired drawers and secreted documents was to disembody himself and yet, in that state, he couldn't riffle the pages of a file or pick up a stack of photographs. The only thing he could do was to pick up a paper cup Barry had left behind in his flight. Coyote had been in Barry's mind enough to know he had a desperate fear of having any trace of himself in the possession of someone else and the raised greasy fingerprint ridges on the waxed cup, the miniscule particles of dried saliva on the rim, were enough to convince Coyote he'd struck gold. He vanished, taking the cup with him.

Were there any more important events to occur that day? It would depend on what one considers important. The earth hurled through the cosmos on a fixed track at such a speed, that humanity, if it could watch it pass by, would find astounding. The rotation of the planet decayed infinitesimally, as it has done since it came into being, but without anyone noticing. Shadows grew as the rotation continued, until they stretched out towards the east, aching for the horizon. The diurnal blossoms twisted or spread their petals open and released small dispatches of pollen and fragrance in order to attract the bees and butterflies and hummingbirds that acted in sympathy with their need to propagate. Lizards looked for the last of the sun-baked rocks while those creatures less tolerant of the heat beating down at noon moved out from the shadows that protected them during the apex of the day. The more familiar type of coyote emerged from dens and moved across the fields and arroyos; looking for whatever small creatures they might take advantage of. The sky ran through a myriad of colors as the sun vanished behind gilded peaks and the moon went from the ghostly blue watermark in the sky it had been in the afternoon to the bright signal light of a summer night.

Angel flipped on his neon sign, supplied by the Coors/Corona brewing concern, as Bob's Big Boy and Reddi Killowatt came in for the Tuesday night special and a couple of Modellos. They'd hunker down in the Acapulco room for the evening, wasting dozens of napkins as they tried to figure out the symbology of their people. Before long, Angel and a half a dozen customers would be throwing their two cents into the mix until the whole enterprise degenerated into a bawdy game of Pictionary.

John greeted his visitors and spent the rest of the day showing them around the facilities, discussing the industry in general and fixing dinner for them. Steve listened with half an ear to the conversations while his mind churned over ideas, mostly in an embryonic form, that might quickly help him bury the big Kahuna. Ted felt his buoyancy rise as the evening progressed. He felt as though he'd shed a skin and was emerging as something familiar but at the same time new. It was an exhilarating state he'd never experienced before and hoped it would last for a while. Carl was feeling pretty exuberant himself. Between his audience with the Maestro and the trip up here, along with the style and ease of their host, he was having as remarkable day as he'd ever experienced. Dinner was served on the patio that overlooked the pueblo below. The block-like adobe structures, now glowing with incandescent light spilling out the windows or up the smoke holes, fascinated him. He was a pokey kid from Des Moines and the denizens below struck him as something mysterious and exotic. Outside of one building sat an old man in front of a small fire. He tossed something and blue flash appeared. "Copper, probably," Carl thought to himself.

Doctor Pepper had indeed thrown fine copper shavings into the fire. He stared at the blue tendrils of smoke and sparks rising upward into the indigo sky and let his thoughts follow them. He was still in a fugue state, thanks to the visitation of the something unforeseen and ancient. While he didn't know exactly what it meant yet, he knew he'd been given a great present this day. All the inadequacies that had plagued him for so long were sloughed away. He let his eyes drift from the smoke, across the roofs of the Pueblo to the mesa rising behind them, silhouetted against the night sky. Moonlight glinted on the ebony finish of the helicopter and he wondered if the prophecy he'd been given referred to the people who'd arrived on that contraption.

Rick saw his potential clients off and sat in his Range Rover for a while, mulling over their reaction. At least they'd seemed receptive but no promissory deals had been struck just yet. The signal glimmer of hope he'd received was a well delivered, "we'll call you after we've discussed this." The more he chewed it around in his head, the more it felt like a lock. He decided a premature celebration was in order and drove off to Irene's house. He'd pick her up and they could run down to Santa Fe for a late evening, check into a motel and come back in the morning.

The rest of Mesa Azul went on with their evening as well. It was a good night for television as Telenova from Argentina was broadcasting the annual grudge match between Buenos Aires and Santiago. The Pep Boys had been looking forward to it all week. Manny and Moe were big gaucho fans while Jack was a Santiaguan through and through. Their excitement led to several fistfights and before the game was over, they went to see Betty Crocker about a poultice and stuffing for Manny's newly broken nose. Other parts of Mesa Azul were heavily addicted to Japanese game shows, especially "Kazahita no Kazi", which required no translation. As a matter of fact, a grasp of Japanese might have lessened the enjoyment as a shrieking host cajoled contestants into being human fruit bats or sitting in frigid artic waters off the coast of Alaska drinking gallons of beer.

People cleaned up kitchen messes and put out dogs and cats. Across the valley, lights began to wink off. As the ground lights diminished, the starlight seemed to gain strength. By the time Angel chased Bob's Big Boy and Reddi Kilowatt out into the street and snapped off his own sign, the boys had to find their way home by the lights of the heavens.

"Look at that big old moon," Bob's Big Boy said happily.

"Hello, moon!" Reddi Kilowatt called out amiably.

Bob's Big Boy squinted and rocked back on his heels just a touch. He and Reddi Kilowatt had consumed a bit more Modello than was probably good for them in the course of an evening.

"I used to look for the man in the moon when I was a kid," Bob's Big Boy said wistfully.

"Everyone looked for the man in the moon," Reddi Kilowatt agreed. "Then we went to the goddamned moon and ruined it."

The two of them stood in the middle of the single blacktop that ran through the valley, unconsciously propping each other up. They studied the wrinkles and crenellations they could make out on the surface. Their faces were bathed in the light reflected by the Sea of Tranquility.

Finally, Reddi Kilowatt said, "if it had been me, I would have brought beer."

"Huh?" Bob's Big Boy was perplexed.

"For the man in the moon," Reddi patiently explained. "If I'd gone to the moon, I would have brought some beer. When I come over to your house, I bring beer."

"You're a good man," Bob's Big Boy agreed. "A courteous man."

"Damn straight."

Bob's Big Boy shook his head. "I never thought how rude astronauts are."

Their conversation continued in that vein as they wound their way home.

Bob tumbled into bed and dreamed of drunken moons.

Angel's mind was on the Mayor as he locked up the Marguerita Bay Club. He hadn't seen hide nor hair of his Honor since the near miss traffic accident earlier in the day. He got in his car and drove around for a while, checking out the Mayor's favorite haunts. He gave up after a half an hour and went home. "That helicopter probably upset him," Angel decided. "He'll show up again after it goes away."

In point of fact, the Mayor had become distracted in the course of his afternoon duties and had fallen asleep hidden from view in Ms. Ryland-Bowles' hollyhocks. He'd wake up in the morning smelling like honey.

Before long, almost all the sentient life in Huernafano valley was slumbering. This wasn't a world of high drama or great social dissention. People's troubles were rarely so large that it kept them awake and the normal rhythm of the place was for consciousness to wink out within a half an hour of the last light being extinguished. By one o'clock, the only beings processing abstract thought were Barry and Coyote.

Barry had found the measure of himself and was grimly pleased. He'd stayed in his bolthole until he knew most of the residents of the valley would be asleep, then blackened his face and stealthily moved back into town. Until this afternoon, all his planning and exercises for this eventuality had been abstract. A man never knew exactly how he'd hold up in a crisis until the moment arrived. He was happy to discover he'd kept his cool and now slid about like a natural born guerilla. In his dark clothes, blackened face and watch cap, he moved like a ninja, darting from shadow to shadow. By one thirty, he'd made it through town, past the pueblo and was travelling through the black firs that covered the lower slopes of the mesa. He reached the crest undiscovered by two in the morning.

Well, undiscovered except for Coyote. Coyote had watched the progress of this shadow from the moment he emerged from the cliff face kiva and puzzled over what he could be up to. He drifted along behind Barry, sending small probes into the man's mind but it was like sorting through a jumble sale in there. A million disconnected thoughts ricocheted about his cortex without a single defining image other than a vague ghostly face. It appeared to be something gray, bland and with large insect eyes. Coyote was at a loss as to what this image meant.

Barry managed to reach the helicopter undisturbed. He was surprised, although he had no frame of reference to judge against, that the cockpit doors had no key locks. He slipped inside and quickly looked for any evidence of who these strangers might be. There was nothing of any great alarm; the only material he was able to run across were brochures for Black Mountain Air Tours. "This is a good cover," Barry thought to himself.

Frustrated over the lack of anything substantive in the chopper, he looked towards the house. The whitewashed abode seemed to glow in the moonlight, deepening the blackness of the windows. Barry debated the possibilities of entering the house unnoticed. He assumed that John had to have some sort of security system. After all, the man's cover was as a cutting edge technology company; there was possibly millions of dollars of equipment and proprietary material in there. He moved back into the shadows of the trees surrounding the house and did a visual recon of the property. No motion detectors or connection tape on the windows. Most surprising of all, the patio doors were wide open. He cautiously slipped inside.

An amused Coyote hovered like a ghost behind Barry as he crept through the house. At one point, Coyote was tempted to quickly re-embody and knock over a lamp or something, but the nervousness of Barry and the large K-Bar knife he had strapped to his leg dissuaded Coyote of the notion. He had no desire to see Barry accidentally shed anyone's blood.

"The man's very good at this," Coyote observed as they continued their progression through the house. Barry was able to enter every bedroom undetected, although it was a near thing when Barry recognized Ted Marquis sound asleep and inadvertently exclaimed "God damn!" under his breath. Ted made a grumble and shifted his position while Barry imitated a statue. Several interminable heartbeats later, Barry backed out of the room and exited the house.

Once Barry was outside, Coyote flicked on the exterior house lights just to see how quickly Barry would scramble for the lip of the mesa. Coyote wasn't disappointed either. The moment light flooded the open space around the property Barry frantically dove into the brush and rolled off the plateau, crashing down the slope for a hundred yards.

Once he'd collected himself, Barry decided that he could venture back to the compound. It was apparent that no strike force had landed on Blue Mesa, merely an advance unit for the company. The question that gnawed at him was the presence of Ted Marquis. Barry wanted to access his files on ByteStream, he felt like he was missing something.

It has been advanced that while a number of conditions need to occur, the thing that finally triggers an avalanche is the settling of a single snowflake. True or not, it makes an excellent metaphor for the consequences of seemingly insignificant acts. It is an open question as to whether or not Coyote later regretted his prank of spiriting away Barry's paper cup, as Coyote is not a creature with a conventional sense of morality. But, it cannot be argued that Barry's discovery that someone now had access to his DNA altered everything. Barry disappeared from Huernafano County that night into the bizarre underground railroad of safe houses and fellow denizens of the twilight world of conspiracy nuts.

In that moment, that space of time before the sun is anything but a slight line of pearl glowing on the eastern horizon, in the subtle shift of light that causes birds to withdraw their heads from under their wings and begin the soft cries of identification throughout the quiet valley, Coyote watched a tarantula wasp paralyze a large spider and then gently bury her eggs in its' thorax. The tarantula would be immobile for about twenty minutes, just about the time it would take for the sun to emerge from concealment among the hills to the east. It would live for another eight or nine days while the wasp larvae ate at it, going about its' business not knowing it carried its' own demise within it. Coyote watched all this and then turned to look at sleepy old Mesa Azul.

Chapter Four -

Ted comes to a decision, Carl goes to the Pueblo and the Doc gets an acolyte.

There was a rainbow over Saint Amandus' head when Angel woke up. An ancestor of his had built his house in 1720. The glass in most of the windows had been made in Mexico and was thick, slightly green and full of of bubbles, warps and imperfections. One of those imperfections caught a ray from the rising sun and split it like a prism, casting the spectra above the carved Santos in a niche on the far wall of Angel's bedroom. Angel's house was cluttered with Santos, but Saint Amandus was his favorite, since he was the patron saint of bartenders.

Angel's grandfather, Ameranté, had given special attention to Saint Jude when Angel was a boy, laying out tamales or rice for the saint every morning. Angel left an offertory to Amandus on his way out the door as well. He placed two fingers of Jack Daniel's, neat, at the saint's feet. In the evenings when he got home, he checked to see if the liquor had mysteriously vanished. It never had, so, raising the glass, he offered the saint a toast and knocked it back.

Angel lay there watching the rainbow move and slowly dissipate. He mulled over the events of the previous day, which had been a remarkably busy one by Mesa Azul standards. He'd lived his entire life in the valley and as far as he could recall, there had never been a helicopter flying up the canyon before. Actually, there had never been a helicopter anywhere within the environs of town. Everyone had spent the afternoon and evening calling each other to speculate on who had arrived in town in such a flamboyant manner. Angel smiled to himself. "I'll bet I know before nine this morning."

While getting dressed, he held a one sided conversation with San Lorenzo, who, thanks to being roasted to death on a griddle, was the patron saint of restaurateurs. "There's a lot of things to find out about today, patron. The helicopter, who those people were with Rick yesterday afternoon and where the hell the Mayor disappeared to."

Now, most people would be of the opinion that Angel was being nothing more than a gossipmonger, but in his heart, Angel felt he was following a long and noble family tradition. His lineage was handed down from Los Hermanos

Penitentes de la Tercer Orden de San Francisco who originally founded Mesa Azul. The Penitentes were sort of the civic council and infrastructure of the town. They acted, among other things, as a council of resolution for disputes among people in the valley. Angel felt that as long as he had such a background, getting the dish on anything going on was his duty to his ancestors. Not that he ever helped resolve anything, but he was usually the person everyone in town came to for the straight dope on events and activities in the Huernafano valley.

Part of the straight dope was sitting in John's jeep when Angel pulled up in front of the Club. John had mentioned Angel's frittatas to Ted the night before and Ted woke this morning with two things on his mind; frittatas and the possibility of building a development campus in Mesa Azul. He'd mentioned the former to John, which led to their presence at the Club doorstep but was saving the second issue for a more involved conversation over breakfast.

Introductions were made as Angel opened up the Club. New customers usually found the décor quite amusing. Everyone's first visit to the Marguerita Bay Club invariably elicited the same reaction. It was a space that never had quite made up its mind what it wanted to be. Angel liked to refer to it as a work in progress. Angel's father Arturo had been the original proprietor of the Club, then known as the Liberty Bell Diner. The old lunch counter and café tables were still in the front room, although Angel had converted the lunch counter into a bar of sorts. Soon after taking it over, Angel changed the name and knocked out the rear wall, adding on a larger dining room. His brother Hiraldo, a low level bureaucrat for the Department of the Interior in Washington had sent him a postcard from Toby's Pub in Georgetown and the collection of tin signs, stuffed animals, pool cues and other gimcrackery collected about the walls caught Angel's eyes. For months afterward he went on forays looking for decorative junk to hang on his own walls. Angel had many attributes, but a sense of design was not among them. The collection of garbage he assembled and bolted to the walls looked more like the hoard of a psychotic delusional than a fun and funky design statement.

Because the new dining room had a creepy feel to it, he removed all the crap from one wall and hired an itinerant sign painter to do a large mural there. It was supposed to be a beach scene, but the painter used odd references to work from; most notably Ron Nagle illustrations from old issues of Playboy magazine. At least it brightened the place up a little. Angel had christened it "The Acapulco Room".

While tucking in to the culinary delights of Angel's frittatas stuffed with home made chorizo, Ted broached the subject of opening a division of ByteStream in the Huernafano valley. "There's something about this place," he said to John, "that makes me more, I don't know, in tune with myself, I guess."

John choked on his eggs. Instinctively, he glanced through the doorway to where Angel stood behind the bar, polishing the countertop. "This isn't the place to have that discussion," he gasped.

John's mind was flooded with images of how bad things would get if ByteStream decided to build here. Every single reason he had for settling down in Mesa Azul would be gone. Ghastly visions of tract homes and shopping malls where the old pokey town had been swirled about in his head and sent ice water straight into his heart. Injunctions and rights to access petitions for dish space on his mesa danced like horned demons over his cortex. This was the worst news he could have possibly imagined and he frantically began thinking about a way to quash the idea.

The only other person to be mulling over the ramifications of what Ted had proposed was Steve. Off the top of his head, it sounded idiotic. Any and all infrastructure needed to support both a development center and the potential employees it would attract didn't exist. From what he could tell, the great State of New Mexico couldn't give a fart in a windstorm about this blowhole in the back of beyond. You might as well build a campus on the moon. Sure there was land aplenty, but that was about it.

The moment that last thought ran through his head, Steve could feel the hairs on his arms raise. What if someone owned this land? Someone who was privy to what the richest corporation on earth wanted to do with it? What if that someone knew that a complete babe in the woods ran this corporation?

"What a revolutionary idea!" Steve burst out, raising his glass of orange juice to his boss. Ted beamed. John scowled and asked everyone to put a sock in it. In a sotto voce, John hissed, "unless you want the entire county to know what you're thinking, we'll save this discussion for my house." Assuming a normal tone again, he deftly asked his guests what they thought of Angel's cuisine.

The entry of Bob's Big Boy distracted everyone. Normally loud, boisterous and full of energy, especially in the mornings, the huge Indian was suffering from the overindulgences of the night before.

"Angel, you son of a bitch," he moaned while shuffling to the bar, "what did you do to me last night?"

Angel grinned. "You look like someone's playing the anvil chorus inside your head. You in shape to drive the Blue Bus today?" Bob's Big Boy delicately perched on a stool and laid his head on the cool linoleum of the counter and groaned. Angel solicitously patted the Shantis' broad back and started pulling down the ingredients for a hangover cure.

In the other room, John's guests had watched Bob's Big Boy's entrance in silence. Carl quietly asked John if Bob was one of the people that lived at the Pueblo. "Well," John chuckled, "looks more like he was dying at the pueblo." He raised his voice and hollered to Bob's Big Boy, "firewater bad medicine, eh, bro?" John enjoyed the reaction his booming voice had on Bob's Big Boy; a severe quiver running the length of his frame and an extended moan.

After knocking back a hellacious mixture of Tabasco and Worcestershire sauce, V-8, raw eggs and ground aspirin, Bob gratefully accepted the cup of coffee Angel handed to him and walked into the Acapulco Room.

"Goddamned last of the Mohicans," he rumbled while sitting down at John's table. "Why don't you go back where you came from?"

"Seneca," John happily corrected him. "No, I was commissioned by the American Indian Movement to sit on your doorstep and keep you friggin' Shantis from embarrassing the rest of the Native American community."

John's cohorts seemed a little nonplussed as Bob's Big Boy was introduced. Even more so when John asked Bob's Big Boy if Doctor Pepper had been performing a ceremony the night before. "Could be," Bob's Big Boy replied, "but I was here with Reddi Kilowatt so I can't be sure. Ask the Pep Boys, they were watching soccer last night."

"Wait a minute," Steve interjected. "Am I right? All you people are named after products?"

"Yeah," Bob's Big Boy replied. "A couple of years ago. I'm always in the market for ways to raise revenues for the tribal coffers, right? Anyway, I read this article in Fortune about how companies are paying big bucks to get stadiums and stuff named after them, so I thought, why not sell our identities to the highest bidder? It's worked out great. I get fifty bucks a month for changing my name. Most of the tribe get anywhere from fifty to a hundred and ten. Steady income, bro."

It was true. After the initial inspiration, Bob's Big Boy had run ads in Fortune, the Wall Street Journal and Marketing Today. It became a measure of cachet among companies to have a Shantis Indian bearing their corporate identity. The Pep Boys scored the largest coup by not only being paid as the native representatives of the corporate title but garnering additional cash by taking the names of Manny, Moe and Jack. Missus Butterworth was currently in negotiations with General Mills to have her children be known collectively as Rice Crispies and then individually referred to as Snap, Crackle and Pop.

"Unbelievable," was Steve's only comment.

Bob got up from the table with the announcement that he had to get the Blue Bus on the road. "Last day of school," he sighed. "Too bad nobody in this town ever wants to go anywhere. I'm going to miss the song of the open road."

"Are you the taxi service for this place?" Steve enquired.

"Sorta," Bob agreed. "No chauffeur's license or medallion though. You need to go someplace? Gotta be cash and under the table."

Ted raised an eyebrow. Steve squirmed just a little under the scrutiny but he felt he needed to get down to the land offices and do some searching through the public records. Not that he was going to tell the Big Kahuna that.

"I didn't think we'd be spending more than a day here, Mister Marquis," he explained unctuously. "I can't get my cell to call out of this valley and I have some business to take care of back at the office."

"Take the helicopter," Ted said nodding to Curtis, their pilot. "I'm sure Mister Monroe has better things to do than watch the scenery change. I want to stay down here for a few days, I'll call your office when I want to be picked up."

Bob's Big Boy looked crestfallen at that exchange. Mentally, he'd already pictured himself whipping the Blue Bus through the curves of the Rio Grande road down to Santa Fe. He'd had a dream the night before that the entire tribe had decided to become nomads. Packing them into the Blue Bus he'd gone roaring up and over La Vida Pass into the Rocky Mountains, loudspeakers blaring and flags flying. He woke up aching with wanderlust.

Doctor Pepper was perplexed and a little disappointed. After his connection with the greater forces of the heavens the day before, he'd spent the rest of the day and the evening waiting for some sort of follow-up communiqué. He'd even used up the last of his powders and pollens sending sacred smoke into the night sky and nothing. He had a cryptic message that meant next to nothing and he'd worn himself down trying to divine an additional meaning.

He'd fallen asleep cross-legged in front of his fire and woken up stiff. He was too old for such shenanigans. At some point, Betty Crocker had thrown a blanket over him and he was gimping his way across the pueblo to return it to her. All the Shantis kids were waiting on Bob's Big Boy to haul them down to Taos for their last day of school. A number of them were playing hackey-sack and he envied their youth and energy. Chuck E. Cheese popped the sack viciously and the Doc followed its' arc high into the morning air, where his eye came to rest on the peculiar machine that rested atop Blue Mesa.

It might be a logical assumption that the epiphany he'd received was related to the people the helicopter had brought, but the Doc was never a man to assume anything. He thought he might go down to the Marguerita Bay Club and find out what Angel knew. Watching out for the spiritual welfare of his people wasn't as easy for him as was for a lot of other mystics he thought to himself. Christians and Jews and Muslims and Buddhists had lots of texts to draw from. Most other tribes had at least a tradition to draw from, whereas he wandered lost and without direction in the cosmos. "I make it up as I go along," the Doc muttered to himself as he walked into town.

The departure of the Blue Bus was the tacit signal it seemed, for the inhabitants of Mesa Azul to get on with the day's work. As it rattled out of the valley, leaving behind an aromatic trail of diesel fumes, people emerged from their homes and got on with the tasks at hand. Camilla Ryland-Bowles came out to attend her garden and discovered the Mayor asleep in the hollyhocks, shooing him off like he was a crow in a cornfield. The Mayor dashed out the front gate and fell in step with the Doc. They passed by Corky Gonzales' garage and listened to the musical ringing of Corky's hammer trying to knock loose the kingpins of a rusty International Harvester truck. The air was sweetened by the smell of corn tortillas being fried in Julie Modesto's house. Her boyfriend Herbie, whom she'd met on the internet and just recently moved to this little chunk of nowhere and found everything more of a challenge than he'd supposed, was on the front porch examining the ancient railing of peeled pine poles that Julie had asked him to repair. He was looking at the hammer in his hand with trepidation.

A little further up the road Mickey Esposito had spread out a tarp and disassembled the gas feed valve of his propane tank. The Mayor wandered over to inspect the process and was greeted with a sharp retort and a hurled rock. He quickly rejoined the Doc. It occurred to the Doc that he and the Mayor where the two most useless denizens of Mesa Azul. Everyone else, it appeared, was busy fixing things or making things, growing things and doing things that were of benefit. The Doc felt he lacked the vision necessary to look after his people and the Mayor didn't seem to care what happened to anyone. The Doc was about to mention that to his Honor when the Mayor abruptly departed, having been distracted by the scent of fresh sopapillas emanating from Magdalene Ortero's kitchen.

Two strangers almost knocked him down as he entered the Club. One flashed a smile of stunning brilliance and said, "Sorry, chief! Didn't see you coming," while the other merely danced around him in an irritated manner, looked at his watch and said to his companion, "let's shake a leg. I'd want to get back to Albuquerque before ten."

The second man appeared to have a nimbus around him, a dark purple like a bruise that shifted to a brilliant crimson on the edges and pulsed outward in waves. The stunned medicine man stood in the doorway looking after them for a moment and then discovered as he looked inside the Club that another set of coursing rays seemed to be leeching out from the Acapulco Room. Angel hollered at him to either come in or go out, as it was, he was letting flies in.

"It's too early for flies," Doctor Pepper said distractedly. He entered the Club warily and peered around the corner into the dining room. The strange lights had receded and he merely saw John Elkhorn and two strangers. Even with that, the shaman sensed he was in the grip of something that had taken control of him. The Doc felt as though he were a helpless spectator in a runaway truck, unable to control any part of himself, yet calmly detached from the process. It posed some interesting questions to the old healer. He wondered if this was finally the way his life was going to work out, as the awkward and vaguely unwilling doorway for the great forces of the universe to interact with humanity.

He kept moving forward and turned to the tall fellow sitting to the right of John. "Your life just changed," the Doc said to the stranger, while in his mind he was shocked at what was emanating from his lips. It sounded almost like an alien voice, even though he recognized it as his own. To John he said, "you think the lives around you are going to change and you don't know what to do about it." The Doc was appalled at his rudeness and discourtesy. Finally, to the kid at the table, he uttered, "your life changed the moment I walked in here." Then he collapsed into a chair.

Coyote was drifting. He hovered among the acoustic tiles on the ceiling of the Acapulco Room, watching the scene play out below him. The Doc's heart was an open door he could walk through as easily as the very air he inhabited. The old man's need to connect with something outside of himself was a beacon to him. Any small event he created was received with such deep gratitude and reverence by the ancient shaman that it moved Coyote as much as anything could.

He'd found John's guest Ted an interesting thing as well. He'd entered the man's dreams the night before and found someone who was terrified of their own life. The poor fellow was plagued with a sense of powerlessness. His life had spun out of control and in the darkness of his mind he yearned to get a handle on it. Coyote watched as he dreamed of his teeth falling out, sensed the absolute terror that coursed through the fellow as he held a bit of broken ivory in his fingers. It was such an agonizing experience that Coyote altered the course of the dream.

He had the dreamtime Ted drink from the waters of the Huernafano. As he did so, teeth grew like new buds from his impotent gums. The person he had been cracked like dried mud and fell away, revealing a new and robust man, glistening in the morning sunshine. Coyote felt the joy of shaping this man's rebirth.

John's consternation at Ted's decision to build a company here was merely a bonus. Coyote had found his friend's unflappability grating to a certain extent. It was nice to know John was vulnerable. It ought to make for some interesting conversations later.

Carl was unshaped clay. The boy was as formless as anything Coyote had ever experienced. Carl's dreams were undirected masses of random imagery, dense in symbolism and steeped in an overwhelming sense of mystery. Coyote wandered in there and saw things even he strained to interpret. An arrow shot into the sky and trailing a chain. A blossom that opened and revealed a beating heart. A book on a windblown and rocky slope. As a gust blew the cover open and riffled the pages, leaves flew out and were carried spiraling upwards where they transformed into white birds. These were the sorts of dreams someone looking for a direction in life had. Coyote felt the kid cast a wide net; whatever he'd pull in he'd look at with open eyes and eventually keep the thing that glinted.

Steve's dreams held little interest for Coyote. They were furious little tempests. Angry squalls without purpose but full of a roaring need to tear, beat and rage against everything they came in contact with. A cacophony reigned there as the dream man pounded the dents out of a sheet of metal that was as rippled as water and every blow that landed didn't smooth the steel but caused even more buckling. He vehemently beat a misshapen thing into an even more formless mass. Coyote dismissed him from any possible interest at that point.

What was left however, struck Coyote as interesting material to work with. The universe is a series of dynamic forces, tensions that support and pull at each other at the same time. It is a delicate balancing act that humanity has always sensed but never fully understood. The relations between human beings weren't that dissimilar and Coyote recognized that people had as little an understanding of those forces within themselves as they did the greater forces of the cosmos.

It was the point at which faith was born. People, overwhelmed with the vastness of things, spun fragile cobwebs over titanic chasms and called it faith. They danced over these voids on gossamer threads. It was a heartbreaking and yet breathtaking ballet to watch. Every person found a mantra, a catechism to hold on to like a balancing pole. Coyote heard them spiraling up and out on a consistent basis. These testaments of faith caressed him like a warm breeze.

It struck Coyote that it always boiled down to power. They sent out supplications to the strength of something outside of themselves. God, love or self-determination; there were a million variants of a single thing. It fascinated Coyote. He loved to play with this thing, to feed a belief or to challenge it. The reactions were unpredictable, perhaps the one unpredictable thing about humanity.

"Jesus, Doc," John said in alarm, "are you okay?"

Doctor Pepper looked at John for a long beat; his face a blank slate and then a beatific smile wreathed his face. "Yes, maybe for the first time."

Angel and John fussed over the Doc for a bit, while Ted and Carl exchanged the embarrassed look people will give one another during alarms they aren't a part of. The shaman protested that he was fine, no matter how insistent his two friends where that had to be suffering from something. Finally, the Doctor went over the extraordinary events of the past twenty-four hours. It did little to soothe John, while Angel shrugged it off.

"Guy spends all his time trying to commune with spirits," the barkeep said with a shrug, "he's bound to get a little loco after a while. I'm surprised it took this long."

"I don't know," John said. "I've read about stuff like this. You might have had a stroke or something. Let me drive you to the hospital in Taos."

"Seriously," the Doc said, while looking anything but serious. He was almost giddy with elation over finally hit some sort of plateau of spirituality, "I'm okay. I'm exactly where I'm supposed to be."

Things went back and forth until Carl volunteered to walk the old man back home. "I've been wanting to take a look at that pueblo since we got here."

"You sure?" John asked.

"It's not that big of a place," Carl said. "I think I can find my way back eventually."

This little piece of earth had never, in its' long existence, experienced so much movement, so much change, so rapidly. As Carl led the old shaman back to his earthwork home, he became a modern Saul on the road to Damascus, as uncomprehending of the future as that ancient venerable had been. Steve, riding a black helicopter that tattooed out a series of harsh booms and cast its' wicked shadow over the valley as it departed, schemed out how he could leverage the country he was leaving to his advantage while his boss dreamed of how this land would save him from the hollowness and disconnection he felt in the rest of the world. It's a wonder that the earth itself didn't shudder.

How capable is anything of noticing change, however? Things occur in stages that are hardly recognizable except in retrospect. The universe hurls along and all that dwells inside it is churned and polished like rocks in a tumbler, broken down and smoothed, but with such a motion and over such a time that the violence of it all is hardly noticed. At best we feel a little grit in our eyes.

John, for example, rubbed his eyes and went on with the business at hand. Perhaps, he thought, if he could involve his new potential business partner deeply in the world of fractal compression, Ted might forget about the larger and more tangible world around him. The magic of patterned relationships and reflecting pairs would absorb his focus and the buttes and mesas, the purple sage and yellow yarrow and the meadowlark's song would be forgotten and left alone.

As John lured Ted into a world of cutting edge technology, Doctor Pepper inadvertently brought Carl into a more ancient, but just as mysterious type of specialized craft. As they walked along the blacktop, the Doc subconsciously recognized he had somehow acquired an acolyte and expounded on the topic of mysteries.

"Everyone accepts electricity," he began, while pointing at the line of high-tension towers marching down into the valley, "but if I stopped anyone and asked them how electricity travels through those wires or turns into something like heat, they'd probably be at a loss." He looked at Carl. "It's an acceptable mystery. Tell me," he went on, "how do the pictures from around the world go from whatever the satellite sends to that thing," he pointed at the old Army Dish and transmission monitoring station, "to my house and turn back into images on my TV?"

"They're broadcast waves, sir," Carl began.

"Uh huh, go on."

"Well, they're broadcast and then received by your television."

"How do they go from these waves you mention to a picture?"

"I'm not sure," Carl stammered. "But you could probably look the process up and learn about it."

The old Indian smiled. "See? An acceptable mystery. You don't know how it works but you accept that it does."

"I guess."

"No," the shaman said, "I guess. I guess a lot. Things aren't always easy to divine. But I'm getting there."

And so they went, walking and getting somewhere. Doctor Pepper had never had such an interested ear before and it was rather novel for him. Most of his people just looked at him as a necessity for their social structure. They didn't really think about what he did or tried to do. They'd always had a shaman and since he was their shaman, the world was intact. It wasn't so different from being the King of England. It was a position that filled a need. A need that was no longer relevant.

Now, he seemed to have a function, a place in the broader scheme of things. He saw himself as a conduit, a conductor for the forces outside the sphere he existed in. He described himself as a spiritual battery to Carl.

Carl, for his part, found himself intrigued. His teenage years had been spent either learning computer languages, codes and development or playing games on his computer wherein he was a wizard in a magical landscape of supernatural forces. These games filled a need for mysteries. Now he was with a man who actually lived with mysteries. A man whose landscape was unseen by most people, who held a key to a vast doorway he'd been curious about for years. All he needed was one sign; one verification, and he'd happily walk away from the world he was familiar with.

Coyote, drifting along with them as they wound their way back to the Pueblo, listened to their voices, inside and out. The boy's yearning tickled him and he decided to urge the situation along a bit.

If there was a single thing that Coyote understood that was beyond the grasp of humanity, it was that everything is sensate. Men, in their desire to understand the structure of the universe, made distinctions between the animate and the inanimate, the organic and inorganic. This was the fatal flaw in their logic. There was a sensory level to every molecule, an ineffable vibration that could be called upon and manipulated. All matter was interrelated and interconnected on some level. To Coyote, it was palpable and he employed it easily.

The alluvial floor of the Huernafano valley is riddled with particles of iron oxide, giving the dirt a red cast. This iron has certain properties of conductivity that make it an excellent toy for Coyote to play with. He charged a small percentage of this iron dust and caused it to glow like the rings on an electric range. The old Indian and the kid froze as this pattern of glowing red concentric rings appeared in the earth near the edge of the black top road. They watched uncomprehending as Coyote made these luminous particles slowly rise from the soil matrix they where in and drift into the air, lazily spinning like leaves caught in an updraft.

Gradually decreasing circles of glowing, pulsing iron hovered in the air and then drifted over the Doc. They descended and enveloped him; gracefully creating a transparent bubble that enclosed him. The interior molecular vibration of these particles increased and glowed like white-hot magma for an instant, then backed off to a fiery orange. The top edge of the iron egg the shaman was encased in separated into a ribbon shape that unwound and floated like a serpent towards Carl, who stood fixated on this phenomenon. The particles curled around his feet and then spiraled outward. They lay there for a few moments, pulsing and then suddenly flared into brightness again, burning the last of the oxidation that coated the iron and leaving a black spiral fired into the tar of the road.

"Triangles," John explained to Ted. They were in John's studio as John walked his guest through the process of creating digital worlds and beings. "Everything is modeled on triangles in a three dimensional space."

Ted was fascinated by the mindset it took to design in these parameters. His life had been linear, as had been his thought processes. He worked inside a constant process of going from point A to point B. Now he was asked to look at existence as a multi-dimensional experience.

"Look at yourself as being a point in space," John said, "the central point from which all dimension radiates. Within you is the core axis. Your external dimensions are measured from that axis using a triangulation of X, Y and Z. Everything outside of yourself is related to that point on the same principle."

"You make me sound like the center of the universe," Ted laughed.

John smiled and said, "to a certain extent, you are. At least," he went on, "of your universe. Depending on the camera angle I need to replicate, that would be the argument."

"That's the thing that has fascinated me about CGI work from the outset," John said while moving a digital stylus over an artpad. On the computer monitor, Ted watched as a matrix of triangles slowly defined a creature made of yellow intersecting points in a black void. A blue crosshair was positioned in the center of these interconnecting lines, illuminating the center of the universe. John worked rapidly, highlighting points of the yellow matrix and explaining the assignment of properties to them. "Skin and muscle," he told Ted. "Once I've assigned control points to them, I'll put the bones in." Now red bars were placed on the screen. Eventually they began to look like a weird skeletal structure within the now defined external parameters of a wire-frame monster. John pulled green threads from these bars and attached them to various points on the yellow matrix.

"Bingo!" he said more to himself than his guest. "Okay," he said straightening up and smiling at Ted, "time to introduce Throgmor to the rest of the cast." He walked over to a bank of monitors and turned them on. Actors capering about a blue void appeared. "This is the blue screen stuff I get from the production company," John explained. "Watch this." He activated an optical print program and suddenly a blasted landscape of smoking ruins and twisted trees surrounded the actors. They appeared to be fighting a stagehand in a blue body suit that was waving a cardboard studded with red ping pong balls on a pole around.

"First I key the model marker you see," John said while pointing to the cardboard bounding around in the blue screen on one of his monitors, "to the height and position of the monster I've created."

Ted watched entranced as his host launched two more programs and then banged out some arcane commands.

"Now, I take the model I created and have it interact with this motion capture suit," John explained, while pointing out a sort of body stocking hanging on the wall, studded with fifty or so sensors trailing long cords that plugged into processing box. John's motion capture actor would put this suit on, along with a pair of goggles that had small liquid crystal display screens embedded in the lenses. The actor could watch his interaction with the characters in the blue screen world and adjust his movements accordingly.

"Can I try it on?" Ted asked shyly.

John helped him into the suit, turned on the motion-processing box and checked the action against his model on the monitor. He directed Ted in some simple movements such as raising an arm or moving a leg. Once he was satisfied with the interaction, he flipped on Ted's goggles.

"I can't see anything," Ted commented.

"Shit," John exclaimed. "Sorry," he grabbed Ted by the arm and led him to a large white cross painted on the studio floor. "You need to be in the center of the universe."

Ted's world suddenly came into view. Before his eyes were the apocalyptic landscape he'd seen on the monitors, as well as the actors. The new element was a huge hunchbacked figure with stunted legs along with lanky muscular arms that ended in viciously clawed hands and a hideously misshapen head. He raised his arm and the creature mimicked his movement. "Is that me?" he asked John.

"Yep," John said. "Watch the actors you see and make yourself respond to their movements."

Ted spent the next hour trying to control the being that he viewed through the goggles. It was an odd sensation to be watching his movements from a third person perspective. Sort of an out of body experience, Ted found himself to be a monster at the center of the universe.

He'd never been so happy.

Chapter Five -

In which we learn what hurts and what doesn't.

There aren't a lot of hidden places in Mesa Azul. For the most part, everything is visible from anywhere. Discounting Barry Moss, it wasn't a place for the secretive to live. Of course, the lives people have out in the open is often a far cry from the things they dream of or yearn for.

Angel, looking out of the front window of the Marguerita Bay Club, dreamed of a Mesa Azul that resembled a celluloid Casablanca, full of interesting and intriguing events, where he could stand at the top of a sweeping staircase, martini in hand and draped in a summer dinner jacket and look down on the sea of mystery spread out on a casino floor. As his eyes traced the long shadows of the late afternoon, his mind cast him as the one man who's lifetime of experience, who's streetwise and sage wisdom of human nature could alter the destinies of anyone who asked. "It would just be nice to do it in classier surroundings," he muttered to himself.

The little town was an odd creation. It never looked prosperous and yet it didn't seem run down either. People took care of their properties. You never saw a canted fence or piebald adobe. As a matter of fact, if one listened carefully, you could usually hear the faint thud of new mud being thrown on a wall somewhere. Patching adobe was one of the few house maintenance tasks on earth that was actually fun to do.

No, the fences were painted and the gardens tended. People that lived on the dirt cutoffs from the main blacktop took good care of their sections of roads. The dirt was raked and planed regularly and the roadside edge of the culverts lined with whitewashed stones. Geraniums, snapdragons, verbena and marigolds grew in neatly fenced gardens or pots hanging from veranda roofs. Two or three anglophiles struggled mightily to keep neat squares of grass in their front yard; their lush green blades a testament to a daily battle with the arid climate and the hearty varieties of bindweed and choker that called the valley their home.

With all that, aside from John's place atop the mesa, there hadn't been a new building raised here since the Army built the tracking station. It could be argued that the group of bohemians who arrived in 1967 and attempted to start a commune to the north of the pueblo erected buildings of sorts. That is, if one considered a converted school bus and three canvas teepees buildings. They were also the last folks to try starting a new industry in Mesa Azul until John Elkfoot arrived. They scoured the countryside looking for herbs as the central ingredients for a natural, non-caffeinated tea.

Angel smiled wistfully as he thought about those hippies. The first car accident he ever had was indirectly caused by one of them. He was driving his dad's old four by four down the western side of Doloroso Pass into Mesa Azul during a rainstorm when he encountered one of the girls from the commune. She was soaked to the bone and her muslin peasant blouse had taken on the consistency of a soggy tissue, which inspired his sense of chivalry while at the same time rendering his common sense inoperative. He stomped on the brakes in order to pull to the side of the trail and give her a lift, however, the rain slick and muddy track, combined with the gravitational force decided otherwise and he slid into a tree. Still, the sight of her cornflower eyes, open smile and jaunty breasts was worth the cost of a cracked radiator and two weeks in the doghouse when his old man found out.

The commune lasted for a little more than a year. The herb tea business never took off as it was a little ahead of its time, Angel supposed. The mainstay for the enterprise had been the steady stream of letters out of the valley to places like Forest Lake and Newport where the parents of these vagabonds sent stipends in return. Eventually, even that sort of funding ran out and the members drifted off, one by one; back into the tailored and plush bedroom communities they fled years before. Two hard winter snows eradicated any trace of the teepees and the bus was devoured for parts just as quickly. Today the only sign that it had ever been there was the rusted chassis nearly enveloped in columbine and Virginia creeper.

All together, the businesses in town consisted of Angel's restaurant, Corky's Garage and Repair shop where Corky would tackle anything, even if he had no clue as to what it might be, what was broken or how to go about repairing it. Hodel's Hardware, probably the oldest established business in Mesa Azul, had gone from selling leather harnesses to chain saws as time and need went by. Mullin's Dry Goods and Grocer limped along on a subsistence basis, selling any and all necessities folks needed on a daily basis. For anything important or for real groceries, people traveled twenty-five miles to Taos. Finally there was John's business up on the plateau. Everyone else was either a farmer or odd artisan, whose products found their way down to the valley to the more prosperous places.

One curious attribute of everyone in the community was cattle. It didn't matter who you were or what you did, before you'd been in Mesa Azul long, you found yourself owning cattle. For some people, such as Ms. Ryland-Bowles, it might be a single white-faced heifer that she bought merely to feel as if she belonged to the community, while for others, they would run several hundred head on the government land across Hernafano Creek. John bought a blindingly white Brahma he named Gizmo. On Sunday afternoons, he'd stop by Camilla's house and escort her across the stream so they could commune with their livestock. She'd named her cow Georgia, to no one's surprise.

They were all beef stock but only half of the folks ever seemed to send their beeves off to the stock pens in Pueblo. Angel himself kept a few head that he'd regularly have shipped to a butcher in Alamagordo. They'd split carcasses fifty-fifty and it cut down on his meat bills at the restaurant. A lot of his customers would ask if one of his cows was on the menu on a given night as the local beef browsed heavily on sage and it rendered the meat a bit savory for some folks' taste.

As much as Angel liked to think he was the lynchpin of society in the valley, he recognized that the cattle were the real catalyst binding everyone together. Managing those animals was a group effort and an informal committee had developed over the years that dealt with issues of ownership, health, grazing and the myriad other small details running livestock entailed.

There were a couple annual chores that required most of the town's participation. The big event of the year regarding the herd was the spring roundup. Every cow had to be examined, doused and assayed before being turned back loose on the range. It was also the time when the new calves were castrated, debudded of their horns and branded. This demanded a lot of bodies and the whole town turned out to give a hand in one way or another. It had developed a real carnival atmosphere over the years. New traditions had been layered on old over time until the whole event had a ritualistic atmosphere. Even the relative newcomer, John Elkfoot had triggered a new wrinkle when he attended his first roundup garbed in a huge fingerroll brimmed Stetson, spangled shirt and wooly sheepskin chaps. Ever since then, folks tried to outdo each other in their resemblance the singing cowboy movie stars of yesteryear.

Angel's favorite event of the spring roundup was the ownership tribunal. Most of the calving occurred right around the spring equinox, but that was an uncomfortable time in the low foothills where the herd ranged so hardly anyone meandered out in late March looking for newborns so most of the calves that came in at roundup were assigned ownership based on what cow they were following. This was an inaccurate system as there might be a dozen calves that were late winter births and already weaned and they didn't seem to be attached to any cow in particular. In those instances, Corky, Freddy Apodokas, Randall Webster and Angel reviewed claims for disputed calves. It gave Angel a sense of Solomon-like wisdom to discuss the merits of a claim with his fellow board members. It was lessened to the extent that they tended to decide a case by either recalling which claimant had been awarded a calf recently and giving title to the opposing claimant or by flipping a coin.

In mid-summer, when the cattle had been on rich grazing for a few months and recovered their weight from the previous winter, those cattle that were going to the stockyards were culled from the herd and driven eighteen miles to the rail spur of the Denver and Rio Grande. Anywhere from fifty to a hundred head were cut out and sent on a two day drive to cover the distance. It had become a ceremony to drive them across Huernafano Creek and onto the blacktop that ran through the center of town. John Elkfoot described it as "the Walking of the Bulls".

"It's just like the Fiesta di San Fermin in Pamplona," he said to Angel once. "Just not as colorful or exciting."

Now that school was out, it was time to move the herd up into the foothills and lower slopes of the Sangre di Cristos. Three or four teenaged kids with horse sense would spend the summer up at the line shack and Angel began thinking over possible prospects. He and his brother had done their turn up in the high country thirty years ago, along with a seventeen-year-old girl named Ruby Mora. It was the one and only time Angel ever fell in love.

Ruby had actually asked to be part of the line camp that summer. A natural horsewoman, she'd been curious about how well she'd fare as a working cowpoke. While her equestrian skills weren't in question, her ability to handle obstreperous livestock, primitive conditions and two boys filled with more hormones than common sense was. Angel and Hiraldo's father had volunteered them, in the hopes that it would put a little coat of self-reliance on his sons. On the first of June, the three of them, along with six spare horses and four hundred and twenty head of cattle moved up to the La Garitas highlands, where they would stay for the next three months.

It was pretty country up there, filled with open meadows that spilled out from dense stands of Blue Spruce and lodge-pole pine. As the late spring gave way to early summer, the meadows became dotted with asters and mountains daisies, columbines and paintbrush. The serenity and beauty of the place brought out a chivalrous side in both of the Ramirez boys and they decided it would be in everyone's best interest for them to sleep under canvas while Ruby got the line cabin to herself.

At first, Angel merely had typically adolescent fantasies late at night about Ruby. She was iconographic, without personality at that point. As they worked together, however, she became a fully rounded individual and Angel found blushed inwardly when he thought about his fevered dreams during those early days. All sorts of romantic notions began seeping into his head and often lay awake staring at the canvas roof wrestling with his own inhibitions about making any sort of advance towards her.

Hiraldo didn't bear the same affliction, it seemed. More than once he got under his brother's skin when he speculated on what sex with Ruby would be like. "I like those jeans," he said lecherously one morning while they watched Ruby cut her painted quarter horse down the crumbling slope of an arroyo where some calf had gotten stuck in a wallow. The lizard part of Angel's brain had to agree, Ruby was posting at the time and the denim fabric clung like a leech to the tautest buttocks he'd ever laid eyes on. On the other hand, that sort of objectification of a woman with the poise, acumen and grace that Ruby possessed rankled Angel's delicate teenage soul. It only grew worse at night when he could hear his brother frantically masturbating, knowing what was running through Hiraldo's grimy little mind.

Ruby was apparently oblivious to both Angel's tender interest as well as Hiraldo's seamier focus. She treated both of them with the same happy attention she gave the cows. Conversations tended to focus on the practical or observational, partly due to Angel's reticence to plunge deeper into human relations for fear of rejection as well as Ruby's seeming indifference to anything else.

As the days moved on, Angel felt himself sinking deeper and deeper into this morass of unrequited love. Tiny, snatched moments of revelation were burnt into his mind. One late afternoon in July, for example, as he was coming back through a stand of aspen chivvying three yearlings that had wandered way up the slope until they found themselves corralled by thickets of currant bushes, he heard a sharp hiss and looked down the slope to where Ruby was cautiously waving him over. Hobbling his horse with his reins, he gave each of the calves a boot in the ass to hurry them down the hill and walked to where Ruby stood. She'd found a hummingbird nest in the fork of an aspen.

While the male hummer darted about their heads like an angry, iridescent jewel, they peered into the tiny, meticulously made bowl that held three eggs the size of a nail on Angel's pinky. In order to see the nest, Angel had to put his head so close to Ruby's that he imagined he could feel the downy hair on her cheek brushing his face. His eyes darted rapidly between the nest and Ruby's face, memorizing the curve of her lashes, the color and texture of her lips and the flash of her neat, brilliant teeth. He inhaled the scent of shampoo left on her hair and the fragrance of Juicy Fruit that emanated from her mouth. Even now, thirty years on, the smell of that gum caused Angel's heart a momentary glitch. There was a tiny little scar there and he protected it like a child.

Another time, when Angel was putting bit in his buckskin mare's mouth, Buttercup decided to be ornery and snapped hard at his thumb, opening up a gash that erupted like Vesuvius. He dashed into the line shack for some tape, gauze and Mercurochrome, only to interrupt Ruby while she was taking a cold-water bath in the galvanized tub they used to clean both themselves and their laundry.

"Dios Mia!" he exclaimed while backpedaling frantically. In his efforts to move back out of the door, he caught a boot heel on the rough-hewn threshold of the cabin and fell flat on his back, knocking the air out of him.

As he lay there gasping for air, he could hear Ruby laughing hysterically. It seemed to be coming from a far distance though, as he was still lingering on some level in the previous moment. When he came bursting in, she was pinning her hair up before settling down in the tub. The position of her arms gave that exceptional line to the shoulders, neck and sides of a woman that artists have pursued since time immemorial, as well as a lift to the breasts, which were limned in the dusty morning sunlight that streamed in from the cobwebbed east windows of the cabin. The whole picture in Angel's mind seemed to be suffused with a saffron glow. He felt as though he'd had a glimpse of heaven.

From that moment on, Angel was lost. Ruby had become elevated past the realm of mere mortals into something beyond this world. No matter what she did, it seemed to him an act of grace or beauty beyond this world's scope. Hiraldo, however, kept bringing things back down to a much lower plane.

He seemed to have no problem interacting with Ruby at all. There was no nobility in his brother, the young Angel had decided. One evening when Hiraldo challenged Ruby to a farting contest after they'd discovered the pinto beans they'd consumed were particularly explosive and Ruby happily took him on, Angel departed their company with wounded dignity and sought solace in the wilderness. As he walked off into the darkness, he heard his brother exclaim, "Angel can't fart, he's too constipated." While the remark stung a little, Ruby's ensuing gales of laughter cut to the bone.

That unpleasant memory snapped Angel out of his reverie. He was surprised at how long the shadows had become, blue stripes running across the road and enveloping the front of his café. It wouldn't be long before his evening customers started dropping in. Pleasantly melancholy, he felt company wouldn't be a bad thing about now and turned on his heel, back towards his station at the bar, swinging a bar rag like a lariat.

"A sense of belonging, mostly," John said. He and Ted were sitting on the patio, with its view of both the town below them and the mountains above them, being tinted by the last rays of the day's sun. A corona of light appeared between Los Hermanos, the two peaks that bore that name and seared the clouds above them a fiery orange. Everything else was caught in the cool blue of the mountain's shadow and from their vantage point, the two men watched the neon sign of the Marguerita Bay Club wink on.

Ted had wondered out loud why John originally settled in Mesa Azul since he seemed so adamant that Ted not do the same thing.

"Until I came here, I always felt like I was watching the world through a plate glass window," John went on.

"I can appreciate that," Ted said dreamily. John looked askew at Ted, whose glasses had picked up the fire in the sky and the lenses seemed to glow at him eerily. Ted had been acting strangely all day. It was a little disconcerting.

Shrugging it off, John went on. "Well, I guess everyone feels disconnected now and then, but honestly, I felt like everyone else was living life while I was just observing it."

John had been the complete outsider for most of his life. It was evident at an early age that he had an intellect of unusual capacity. His quickness and ability isolated him from his classmates and caused the school system he was in to constantly promote him in grade levels as it became apparent that anything they could teach him didn't challenge his gifts. He graduated from public school at fourteen and started college the very next year.

While still an undergraduate, he'd been approached by the Artificial Intelligence research group at MIT in regards to his formulas for particle mapping. At the Institute, he found himself in a closed and sterile environment that pursued him for the next twenty years. Everyone interested in his abilities in applied mathematics and programming looked at him as if her were some sort of secret weapon to be shielded from prying eyes and the general populace. When he took a position at Los Alamos ten years later, he had begun to feel burnt out, exhausted by the surveillance and protection that he'd been cloaked in ever since his early college days.

By that time, the cold war was a thing of the past and security at Los Alamos could kindly be described as lax. It gave John an opportunity to get out into the hills and the desert and begin to find out who he really was.

He quickly dropped into a routine of turning in his key card on Friday afternoons, throwing a sleeping bag and a change of clothes in the back of his jeep and heading out to explore eastern New Mexico on the weekends. The clarity of the air and the stark purity of the landscape revived long dormant feelings of wanting to connect with something; anything, that would make him feel a part of the real world again. He'd lived in abstractions for too long.

Like most people, his initial attempts at belonging revolved around romance or sex. While sexual connections were easy enough to achieve thanks to his appearance and personality, they never really went anywhere. John didn't have the personality to create long, deep, lasting and meaningful relationships. After a couple of years spent trying to understand the chemistry between men and women, he turned to reconnecting with his family.

His brother had been pursuing a lackluster career in Hollywood, producing and directing television shows for various networks. Every now and again, he'd pump John for information regarding the type of work he was doing for the government in hopes that there was an idea for a series buried in there. Unfortunately, the Official Secrets Act covered most of what John worked on, so they tended to talk about their parents and the weather a lot. On one occasion, John mentioned role-playing games, specifically multi-user dimensions, or MUD's as they were referred to. As John described them, a bell went off in his brother Kyle's head.

"Jesus! You're talking about those nerd fixation games like Dungeons and Dragons, right?"

"Uh, yeah. Sort of."

And from those humble beginnings, the syndicated phenomenon that was known as "Warriors of the Whirlwind" sprung to life. It was a hard sell at first, which is why they peddled it as a syndicated series, but the production costs were extremely low, and within it's first few months of being on the air, their ratings numbers were nothing short of miraculous. John happily resigned from his government position and moved to Santa Fe, where he set up his first production facility for the computer generated effects and characters he created for the show.

While he loved the feel of the place, Santa Fe was like every other moderate to large city he'd ever lived in. The ability to connect with neighbors or even have the sense of becoming a "regular" at restaurants and taverns he frequented just didn't exist. The pressures of an urban environment had afflicted this city well. Walking along Water Street or soaking in the sunshine of the Plaza, even catching a meal at the Zia Diner, John felt hermetically sealed off from everyone else. His friendly overtures met with bland, glassy faces that momentarily acknowledged his existence and then disconnected from him.

He wound up ranging a lot. A sense of restlessness, of rootlessness, pervaded him. The only moments where he felt completely at peace and all of a person was out in the wilds of the desert or the mountains. Partly, this travel was a requirement of his job. He had to collect textures and patterns and surfaces to skin his digital creations with. Camera in hand, he would explore everywhere, peering closely at adobe walls or brick walkways, cement, sand, tree bark and sky. The desire to create drew John ever deeper into creation. He studied everything there was out in the grand wild world in a manner similar to his Paleolithic ancestors. How the light changed incrementally as the sun arced across the sky. How the wind moved and rustled things in its passage or the manners water took on in rest or at motion. He took these things and replicated them in algorithms and then ventured out again for more.

He first saw Mesa Azul as a glimmer through ground haze when he crossed the Madre di Cristo at Doloroso Pass. Something winked at him and lured him on. While the analytical part of his mind had assured him ever since that it was merely the sun reflecting off the satellite dish down below, some other part of him felt Coyote reached out to him. He'd asked the rascally old spirit point blank on several occasions and never received a satisfactory answer. It was a small point, as John had never regretted venturing down into the valley to investigate.

While the location and construction of the town held more than enough charms for him, it was the demeanor of the people that captured his heart. He had just finished stopping his jeep in front of the Marguerita Bay Club when Bob's Big Boy heralded him.

"Is that an Army issue Willy's?" the large Indian exclaimed.

Before John had a chance to say anything, Bob's Big Boy had undone the hooks and flipped back the hood. "Now that's a great engine," he said enthusiastically while disappearing into the bowels of the jeep, "Simple, straightforward. None of the dumb crap they hang on engines today. Anyone could fix this sucker."

And so it went. Wherever he wandered throughout Mesa Azul, people began conversations with him as though he'd lived there forever. The only thing close to either big city indifference or small town hostility he came across was when Barry Moss accosted him. Even Barry, telegraphing his paranoid concerns so clearly, was a source of charm for John. He felt as if he'd arrived at home.

Soon after he relocated, John had developed a patriarchal attitude towards Mesa Azul. A slight childishness pervaded the place and the sweet naiveté of the residents made him feel very protective. It was the taproot for his concern over Ted wanting to build a campus here.

"I have a craving for menudo," John said suddenly, getting up from his chair. "Let's go down to the Bay Club."

"What's menudo?" Ted asked as the walked towards the jeep.

"Try some first," John advised while turning the engine over. "Once you love it, I'll tell you what's in it."

Angel, his mind stuck on his unrequited teenage love, was dreamily studying a picture of Ruby, Hiraldo and himself that hung over the bar when John and Ted came in. Angel's father had taken it when they first mounted up to drive the community herd into the mountains that long ago summer. The time yellowed photograph showed them all frozen forever in their youth and joy. Hiraldo, with his straw cowboy hat kicked way back on his head, whooping like an old cayuse; Angel himself, grinning shyly from the shadows of his low-set Stetson and Ruby, hatless and hair plaited in two thick braids that ran all the way to the pommelhorn of her saddle, waving and smiling into eternity.

"Who's that?" John asked, startling Angel. He'd been so lost he never heard his customers come in.

"Oh, my brother and a girl who went up to the line shack with us," Angel informed them once he'd regained his composure. John took the picture down from the wall and studied it. John surreptitiously fired looks at Angel and the picture he'd handed him, trying to figure out where in the plump, gray-templed bartender the wiry high-cheeked kid in the photograph had disappeared.

"What is it about old pictures that fascinates us?" he said more to himself than to his companions. "That girl," he went on, tapping the glass, "looks like a real pistol. I bet you and your brother had a few arguments about her."

Angel was stunned speechless for a moment or two. "What do you mean?" he finally blurted out.

"Hell, man," John said expansively, while handing the photograph back to Angel, "look at her. She's beautiful and every bit of her shoots off personality even in this old print. I bet you were tripping over your tongue all summer long."

Angel shrugged and hung the picture back where it belonged. John ordered a couple bowls of menudo and some Coronas and wandered back to the Acapulco Room.

"That she was," Angel said when he served the two men their orders shortly afterwards.

"Who was," John asked. He still had other things on his mind.

"Ruby. The girl in the photo you looked at."

"Oh," John grinned, "yeah. Very nice looking. What happened to her? She marry and move away?"

"No," Angel sighed, "she died."

"Sorry to hear that. Judging by the tone of your voice, I'm guessing you liked her a lot."

"I didn't really know her," the bartender went on, "but I loved her."

"We spent the whole summer up there and I ached for her every day. I was working up the guts to say something about how I felt but then it was too late."

"Hey, amigo," John said sympathetically, "at least you found someone you wanted to say that to. That's something."

"It's not much. Not in the end." While his voice stayed calm and even, a tear crept out of the corner of Angel's left eye and followed the rough topography of his face downward. "At least you still have a heart to break. Me, I'm done with it all."

It happened about a week before the end of the season. At that time of year, all the bulls that never got castrated start feeling their oats. For the most part, it didn't present a hazard to the kids looking after them as the bulls, when they were calves, while retaining their nuts, had the buds that would eventually grow into horns burnt off. Polled animals are easier to deal with but not completely safe.

By the time the columbines had retreated from the winter ahead and the lush summer grasses had begun to lose their chlorophyll, the herd began to range a bit more in search of anything green and tender. All three of the teenagers spent most of the day wandering the middle slopes of the foothills looking for animals that strayed. The bulls created an extra chore in that they often wandered far down the slopes to more level meadows so they could butt heads in their annual contests for dominance. They would tear up the earth with their hooves and attempt unsuccessfully to throw dirt in the air with their non-existent horns. Their bellows would echo through the blue arroyos and golden aspens of the mountains. After a fair amount of time spent posturing, they'd slam their naked heads together with a thump similar to whacking a coconut with a ball peen hammer. These contests could carry them all over the countryside.

Hiraldo was the best of the three with a lariat. Every time he came across some of those strays, he'd goad his horse into a hard gallop, stand up in the stirrups and swing a large rope. Racing along beside the recalcitrant critter, he spun his lasso until it whirred like a hummingbird's wing and took on the appearance of a rigid hoop hovering over his head. Leaning over his horse's neck, he let fly and it would fall, pretty as a picture over the dogie's head. The second it dropped, he'd pull in half the slack, rapidly wind the rope three times around his saddle horn and haul on the reins. His horse would skid to a stop and the rope would snap taut, throwing the bull ass over teakettle in an impressive display. It usually knocked the ginger right out of him and turned the formerly horny bull into a creature as mild as a brood mare and twice as tractable.

Angel, on the other hand could miss three or four times before finally dropping a loop. Even then, he was never as foolhardy as his older brother, preferring to pull the rope in and hitch it steadily around his saddle horn. It would slow the bull down and eventually wear the bastard down. The only risk he faced was getting his leg bruised now and again as the bull slammed against him in frustration. It wasn't a showy method, but it was practical.

Ruby was handless. She couldn't toss a rope to save her soul. Both Hiraldo and Angel spent a lot of their limited spare time trying to coach her but it seemed impossible. They'd set a sack of potatoes in a clearing and at first tried to teach her how to handle a houlihan, the short rawhide rope used to lasso horses in a crowed stall. Both boys enjoyed standing behind her and pressing against her as they guided her loop hand in twirling and then the toss. Angel was of a mixed mind regarding her lack of progress and his joy at continuing her lessons.

Of course, not having a facility for something doesn't prevent most people from attempting it every now and again.

Angel was leading a cow through the lemon-tinged leaves of a stand of aspen, enjoying the color of the light inside the grove, the snap in the air and the general feeling of lassitude that sunshine in the fall tends to bring. He lazily popped the cow's ass with the end of his rope to get her to kick up her heels and hurry down the slope, but all she did was turn her head and look at him with a rolling eye, switch her tail a time or two and continue with her slow mosey through the trees. When they finally emerged into the clearing, he saw two bulls getting ready to knock heads and Ruby riding towards them, awkwardly swinging her lariat.

Angel pulled up at the edge of the trees, his toes curling inside his boots and a prayer on his lips that she succeed into throwing the rope for once. Ruby tended to throw a wobbling loop that lacked the aerodynamics necessary for a good flight and it usually collapsed and fell halfway to the target. For once, it seems she'd gotten the mechanics in place and out shot a nice flat loop, racing like an arrow to the nearest bull's head. It dropped perfectly and she gave a yank to set it snug.

Tragically, Ruby had never been given a single lesson on horseback. No one had bothered to let her know that a bull can easily yank a rider off an animal if you didn't secure the lasso around the saddle horn. The bull shook his head twice and then took off for the trees on the lower slope, pulling Ruby off her horse. For one heart-stopping second, Angel saw her stretched like a wishbone between the bull and her pony, as her boot twisted in the stirrup and got hung up. He heard a faint pop as her ankle broke and her foot slid free of the boot, then she disappeared into the trees behind the bull.

Angel ran like lightening across the clearing after them. It didn't take very long for him to find Ruby, as her passage tore up the undergrowth pretty handily. She'd been slammed hard up against a tree.

"I've heard," Angel said to his guests, "that a broken neck doesn't hurt at all."

"Is that what she died of?" John asked.

"Yep," Angel said as he walked back toward the bar. As he walked around to the back of the bar counter, he paused and looked again at the faded color photograph on the wall. There they were, the three Caballeros, as Ruby joking called them. Caught forever in their youth and their glory. He lingered on the heart shaped face, framed by those thick braids and took in the joy that danced about the eyes and the mouth. It was a poor, weak tracery compared to the images that existed in his mind, but it was there. A record, a memory, a sad, sad song. He kissed his fingertips and pressed them against the glass.

"A broken heart can't kill you," he said, "but it damn sure hurts."

Chapter Six -

Coyote asks a question and gets no answers.

While many people would say that Ted Marquis' best attribute was knowing a good idea when he saw one, he himself felt that knowing the right course of action and sticking to it was the key to his overwhelming success. ByteStream had been the beneficiary of his inflexibility on certain issues. Once he made his mind up, he was impossible to dissuade.

John was discovering this characteristic and it was frustrating him no end. The negotiations for licensing rights to his compression technology had been wrapped up in short order whereas John's attempts to talk Ted out of building a facility in Mesa Azul went nowhere. Better men and stronger enterprises had gone up against Ted and walked away limping. John felt as though he was being pummeled with large, heavy pillows.

Without meaning to, Ted had a debate tactic that usually left his opponents boiling over with frustration. He was bland, myopically happy and seemingly unflappable. While John argued with passion and acumen, histrionically reeling off point after point, Ted would peer like a mole popping through the soil with a soft smile on his face, nodding in agreement and then stating that whatever point had just been presented was irrelevant.

"Irrelevant?" John nearly shrieked. "How can you say the cost of creating an infrastructure is irrelevant? It could be twenty years before your company recoups the investment based on what you do here."

Ted blinked and mildly went on. "No, R&D is a loss leader in any industry. We just spread the capitalization around the other divisions. It's a drop in the bucket at the end of the day. The investors won't even notice it."

As to the nagging question of why Ted wanted to build a facility in this valley, it inevitably came back around to Ted "feeling" better here. John was used to pummeling irrationality with logic, but in this instance, he made not one dent, scrape or impression on Ted's construct. He was determined to go ahead with this folly.

Coyote, of course, was having the time of his life. He could almost feel

John's synapses blowing. That wasn't the only cranial explosion going on in Huernafano County either. Down in the Pueblo, the Doc and his new acolyte were experiencing similar shifts in their consciousness.

Thanks to the ancient spirit dogging his tracks, nearly everything the Doc encountered now contained an element of mystery. His hand could touch an adobe wall or wooden cross beam and sear an impression into it, even though it remained cool to his touch. He had flashes of revelation regarding the dreams of anyone he encountered. To Doctor Pepper it was as if a lifetime of mysticism had been bottled up and suddenly let loose in one raging torrent. Paradoxically, he wished it would tone itself down while at the same time he reveled in the experience.

Carl was in awe. He felt as though every nagging question that had hidden in the deep recesses of his consciousness was being validated. Being an empirical thinker, these inexplicable events thrust his veiled beliefs of powers and experiences beyond his understanding to the fore. To him, it was if he'd finally dropped through some trapdoor just past the realm of human understanding into the world he'd longed for; where wizards exist and magic is common coin. During all of his adolescence, fantasy role-playing games were never just a diversion for him, but an almost tangible place that felt more comfortable to him than the plane of logic that existed outside of these pastimes. Now, he began to feel as if he was living on the fringes of it.

The Doc was in a rather peculiar position. Suddenly imbued with seemingly mystical powers, he was at a loss to explain most of them and he now had a follower who asked awfully probing questions. He floundered for answers, sifting through the various speculations he'd made over the years on the nature of existence, turning each proposition over in his mind and discarding most of them. He'd love to be able to turn to this young Anglo, shrug his shoulders and say, "you got me, kid. I'm as puzzled as you are."

For the moment, he avoided the issue by talking about the transitory nature of things. "Everything shifts," he mused sagely, "even our powers."

"The universe swirls around like the rainbow gasoline makes in a water puddle. It curls in and out of itself, changing color and position all the time. We wake up to a new existence every day, whether we know it or not." Carl found the symbolism a little mundane but grasped the point. He liked the idea of a cosmos in motion, but the real question to him was what drove it, what gave the initial impetus to everything.

Coyote laughed. It was the ultimate human statement. Of all the consciousnesses that drifted through the ether, only mankind ever posed the question as to what drives the cosmos. Nothing else cared. Nothing Coyote encountered ever questioned these things; they all existed in the moment. Even Coyote didn't care. Coyote, for all understood, he'd always been and always would be. It was all Coyote needed to know.

Steve Abrams needed to know a lot, and quickly. God only knew when that moron Ted would finish farting around down in the middle of nowhere. While he had the time, he had to find out who owned what down in Mesa Azul and what it would take for him to grab it. Two hours after he'd gotten back to Albuquerque, he was at the State land offices, looking up property records.

It was a crazy quilt of deeds, land grants and history. There was also a curious anomaly that was making him a little nuts. Every street and road in the Huernafano valley was called Oak Street. There were no maps of the town itself, and any regional map only showed the state blacktop running through the center of town. He might as well have been looking at an ancient mariner's map from the 14th century where the edge of the world was marked with "Here Be Monsters".

He spent most of the day just trying to figure out how the land lay. Between the lack of survey maps, county maps or any sort of cohesive organizational plan, it was impossible to determine who owned property that had any development value. By the time he went home and was making a blue martini, he'd decided any suffering his intended schemes for Mesa Azul caused the local residents would be well deserved.

The next day, he ventured on a different tack. He'd start by calling the General Mail Facility for northern New Mexico in Santa Fe to see if they could at least talk him through the layout of the valley, based on the various Oak Street addresses he'd garnered from the Hall of Records at the State Capital. The second he mentioned the zip code for Huernafano County, a palpable shudder ran back down the line.

"There's really nothing much we can tell you about the area, Sir," the disembodied and slightly distressed voice on the other end of the line said. "Due to certain amendments to the town charter in Meza Azul, home delivery is impossible. All mail is delivered to the regional mail concession office and the locals go there to pick it up."

"It's that Oak Street thing, isn't it?" Steve growled back into the receiver.

"Yes, Sir. The regional mail facility is on Oak Street," the postal authority on the other end agreed. "17 Oak Street to be exact."

"No," Steve snapped. "I mean the difficulties you have in delivering mail have to do with every friggin' road being called Oak Street!"

The unknown worker on the other end coughed, paused for a long count and then agreed.

"What's the deal on that? Shouldn't it be illegal or something?"

"I wish," the voice said with a hint of sadness. "Unfortunately, there are no enforceable conventions regarding how municipalities are laid out. It's their charter to do with what they please. It used to be a fine place for mail delivery," another long pause, "until everyone went nuts."

It seems that the introduction of the extended eleven-digit zip code caused an unprecedented uproar in Mesa Azul. Even after their rural carrier explained that it wasn't critical they use the additional four numbers, the town took umbrage at the principle. In protest, the town council voted to rename every street Oak and change the addresses of every resident. Address numbers where assigned by lottery to insure that nothing remained sequential in any direction. The main drag Oak Street that ran through the middle of town, for example, had a numbering sequence for the east side of the street that went 1, 22, 7, 255, 43, 40, 56, and 18, running north to south. It was a roaring success. Strangers were completely bewildered on how to find anything. As Corky Gonzalez told their last rural carrier before he quit in disgust, "there! Now you gotta work for your goddamned zip code!"

Steve was close to beating the handset of the phone into rubble. He'd never encountered anything quite as tantalizing and yet frustrating as this situation. He decided to blow off work for the rest of the day and go back down to the hall of records, make notes on the survey lines of every property abstract, then get a USGS map and start laying things out by co-ordinates.

If Steve had been a historian, he'd have found the abstracts fascinating. Nearly every title was as thick as a book, containing facsimiles of the original Spanish land grants, the revised Mexican partitioning, redistributions done after the Treaty of Guadalupe Hidalgo and so forth up to the current title. Anyone less avaricious and more imaginative would have had a cavalcade of life running through his mind as he perused the records. Conquistadors and missionaries, soldiers and statesmen all were bundled tightly in those dusty accordion folders. Everything was in there. Everything, that is, but proper survey points.

Thanks in large part to the area's relative obscurity, the region was overlooked during the United States Geodesic Survey of 1931, the massive public works initiative that Hoover started and Roosevelt finished in order to lay out a comprehensive grid of the country and resolve a number of "patchwork" title disputes. Before the USGS, surveying was a sketchy business at best, with plot lines and survey marks overlapping each other from generation to generation. In Huernafano County, they still did.

It wasn't really an issue in the valley either. Most folks calculated the edge of their property by eyeball. During the days of open range, a set of agreed upon landmarks marked the beginnings and ends of things and the only things that had fences were the garden and grain acres. Even those were put up to control the creatures that had no concept of property, such as mule deer and raccoons, but had a fine grasp of good eats. If you lived there, you knew where the edges of your claim were, as well as your neighbors.

People who didn't live there, however, owned a large amount of real estate. People who'd never even laid eyes on Mesa Azul held substantial acreage of the area. This phantom ownership had been brought about by the Civil War.

It wasn't a phenomenon peculiar to the Huernafano valley, but to the West in general. During the Civil War, government contracts for beef went begging and the few enterprises able to meet those contracts became obscenely rich. The lesson of a demand that exceeded the supply wasn't lost on a number of wealthy families in New York and soon after the restoration of the Union, these princes of commerce cut deals with the Department of the Interior to buy vast tracts of country from the government. It was the beginning of cattle as an industry.

Coyote himself had enjoyed that period of time. Not so much in Mesa Azul, for a number of reasons. In the first place, the country wasn't really contoured to run large herds and the distance to a railhead in those days was such that any beef driven north or east towards the cattle towns showed up looking like skeletons with horns. Secondly, it was peculiar but no less a fact, just about everyone who set roots down in Huernafano County wound up benign, happy and rarely prone to generating conflict of any sort.

The early days of cattle ranching were more entertaining to the southwest, towards Lincoln County. Down there, it was a serious and deadly business. Range wars elsewhere in the west usually consisted of one bunch throwing up a fence and the other cutting it down. It was a piddly little bad neighbor issue in most places; in Lincoln County, it was bloody.

Coyote missed the open range days. People acted in a most amusing manner at that time. Any neighborhood where a man could wind up being dangled from the limb of a cottonwood for owning a bent piece of iron, known as a running iron, which was used to alter the brand on cattle, was one he enjoyed observing. Coyote made mental bets with himself regularly regarding who'd wind up at the top of the heap on range disputes that flared up with alarming frequency. Ambushes and shifting alliances were like a chess game and he itched to move the pawns about to make it even more interesting but these Americans seemed immune to his powers of suggestion. Fortunately, they showed a capacity for irrational behavior on their own that he came close to admiring. He followed the short career of Billy the Kid with considerable interest.

Some chunks of Huernafano County were purchased in this manner and the deeds sat moldering in family vaults for generations and these records were the ones that had caught Steve's eye. The Address of Record for these people tended to be in civilized parts of the country, which gave Steve hope that they might be less irrational than the locals of Screwball County, as he mentally began to refer to the valley. He copied down the information he could garner and headed home.

"They probably use the damned deeds as cocktail napkins," he muttered to himself as he began dialing.

Much to Angel's amusement, Rick and Irene weren't speaking again. They had the most on-again off-again relationship he'd ever seen. While Rick seemed to maintain a constant state of smarmy sleaze, Irene bounced between emotions like a pinball. She seemed to be either in the grasp of romantic bliss or poisoned depression, with only hours separating each.

She'd popped into the Bay Club late that afternoon with sparkling eyes and a rapturous smile, bending Angel's ear for an hour or more about the night she'd had with Rick in Santa Fe. "It was wonderful, cholo," she said. "We had dinner at the Coyote Club, danced in half the nightclubs in town and then spent the rest of the night at La Fonda."

Angel smiled and nodded. Considering that Rick had been in for lunch and bent Angel's unwilling ear about the sexual hijinks he and Irene had indulged in without so much as a word regarding anything else that may have occurred down in Santa Fe, Angel was reasonably sure that the two of them existed in completely different worlds. He wondered to himself how long it would be before they collided again.

There were certain downsides to being the town confidante, Angel realized. Many times he learned things about people he really didn't want to know. For example, listening to Irene rhapsodize over her weekend, he couldn't shake the mental pictures that Rick had planted in his head regarding what orifices Irene liked having filled and what she preferred to have them filled with. It wasn't necessarily distasteful, merely distracting.

These moments where he would listen to one person's reality and have another's version of the same events kicking around in his head often created a crisis of conscious for the barkeeper. Irene was a sweet, but terribly mixed up woman. Without a shingle but having the occupational hazard of becoming a psychiatrist for the price of a drink, he could easily label Irene as a woman with horrible self-esteem who compensated by creating a false environment for herself in her dress, her physique, her interests and her choice of boyfriends. She didn't see Rick for what he was but for what he could be with a little guidance.

Irene's expectations of the world were wide of the mark, as was evident when she talked about her boyfriend. Almost everything she said about Rick caused Angel to cringe internally. Angel had no interest in Irene himself, assuaging her insecurities would be more work than any rational man would want to take on. Still, he liked her as a person and hated to see her waltzing to the precipice in regards to Rick. He longed to knock the scales from her eyes. At the same time, he felt it would violate some unspoken trust he'd created with the townspeople, so he only nodded and wiped down the counter with his bar rag.

"How's the real estate business for him these days?" Anything to change the subject.

Irene beamed. It seemed that Rick was on the verge of tremendous success. A number of high rollers had been in negotiations with him regarding the properties he represented to the north of the Pueblo. "They've all got big plans for the area," she said. "Rick says the potential for this county to turn into a prime recreation destination is huge."

Angel arched an eyebrow. "Really? Huh."

"What's that supposed to mean?"

"Nothing," Angel mused. "I'm just surprised that anyone would consider our little hunk of earth a place to go for entertainment."

"Not entertainment, dummy," Irene snapped, "recreation. You know, hiking, fishing, hunting. Stuff like that."

Angel could agree that the area offered plenty of opportunities for hiking. They were a fair piece from anywhere. Fishing used to be good until the State hatcheries got some trout food from Denmark that was infected with whirling disease. Once introduced into the streams on the Eastern Slope, it had run like wildfire through the native trout, the cutthroats and the rainbows, that had never been exposed to such a thing. Angel wasn't sure exactly what the internal effects of the disease were, but the external ones were alarming enough. The fish seemed to lose the ability to navigate streams properly, chasing their tails until they finally would die inside of a season. Now, the only fish in the Huernafano were German browns that were hardly a big attraction to serious fly fishermen.

When Angel was a kid, the fall game season was pretty impressive. The mule deer population had benefited greatly from mountain lions being classified as vermin. Back in those days, the State paid a twenty-dollar bounty on cat skins, prompted by the stockman's association. By the time a sense of environmental consciousness had dawned in the Seventies, there wasn't a tawny phantom to be seen anywhere in northern New Mexico and the deer population had exploded. Mule deer began to be looked on like overgrown mice. They got into to everything that wasn't locked in a cupboard. The hunting season was extended in both directions, starting in August and wrapping up in March and it didn't seem to stem the advancing wave of flash tails one bit. Just when it seemed that it might be in everyone's best interest to walk away from the Sangre di Cristos and leave it to the mulies, two years of drought capped off by the toughest winter on record did the trick. Mule deer died off in the hundreds of thousands. By spring it seemed they were plagued with a new disaster. There were so many carcasses the natural disposal critters couldn't handle it and diseases from rotting, flyblown bodies nearly eradicated the few surviving deer. It was a boon for the coyote population.

The new influx of coyotes played havoc with the game bird population. Pheasants, grouse and quail were quickly consumed and Angel reckoned within a year or so, coyotes would start dropping dead from starvation. It didn't leave a lot for the sportsman to chase after.

As Angel enumerated the reasons why we felt that Mesa Azul was less than an ideal vacation destination, Irene grew increasingly prickly. "God damn it," she yawped, "that's the sort of thinking that keeps this place from ever becoming anything. Wait and see, cholo. Rick will turn this place into something to be proud of!"

"I never said I wasn't proud of the joint," Angel called after the departing Irene, "I just said I wouldn't come here for vacation!"

Irene was fuming. It seemed that anytime she was in a content mood, life popped her in the kneecaps and put her off her feed. It was almost as if fate never wanted her to be happy. Every time she thought about how unfair life was to her, it set her blood boiling. All people had expectations, how come hers couldn't be met? She didn't want much, just her due. After all, she was pretty, vivacious, as intelligent as anyone else. Why did it seem like the rest of the world got what they'd set their caps on and she couldn't? All she really wanted was someone to make her happy. Even the things someone would have to do to keep her smiling weren't as hard as all that. A nice house in a nice city that had plenty of nightlife and the sorts of sophisticated people she'd always imagined she'd have as friends.

But, no. She got to slowly age in a backwater community that offered little in the way of creature comforts. When the hottest place in town was Angel's joke of a club, she knew she'd been condemned to some sort of purgatory. Rick Arnold was the closest thing to a ticket out of there she'd ever discovered. When she first met him, he was a spectacularly unsuccessful penny stockbroker in Santa Fe. At first, she'd done everything but rape the guy to get his undivided attention and the moment she did, he went and moved here, of all things. In the five years since then, he'd come up with a number of ideas that failed to pan out. She kept her fingers crossed that this time he'd hit the mother lode and they could run away to San Francisco or Aruba or someplace fancy like that.

She thought she'd stop by Rick's house and see if he'd heard anything from those big wigs that had shown so much promise last week.

Rick had been on a real roller coaster all day. It started off with another of those "thanks, but no thanks" phone calls from the last bunch of speculators that had come down to look at property he handled. After that, seeing as he was running precipitously low on funds again, he'd called his Dad in Grand Rapids for a little "leverage" money and after enduring another of his father's lectures on fiscal responsibility, discovered that the reward for listening quietly to all that yammering was that the wallet wasn't coming out. He was cut off. Close to panic, he was frantically mulling options on what he could sell, hock or bargain with to meet his rent when a life preserver fell right into his lap.

Some guy in Albuquerque was interested in the holdings he represented. If there was one thing Rick was blessed with, it was ability to hear avarice in a person's voice, no matter how cool they might sound. This guy was a cucumber, but underneath the ice was a hot ember of anticipation. Working this guy was going to take some finesse, some patience and Rick sensed that if all went well, the payback would be enormous.

They were playing a game of hold 'em. There wasn't a single card showing at this point, other than the guy evidencing a supposedly mild interest in the property available north of the pueblo. He'd done his homework in regards to the patchwork survey lines, adjoining encumbrances and water issues; so all that was left for Rick to dance with was topography and price. He was trying to figure out a way to pump this guy on what he thought he could get the acreage for when Irene popped in unannounced.

He jumped out of his chair when she let the screen door slam, then he closed his eyes and began grinding his teeth as she began tromping like an elephant towards his back office, all the time bellowing "Hello?" He calmly asked the guy on the other end if he minded being put on hold for a few moments, then pushed the button and whirled his chair around.

"God damn it, Irene! I'm fucking working here!"

He mentally slapped his forehead as her face crumpled. The spark died out of her eyes and lines formed between her eyebrows. For a moment, her face was a montage of shifting emotions, quickly flitting through shock, sorrow, bewilderment and then outrage. Her mouth hung open for a moment or two while her jaw and brain tried to come to some sort of concord on what they would answer him with. Finally, an explosive "fuck you!" erupted from her and she whirled around, thundering through the house and bursting through the door again. Rick was up and after her like a shot but by the time he caught up with her, he had to dodge gravel from her spinning wheels and watched her car fade quickly over the rise, a single extended finger on a rigid arm thrust out of the driver's window being his final image of her for the time being.

"Great," he thought to himself, "my timing is shot now." He walked slowly back to his office, trying to reassemble himself, knowing that he probably couldn't.

Angel was hardly surprised to see Irene show up again at the Marguerita Bay Club so soon after her departure and even less surprised that her mood had altered so quickly. She was like the afternoon thundershowers that occurred with such regularity in the summertime around there that you could set your watch by them.

"What a Bozo," Steve thought to himself after getting off the phone with the real estate agent. The guy was as easy to read as the morning paper. He was clearly unsuccessful, tapped out and clinging by his fingernails to any opportunity to turn his life around. Another of those loser sales types he'd spent his career walking over. Steve had had to dig his fingernails into his forearm to keep from laughing as this idiot tried to paint Huernafano County as the next Aspen. He'd sung that line for so long he probably believed it.

This was going to be easier than he thought. This Rick Arnold guy was pursuing a vision that was demented, while Steve himself sat on information that no one in their right mind would possibly believe. As long as Ted kept his yap shut for a month or so, Steve could snatch up the available ground for a song.

"Vacation paradise," Steve cackled as he started running some numbers on a legal pad. "Yeah, welcome to Mesa Azul, home of New Mexico's finest quality nuts."

Even after watching humanity for several millenniums, Coyote had only a vague understanding of what drove them to deviate from the natural order of things. It was a spectacular and mysterious thing, to his mind. These titanic desires that had nothing to do with the basic principles of existence entranced him. As often as he'd heard the call of humanity, that ever echoing plaint of "why", rise up to whatever entity they beseeched, he himself bounced the question back to them, and had yet to get a satisfactory answer.

The things they did that had no bearing on the primal drives every other creature had amazed him. The structures they built, internally and externally were fascinating. The arguments and presumptions they indulged in; to Coyote, it was as unfathomable as the reason an octopus changes color to reflect emotional states or why a gorilla cries. Observation hadn't given him a clear answer and interviews with his subjects gave up a million differing views, all of them as valid or invalid as he chose to make them.

He had his own theories, just as any observer will. For the most part, they tucked neatly into what he knew of the cosmos and how it was supposed to function. Much of what people did, he tossed into the large and overflowing bin of creation. Everything, sentient or not, had an urge to create. It was the single simple principle of everything. For the most part, creation meant replication or dissolution. Mountains created sand just as wolves created pups. There was continuity to this, a logic that was comforting. "Whatever was," Coyote mouthed to himself, "is and will be, in some form or another."

Except for certain things. A sound reached up to Coyote; plaintive and harmonic, it drew his attention to John's patio. John was sitting on a plank chair as the nearly iridescent colors of the sunset washed over him, playing a bottleneck guitar. These were the forms of creation that went far beyond any theory or concept Coyote could form. Playing instruments, drawing things, they were ephemeral creations of humanity that puzzled him. They didn't protect or feed or propagate the species and yet they seemed as essential as air to their existence.

He thought back to when he'd first seen human beings in his world. As the ice caps retreated and cut great alluvial swaths on the land, they cracked and shattered, creating sheltering gorges that these new creatures used to traverse the frozen land into a new and greener world than they'd come from. The spark of their fires, brave little lights in a vast and seething darkness drew him, but it was the sound of a bone whistle and gut drums that made him stay and watch and puzzle over these beings.

They sensed him then and soon above the whistles and the drums and rhythmic feet came the sound of singing, and his entity was framed within it. They were singing to him and it touched him deeply.

"On a Monday, I was arrested. On a Tuesday, I was locked up in jail," John sang. Coyote drifted down and settled a few feet above John's head. The vibrations of the guitar ran through him and set his molecules on fire. "On a Wednesday, my case was attested. On a Thursday, nobody would call my bail."

Hardly anyone sang about Coyote anymore. He'd been shuffled off to the side in favor of love and work and hardship. Still, these bits of nothingness, spun out into an uncaring world; so full of the needs and love of their creators, filled Coyote with something akin to rapture every time he encountered them. He imagined that if humanity needed a succinct answer to why they existed, he'd have said, "because you sing".

He loved watching people make music. John's hands worked independently of each other, the right hand sliding the glass sleeve up and down the fret-board while his left plucked at the strings. Coyote watched him bend and shape and alter the melody as the song went on and wondered how John knew when to bend the note or change where the line was going.

From there, Coyote's thoughts drifted to a number of things. It's a common occurrence to anything that listens to music, that sense of being carried away. While John went on with Leadbelly's jailhouse blues, Coyote drifted back over the things he'd set in motion. Sometimes he wondered why he did what he did, as there seemed to be a commonality, a connection to these things that he couldn't see until much later. Did some unseen being influence and manipulate him just as he did these human beings? It was a little disquieting to think so and Coyote metaphorically looked over his shoulder for a moment.

He couldn't see, but definitely sensed that the powers he'd imbued the Doc with, the flight that he sent Barry into and the resolve to build in Mesa Azul that he'd set in Ted all had a connection, but he was stumped to figure out what it could be.

Ironically, Coyote sent his mind out into the cosmos for a beat or two, unconsciously framing the same question he'd mocked humanity for posing. Among the nimbi, the stars, the planets and the great yawning void, there were no answers to be found. Things hung on the celestial pole, swirling in the vastness of being, some accelerating and some decaying and nothing called back to him.

It's a tricky thing, Coyote thought to himself. Perhaps he'd spent too much time with humanity. He was starting to wonder about things it didn't pay to think about, other than to make yourself a little nuts. Coyote, like most things that filled the universe, was a creature of the moment. It was hazardous the moment he started thinking beyond the immediate instant he existed in. A shudder ran through the cosmos and somewhere, a star collapsed.

"Almost done," John sang, snapping Coyote's concentration back to the zeitgeist. "I'm almost done."

No, Coyote thought. Nothing is ever done.

Chapter Seven -

Ted heads into the wet and Barry runs down the Trail of Tears

Bob's Big Boy was ecstatic. He was going to run the Blue Bus all the way to Albuquerque. The rich guy staying at John's had chartered his services and not only gave him an excuse to go tearing down the canyon, he was paying some beaucoup bucks to boot.

"You wouldn't rather fly in a whirlybird?" he asked when Mister Marquis approached him the evening before in the Marguerita Bay Club.

"Nope," Ted said. It seems he wanted to invite as many people as wanted to ride along to go down to the state capital with him so he could tell them of his plans for Mesa Azul and then field questions. "It'll be like a town hall meeting on wheels," he said happily.

Bob's Big Boy wondered what the plans were. Whatever it was, it seemed to be bad news for John, who looked rather dispirited. Bob's Big Boy was surprised to see him in such a condition. John usually appeared as a master of all he surveyed; calm, steady and mildly optimistic. That evening he looked as though he was about to start banging his head against the wall. You could almost hear his teeth grinding.

Well, it was no skin off his nose. He was going to get to hit the road and that was all that mattered. It had been a week since he'd been able to do any gear jamming and the summer hiatus usually drove him nuts. Just the feel of that big diesel engine, the bite and hiss of the air brakes was enough to make the hairs on his arms rise up.

Ted also requested that Bob's Big Boy spread word of this junket to the residents of Mesa Azul. Bob wondered if Angel would let him use the club phone. Angel was very protective of the phone; he seemed to think that anyone else tying it up would prevent him from receiving some critical call, although he was never really clear on what that might be. As usual, Angel gave him a firm no and Bob wound up having to get ten dollars from Ted, get Angel to convert it to quarters and then head outside to the phone booth in front of the Club. As he started going through the phone book, Reddi Kilowatt came by and Bob drafted him to spread the word down at the pueblo that free rides to Albuquerque and back were being offered by the rich guy at John's house.

76

John himself was now being surreptitiously pumped for information at the bar. "What's the story, cholo?" Angel inquired.

"Bad news, ese," John said wearily and then ordered a straight shot of Jack. As John laid out Ted's plans, Angel mulled them over and tried to see why John was so bent out of shape over the idea. Most of the people in Huernafano County owned their property outright. Land there had always been dirt cheap and appraised even cheaper. A few years back, Angel had tried to use both his home and the bar as collateral on an expansion loan and the most that the Bank of Santa Fe was willing to extent him had been fourteen thousand dollars. Even at that, they felt they were being generous.

"That'll change in the blink of an eye, bro," John informed him. "You think the people that will come to work here want to live in mud houses and have to mess around with well water and septic tanks? Or have their kids hauled all the way to Taos to get an education? Nope, progress is coming to Huernafano County and you're going to see your taxes go up to pay for it. What do you clear on this joint, per annum?"

Angel saw John's point but felt he was being a bit alarmist about it. "You're talking to the head of the town council, vato. We're not going to go nuts on this thing if it happens." He swiped the bar top with his rag, mulling over what the future might bring. He'd probably have to bring on some help. Everyone that had a business in town would. Businesses would have to expand, diversify a little more and probably reap some nice benefits in the process. He thought of the town's operating budget. They'd have to blacktop some roads around here for certain and more than likely replace the wooden sidewalks with cement. Right now, the town coffers couldn't cover the cost of half of the main drag Oak Street. Sales taxes would go up, probably from their current one and half percent to possibly three percent. Property taxes would too. Still, all that new money flowing into town should cover the costs and keep things reasonable for the old timers.

"Dream on," was all John had to say.

"Maybe we could put in some parking meters." That gave John the first good laugh he'd had all day.

Ted joined them at the bar, wearing his usual bland smile and myopic gaze. He patted John on the back. "Still preaching the isolationist stance, partner?"

Barry longed for isolation, or at least insulation. In the three days since he'd had to flee his compound, he hadn't slept for more than an hour at a time. He wasn't comfortable unless he was in motion, preferably in a truck where he could slide down in the passenger seat and stay out of the eye line of passing motorists. He'd done a fine job of cocooning himself down in Mesa Azul. He didn't realize what a good job he'd done until he didn't have it as a refuge anymore. He felt like a bug on a pin.

Everything was subject to scrutiny. While cloaked in copper mesh and pirated lines, pulled completely off the grid, he'd come to a stronger and stronger realization that the Estes Foundation was doing an effective job of slowly taking over the planet, but he'd felt relatively secure. Now, his bolthole blasted apart and his DNA on file, he knew it was only a matter of time before they got him.

The hardest part of his new life was trying to look as if he fit in. He'd forgotten how unaware most of the people on the planet were to what was happening to them. When he'd initially worked his way to the interstate he was shocked to see how many chemical trails crosshatched the sky. He wanted to veer away, or at least slap a particulates mask on, but he had to appear as oblivious as the people he moved amongst.

He felt like the only alert man in a world of zombies. When he walked into a truck stop the first morning after fleeing his home, he nearly recoiled in horror at the number of people with cell phones pressed up against their heads. He could almost hear their synapses frying and the tumors beginning to grow. This was the new Hiroshima; he was running through the wasteland.

Sanctuary was only 350 miles away. Barry had a list of addresses and contacts based on subscribers to his newsletter, and just outside Amarillo was one of his most trusted associates. Tom Calhoun had corresponded with Barry for a number of years on the issue of global banking, the New World Order and the Estes Foundation. Barry had even published one or two of Tom's research pieces. In the event of an emergency, such as Barry was currently experiencing, they'd worked out an elaborate method of communication and contact. When Barry hit Taos, he'd sent a letter to a re-mailing service in Kansas City, which in turn sent it on to a mail drop company in Denver. From there, an unknown associate of Tom's who could reach him in a manner undisclosed to Barry would pick it up. In Santa Rosa, Barry would stop at the Western Union office for more explicit instructions on how to find the Calhoun compound.

Such elaborate planning soothed Barry in the same manner as a string of prayer beads. It was an exercise in faith. Faith was a hard commodity for Barry and trust was even tougher. He'd grown up having his eyes peeled consistently by his old man.

It had begun with the assassination of President Kennedy. Barry was five years old at the time and it barely impressed itself on his consciousness. For his father, however, it was a watershed.

Like a lot of men of his generation who'd gone off to Europe or the Pacific Theater cloaked in patriotic zeal, he came home more than a bit disturbed by the experience. As he told Barry when he was little, "Just because I love my country, doesn't mean it loves me." He'd experienced the difference between his perception of things and the reality. Since then, he tried hard to peel back the cover of anything and look for the substance. He'd raised his boys to do the same thing. With Jerry, it was water off a duck's back, but with Barry, it stuck.

While other fathers spent Saturdays teaching their sons how to throw a ball, Ken Moss taught them how to comb the Warren Commission Report for inconsistencies. Barry was fascinated. As he grew, he outpaced his Dad in finding threads, links and connections into the inexplicable and slowly traced them back towards a shadow world that seemed to have its finger in everything.

Eventually, a million diverse threads led towards the Estes Foundation. This was a think tank for global economics that had been set up during the 1920's when America was having its first fling with international fiscal policy. The foundation's board originally consisted of American financiers, manufacturers and heads of commodity-based companies that had international concerns. After World War Two, the structure changed so that there seemed to be a triumvirate of an ancient Swiss banking house, an old American concern whose roots went back two hundred years and a synthetics development company whose profits rose with the level of armed conflict going on about the globe.

Barry had a knack for comparative analysis that his father lacked. He could find connections between seemingly disparate things and slowly string them together. For example, he might read an article about a drought affecting part of Africa, put that together with an announcement several months earlier by Trans Global Airlines of new routes to South Africa and combine that with patents filed by the synthetics corporation on a new jet fuel additive. A little supposition and it was clear that the contrails left by jets passing over that portion of Africa were in fact chemical trails that blocked the thermal up-thrust of the earth to make clouds tall enough to create rainfall. Naturally, this led to social unrest, government upheaval and civil war. Financing for arms purchases and the actual purchases of weapons technology in the region soon fattened the coffers of the companies controlling the Estes Foundation. It was a clear-cut conspiracy, and it was terrifying in its implications.

The responsibility of this knowledge proved too much for the old man. By the time Barry was sixteen, his father was a heavy drinker. Heavy enough to alienate his family and find himself divorced and without access to his kids unless he had court appointed supervision.

To Ken Moss, this was proof that the shadow forces had grown aware of him and were determined to destroy him. When Barry was a sophomore at the University of Colorado, he was informed that his father had killed himself. Ken Moss left no suicide note, no rationale for wrapping his lips around a 12 gauge Mossberg 500 and sending his gray matter on a very short trip towards the wall behind him.

When Barry returned from the funeral in Lexington a week later, he found a long and rambling letter from his father that he'd mailed only hours before he died. In it, he explained to his son how everything had built up in him, how the burdens of his knowledge had finally caused him to surrender. Barry studied that note for days on end. He compared the handwriting in it to other letters from his father. After a month of more of soul searching, he came to the conclusion that the letter was a plant. There was no way on God's green earth that the jittery spider writing on those four wrinkled pages was his father's. His father had been emotional and reckless. Bad attributes for a spy, and there was no doubt that both he and his father were engaged in espionage. It was a great game and Barry would plot his course at least fifteen moves ahead for the rest of his life.

Moments after seeing Ted onto the Blue Bus, an odd sensation crept through John which convinced him he wasn't alone. "Hey stranger," John said, without looking around. Smack dab in the center of Oak Street, the arrival of Coyote would be announced by thickened air, a palpable wrinkle in the atmosphere and nothing worth turning around for. "I imagine I have a few bones to pick with you."

"What did I do?" Angel asked. He had just emerged from the club when he was greeted by John's accusation. John jumped just a bit when Angel responded. Then he turned and ducked sheepishly in Angel's direction. "Sorry, Angel," John said, grinning. "I didn't know you were there. I was talking to myself."

"You pick bones with yourself?" Angel was perplexed.

"Ah, yeah," John shrugged as Coyote's laughter hung in the air. "Why not?"

"I don't know, ese," Angel said. "I don't argue with myself much. Normally I know what I'm doing."

"Yeah," John said distractedly as he watched the dust and diesel of the bus slowly vanish down the canyon, "I used to think I did too."

"You sorry you didn't go with them?" Half the county and all of the Pueblo had piled into the bus that morning.

"No," John said while climbing into his jeep. "I've seen lemmings plummet off a cliff before."

The lemmings themselves were entranced by the future that Ted painted for them. It seemed as though they were going to be shot straight from the nineteenth century into the twenty-first. Ted himself was pleased that his proposal was greeted with such enthusiasm and was quickly cornered by most of the town council in the front of the bus. Corky Gonzales, Freddy Apodokas, Randall Webster, Jenny Patton and Winnie Cameron unconsciously crowded around the Big Kahuna and bombarded him with speculation. Each of them was a little distracted by the dreams of avarice dancing about their heads. It was a curious thing, until this vision of a bright and shining tomorrow was unveiled to them, none of these folks was particularly grasping. They'd been content with their lot in life, but now, they saw vast fortunes and power, laid out on a golden road.

Ted couldn't be happier that he seemed to have a consensus vote in his pocket already, the only person on the town council who wasn't there and peppering him with questions was the owner of the dumpy restaurant he'd spent half his time in, and that fellow seemed pretty malleable in Ted's estimation. He asked a few questions of his own in regards to the governmental structure of the town. He was surprised to learn that Mesa Azul did have a Mayor and slightly disappointed that his Honor hadn't come along for the trip.

"No one's seen the Mayor for three days," Freddy Apodokus said. "I think your helicopter scared him and he's hiding out somewhere."

"Gee, really?" Ted said. "Doesn't sound like much of a Mayor."

"Until you came along," Corky told him, "it wasn't much of a town."

Ted's concerns about lack of representation regarding the executive office were laid to rest in short order. It turned out that the office of Mayor was merely titular and decorative. The council had always handled the business of the town while the office of Mayor was put in place at the request of the Penitentes a long time ago and no one could recall a Mayor that had actually ever gotten involved with municipal business.

"Besides," Jenny Patton said, "the ballots we buy from the State Election Office have a slot for Mayor on them. It would seem like a real waste not to have a couple of names next to them."

"Talk about a waste," John said to Coyote as they rattled up the track to the crest of Blue Mesa, "the energy you expend on nonsense is amazing. I don't get you at all. Here you are, some sort of supernatural entity and what do you do? Alter the cosmos? Create a universe of harmony and good will? Nope, you fart around with a few people in the middle of nowhere just to see what happens."

Coyote was indulging in a little mimicry. Once the jeep had gone out of sight of Mesa Azul, he collected his molecules in to a wonderful simulacrum of John. "How do you know the long range ramifications of what I'm doing?"

John glanced over, did a double take and then responded sharply, "because you never think farther than the next second! Stop looking like me, it's unnerving."

Coyote-John was doubled over with laughter. "You're so easy to get to." He started to unzip his jeans, saying, "check this out. I decided to make some improvements on the basic package." Curiosity getting the better of him, John glanced over at his twin's genitalia. "No," John said matter of factly, "you got it just about right." Coyote made it grow another four inches just out of spite.

"You look like a god damned tripod."

"Actually," Coyote said while zipping up, "I do want to talk to you about actions and consequence."

Ever since Coyote's revelation the night before, he'd been mulling over the idea that something was operating him the way he manipulated some human beings. It was disturbing to him, as if he'd discovered he was nothing more than an extension of something else. The concept robbed him of his sense of identity and he wanted to find a way to get it back.

It took him a little while to articulate what he was feeling, following John through the house and standing around while John knocked together a sandwich and fetched a beer. They wound up on the patio, where Coyote began laying out a series of questions.

"Something bigger than me?" John started out. "Sure, I guess. I mean I've always had a nagging feeling that there had to be some sort of cohesive force that keeps everything from bonking into each other or imploding or something. Anything's possible."

John tipped the neck of his Corona in Coyote's direction. "A few years back, if I met someone who interacted with you the way I do, I'd have called for the straight jackets and sedatives. You should be merely a myth or something, you know?"

"That doesn't make me feel a lot better," Coyote sulked. "I'm not dismissive of you."

John chuckled and took a bite of his sandwich. "Sure you are, amigo. You're dismissive of humanity in general. You treat us like something in a petri dish or a bunch of mechanical toys. Wind us up and watch us go."

"Well, with some people, that's true," Coyote agreed. "I can't get into your head though. I can't get into a lot of people's heads anymore."

There had been a time when everyone was receptive to Coyote. As time passed, more and more consciousnesses were locked off from the old spirit. He felt it had something to do with the rise of logic over mysticism. When people had no explanations to certain phenomena, they were more receptive to him.

"I don't know," John mulled it over, while sucking on a tooth. He looked up at the wide, arcing sky. Deep in the blue, he tried to penetrate the ionosphere, into the depths on the cosmos, but his own limitations left him with nothing but air. "I like rational explanations as well as anyone else, but that doesn't mean I'm closed off to the mysterious."

"You're an oddity, in my experience," Coyote said.

"Yeah? Well, you're an oddity in mine."

"What I can't figure out," Coyote went on, "is why you can see me, interact with me, but aren't open to me." When John gave him a puzzled look, Coyote went into more depth. "I can't penetrate your mind. I can't play in your dreams or alter your structure. You're impenetrable."

"So," John asked, "guys like the Doc that you mess around with, they can't see you?"

Coyote thought about it for a bit. He rarely appeared to anyone. People like John seemed to send out a signal to him that stated it was right and normal, part of the order of things, to solidify and appear before them.

"You know what?" Coyote declared, "I'm not sure I ever tried."

"Well," John nodded. "There you go. If I were you, I'd give it a shot. I mean, of all the people around here that you could materialize in front of, the Doc would probably be the one guy who wouldn't completely freak out."

"Maybe later," Coyote agreed. "I got other things on my mind right now." As Coyote thought about what he wanted to say next, his physically being began to dissipate a little.

"You're breaking up on me," John commented blandly. Coyote now looked like a fuzzy projection of John. He could vaguely make out the mountains behind Coyote.

"Tell me what you think of free will," Coyote said while he became more and more of a ghostly presence.

"What do you want to know?" John asked. "Do I believe in it? Pretty much. Although, there's a lot of people I know that feel it's an absolute canard. I like to think that I'm exercising choice, not being set up in some sort of cosmic three card monte game." He took a sip of beer and then added, "I could be wrong though."

"You're not as reassuring as I'd like you to be."

"Nothing's concrete, bro." The irony of making a statement like that to a creature that now resembled nothing more than a fine mist wasn't lost on John. He snorted through his nose a bit. "You're not used to asking questions, are you?"

"Until I met you," Coyote said as he disappeared, "I never had to."

By the time the Blue Bus reached Albuquerque, Ted knew he had a lock on the community. Everyone was enthusiastic about the opportunities ByteStream presented to Mesa Azul and he could see that all of them were taken over by dreams of avarice. He'd ended his little gathering by passing out nondisclosure forms that held every individual on the bus liable for suit if a single one of them breathed a word of what they'd talked about. One thing he didn't need was for some speculator to buy up the available property and hold it for ransom. He'd made sure that neither Johnny Gee nor Rick Arnold were invited on this junket and he explicitly pointed out that it was in the town's best interest to keep them in the dark.

While Bob's Big Boy was extricating Ted's luggage from the side compartment of the bus, Bob leaned into Ted and whispered, sotto voce, "I'm assuming the Native Americans that will be your neighbors will be quota-ed into the workforce? You know, building bridges between the capitalists and the residents, right?"

Ever since his company had risen to any level of prominence, Ted had had to deal with the soft hand of equity blackmail. "ByteStream is an EEO compliant company. Diversity is our watchword."

"That's good to know," Bob's Big Boy grinned. "You got a card? I can give you a call next week and we'll discuss what you have in mind."

Ted patted Bob's huge shoulders. "You're sort of rushing things, friend. I have to get approval by the board, then come up with a development study, resource allocation. A bunch of stuff like that. Come fall, you'll see a ByteStream team down there and I'll personally recommend that non-essential staff recruitment starts at your Pueblo." It was a speech Ted had given a hundred times to a hundred different groups. He could say it in his sleep. Cafeteria and janitorial positions were the easiest panacea for local harmony on earth.

Just at that moment, Bob's Big Boy had an instance of déjà vu. The instant had locked into place, he felt absolutely everything was a replay of a dream he'd had a few days earlier. He felt afraid to move, one wrong step and he was certain everything that was about to happen would fall apart. Moments from now, he knew he'd be climbing back aboard the Blue Bus, jamming it into gear and heading north for Colorado, music blaring out of the loudspeakers and banners flying, he was on the cusp of his favorite dream. All he had to do was to let the moment catch up to him.

Ted slapped him on the back and he felt the moment shatter. Crestfallen, he turned to look at the future Mesa Azul, the blood roaring in his ears, deafening him. He saw Ted's mouth move but couldn't hear what he was saying. Then he watched as the richest man on earth jogged awkwardly towards his private jet on the tarmac, climb the ramp, disappear from view and then, after the roar of the jet's turbines penetrated his consciousness, rocket off into the blue.

While Bob's Big Boy was moping around Albuquerque, mourning the loss of his dream, Ted was mulling over the birth of his. What a place he'd stumbled on to. It was as if he'd found the Philosopher's Stone and the Fountain of Youth rolled into one. It had been years since he'd felt as energetic, as bursting with ideas and as revitalized as he had in Huernafano County. He couldn't wait to see what would happen when he culled the best and brightest from his company and set them down in this magical place.

Thinking about it, he dreaded going back to Seattle. When he'd first relocated there, he'd found it a nice change from the constant blistering sun and heat of Phoenix. After twenty odd years, he was thoroughly fed up with rain. After his brief interlude in Mesa Azul he looked at Seattle as a place to be unhappy in. Where once lights sparkled off of rain-damped streets and the fog rolling in from the Pacific entranced him, he now looked at it as a place that embraced melancholy. As he got closer, Seattle began to take on an almost ominous feel, as if it were a city designed for people and dreams that were played out, ventures that flopped and songs that were stillborn. He felt damp.

The world scatters. The land expands and contracts. It buckles and heaves from internal forces and collapses under the movement of wind and water. Extracted from the Sun, the Earth becomes its delicate blue daughter, dancing with celestial grace in an imperceptibly collapsing spiral, slowly being drawn back in to the source of her creation.

Everything of the earth is affected by this dance. Swallows feel the tug of the seasons and fly thousands of miles when the shadows change and point the way. Sunflowers bull their way from a resistant soil, daily reaching upward with a blind yearning to turn their blank heads towards the Sun and trace its travels across the heavens. Even deep beneath tons of bedrock, in subterranean pools, blind white salamanders feel the urge to find their kind. Everything shifts and things become restless.

People feel the tug. The days lengthen and call to them. Chevrons of geese, passing overhead act like signposts and beckon the human foot out of the doorway and onto the road. For the most part, only their spirits wander while their beings stay root-bound with responsibility. But the yearning is there.

America is a temptress for this wanderlust. Girdled and bound by interstates and the blue highways, stitched together with iron bands and skyways, America sings out to her people to get a move on. The song of America is the song of the open road.

A full moon rises into an empty sky and shines down on the little town of Mesa Azul. It lights Angel's way home from a dead evening at the Marguerita Bay Club. All his patrons are on the Blue Bus, being piloted home by a still woeful and heartbroken Bob's Big Boy. It sparkles on the crushed stone of the patio on top of Blue Mesa were John sits, nursing a nightcap and looking out on an empty town. He sees Angel climb into his truck and he sees the Mayor trotting down the center of the main drag, looking like he actually has some place to go tonight.

Elsewhere, Ted Marquis has already arrived. There is no moon for Ted, only rain and the dismal passage of time until he can pull together the votes on the board he needs to make his latest inspiration a reality. A fog as thick and heavy as the one on the bay has settled into his soul. He feels dull and listless. He yearns for the bright clarity of Mesa Azul. The fire in his belly has banked to an ember, but it's enough. It's the heat he needs to drive him forward.

The moon sits just atop the trees that fringe the wall of the canyon the Blue Bus rattles through. Bob's Big Boy dreams of racing the moon, chasing it to someplace wild, wide and open where there is so much space and air that it could cause your heart to leap out of chest at the exuberance of it all. Most of his passengers are asleep, lulled by the motion of the bus and those few still alert are falling. Reddi Kilowatt comes up to the front of the bus and leans over Bob's shoulder to look at the night sky. He whistles at the stars and then goes back to his seat. He never notices the tears in Bob's Big Boy's eyes.

Barry is on the road tonight. The moon shines in the cab of the truck he's caught a ride with. He listens to another trucker's story. He's heard a lot of stories in the past couple of days. He's a good passenger, a good listener who doesn't say much at all. These truckers talk about the country and their lives and their dreams with no prompting. They're men of the road, people that live in a polar opposite to most of society. They have been too long in the open and crave human companionship, even if it's merely a voice on the CB radio.

They talk of a country that Barry's never known. The government they live under is sinister only in the application of taxes and fees and regulations. They see a government consisting of little men and petty bureaucrats. They tell him of a land with moderate pressures, the kind any nation feels as it fumbles through the void of international relationships. The tiny fears this creates are far outweighed by the joys of a new boat or a girl they met in Tulsa two days before. The gears click, the clutch releases and the road rolls on.

The vibrations from the gearbox rattle Barry and he realizes he's nearly fallen asleep, he drifted down into a place where the land the trucker tells him about might actually exist. Barry nearly dreamed of such a place and a smile of wistful regret flits across his lips. In his drowsy state he muses for a little while on what it would have been like to not have the great weight of knowledge he has, draped about him like Marley's chains. He thinks about his brother Jerry, happily out in the great American night, without a concern other than getting to a gun show in Barstow by Friday afternoon. Jerry shook off everything their father taught them like water flying off a dog coming out of a creek. At some point he decided that their father's legacy wasn't something he wanted to carry. Jerry liked to move fast and with very little gear.

One time, when he was back at the compound loading up on pamphlets and beer, Barry asked his brother how he could turn a blind eye to this shadowy presence that was spinning the globe however it wanted to. Jerry, tapping the sides of his beer can to release the bubbles clinging to the sides before he popped the top, smiled and said, "Nobody cares, bro." Carbon dioxide made a soft hiss and Jerry took a long, satisfying draught. "Well," he corrected himself, "some folks care, at least enough to keep you and me in beer and pretzels. Even if it's true, what does it matter? Say we're all under the sway of some evil secret outfit. We're not suffering, are we? The sun comes up and the girls go down. That's what counts, right?"

"No," Barry said to himself, "that doesn't count at all."

"Huh?" the trucker who'd been talking about his upcoming vacation said.

"Sorry," Barry replied, chagrined. "I was thinking of something else."

The trucker shrugged and went back to speculating on how much his kids would enjoy Disneyland.

"He's frozen, you know."

Another confused exclamation from the trucker.

"Walt Disney," Barry explained. "When he died he was cryogenically frozen. They have him in a special chamber, ironically built under Sleeping Beauty's Castle."

"Yeah? Ain't that something? I can see why you'd want to use iron though. You know, they have a lot of earthquakes out there. Gotta have something that can stand up to 'em." And the song spun on as the miles flew by.

Chapter Eight -

Barry goes down the hole, the Doc goes to water and John stays on his patio.

Barry was standing at a crossroads. A big X in the Texas panhandle with nothing but mesquite and sage as far as the eye could see. If the land rose and dipped, it was in such deceptive increments that it fooled his eye. He felt like he was standing on a glass slide and someone was about to crank the focal lens down hard enough to smash him. In other words, he'd never felt this exposed.

The only thing that made him feel a little easier was the wide-open sky. A couple of cumulus clouds dotted the heavens and far to the east, where the actual city of Amarillo was, he saw the faint, blurry streak of a single contrail. There was a slight wind moving from the west, so that chalky line in the sky held no menace for him. He sniffed the air and all that came back was sage, creosote and dust. He'd been waiting for about an hour for a ride to show up and take him to the Calhoun compound. The telegram addressed to Billy Sol Estes that was waiting for him in Santa Rosa gave explicit instructions to find this spot where two rural roads intersected and make sure he found it by 10 a.m. on June 25th. A blue 1975 Ford pickup was going to make one run down the road and if he wasn't there and ready to jump in, that was it. No second chances, no do-overs. Barry looked at his watch. It was 10:04.

He strained his ears trying to pick up any vibrations in this big hunk of empty. There were a couple of donkey pumps out there making a rhythmic thump, some birds chirping listlessly and occasionally the dry rattle of dead mesquite branches knocking against each other during particularly exuberant wind gusts. Tucked down underneath it all he could possibly make out an engine, running too high on a gear, or maybe not. It was faint enough that he considered it might be his own hopes creating it out of nothing. It was now six after ten. He began to debate how long he'd stay there, until he realized that he didn't have a lot of choice. Whatever came by, he was going to flag it for a lift.

As usual, whenever things didn't go exactly as he'd envisioned them, Barry's paranoia would rise to the fore. Why had he been foolish enough to contact this Calhoun character? The guy was wired in almost as tight as Barry himself, possibly too tight. Double agents and disinformation began to drift into his consciousness. Christ, he'd let himself become too complacent. He'd probably been under scrutiny for years; the Estes boys had lured him into a sense of false confidence until they could draw him out, here into the middle of nowhere and get rid of him. As far as the rest of the world knew, he'd run on his own, prompted by God knew what. He could wind up in a culvert and his brother would shrug it off to Barry finally losing it, heading out and getting killed for his cash in the Texas boondocks.

A more likely scenario would be finding himself abducted by the dark suits of the foundation, debriefed and then eradicated without a trace. Two weeks from now, his clone would show up in Mesa Azul where everyone, including Jerry, would accept that it was him and the clone could slowly pry out all the enlightened who subscribed to his newsletter, corresponded with him or bought his books and pamphlets.

Off to the east, a dust cloud was growing. Barry swam in paranoia as it grew closer. Before too long, he could see a faded navy pickup with the nose of a boxer who drops his right pulling the cloud along. Barry took his backpack off, set it on the ground in front of him and then put it back on as he'd been instructed to do in the telegram. The truck flashed its lights once. It was Calhoun.

He'd expected the man to stop but all he did was kick open the passenger door and slow down to around five miles an hour. Barry jumped in and the truck picked up speed. Getting his bearings in the cab, Barry took a gander at the driver. Calhoun was an ox, no neck and hulking shoulders. He had the side of a mountain for a face and tightly wound gray hair surmounting it all. "Hey," came out as a growl.

"Hi," Barry said. "Thanks for helping me out."

"Not a problem," the driver rumbled. "Not yet, anyway."

Doctor Pepper had a problem. He'd assumed that Carl would go stay in Albuquerque once the Blue Bus had arrived, but when everyone from Huernafano County was assembled again for the ride home, there was Carl, with a suitcase and a graduate student in anthropology from the University in tow.

"What are you doing here?" the Doc asked, perplexed.

Carl explained that he was on summer hiatus and decided rather than going back home and mooching around until the fall semester began, he decided to spend the summer at the Pueblo, learning what he could from the Doc. The kid with him was Troy Derlinger, Carl's roommate off campus and interested in holistic healing techniques. "Anthropological Botany, to be specific," Troy explained.

"I see," the Doc said. This was going to be difficult. He had no idea how to explain what was happening to himself and having two curious puppies underfoot wasn't going to give him much time to figure these things out on his own. He rubbed the back of his neck to ease the tension that was growing there and blue flames erupted.

"Wow!" Troy exclaimed.

"I told you," Carl said. Both boys were nearly vibrating with glee and excitement.

Troy immediately reached out to the Doc's neck where a little nimbus from the momentary fire still hovered. The old shaman slapped the boy's hand away and snapped, "look, if you kids are going to be trailing after me, we've got to set up some rules."

It was going to be a long summer.

It turned out to be a long summer for everyone in Mesa Azul. As far back as anyone in the county could remember, there was never much to cogitate on, the place had a rhythm all it's own. The sun's motion and the state of the land set the calendar and people played along with it. June was the time that the yearlings were separated out and branded, as well as when the communal herd was staked out up in the high meadows of the Sangres.

After that, folks repaired all the damages from the winter and tended their summer gardens. No one but the transplants such as Rick Arnold and John Elkfoot took regular summer vacations, for as Corky Gonzales once remarked, "I don't think anyone works hard enough around here to need a vacation". Surprisingly, in the shank of June, Angel closed up the Marguerita Bay Club for a week and went to visit his brother in Washington D.C. Bob's Big Boy took it as a personal affront, especially when he offered to run the place while Angel was away. "Uh, yeah," Angel said sardonically, "right after I find a burglar to look after my house."

"I resent that," Bob's Big Boy said huffily. "I got ethics."

"I'm not sure what ethics are," Angel said as he got into his truck. "But if you got 'em, I'm sure they used to belong to someone else."

Bob's Big Boy and Reddi Kilowatt moped around for a day. The closure of the Bay Club was tantamount to closing their boardroom. Most evenings, they hunkered down in the Acapulco Room to kick around ideas on how to improve the tribal fortunes.

In regards to tribal fortunes, the two Shantis were still wrecking brain cells trying to come up with a visual identity they could market. Camilla Ryland-

Bowles had gone ahead shaping and refining her idea of what the Shantis ought to embrace as their talisman and showed up unannounced at the Pueblo one day with an oversized portfolio.

Bob's Big Boy nearly choked when he saw what she'd done.

"Geez, Ms. Bowles," he finally stammered out, "I don't really think that'll work."

"Nonsense," she replied lightheartedly. "I've worked it all out. I researched Native American iconography and I can assure you you'll have a very unique identity." She held one of her drawing in Bob's face and he inadvertently back-pedaled as if he was afraid it would snap his nose off.

"Well, yeah," Bob agreed, trying to get at least an arm length from the paper she so aggressively held out, "no one's nuts enough to want that!"

"Please," Camilla said, "grow up. You're acting like a little boy looking at a naughty drawing on a bathroom wall."

"It IS a naughty drawing," Bob insisted.

"It's an icon for the female life force," the artist said primly. "It's a celebration of the primal roots of matriarchal society."

Bob had reached his breaking point. Like most Shantis, when it came to certain things, he tended to be slightly puritanical. "It's a snatch!" he screamed.

"There's no need to be vulgar," Camilla said huffily. "It's a geometric derivative of the essence of woman, yes. It's the seat of her power." She when on in rapid fire about the essentially matriarchal nature of Shantis society, the obvious allure to empowered women to reconnect with their primal roots and the simplicity of the design.

Bob's Big Boy's head was swimming. He could imagine the riot that would ensue if he presented her designs to the tribal council, let alone the horror of seeing such a thing emblazoned on pots and moccasins or worked as a pattern into rugs. He could kiss off any sales deal with WalMart, that was a certainty.

Unlike his previous visit with Ms. Bowles, she'd invaded his turf and as such, he was having a hard time extricating himself. Frantically throwing out various rationales for her departure, all of which she handily dismissed, he began to despair of ever being clear of her presence or the nasty drawings she kept thrusting in his face. Just as he had abandoned all hope, in popped Reddi Kilowatt.

"Hey, Bob," Reddi said, then catching sight of Camilla, amended his greeting to, "oh, Hi Ms. Bowles. Whatcha got there?" He snatched a drawing from her hand. "Holy crap!" He dropped it as if it were on fire. "What the hell is wrong with you, lady?" Then he grabbed Bob by the arm and pulled him out of his doorway.

"She's nuts," was Reddi's final statement on the matter and then he led Bob to the Pep Boys place, as they'd come into possession of a keg of beer and the

Denver Rockies were getting ready to duke it out with the Padres.

"You're nuts!" was the first thing out of Rick Arnold's mouth when Steve Abrams made a per acre price offer on the land north of Shantis Pueblo. The two of them had been dancing around each other like a pair of fencing masters for weeks, searching for vulnerable spots. Each of them was certain the other wore a big sign around their neck that said, "Chump!" and they each believed they were the princes of street savvy.

Their little duet had been as effective as shadow boxing, so Rick had finally called Steve and asked for an offer. Steve, in turn, sensing frustration and panic on Rick's part had low-balled so much that it almost went underground. "You can't be serious," Rick continued.

"Serious as cancer," Steve said. "I think I've wasted as much time as I care to on this. I've looked around and considering the amount of money I'll have to spend to turn Bumfuck, New Mexico into anything of real value, I think I'm pushing out a fair price." Steve had sweat pools underneath his arms that were spreading to meet in the middle of his back as he played his bluff. He prayed under his breath that Rick would blink.

Dead silence on the other end of the phone. "You blew it!" his mind screamed at him.

Rick's mind was racing. This guy flabbergasted him. He was coming to the table with about a third of what he was hoping he'd get. Was he serious? If Rick tossed back his own number would the guy hang up on him? If he could look this character in the eye, he could get a better read on him. He needed a face-off.

"Look, you haven't even seen the property," Rick said as coolly as a man whose heart was ready to pound its way out of his sternum could, "you don't really know what you're bidding on. Why not come up here and have a look see, then we can sit down and run some realistic numbers."

Steve breathed a little easier. The guy wanted to play Abdul the rug merchant. Fine. There was no way in hell that he was going to show his face in Mesa Azul, though. All it would take would be for some local boob to recognize him; eventually word of his arrival would get to either John Elkfoot or that kid Carl, who had gone native, and someone would drop a dime on him to Ted Marquis. Bye bye bonanza.

"Look, I've seen the abstracts," he said. "The acreage structure is fine, the grade is workable, I'm sitting on an artesian spring for crying out loud, what more do I need to know?"

"The intangibles," Rick said. "The view, the air, the feel of Huernafano County."

Steve laughed. This guy was flailing around like a blind man who had dropped his cane. "You're not selling time shares, are you?"

Rick collapsed. The man was intransigent. As much as he hated to, he was going to have come clean. "Look," he sighed, his hand whitening from his grip on the phone, "you know and I know you're tossing out ridiculous numbers. How about I run down and see you if you can't come up here? We can come to some sort of equitable agreement."

Steve mulled it around in his head. The man had blinked, he'd won but he was still balking. Some people had no sense of grace. Still, it might not be bad to pump the guy for a little more information. As far as he knew, he was angling for the only chunk of contiguous property in the valley. The only piece big enough to support a campus such as that boob Marquis had envisioned. Still, considering how fucked up the abstracts around there were, he might have missed something. This Arnold guy might save him a nasty surprise.

While he didn't relish piddling around with some small timer, he figured he ought to send the guy the right signals and make an ally. Might not be bad to have someone on the ground around there to keep him informed of anything that might start to gum up the works. Besides, he pictured himself and this loser setting down to final negotiations. The guy would try to hotbox him; make him feel as though there were offers flooding in for this chunk of crap in the middle of nowhere. He could turn it around in the blink of an eye and watch this schlub dampen his armpits. Hell, he might even ease up at the close of the deal. Throw the guy a bone and feel a little righteous at the end of the day. He'd have still paid chicken feed for gold at twice his current offer.

"Sure," Steve finally relented, "come on down next week and we'll see if we can't come to terms."

Rick felt his confidence come flooding back. Damn, he was good. He could play this guy like a fish. He'd floated the hook into his mouth and the guy had bit. All that was left was to set the hook and then he'd reel him in. Let him gasp for air on the bank for a while and wonder what the hell had happened

They each said their goodbyes, set their phones down and leaned back grinning. The same thought danced around each of their cortexes, "idiot".

For John, things in his life were pulling at each other. On the one hand, the royalty structure he'd negotiated with Ted would insure that for the rest of his life, the one thing he'd never have to worry about would be money. Added to

that was the ever increasing popularity of "Warriors of the Whirlwind". His brother mentioned that one of the regular broadcast networks was interested in picking the show up next year, which would mean bigger budgets and better production values. John could really push the boundaries of what he was doing in computer effects if that came to pass. The business side of him was happy as a clam.

On a more personal level, he found himself spending most of his free time on his patio, looking down at his adopted town. He was as happy as he'd ever been or could have dreamed of being since he moved there and now it appeared it would all be pushed out by progress. Somehow, a WalMart wouldn't hold the same appeal that Mullin's Dry Goods did. He liked Stacy Mullins' idea of window dressing. One month, she'd filled the entire display window with wax teeth and overhead hung a sign saying "The Sun Can Turn All These Teeth into a Perfect Smile! - Guess the day they're all melted and win a free hotplate!"

Any charm Mesa Azul would possess after ByteStream came to town would be artificial. The Marguerita Bay Club might survive, although the dusty animal heads that occasionally shed flies into a bowl of menudo would definitely hit the bricks, as would the menudo itself. He could see Angel bowing to the pressure of these newcomers for a lighter and less suspicious menu. Before long, even the bar would probably carry an assortment of flavored vodkas and call itself a "martini lounge". The Acapulco Room would have its murals redone by someone actually skilled at it and any funkyness left would be completely contrived.

It wasn't the stores or the layout or the climate that made Mesa Azul what it was. It was the people. The crazy amalgam of folks that had set their roots down here and found a way to live outside of the mainstream. They'd evolved their own unique culture and it was on the verge of extinction.

He'd seen, since he was a kid, the slow homogenization of the United States. There were times in the past few years when he was slightly unsure of where in the country he was. The same chains of stores and restaurants and hotels dominated things. Accents deteriorated and gradually became some sort of medium tempo mid-Western thing that was spoken from the center of the tongue. No twangs, brays, honks or wonks. John was one of those people that usually asked natives in a strange town, "where's your favorite place to eat?" and more often than not when he was still a green twig, the question was rewarded by a recommendation to a dive that had the best ribs he'd ever sunk a tooth into or catfish that tasted like ambrosia. Strange regional specialties used to dot the landscape; little bonanzas of food, music, festivals and customs that reinforced what a wild and magical place America had started out to be.

Now, it seemed everyone dressed about the same, dreamed about the same things and ate off of the same menu, which held possibly thirty different items. He heard America singing, "I am unique!" in one voice and in one outfit and in one tune. He didn't want to go back to that, but he'd learned most people, given the choice between fitting in to the largest mass possible, absorbing themselves into a collective animal, such as a coral, or coming into their own without a care as to what someone else would think; these people usually burrowed as deep into the center of the mass as possible.

In a few days, Mesa Azul would be throwing its Fourth of July celebrations. Like a lot of places, they had a parade, but unlike a lot of places, everyone in town was in the parade. Jesus Mondragon started this tradition in the 1940's after he'd gone to visit his cousins in Pasadena at Christmas and seen the Rose Bowl parade. Describing the floats to his friends set off a float mania among the town. Mesa Azul, unlike Pasadena was a little sparse of flowering plants in the middle of winter so the idea hung in folk's heads until the Fourth of July. Gardens were stripped of every blossom and there wasn't a tube of Elmer's Glue-All to be found in town by the 3rd. The next morning, sedans, pickups and even a tractor raced up and down Oak Street, scattering petals in their wake. Several accidents occurred.

Since then, the whole thing had become organized in the interests of public safety. The entire populace would pull together bands and floats and assemble at 10 o'clock near the Pueblo and start marching down the main Oak Street, past the Mayor, who, by tradition, was the only person not allowed to participate in the parade. As old Jesus pointed out once, "what good is a parade if no one is watching and cheering?" The general consensus was that the only reason to even have a Mayor was to have someone to cheer the rest of the town on. Nominee's spectating abilities soon became the serious criteria for gaining elected office.

Once past the reviewing stand, which was a lawn chair, the parade continued on down the road, all the way to the meadow they liked to refer to as Dean Rusk park, in honor of the effigy the tea hippies had burned there in 1966 and then stay for the rest of the day having a barbeque and then the flourworks.

The flourworks was an invention of Corky Gonzales. The town coffers never had income enough for a civil fireworks display put on by professionals and the random amateur stuff that went on was impossible to choreograph into anything that was truly entertaining. The year after Bob's Big Boy and Reddi Kilowatt accidentally set Corky's garage on fire with a huge roman candle, he was determined to come up with something entertaining and safe.

He thoroughly enjoyed the flourworks. It fed his creativity as well as his marksmanship. For weeks before the 4th, he'd stay up evenings sketching out how the display ought to go together and building the necessary bags. He'd fill bags with colored flour and "chamber" them, as he used to refer to it. Then he'd number them and figure out the timing. A number of people petitioned him every year to act as his assistant but after a couple of bad performances, he'd discovered that the Pep Boys acted like a well-ordered drill team and he stuck with them. He'd built a catapult that flung the various bags of colored flour high into the afternoon sky and then blow them asunder with his over-under 20/20. The brightly hued flour exploded in beautiful flowerlike clouds and then hung in the air, becoming distorted by the passage and explosion of the next bag. The Pep Boys would labor like fiends, cranking the catapult's windlass down, loading and then hurling the next bag. Corky would fire and before long the sky above the spectators looked a gigantic action painting, brilliant smears and blossoms and trails of reds, blues, yellows and greens hanging in the air and slowly sifting back down to earth. By the end of the afternoon, the spectators themselves would be coated and colored with the fallen flour. It made for an oddly enjoyable spectacle and as John discovered his first year there, a lingering experience. As he told Angel two days later, "I'm still sneezing blue." Not only that, the south end of town looked like a crazy quilt until the wind and the rain cleaned everything off.

John closed his eyes and massaged his temples. He was in preemptive mourning for the loss of these things and damned if he could figure out a way to stop it.

Doctor Pepper was mourning the loss of both his anonymity and his freedom. Carl and Troy never seemed to be more than an arm's length away from him. From the time he arose to the time he fell asleep, they were as constant as his shadow and as closely attached. While they were nice enough fellows, their constant attention was draining, especially since he was still trying to work out what had happened to him and what exactly these new experiences and powers meant. For the most part, the things he could do were all flash and dazzle. They looked spectacular but didn't carry much in the way of practicality with them.

People he'd known his entire life were reacting to him in a completely new way. Not aversion, per se, but most of his friends and acquaintances had a demeanor of cautious perplexity towards him. Sort of the same reaction he imagined he'd get if he'd sprouted antlers overnight. "Nice rack, Doc," they might have said, followed by a moment of discomfort as the silence stretched a beat too long, a little fidgeting about awkwardly and then, "well, I got to go. I got to see a guy about a thing."

He missed folks popping in for a poultice or a salve or some dried willow bark to treat the various calamities his homeothapy dealt with. The first time he encountered Mrs. Butterworth at Mullins' with a bottle of aspirin, it broke his heart. She was flustered to run into him and fumbled about until she finally said,

"Well, you know, you have those boys with you all the time. I just felt as though I'd be intruding." She started to give him a pat on the arm and abruptly stopped, her hand hovering about ten inches away from him. Then she smiled and scurried away.

The boys, on the other hand, were fascinated. He was drowning in questions he couldn't answer. Carl dwelt on the mystical while Troy focused on the practical. Troy had taken samples of all of the shaman's homeopathic stock and now concentrated on the Doc's diet and environment. Anything he wanted to eat or drink was almost snatched from his lips and a sample quickly bottled and labeled and frozen for analysis later. Yesterday morning, Troy asked if he could get a urine and stool sample from the old mystic. Doctor Pepper politely declined.

He might not have minded his new condition if it had any value to it. Unfortunately, visions or insight into the human condition were not part of his ability to create cool flames or char wood or have arabesques of pollen and dust appear when he moved his hands. He felt like a dime store novelty. Any wisdom he had, he'd gained through basic human existence. He wasn't any different than any other old geezer that gimped along this old world.

That morning, he'd awoken a few hours before the sun came up. He stared at the kiva beams on the ceiling and repeated his usual early morning analysis of who and what he was and what to do about it. Perhaps there was too much noise and clutter in his life; the constant yammering of his acolytes might be drowning out any spirits or gods trying to contact him. He needed a sabbatical or a pilgrimage or something.

He got out of bed and climbed into some clothes. When it came to matters of dress, Doctor Pepper was a traditionalist. Velvet shirt and ropes of corn beads, then leggings he'd made from a pair of jeans. He was probably the only Shanti left that wore a breechclout, held up by a wide leather belt adorned with a buckle from the 1964 Cheyenne Stampede. He also wore traditional long moccasins; an idea pilfered from the apache peoples eons ago. They tied just below his knee and had bone buttons on the toes to keep cactus stickers from jabbing into his toes as he walked along. He crept through the darkened rooms of his adobe and quietly assembled some dried foodstuffs that he put into a plastic bag from Mullins Grocery. While Carl and Troy slumbered, he tiptoed away, into the dark and headed north for the spring at the base of Madre di Cristo that helped feed the waters of Huernafano Creek.

Calhoun wasn't a man who treads lightly. His physical appearance accurately reflected his demeanor. He bulled his way through the world. Intelligent enough, he was also physically intimidating and so sure of his own mind that very little stood in his way. Barry learned this almost from the moment he hopped into the guy's truck.

Calhoun's compound was exactly the thing Barry envisioned owning some day. Completely underground, the only signs a structure existed where a couple of screened and roofed pipes sticking up inside strategically planted mesquite bushes. Once they'd entered it, Calhoun put a Desert Eagle 640 to the back of Barry's head. "Now," Calhoun said calmly enough, "let's find out if you are who you say you are."

Fourteen hours later, Tom Calhoun grudgingly conceded that the man he'd strapped to a chair and interrogated relentlessly might, in fact, be Barry Moss. "You're on notice," he rumbled while unstrapping Barry from the chair, "that if you give me cause to feel uncomfortable letting you in here, I'll make sure no one ever finds a trace of you." It was as good a welcome as Barry could expect. He didn't pay a lot of attention to it, however, as the pain in his ass and thighs from the rivets on the seat of the chair, coupled with the burning sensations his own slowly drying urine had left him with took precedence over anything else.

Barry had spent most of his life walking on eggs. Just now, he was in a situation where those eggs had much thinner shells. Calhoun, he recognized quickly had come to his enlightenment much later in life and from a very different path than Barry had. As such, he was still in the fanatical stage; something Barry had grown out of in his youth. Barry viewed things as just the matter of course, albeit a little more aware of the true nature of things than most folks, while Calhoun burned with the holy fire. Barry just had to make sure he didn't get singed during his stay.

Tom Calhoun had grown up in the energy industry, or as he preferred to call it, "the all bidness". His father had been a wildcatter in the thirties, finally hitting the north end of the vast Smoky Hill deposits just as his creditors were about to reclaim every bit of his drilling rig. Before World War II came to America, Calhoun senior had leases all over the north Dallas hills and his son Tom was born in very comfortable surroundings.

His father had some definite ideas of how a man develops character and just what that character should consist of. A typical southern democrat, he endorsed "Johnson's War" and encouraged young Tom to do his bit in Southeast Asia. Tom Calhoun entered the Air Force and soon was a lieutenant in an F-4 Phantom, spreading napalm and tracer lines through two tours of duty. When he first went overseas, it was only during bull sessions that any questioning of the war came up. By his second tour, his entire squadron, probably his entire flight wing was fed up with the inability of the people in charge of this debacle to reach for a big stick and end things. "Hell," Calhoun said to Barry over dinner one night, "I used to wonder why them strategists didn't ever ask us. The way we looked at it, all we had to do would be to load up some bombers with enough nuclear weapons to turn Hanoi into a smoking crater, send 'em up and tell ol' Ho Chi Min they was there. He'd have capitulated sure enough."

Barry grinned cautiously and said, "given the knowledge you had at the time, yeah, it makes sense. All you need to do is look at who was making the money off the war and you can see just why it was a limited engagement."

Calhoun grunted in agreement. After the war, his confidence in the country was only slightly dented and he readily took his place in his father's company. Things were looking up then too. The oil embargo made the Calhoun holdings nearly priceless and a desperate government prompted Chickasaw Oil to do a lot more exploring for new resources. "We punched a lot of holes and signed a lot of leases that turned around and bit us in the ass when OPEC opened the floodgates." It left Chickasaw Oil and Calhoun's father debt-ridden and worthless. Tom's father died with his boots on, arguing for a debt restructure when he was slammed by a massive coronary. The only thing he left behind was an insurance policy that wasn't attachable. At 35, Tom Calhoun was a millionaire several times over and highly suspicious of international finance. He took most of his fortune and surreptitiously began buying Krugerands and diamonds. "Fifty-fifty, right down the line," he said to Barry. "That was the first valuable thing I learned from any of your books." Barry took the reference to his 64 page mimeographed pamphlet, "The Great Diamond Hoax", as a book as a compliment. It was a detailed account of how one family controlled all the diamonds in circulation as well as ninety percent of the world's existing diamond mines. By strict manipulation of the number of diamonds in circulation, they kept the price of a relatively common commodity astronomical.

Thanks to fluctuating gold and silver prices, Calhoun had seen his resources reduced and each time he took a hit, he did more research into market manipulation, which usually led him back to another publication by Barry. Naturally, Barry tied them in to the Estes Foundation and before long Calhoun was a true believer. Barry was pretty good at predicting certain trends. A lot of things that were pure supposition on his part came to pass, such as the technology revolution in the 1990's and it fed Calhoun's sense of paranoia. By the turn of the millennium, Calhoun had gone underground, both figuratively and literally.

After two weeks, Calhoun was less wary of Barry being some sort of fifth columnist for the New World Order. The two of them spent a lot of time talking over various theories, suppositions and connecting threads. Pretty soon, Calhoun jokingly referred to the two of them as the "Brain Trust" and "Mankind's Last Best Hope".

"You and me have to open their eyes, somehow," Calhoun rumbled.

Chapter Nine -

In which we find the summer in locked in amber and the world as seen through compound eyes.

Anticipation is a terrible thing. Time, which physicists tell us is relative, has a stronger relation to our emotions than most folks would like to admit. When a body is holding their breath, time stretches and slows, it bends and warps and plays hob with our sense of passage. The days themselves may seem normal enough, but there are moments, trapped in a crystal matrix where it seems as though the molecules of creation slow their vibration and everything is thick, gummy and slowed. There are moments when the sands of time stick in the clockworks and a cosmic grinding invades everything. Such a thing will make one's bones itch.

That's how things operated in Mesa Azul throughout the summer. John hovered in a fog of apprehension while down below, past the spruce and cedar and junipers that cloaked the sides of Blue Mesa, the town itself sputtered and jerked through the suspense of fortune to come, the golden moment that would blossom and transform them all. There was a dreamy cast to their faces and often, for no reason other than some beautiful vision of the future popped into their heads, smiles of serene warmth spread across their faces.

Angel would spend the languorous hours of the afternoon flipping through various catalogs from restaurant and saloon outfitters. In his mind's eye he constructed the next incarnation of the Marguerita Bay Club. It would be a tropical dream, with fake palm trees and scalloped aqua colored neon waves along the walls. It would be equal parts Miami Beach, the Trocadero Ballroom and Trader Vic's Tiki lounge. He'd doodle little sketches on cocktail napkins and quickly snatch them from sight when the first customers of the evening arrived.

Corky was filled with both excitement and concern. The soon to be arriving populace would undoubtedly be driving newer cars than his current clientele could afford. Corky was a shade tree mechanic of the old school. If it was built before 1985, he could fix it. Rick Arnold was the only person in Huernafano County that had a car built in the last 15 years and once when he was having engine problems, he had Corky take a look at it. Corky was dumbfounded by the computer system that monitored and regulated everything. Every part of the drive train he looked at had a monitor of some sort stuck in it. He found it frustrating. It was if they'd taken a perfectly sound engine and infected it with technology. It spread like a cancer throughout the system and left him impotent. Eventually, he slammed the hood down and told Rick he needed a computer repairman, not a mechanic.

Corky mulled over the possibility of going down to the trade school in Santa Fe for a quick course on these joke engines. His son Ramon was hell with a hammer and a devil with a blowtorch so the shop would be in good hands while he got up to speed. Still, it wasn't something he had to deal with today. He decided to take a wait and see attitude. It kept him awake at night, though.

This golden future plagued everyone. People whom for eons had never wanted more than what the valley provided had discovered the joys of salivating. Strange things, such as catalogs from Land's End and the Sharper Image began to appear at the post office and the Julie Modestos, Mrs. Butterworths and Fred Platts who ordered them flipped through their glossy pages with hungry eyes. Mesa Azul had turned into a valley of dreamers.

In the evenings, they all came in to Angel's joint to soak in the collective vision of things to come. As Mister Marquis had advised them, they talked about what was going to happen without talking about it. Whenever Johnny Gee or Rick Arnold came in, there was a beat of silence as everyone gathered their wits, tried frantically to find a topic that wasn't on the collective mindset and then expound on whatever came to hand. Johnny Gee was slightly alarmed that people had so much interest in the weather. For weeks, when ever he popped into the Marguerita Bay Club that was all he heard. It was odd in that the weather in the valley was as predictable as the first belch on a beer.

Rick didn't pay a lot of attention to what was going on around him since he was holding his own secret close at hand. He and Steve Abrams had reached an agreement in principle regarding the acreage north of the Pueblo, although it had taken a lot of effort on Rick's part to get the numbers up to where they made sense.

Every time Rick reflected back on the time spent in Albuquerque in Steve's office, he felt a shiver run through him. It was one of the most intense periods of extended effort he'd ever been through. The mere thought of it, revived the sour taste in his mouth, the stiffness in his neck and the prickliness in his scalp that had been a constant during his talks with the man. Still, by the end of the weekend, he had a contract for three quarters of a million dollars and a good faith deposit of five thousand. In less than sixty days, he'd have an additional forty seven thousand. Life was sweet.

The biggest trouble was, he was sworn to secrecy on the proposition. Steve had been insistent that if a single breath of his impending purchase leaked out before the title was closed, the deal was dead. That covenant was torture for Rick. He ached to tell someone, especially Irene. Unfortunately, mentioning such a thing to Irene would be tantamount to driving down Oak Street with a loudspeaker. Still, it was less than two months until the enterprise was wrapped up. He could hang tough.

The Doc had dreams as well. As a matter of fact, that was almost all he had. Less than a mile from the pueblo, he might as well have gone to the dark side of the moon. Using deadwood, he'd built a horrible looking wickiup and was on a fast. Fasting tends to lower one's motivations to the degree that all one eventually does is sleep.

Coyote strolled through the dreams that the Doc had. They had a monotonous sameness to them and nothing Coyote suggested in this dreamtime altered their construction or outcome. The internal Doc wandered in darkness, fumbling blindly for some sort of illumination. Coyote would create glowing cones of light, brilliant rivers of light, soaring pillars of light and the Doc's dream persona walked past them without seeing. The shaman moaned and cried and beseeched in his sleep. Coyote talked softly to him but it was as if the old man was locked in obsidian, a black impenetrable mass to which there was no entry or exit. Coyote was concerned.

Carl and Troy were equally alarmed at Doctor Pepper's disappearance. At first, they wandered about the pueblo asking everyone they encountered if they'd seen the old man. "The Doc?" Manny Pep Boy mused, "I think I saw him about a month ago. I got my nose busted and he packed it up real good." They encountered the same sort of answers from the rest of the Shantis. This blasé indifference puzzled them until Bob's Big Boy set the two of them straight on the matter.

"Shantis have a high regard for spiritual types and being as the Doc is all the time communing with spirits, we give him plenty of elbow room. We're a rowdy people and you never know when me or the Pep Boys might disturb one of the spirits ol' Doc Pepper might be yakking with when we come by. It wouldn't do to have an angry god raining all sorts of hoodoo down on our heads, would it?"

Aside from the hoodoo reference, which seemed distinctly un-Indian, the boys accepted Bob's explanation of the matter. Since the Doc wasn't accounted for in the pueblo, they moved their search in to town.

"The Doc's gone?" Angel replied. "Oh, well," the bartender shrugged and half listened to the boys while visions of his soon to be realized new establishment danced about him, "he might have gone off to gather some medicine weeds or something. He tends to vamoose now and again. I wouldn't worry too much about it."

"No," Troy interjected. "He would have taken us along if that was the case. That's why I came down here, to do a little ethnobotany."

"Ethnowhosits?" Angel asked.

"For gosh sakes," Carl said in frustration, "what sort of town is this? The oldest guy around here walks off into nowhere and you just act as if it's no big deal?"

"Everybody," Angel said placidly, "who goes for a walk around here walks off into nowhere. That's the one thing we got plenty of."

Angel felt the need to mollify these college types. They were getting awfully red in the face. Troy, with his beanpole build resembled a thermometer, which had had all the red mercury shaken to the top. Squat little Carl looked like a tomato.

"Look, boys. You forget that ol' Doc is an Indian. He learned how to live off the land when he was a brocito. I imagine those hills are like a grocery store to the old coot. I bet he's up there somewhere in a pine bough hammock, swinging in the breeze and sipping on coconut milk." Angel's current obsession had affected his judgment regarding the local fauna.

"Coconut milk?" Troy exclaimed, "where's he going to find coconuts around here?"

Angel waved his hand dismissively. "Chipmunk milk then. You know what I mean. The guy knows how to live off the land."

"Where would we file a missing person's report?" Carl inquired.

Angel glanced sidelong at the boys. They certainly were a pair of enthusiastic pups. "Taos, I suppose. We don't have much call for that sort of thing up here. Not that the county sheriff in Taos can do anything. I guess you'd really have to call the New Mexico Bureau of Criminal investigation in Albekew."

"So, a body can vanish off the face of the earth and nobody in this town cares?"

"Oh, no," Angel said. "We care, sort of. We just reckon if someone doesn't want to be around, they have their reasons. Barry Moss has been gone for a month and the Mayor disappears on a regular basis." Angel impatiently tapped his fingers on the bar top. He was anxious to get back to his catalogs. "They always show back up."

The dearly departed Barry Moss was vaguely missed by his brother Jerry, who was a little surprised not to find Barry either at the compound or at the Marguerita Bay Club. Barry hadn't ventured more than half a mile from his copper netted sanctuary in 10 years. After checking the supply of pamphlets, books and newsletters, Jerry realized that all he needed to stay in business was a reliable printer. He got on the phone to a couple places in Denver and eased his mind. Then he left for a gun show in San Diego.

Barry himself was undergoing a transformation of sorts. His host was a man who believed in action, not passive observation, as well as organization. He was slowly converting Barry to his point of view regarding resistance to the insidious Estes Foundation.

People with passions tend to suffer from a diminished range of sight. The higher the passion goes, the narrower the vision. This afflicted both Barry and Calhoun, but their eyes were pointed in different directions. Combining both their views gave them a sort of binocular perception; it was a potent union.

While Calhoun would be the first to agree with Barry's belief that knowledge is power, at the same time, he felt that real power rested in applying knowledge to the issues of organization and force. "Knowing your life is threatened and acting on it is a whole different ball of wax than merely meditating on the issue," he told Barry. Barry saw his point and slowly began to reposition his mindset towards the same horizon his host pointed at.

The way Calhoun saw it, as long as the people most capable of resisting the inexorable encroachment of the Estes Foundation remained isolated and unorganized, the less chance they had to survive. "Hunkering down in a bunker is all well and good while you're figuring out what do to, but it's sort of like a gopher that knows a farmer is going to pour kerosene down his burrow. You can't sit around waiting for the match to get lit."

And so, the two men began an earnest examination of the forces aligned against them and the resources they might assemble to keep from being charred gopher meat.

The single element that Barry had kept to himself for years, partially because it was so fantastic, so wild, that it threw everything else he knew about the Estes Foundation into a questionable corner and partly because he was concerned that if by some chance the Estes Foundation knew he was privy to this information they'd waste no time in eliminating him, was the alien connection. Even Calhoun blinked a few times when Barry first brought it up; but once he'd laid out the evidence, Tom was fully converted.

Barry was the first person to admit that conversations about little green men put the majority of the populace into a state of disbelief. While a lot of people didn't doubt that there might be intelligent life elsewhere in the universe, the idea that otherworldly beings had been slowly infiltrating human existence for centuries was one that didn't go down easily. Stating such a thing usually caused people to want to wrap you up in damp towels and call for institutionalization. Barry understood the reaction. Some things are so vast that people's minds shut down in denial before they can grasp the entire picture. It causes a synaptic overload.

Still, there was no denying the evidence Barry had pieced together over the years. He'd made his first formal connection between alien overlords and the Estes Foundation while researching secret government testing of "black ops" technology in the 1950s. Things such as anti-gravitational fields and particle masking had popped up out of nowhere, with no logical chain of development in the world of physics. It was almost as if humanity had stumbled onto some secret treasure trove of advanced engineering, on a sub-atomic level.

Naturally, Barry wasn't the first person to make a connection between the amount of reported UFO activity in the late 1940s and the rise of cloaked technology just a few years later, but he was the first person to follow the money trail. The United States Department of Defense had a couple of pure research and development arms, known as ARPA, for Advanced Research Projects Agency and DARPA, which merely added the extension "Defense" to the previous name. Most people researching covert development glanced by ARPA in favor of DARPA on the assumption that the military had to be working on the really nasty stuff.

Nothing could have been further from the truth. Barry discovered that DARPA was a red herring, a sop for the paranoid. ARPA was where the edgy stuff was being worked on, in shared funding grants between the Department of Defense and various private agencies. Most of this research was conducted by universities across the nation and invariably, a chair at each university was endowed by the Estes Foundation.

Once he'd found that, Barry methodically combed records for years, building a trail that when back towards the mid 14th century in what were then the Germanic city-states. Illuminated manuscripts of the time talked about a series of celestial events, "burning wheels in the sky" that appeared over the Alpine regions of what would eventually be Austria and France. Shortly after this phenomenon, the Rosemond family became the financial power of Europe. The Rosemonds had a permanent seat on the Estes Foundation since it's inception in 1925. This direct connection between the strongest international financial institution on earth and extraterrestrial beings answered a question that had nagged at Barry since he was a teenager.

Barry believed that there was a purpose to everything and every action. He felt that if one couldn't see the motivation behind something, you were misreading what was going on. That the Estes Foundation was pursuing a strategy whereby it could eventually gain dominion over the planet was patently clear to Barry, but it made him a little nuts when he couldn't find the motivation for doing so.

As an undergraduate, Barry could easily trace the Estes Foundation's manipulation of global politics. Any war that popped up usually had a Byzantine connection to the Foundation, just as any end of hostilities and resulting re-structure of boundaries, treaties, governments and alliances did. For a number of years, it struck him as some sort of pointless chess game, where the same person was moving the pieces on both sides of the board. Try as he might, he couldn't find the rational for it all. The various organizations that ran the Estes Foundation already had as much power, influence and wealth as possible. They were vulnerable to nothing except possibly a cataclysm of global proportions. Even if everyone responsible for the foundation closed up shop tomorrow, re-tired to Bermuda and never lifted a finger to manage their monies from now until Kingdom come, their fortunes would survive a thousand years. So why, Barry would ask himself, do they continue this course of control? To what end?

The alien connection brought everything back into focus. "Imagine," Barry told Tom one night as he was revealing the true purpose of the Estes Founda-tion to his host, "that you are a creature who's current environment is in jeopardy. Imagine that while you have certain technologies that allow you to modify your environment, you cannot control it completely. Let's just say that you've discovered the sun your planet orbits around is going to supernova with then next two thousand years. What do you do?"

"Go shopping for a new house, I reckon," Calhoun mused.

"Yeah," Barry went on, "but you've got a big family with a lot of special needs. You need to find a place with the right specific gravity, the right combi-nation of temperatures, atmosphere, sources of nutrition and all. Let's say you found the right house, fits the bill nearly to a tee, but there's someone living in it. What next?"

"You kick them out, obviously." Calhoun was a straightforward sort of guy.

"Yeah," Barry concurred, "but this family won't go. If you want to get rid of them, you'll wind up destroying the house."

Calhoun scratched his head, flummoxed. Barry pointed out that the next logical step would be to move into the people that inhabited the house. "Create a hybrid that will gradually mutate into something else, mostly alien, but more adaptable to this planet."

It was a neat package. Every loose end Barry had ever encountered tucked quite nicely into this construct. Puzzling or questionable events the Estes Foun-dation set in motion now could be seen in a new light, such as the creation of a controlled hole in the ozone layer, the rise of hormones in foodstuffs and the resulting acceleration of maturation in children around the globe, even some of the curious research projects that ARPA pursued made absolute sense inside this scenario. Barry projected that with the introduction of a pandemic virus that really worked, the human race could be completely hybridized inside of the next fifteen years.

"It's a simple process, really," Barry explained. "They first had to find some-thing to use as leverage. Pry a little gap in the window stripping, so to speak. Look at Europe during the first Crusade. You got a church that will condemn you to Hell if you don't go rescue the Holy Land from the Arabs. You got all these Kings that have to foot the bill and nowhere to get the money since no one wants to lend these Kings money because the church considers interest above one and a quarter percent usury and usury is a venal sin. Along come some Hebrew fellows with money to lend at three percent because they're not bound by Papal law."

"Yeah," Calhoun said, "so?"

Barry grinned slyly. "Only these Jewish guys aren't really Jewish. Hell, they're not even human."

Calhoun's stunned expression was all Barry needed. Calhoun was eyeless in Gaza and Barry happily romped through the man's cortex, bringing enlighten-ment.

Over the course of the next few weeks, Barry related the history of alien in-filtration into affairs of humanity. First, came the Age of Exploration, financed by these ancient money brokers, which allowed them to gain subtle and slow footholds into the Americas and Asia. Next came the Industrial Revolution, which allowed for the earth's population to redistribute itself into easily control-lable urban masses. Naturally, the next steps were a series of events designed to psychologically prepare humanity for the final takeover. World wars, global monetary crises, the advent of super powers and super weapons and now the glint of a New World Order and the rise of biomedical technology.

"Now that most of the planet is thinking globally, all they need to do is find the right pandemic to release that will cause everyone to walk right into their hands and be transformed from human beings into alien autonomatons from beyond the moon!"

Irene was delirious. It seemed as if all the disappointment life had ever handed her was now being eradicated by a kindlier set of fates. Her pokey little town would soon become a hub of cutting edge industry and all the fun and glamour that would accompany it. During the technology boom, she'd read lots of articles in the glossy magazines and special Sunday sections of USA Today about the wild and free spending habits of tech boomers in places such as San Francisco and San Jose. She couldn't wait.

She was getting a taste of it already. She and Rick had patched things up once again, and he'd been on a buzz of excitement and exuberant joy for several weeks, taking her along for the ride. He was flush with cash and made references to an even bigger payday to come soon. Every weekend, they went to Santa Fe or Denver or, as this weekend panned out, Telluride, Colorado.

"Isn't that Kurt Russell?" she exclaimed as they drove Rick's Range Rover slowly up the main drag of the resort town. Rick chuckled and shook his head.

"Jesus, Irene, not everyone that lives here is gonna be Kurt Russell."

"Well," she said in a minor huff, "it could have been."

Telluride had a number of events every summer, culminating in a film festival. Rick had pulled some strings with his old fraternity brothers, one of which had eventually wound up hacking public relations for one the majors in Hollywood. His studio leased three floors of one of the lodges there for the event and got Rick into one of the suites. Irene was ecstatic when he informed her of their weekend plans.

As Irene rambled on about the style and class the town showed and speculated on what Aspen must be like during the height of the ski season, Rick, overwhelmed by thoughts of his impending success, said, "could be that we wind up living like this ourselves before too long." He hoped for a squeeze on the arm and an adoring look when he said that, but a statuesque blond she was certain she'd seen in half a dozen movies distracted Irene.

Rick was scoping out the landscape himself. Aside from the glamour factor he'd decided to run up to Telluride because of its recent transformation from the back of beyond to an A list destination resort. It had a few similarities to Mesa Azul, the primary one being a shortage of land suitable for development. Situated in a very narrow valley and having an annual snowfall that dissuaded architects from building all but the stoutest of cantilevered homes on the steep mountain slopes, Telluride had used up nearly all of its' available ground. Rick studied how the town was laid out and mentally moved the pieces around onto Mesa Azul's topography. Distracted, his focused was snapped back to things at hand by an exclamation from Irene and then a strong "thump" on the fender of his car.

"Chingara, Rick!" Irene shouted, "you just hit that guy!"

"What guy?" Rick said, throwing the car into park in the middle of the street and starting to get out of the door.

The guy he hit was hobbling around in circles just behind him and holding his hip. A bag of some sort was torn open and canisters of various sizes were rolling around on the blacktop.

"I'm sorry, man," Rick said as he approached his victim, "I didn't even see you there. Are you..."

"That's fucking obvious, you Goddamn lamebrain," the guy hollered back at Rick. "Jesus, that fucking smarts!"

Rick started to pick up the things that had spilled out of the man's bag. Lots of them were film canisters, while the larger ones appeared to be lens cases; a good assumption since the guy had an expensive looking single lens reflex camera hung around his neck.

"Fucking turkey," the cameraman went on, "cost me a shot and probably my Zeiss compound zoom. I hope you're loaded, asshole. This is going to cost you!"

As this dialogue went on, a couple more people draped with cameras, light meters and bags joined them. They all seemed to be yelling at Rick while commiserating with the man he'd sideswiped. Traffic was piling up behind them and car horns began to blare. Weaving through the cacophony was the sound of laughter. Rick could feel himself sweating like mad. He looked back at his car and Irene, rather than doing anything helpful, was sitting and staring across the street. "Typical," Rick thought to himself, "Irene can't be bothered to give me a hand." To him, it seemed as if she'd completely removed herself from the equation. If a cop came along, she'd probably say, "I don't know this guy, I was hitchhiking and he gave me a ride."

Actually, Irene was staring at Don Drayton and Sharon Westlake. This couple had been on the cover of every gossip and celebrity rag Irene had picked up in the past few months. They had been walking down the wooden boardwalk that fronted the shops on the main drag of town, seen the accident and quickly run into an antique store. She could see them watching the commotion through the front window. It didn't take a genius to figure out that the guy Rick had hit was a paparazzi dashing across the road to get a couple of pictures. The famous couple seemed to be nearly doubled over in paroxysms of laughter. As Irene watched them, they finally got a grip on themselves and vanished into the interior of the store.

Looking back to where Rick was, it was evident that he was ready to blow his stack. Everyone, now including some sort of law official was yelling and waving their arms while her boyfriend was busily trying to hand film cans and lens cases back to the guy he'd thumped, at the same time trying to see if he was hurt and find his wallet. His face had begun to resemble a beet, which was a sure sign that an explosion was imminent. She jumped out of the car.

"Just move your car out of the street, sir," a guy dressed in a khaki uniform and a straw cowboy hat with a star on the front was patiently repeating to Rick as Irene wormed her way into the clump of people.

"Where?" Rick said, the undertone of his voice drifting menacingly towards and explosion. "I've been going up and down the streets for ten minutes looking for a place to park."

"I just saw Drayton and Westlake," Irene shouted, which caused everyone but the cop and Rick to shut up. "They went into that restaurant over there!" She pointed to Fatty's, a rib joint that didn't have an entrée for less than twenty-five dollars on the menu. Everyone but the three principles and Irene immediately started running in the direction Irene had pointed. Even the injured cameraman grabbed the stuff in Rick's arms, frantically tried stuffing it in his torn camera bag and started to limp away.

"Just a minute, sir," the local cop said. Irene noted that his badge said deputy. "I need to get your statement."

"Fuck you, Gomer!" the victim yelled back while picking up speed. "That's my goddamned shot! I saw them first!"

The deputy told Rick to get in his Rover, gave him directions to the Sheriff's office to file a report and then waved him off. Rick was completely keyed up for a few minutes, his heart racing and every nerve on edge. Finally, after finding a car park only a quarter of a mile from the hotel they were supposed to stay in, he had calmed down enough to turn to Irene and thank her for extricating him from the situation.

"This place is pretty nutty," she observed. "That guy ran out from between a Humvee and a humongous RV. There's no way you could have seen him."

"Yeah," Rick agreed, "still I'm glad we avoided a mess. Thanks, baby." Irene simpered at the compliment and then wondered aloud if they should file an accident report before they checked into the hotel.

"Fuck that noise," Rick said. "Barney Fife back there has his hands full. Fifteen minutes from now, he'll have forgotten all about it. I'm just glad I never gave the guy my insurance information."

Irene was shocked. She lectured Rick on responsibility until he finally slammed his hands on the steering wheel in frustration. "Fine," he fumed, turning the ignition and viciously grinding the gears, "let's go find the county jug."

The afternoon passed in icy silence. Irene regretted going away with Rick and was ready to make arrangements to get home on her own by late in the day. Rick smoldered and walked heavily around the suite they'd gotten. He expected that squirrelly cameraman to show up at any second, complaining of some crippling injury and with a lawyer in tow. Things reached their peak when a hard rap was heard from the door.

"There you go, Irene," Rick said venomously, "I bet that's Johnny Whiplash and an ambulance chaser." Wearily he opened the door and was confronted by a short blond woman with enormous sunglasses on and holding a basket.

"Mister Arnold?" she asked. He nodded and she handed him the basket. "Compliments of Miss Westlake and Mister Drayton."

"Who?" Rick said dazedly while Irene shrieked hysterically in the background.

"Oh my God," Irene babbled, "they know who we are?"

The blonde woman smiled. "Yes, they're anxious to thank the both of you for helping them out of a sticky situation. They're having a party this evening and would like you to attend."

A few more exclamations from Irene, a couple more gracious replies from the blonde and business was concluded. Rick felt as though he'd passed through the looking glass. Nothing made a lot of sense. He'd hit a guy and now movie stars were expressing their appreciation? He lifted the gingham cloth that covered the wicker basket he'd been handed. Muffins. And a note.

While Irene went into rapture over the muffins, Rick read the note. It was an invitation to a party in the Presidential suite of the hotel, signed, "Thanks, Killer - Don & Sharon".

Fate is a diavello; a spinning erratic axle hanging precariously on a string. It tends to go in directions other than the person controlling the string would wish. Rick and Irene were tugged constantly that day by its' caprices, until they both resembled spot-lit deer. Glassy eyed and nervous, they presented themselves and their invitation to the top room in the hotel at eight o'clock that evening.

One thing Rick had a nose for was other people's money. The air was thick with the scent and it acted like a tonic for him. His height grew by at least an inch the second he felt all that disposable income flowing around him. He scanned the room with laser-like focus, seeking out possible marks. Within thirty seconds, he saw six or seven people that were definite possibilities. "I need to mingle a little," he whispered to Irene.

Irene nodded hypnotically. She wanted to slap herself, as this was the culmination of every daydream she'd ever had. Little Irene Naha from the middle of nowhere, haunch to paunch with the rich, beautiful and famous. While everyone was dressed in Telluride casual clothes, she saw that even those rags cost more than she made in a year. Overwhelmed with self-consciousness she nailed herself to the floor and watched enviously as Rick oiled his way through the press of people towards the bar. She had the oddest sensation that she was standing on the breakwater of the old world, watching a ship sail off into the new.

This new world had some rough waters, Rick quickly discovered. The marks he'd zeroed in on only looked stupid. They quickly sized him up for a small timer, an interloper into their world. He'd had enough brush-offs in his life to know when expert escape artists were maneuvering around him. No matter how he approached them, they slid through his conversation easily and without causing him any undo embarrassment. Still, he kept in there, grinning and sweating and trying to make some sort of contact. Anyone who looked at him, however, would see the eyes of a drowning man.

The conversations going in every group were opaque and impenetrable. They talked of above and below the line points, power plays by people he never heard of and credit positions. At first, he thought, naturally enough, that credit had to do with finance. "Marty is screwing the guild by not taking a normal credit position," one fiercely bald man said through a haze of perfecta smoke. Rick felt it was a natural opening as he was right next to this guy and he was looking just past him to a slim fellow with glasses who's bows seemed to have worn little gutters on the sides of his head. The slim guy nodded and Rick chuckled loud enough to be noticed. Both men turned to him quizzically and he seized the opportunity.

"Credit's a bitch these days, isn't it, boys?"

"Sure," baldy said cautiously. "Everyone who thinks they're an auteur wants to fuck around with the rules."

"Tell me about it," Rick went on confidently. "I got clients who never listen to my advice on credit. Breaks my heart. I could put them in a sweet position."

"Clients?" the slim guy asked. "What agency are you with?"

Rick pulled out his card case and handed each of his new acquaintances a pasteboard. They were nice too. Irene had designed them and taken them to the Quickee Print in Taos, paid extra for thermographic printing, where the ink was baked on so it rose from the surface and felt like an embossed card when you ran your thumb over it.

"You're a real estate agent?" baldy asked incredulously.

"Where the hell is Mesa Azul?" the slim guy wondered out loud.

"I'll tell you," Rick said happily, shifting gears into sales mode. "It's where the future is, boys. In less than five..."

"Sorry," baldy interrupted, "I see our hostess. I gotta drop a word in her ear." As one of Rick's new found acquaintances bulled his way through the sea of people surrounding them, Rick focused on his remaining patsy. While the guy wasn't as receptive as Rick would like, he hadn't bolted and listened with at least half an ear as Rick went on about the fantastic possibilities opening up in the gorgeous Sangre di Cristo highlands. He'd just gotten around to telling the slim guy about the recent earnest money paid on the top property in the Huernafano valley when he heard his name mentioned. He turned around and stared into a face he vaguely recognized.

"Hi, Killer," the man said. "Don Drayton." Rick shook his hand and he realized this was the movie star that Irene had been going on about for the past few hours. Personally, Rick didn't see what the big deal was. This Drayton character looked no more handsome than he did. Must be the sheen of celebrity that sticks to some people.

"Marcus," Don said, looking past Rick to the skinny guy, "you don't mind if I steal Killer here away for a little bit, do ya?"

The skinny guy's face was wreathed in gratitude. "Thanks, er, I mean, not at all Don."

Rick was puzzled. "What's this 'Killer' stuff?"

"I was about to ask the same thing," Marcus chimed in.

Don laughed. "He's the guy I was telling you about." Don held his thumb and forefinger a hair's breadth apart from each other. "He came this close to ending that dipshit Terry Bruckman from Black Diamond's career forever."

Marcus joined in on the laughter. "Oh, he's the CSM you were talking about." Marcus slapped Rick on the arm. "Nice to meet you. Get a Humvee and do the job right next time."

"CSM?" Rick asked.

"Camera Seeking Missile," Don guffawed as he steered Rick away from the slim guy. "I've been telling everyone here, we ought to kick in a pot and have you race around LA, running over paparazzi."

Don kept up a breezy chatter as he pulled Rick through the crowd. As the got the edge of the folks crammed around the bar and the buffet, Don nodded towards Irene, who was still frozen in the position she'd taken on first entering the suite. "That your lady?" Rick acknowledged that it was.

"Great!" Don roared enthusiastically. "You just steer her over there," he pointed towards a stunning blonde near an alcove, "and I'll introduce both of you to Sharon."

This was almost too much for Irene to handle. Rick discovered that she could barely remember the basic mechanics of walking and he almost had to drag her over to the alcove. Sharon and Don were so gracious, so at ease with themselves and their guests that Rick could feel Irene slowly coming back to herself. He just hoped that as she relaxed she wouldn't say anything too idiotic. Don and Sharon were consummate conversationalists, feigning a keen interest in Rick's dreams for Mesa Azul and Irene's stammering adulation of their celebrity status.

Irene, after a few minutes of casual small talk with Miss Westlake, caught a snippet of conversation between Rick and Mister Drayton.

"I'm telling you, Don," Rick was pitching, "you'll hate yourself for passing up this opportunity. This is like buying into Aspen on the ground floor. I've already sold a huge acreage on the north end of Mesa Azul to a developer with big plans for a resort, but there's plenty of small lots available on the slope of Madre di Cristo. Just imagine owning Little Nell at the base of Ajax Mountain. Same deal."

"What are you talking about, honey?" Irene asked.

Rick smiled and wrapped his arm around Irene's shoulder. "I'm supposed to keep this on the QT until the title transfer, but yeah, I'm closing on the Morrison property in a few weeks." He tapped a fingertip on the end of her nose, "but you have to keep it quiet."

"How did you find out?" Irene asked, completely baffled.

"Honey, I put the deal together."

Irene chewed on her lip. Something didn't make sense, unless Mister Marquis had contacted Rick. Well, a resort community would be more fun than a development center, Irene concluded. She smiled at Rick. "I'm glad that Mister Marquis contacted you instead of Johnny Gee."

"Mister who?" Now it was Rick's turn to be in the dark.

Of course, Irene realized, Mister Marquis wouldn't have contacted Rick. Someone else from his company would have.

"Who did you talk to at ByteStream?"

Rick smiled benignly at Irene. She was an absolute space cadet, but she was pretty cute when she was feeling good.

"Why on earth would you think ByteStream wants to build a resort community? They're a computer company."

"Uh," Irene was trying to feel her way now. She felt as if she and Rick were having two completely different conversations. "Mostly because that's what Mister Marquis said."

"Ted Marquis?" Don asked. "You know Ted Marquis? The CEO of ByteStream?"

Irene blushed. "Well, I don't think I could call him Ted or anything, but yeah. He was in town at the beginning of the summer. He told the whole town he wanted to build a development center there."

There was a high-pitched ringing in Rick's ears. Ted Marquis. A bajillionaire had been in stupid, pokey, fucking nowhere Mesa Azul and he hadn't known a thing about it.

"You okay, Killer?" Don asked solicitously.

"Huh?"

"You look a little white." Don turned to Sharon and said, "I told you not to get those scallop hors d'ouevres. Guy's got food poisoning." He patted Rick solicitously on the back, "maybe you should lie down for a little bit."

Don had one of the waiters take Rick and Irene to a bedroom. Once they were alone, Rick, trying his damnedest to keep it together, asked Irene what she knew about Ted Marquis and ByteStream. As she explained what had gone on earlier in the summer, the buzzing in his ears got louder and he felt his face grow cold. While he listened, he frantically tried to figure out how he could get out of the closing with Steve. He was sitting on a property worth millions and he'd closed a deal for peanuts.

"Fuck," Rick said almost under his breath.

"What's the difference whether it's a development center or a resort community?" Irene said, stroking Rick's cheek. "You got the contract."

"Fuck!" Rick shouted, pushing Irene's hand away. He stood up and towered over her. "You stupid cow! I don't have the deal! I got shit!" He clenched and unclenched his hands, fighting the urge to strangle her. "You should have told me!"

"He told us not to!" Irene cried, tears burning the back of her throat. "He said we couldn't tell you or Johnny Gee! He wanted to keep the price down."

"Fuck!" was Rick's final comment as he dashed out of the room, heading like a cannonball back to his suite and his phonebook. He had to find a way out of his deal with Steve.

Steve was surprised at the frantic tone in Rick's voice. "Steve," Rick said, "I got to come clean with you on something."

Steve rolled his eyes. God only knew what this Goober was up to. "Really? What's on your mind, old buddy?"

Rick had come up with a brilliant idea as he looked for his address book and dialed Steve's number. "I just found out, while talking to my client that the property you're looking at is primarily bentonite."

Steve smiled to himself. He looked at the clock on the desk; it read ten fifteen. Saturday night and Mister Wheeler Dealer is having a crisis of conscious. He knew. Somehow, the little pischer found out. Oh well, it was all over but the applause, so Steve figured he'd play along.

"It's primarily got who in the what, now?"

Rick calmly explained that bentonite was a clay that was extremely unstable. It expanded and contracted with various degrees of moisture and temperature change. "It's like building on Jello. It can break a building apart."

"Wow!" Steve chuckled inwardly while playing dumb on the phone. "Sounds serious."

Rick felt the muscles in his back unknot. He could do this. He could ease this guy out of everything. "It is," he said sincerely. "Serious enough that if you chose to back out of this purchase now, you'd be well within your rights to do so. Morrison should have disclosed it in the property description. He's violated the terms of sale."

Steve made a "tsk"-ing sound into the mouthpiece. "Yeah, that's mighty unethical. I have to say, Rick, I admire your honesty in telling me about this. A lot of guys would have just let it slide. You'll be losing a hell of a commission."

"I know," Rick said, grinning. "But I have to be able to sleep at night."

"You'd sleep better if you had the property to sell to ByteStream, wouldn't you?" Steve could almost hear Rick's heart stop. He pictured the guy, all color draining from his face while his toes curled up. Small town sharks; you had to love them.

"Listen, asshole," Steve hissed into the phone, "we got a deal. Ironclad and sewn shut. You're shit out of luck." Steve heard the phone drop. He yelled into the mouthpiece in the hope that Rick hadn't passed out.

"If you're a good boy, I'll give you a ringside seat when I fuck over the richest man on the planet."

"Sleep tight."

Chapter Ten -

The Blue Bus Takes Off and the Compound Comes Down.

Bob's Big Boy was debating the merits of Raton Pass and La Vida Pass. On the one hand, Raton was more fun to wrestle the Blue Bus over, but once you were down on the other side, there was nothing but smooth interstate all the way to Denver. La Vida had easy grades on both sides, which held no challenge to a true gear jockey, yet it was part of the blue highways, the state roads that went through the more interesting parts of the world.

His decision was based on the occupants of the bus. The oldest person on board was Mrs. Butterworth. The Doc had wandered off somewhere and it seemed obvious that a road trip held no appeal for the old shaman with the small bladder. Without Doctor Pepper, he'd have a lot fewer pit stops to make, so he turned north for Fort Garland, La Vida Pass, Walsenburg, Pueblo, Colorado Springs and eventually Denver and the Annual Inter-tribal Pow-wow; 300 miles of bliss.

He often thought to himself that the worst thing to happen to America was the Federal Interstate Highway Program. He looked at them as razor cuts across the face of the country, bleeding out anything interesting or unique. At high speeds and no stoplights, the days of the roadside attraction were dust. He liked living in a world where there were three headed calves in formaldehyde and jackalopes.

On the state roads, he could still look forward to a couple statements of individuality. They stopped for lunch at Geronimo's Hideout, which was "home of the Apache corndog". They were the only Indians in the place. The owner was a Norwegian from Minnesota and the few customers were ranchers from Costilla County as well as a German tourist couple who paid Bob eight dollars for his photograph. Mrs. Fields was surprised that Apaches had invented corndogs and disturbed the guy that ran the batter machines by asking whether the Chiracollas, Mescalero, Mimbrenos or White Mountain bunch came up with the idea.

"Christ," the man said in a pique. "I bought the damned stuff from a drive-in in Saint Louis. It must have been the Cardinals."

"I must ask about the Cardinal Apaches when we get to the Pow-wow," Mrs. Fields confided to Mrs. Butterworth later on the bus. "I didn't know Apaches went as far north as Saint Louis."

These were the sorts of things Bob's Big Boy dreamed of. A nation of eccentric individualists, reveling in whatever inspiration came trickling into their hearts at some point and settled in for life. Just north of Walsenburg, where the ability to avoid the interstate peters out, a farmer who'd made extra income by leasing the edge of his fields that bordered the highway to outdoor advertisers until the Highway Beautification Act banned billboards, set out more than thirty towering signs, manically covered with obscene screeds about big government. They were like filthy Burma-Shave signs, suggesting that the Federal Interstate Transport Authority was full of perverse contortionists, capable of amazing feats.

While other farmers spent the winter repairing equipment and possibly putting in a crop of winter wheat, this man attended to his billboards. He constantly edited them, revised them, improved them or added to them. It was worth a stop to study the changes.

"This guy writes like Miz Ryland-Bowles paints," Bob's Big Boy thought to himself. Mrs. Butterworth noted that the farmer seemed to have developed an interest in teabags and tossed salads over the winter. She was relieved. Perhaps a nice cup of tea and the proper amount of roughage a day would slowly reduce the amount of rancor towards the world the poor man seemed to display.

Denver itself was always a bit of a disappointment to Bob's Big Boy. When he was a kid, it had uniqueness; a singularity to it. The intervening years had leached the overgrown cow town feel out of it and all that was left was another big city. He skirted the downtown and headed towards the eastern suburbs, at least the Wagon Wheel Motel was still on East Colfax, which was a bygone a slice of eccentricity. Judging by the way the rooms were furnished, the owner had watched a lot of Roy Rogers as a kid. The irony of a bunch of Indians sleeping in rooms full of cowboy coverlets and lamps made from toy revolvers wasn't lot on him either.

The Intertribal Pow-Wow itself was held in the heart of the city, in the convention center. If anyone wondered what the current state of affairs regarding Native Americans was, the Pow-Wow usually left outsiders with more questions than answers. It was a combination of an Indian Market, ethnic festival, cultural awareness, legal roundtable, protest movement and marketing seminar. Various native costumes abounded, from Zuni cloud maidens to Armani suits. Bob dreamed of the day he could wear an Armani suit and pull it off.

The Shantis exploded like a covey of quail spooked from the brush the second they entered the convention center. Bob strolled leisurely down the hallways on the third floor where the conference and seminar rooms were, looking for Dan Bucknuts, an Arapahoe attorney he'd met the previous year. While Mrs. Fields was attending a workshop on making Indian bread and Reddi Kilowatt was cruising for cloud maidens, Bob's Big Boy wanted to talk to Dan about the impending arrival of ByteStream to his little corner of the world and how to leverage the Shanti's position to the best advantage. Dan specialized in Equal Employment Opportunities lawsuits. Class actions had made him a wealthy man.

"You're kidding, right?" Dan exclaimed after Bob laid out the basic scenario. "ByteStream is building in your fucking backyard and you got some cafeteria jobs out of the deal? That's it? That's fucking it?"

"Pretty much," Bob agreed. "Janitorial stuff too, I guess."

Dan's indignation was spoiled slightly by the glimmer in his eyes. His goal in life was to do well for himself while he was doing good for others and with this plum he could do very well for himself indeed. He was already looking at the suit he could file against Mr. Megabucks Geek for discriminatory hiring practices. This was the deepest pocket on earth and it was wide open to him. Stifling his less savory impulses, he asked Bob a series of rapid-fire questions regarding offers of internship, training programs, vertical integration and the like.

"Hell," Bob said, spreading his hands wide and shrugging, "I only got to talk to the guy for a minute."

"Yeah," Dan said dreamily. "He brushed you off. Typical WASP stuff." He paced up and down the hall for a few minutes until Bob started to fidget. "Look," Dan slapped Bob's shoulder, "come and meet me in the coffee shop on Friday. I'll have some ideas for you by then."

"Is this Pro Bono or are you looking at a contingency fee?" Bob's Big Boy asked nervously. Visions of exorbitant legal bills began to appear in the shape of Dan Bucknuts.

"How stupid do I look?" Dan said. As the color drained out of Bob's Big Boy's face, the Indian attorney said reassuringly, "contingency, baby. Don't worry. The Shantis will come out of this with thirty-five percent of whatever I milk the geek for."

There is nothing that occurs on the face of the earth that isn't noticed by something else. Coyote once had a conversation with John Elkfoot on that subject. His observation was that matter could not be concealed. Coyote pointed out that matter would invariably interact with matter. "Even something as simple as oxygen becomes a known and physically defined substance by its'

existence. You feel its' presence, even when you don't see it." It was a discussion that Barry and Tom Calhoun might have benefited from.

For all their efforts at concealment, they made certain motions that brought attention to them. Usually, this attention was in the form of electronic monitoring systems on phone lines and internet connections. Ever since America had become the victim of terrorism, both internally and externally, security agencies had implemented steps to monitor phone and data lines. Barry and Tom were aware of these systems and used pay phones, internet service provider address masking and other methods to avoid being tracked back to the compound when they were communicating with others.

The trouble was, regardless of the intricacy and caution they took, they had no guarantees that the people they were communicating with were as diligent. The moment a key word or phrase popped up in either a text or voice conversation, sophisticated digital systems began back tracing through routers and switches, looking for the source of each end of the conversation.

While Barry and Tom weren't uncovered, one of their new co-conspirators was. Arlen Jeffers was an old school survivalist having a hard time catching up to the age of technology. Twenty years older than Barry, he was a man who dropped off the grid in the early seventies, when pay phones and re-mailing services were the height of concealment. It worked well until the advent of the internet and most correspondence moved into websites, chatrooms and email.

Arlen lived deep in the Snake River region of Idaho, venturing once a month into Redrum and or Coeur D'Alene to pick up mail and make some phone calls. He had been a subscriber to Barry's newsletter for a few years and the final issue he received had a single article, written by Barry after he'd reached the Calhoun compound.

The story of Barry's discovery and flight set off alarm bells in Arlen's head. If a guy as bright and savvy as Barry could be discovered by the system, what hope did poor old unsophisticated Arlen Jeffers have? Barry had kept pace with the developments of the world and prepared as best he could against every new wrinkle the system came up with. Arlen had just retreated into the mountains and lived a life that would have been considered cutting edge in 1870. Now he felt as though shadowy forces were trailing him everywhere. He needed help and the only guy he could think of to extricate him from this mess was Barry.

Barry got a number of letters like the one he soon received from Arlen. Throughout the nation, isolated people with the same mindset as Calhoun and Barry were sending petitions for assistance. It was clear to Tom that the time had come to pull all these people together and begin the process of fighting back. "We're done sitting, partner," he said to Barry one evening in late July, "it's time to come out swinging."

119

Tom's son Lyle had been fighting the system in his own way for a few years. Ever since he was a kid, he'd discovered the fun in reverse engineering computer programs and figuring out what he could make them do that they weren't designed to do. Before long, he was using the old ARPANET to get into computer systems, then graduated to full fledged system cracking. While he didn't buy into his father's worldview, he had no problem supporting it by using his skills to tunnel past protection networks and romp around sensitive data. Lyle supported himself with stolen credit card numbers, lifted cell phone numbers that he programmed into cloned phones and sold, as well as entering e-ticket orders into every airline database on earth for a moderate fee.

Lyle suggested that they set up a chatroom on a cloaked server. "You guys need to get with the program," he told Calhoun one night when he was visiting the compound. "All this snail mail and pay phone crap is bullshit. There's a whole hidden world of communication you two are either too stubborn or too dumb to access."

Lyle went ahead and tapped into the secure data farm in Langley, Virginia. Part of the United States covert ops system, it had been lagging behind for a good ten years in regards to state-of-the-art security. Lyle found the idea of creating a cloaked network for the enemies of the existing power structure inside their very own intelligence system too ironic to pass up.

"As long as everyone dials in and uses an IP masking device, they'll never catch on," he explained to his Dad after he set things up. "Let me know forty minutes before you want to hold an online conference and I'll get things happening. You guys can yak for two hours and no one will ever know."

Arlen, and all the other acolytes of Barry Moss soon received a letter that explained in great detail how this new underground electronic communications system would work. To Arlen, it all read like gibberish. Computers? The world wide web? He didn't like the sound of that at all. At the same time, Barry was offering him a lifeline and he was damned if he wouldn't grab on to it. He had until August 15th to figure all this stuff out.

August found Arlen in a public library in Coeur D'Alene, reading up on everything he'd missed out on in the past thirty years. Why, the library itself had computers hooked up to this internet thing and he could access an unbelievable world of information. He was shocked to discover the number of people out there who'd put up websites and information similar in nature to the things Barry Moss had discovered. There were thousands upon thousands. The first time he entered the term "Black Helicopters" into a search engine, it returned more than thirty thousand pages of results. The sheer numbers convinced Arlen that there was no way the Estes Foundation could stop the truth from coming out or shutting it down. He soon became an internet addict.

The problems he encountered with his newfound passion were easily resolved. The library computers had ancient modems that ran at a snail's pace. Since he was limited to an hour's access time a day by the library rules, such slow speeds were intolerable. He soon discovered that there were a number of internet cafes in town though. The drawback there was they all required a credit card. Arlen had no credit cards. They increased his vulnerability to exposure and he used cash for everything. Finally, he found a place called CyberJava that would accept cash. He was soon spending up to eight hours a day there, hooked into the brave new world at four dollars an hour.

The guy that ran CyberJava soon became a friend of Arlen's. He explained to Arlen exactly what masking programs were. "Can't use them on these machines, though," he said. "Most people come in here to download music and porn movie files. Masking interrupts the download process." He did recommend online masking services that Arlen could access the rest of the internet through and even set up a bookmark for him. He assumed that Arlen was interested in kiddie porn and didn't want to get caught. The café owner himself was a "Furry" addict. He logged into websites devoted to people who liked to dress up like animals and have sex. He had a rabbit suit and was interested in a woman in LeCroix, Louisiana who sent him home pornography photos of herself in a fox suit. There were going to get together over the Labor Day weekend. He was real tolerant of other folk's obsessions.

"I hope you're pleased with yourself," John was saying to Coyote. "Your grasp on this place is tenuous at best and you've probably just destroyed your final connection to it."

John had just returned from the University Hospital in Santa Fe, where Doctor Pepper lay comatose in the critical care wing. His vital body statistics were barely registering and there was quite a debate ranging on whether or not to administer heroic measures. Currently, he was on oxygen and a saline drip, as well as a slow induction of necessary vitamins.

Coyote was incapable of chagrin. The spirit pulsed in and out of John's focus while considering how to respond to John's accusations. Finally, Coyote solidified, shrugged his shoulders and said, "I answered his prayers. Isn't that the secret hope of everyone that throws out supplications?"

John shook his head. "I just don't get you. You fuck around with things and when they blow up in your face, you have some stupid flip answer for everything. You know what that guy really wanted? Just a rationale, a reason for being. That's all anyone really wants. A little peace, a little respect and a little love. It's not a hard equation."

"That's what you want, John."

"It's what everyone wants."

Coyote laughed. He decided it was a good thing that men like John didn't have his ability to see inside people. He'd go crazy in twenty minutes, tops. The things that people craved, John had no idea. If Coyote had to find an overweening compulsion in humanity, it would be control. Not just over destiny, but dominion over everything.

"Men want to be Gods," he informed John.

John tapped a cigarette on the patio tabletop. The strain of the summer had caused him to start smoking again. He gave Coyote a sidelong glance and absently patted his pockets, looking for a lighter. Coyote caused the tip of John's cigarette to flare and John nodded his thanks.

Several days earlier, those two kids who'd been shadowing the Doc all over creation popped up to the top of the mesa to ask John if he'd seen or heard from the old man. The three of them began quartering the county, looking for the shaman. It was pure chance they found him. The Doc had built a shelter that looked more like a accidental pile of old twigs, branches and brush hard up against the Huernafano spring. The ground there was rough and uneven and John was creeping his Jeep over it when he happened to see a footprint in the dried mud near the spring. If he'd been going five miles an hour faster he'd probably have missed it. Getting out to investigate, the boys noticed there was an opening of sorts in the big brush pile. Carl peered in and gave a shout of alarm. Desiccated, painfully thin and seemingly dead, lay the Doc. John could barely make out a heartbeat and Doctor Pepper's breathing was so slight it was impossible to detect the rise and fall of his chest. The Doc was six feet tall and yet when John picked him up, he was shocked to discover the old man weighed in at well below one hundred pounds.

"He should have been on the cover of Time magazine," John said. "We'd have had UNICEF packages airlifted in here overnight."

They laid him in the back of John's jeep and he took the four wheel track over Madre di Cristo at a bone jarring pace in order to get the Doc to the Emergency Clinic in Taos as quickly as possible. The Doc was there for less than an hour. His vital signs barely registered, except for brain activity, which caused the electroencephalograms to spike like mad. An air evacuation helicopter was called in and he was rushed to the University hospital in Santa Fe. Since then, he'd been a conundrum to the experts.

"He's malnourished and dehydrated," John went on, "and it seems as though his system is shutting down. The weird thing is what's going on in his brain. It's like he's retreated into his mind."

Coyote wasn't surprised. The Doc had vanished into that little lump of gray matter a while ago. He'd tried to reach whatever consciousness the old man had a number of times unsuccessfully. He tried to explain to John that he could see where the Doc was, he could exist in that space, but he couldn't reach him.

John glared angrily. "Why the fuck do you want to go into people's consciousness anyway? That's what started this whole mess."

"Why do you get up in the morning?" was Coyote's reply. "Why do you read? Experiment with logarithms?"

"Oh," John said, raising an eyebrow, "this is all just intellectual curiosity?"

Coyote didn't like being lectured to. At the same time, during the millennia of his existence, John was the only entity that ever shook a finger in his face, so there was still a residual novelty to the act. Inadvertently, during his hectoring, John brought up things Coyote found were worth the time to think about. These sweet spots made bitter pills easier to swallow.

Coyote began to ponder the similarities and differences between himself and humanity. John recognized whenever the Spirit went into deep introspection because the physical manifestation of Coyote began to break up, like a picture on a TV screen that was getting a bad signal. Sections of Coyote's body broke apart or stretched sideways momentarily, before snapping back into position. Other times, he might ripple like a reflection on water, or pulses of color would flash and shift on his surface, as if he were made of mica or crystal. John knew there was no point in continuing a conversation with the ancient entity and looked out over Mesa Azul, nursing his cigarette and wondering what disaster would befall the little village next.

Coyote wasn't the only creature lost to the world at that moment in time. Several hundred miles away, the essence of Doctor Pepper had banked down to a tiny ember, burning brightly in the recesses of his cortex, but at the same time, slowly ebbing away. He seemed completely unresponsive to anything the medicos working on him tried to do. The doctors were flummoxed by several anomalies, not the least of which were the analysis of his blood gasses and toxin screens. One of the specialists spent more than a little time interviewing Carl and Troy. "You're telling me the patient was on no prescription medications?"

"Nope," Carl said and Troy reiterated Carl's statement.

"The guy is an herbalist," Troy explained for the umpteenth time. "That's why I went down there. He has these phenomenal abilities..."

"Yes," the doctor said, irritably interrupting Troy. He was sick to death of hearing about the mystical abilities of the old man, "so I've been told. But the results of his tests indicate that he's been on at least one psychotropic drug."

Physically, the Doc was an anomaly. All his organs seemed to be functioning perfectly, although suffering from deficiencies brought on by what appeared to be two weeks of no food at all. The old man did, however have a naturally occurring alkali in his system at six times the normal levels. This was what alarmed the physicians who were treating him.

"Right now," the doctor said to the two young men, "my concern is how on earth he managed to gets such high levels in his system without being on a drug such as Eskalith. It would explain the comatose state and right now, that's what we're having to treat."

He went on to say that without having a full medical background on the Doc, he was worried that Mesa Azul might have a naturally occurring health risk and asked if the young men would submit to at least a urinalysis. "This is an alkaloid with a very light atomic weight. As such, it can be active in water, plant tissue, animal tissue," he looked intently at the young men, "even in the air itself."

Something was in the air over at Project Genesis, the Department of Defense's electronic surveillance system. In the past few weeks, they'd begun to upgrade their security systems on the data farm at Langley and were disheartened to find that the protections they'd put in place for their networks, commonly known as firewalls, were as impenetrable as Swiss cheese. Hundreds of breeches in their system had been discovered. They had contracted one of the best computer security research outfits in the world to run a review of their security net and were horrified by the results. It seemed as though anyone with even a modicum of knowledge about firewalls and password protected systems had taken the time to tunnel through their security, plant a backdoor code that allowed them instantaneous access and used their servers and data farms on a regular basis.

Kevin Watanabi volunteered to clean up the entire mess. A convinced cyber-terrorist, he'd been given a four year prison sentence and used the time to write the first definitive paper on system protections and on his release, started a consulting firm that was hired by Fortune 500 companies to upgrade and monitor their systems.

"I'm the last gunfighter," he told the DOD's chief of security when he signed on to fix their problems, "if these crackers knew I was taking over your protection architecture, they'd be flooding your machines with denial of service attacks and Trojan horse and God knows what all. Just to show that they can beat me."

The trick, he said, was to remain invisible. "You have no one but the American public to answer to, and it's obvious you don't give a shit about them, so it's best that you make no announcements about what's wrong with your systems or what you're doing to fix them."

"Just keep quiet and let me do my job," he concluded.

Rather than remove the backdoor applications that he found, Kevin instead altered the code in them to send a tracer back to the source computer whenever those backdoors were opened. What this code was designed to do was look for initial keyboard strokes. Unless a system was actually supporting a keyboard that was typing commands reflected by the operation of the backdoor the tracer code was installed in, the code ignored it. Once it found the source computer, it planted itself in the system and sent back a monitoring signal that allowed Kevin to identify the assigned internet protocol address of the source.

Having been part of the Cracker universe at one time, Kevin realized that any and all arrests would have to take place at the same. In order to make sure that his system of traces wouldn't be discovered until it was too late to do anything about it, he insisted that nothing be done until he had a complete list of addresses for all the backdoors, worms, datamines and Trojan horses he found on the systems. Until then, he installed a series of monitoring codes and several DOD security operatives were assigned to review the logs of these illegal users daily. The chatroom that Lyle Calhoun set up was discovered and quickly brought to the attention of the FBI and the Bureau of Alcohol, Tobacco and Firearms. The BATF immediately assigned one of their own computer experts to work with Kevin and within a matter of hours he discovered the covert data fields Lyle had placed inside Langley's database and the message board it supported.

The tone of the messages being exchanged on the board convinced the BATF that illegal weapons were being sold, traded and solicited through this network. While there was nothing so concrete they could get a search or arrest warrant on, even an idiot would understand references such as: "street sweepers available" and "Russian bounty, cold war surplus" weren't in reference to urchins with brooms or instant Borscht.

A small task force of agents was assigned to this message board. Purely by chance, one of the agents assigned to the group had read enough of Barry's newsletters to recognize the writing style of "last_true_patriot", which was the screen name of one the message board members, as identical to Barry Moss. Barry had been in the periphery of the BATF for a number of years, ever since his first series of articles on homemade explosive devices made from common household ingredients. The Bureau had concluded that he was merely a paranoid nut, without the necessary violent streak to start amassing weapons. Something had changed in his consciousness and now the task force looked at him seriously. The messages originated from a compromised telephone switching station in central Texas. Kevin Watanabi was asked to look at the station and was impressed by the technical skill of the Cracker who'd set things up. "Whoever this is, knows the routing ticket system for Nortel and Lucent switches. That's something most network guys and Crackers don't have a clue about. This guy's good. Either he works for Texas Telecomm or he knows someone who does."

In the end, trying to track Lyle down proved to be impossible. The BATF had to set up an old-fashioned sting operation to get a lead. In order to actually arrest anyone, they had to have proof of criminal activities that would stand up before a judge. So far, they had intent, but nothing concrete. They quickly posted a cryptic message referencing fully automatic Kalishnakov rifles, adapted for belt fed ammunition. It was just the thing for Arlen Jeffers to bite on.

Once he'd become wired in, Arlen was amazed at the things available to him. Not just the meeting of like minds, he'd discovered there was nothing on this earth that wasn't for sale. He had a nice stash of Krugerrands from the early seventies whose value had increased precipitously and now he'd found a venue to use them in. He could see himself as a key player in the armed resistance against the Estes Foundation and after seeing the posting for sale of cold war weaponry, was determined to buy as many as he could afford and take them down to Texas, where he was sure Tom Calhoun would welcome him with open arms. He sent off a response to the posting and the BATF snagged and traced it at once.

"Take it to an email correspondence," was Kevin's suggestion. "The guys running this chatroom won't ever allow an overt reference to what you guys are doing. They've set up a keyword filter in the posting panel. It will remove any references to guns, money, the government, militias or anything of that nature. As a matter of fact," Kevin went on with a giggle, "it strikes me that they somehow got a hold of the Genesis keyword glossary and adapted it to their own purposes." Kevin whistled. "I love the guy that set this thing up."

When the BATF tried to type in an email address on their next posting, it never appeared on the message board. Kevin informed them that the system was obviously filtering email addresses as well. "Go on one of the free ISP providers like Yahoo and set up a group in there. Then tell the guy in a posting about it. That probably won't get filtered."

It wasn't and Arlen bit on that lure as well. He was soon logged on to the "FinalWarning" discussion group and exchanging email addresses with the

BATF. Twenty-four hours later he was in custody and charged with buying illegal firearms through the internet.

Arlen wasn't the only person buying guns and he knew it. From his correspondence with Barry over that past few weeks, he knew that Tom Calhoun had been stockpiling anything he could get his hands on for years. The man had weapons ranging from fully automatic machine guns, to Claymore mines and even a few shoulder launched ground to air missiles. Arlen never had to say a word. Between the letters they found in his hotel room, the email they retrieved from the computer he used at the CyberJava internet café and his journals, the BATF had more than enough evidence to go to the Justice department for permission to arrest Tom Calhoun and seize his armory.

At six a.m. on the Saturday before Labor Day, a convoy of jeeps, armored personnel carriers and even a modified Abrams tank was kicking up a cloud of dust as it raced across the Texas panhandle just west of Amarillo. A mile from the Calhoun bunker, motion sensors were tripped and set alarms blaring in the concrete and rebar structure buried fifty feet underground that Tom and Barry called home.

It took the combined strike force of FBI, Justice and BATF agents two hours to find the entrance to Tom's compound. By then, Tom and Barry were a hundred miles away, the dust from their rapid flight mingling in the air and leaving no sign that the two men were on the road to San Antonio. It was noon before the task force had broken down the access door to the bunker and by the time they'd finished recording all the seized materiel and issued a general fugitive warrant to all federal, state and local officials through Texas, Oklahoma, Colorado and New Mexico, the sun had gone down.

By then, the subjects of those warrants were busily altering their appearance in a motel room in Midland, Texas. Barry had dyed his hair black, which looked startlingly incongruous with his skin tones and was shaving his mustache. Tom had shaved his head and was dying his skin as dark as he felt he could get away with, considering his sky blue eyes.

"I'm open to suggestions," Tom said, while smearing walnut furniture stain under his eyes. The fumes made him a little light headed.

"About what?" Barry said while mourning the loss of his mustache. Barry had a long septum and no upper lip. His mustache had given his face a sense of symmetry and balance.

"What we should do," Tom went on. He was finding himself with a slight sense of disassociation to the person looking back at him in the mirror. A dark, bullet-headed stranger stared at him. He gave himself a wolfish smile and liked the way it came out. Now he finally looked like he felt. Menacing. "Where we should go. We're out of resources."

Barry was a little alarmed. "I thought you said you had connections in San Antonio?"

"I've got money in San Antonio," Tom corrected his friend. "Enough to go anywhere. The question is, where do we go?"

It was a good question. Was there a place on this earth that wasn't tainted by the Estes Foundation; somewhere that they couldn't be pried out of as easily as they had this morning? Each of them had developed elaborate and sophisticated methods for effectively disappearing from the face of the earth and yet it hadn't been enough. They were battling an invisible enemy with a global reach. They existed in a suspect world where nothing was as it seemed.

Left to his own devices, Barry might have given up then and there. He'd aligned himself with a bull, a ravening force of nature, who even as Barry stretched out on one of the twin beds in their dingy motel room, stalked across the threadbare carpet repetitively. Calhoun was a bundle of muscle, waiting on the neural impulses only Barry seemed to be able to provide.

Barry didn't want to think. He didn't want to lead. He wanted to sink down into darkness for just a while. He wanted the peace of a void, a vacuum; a deep recess that would allow him to just float for a while. Eventually, he would surface and when he did, he would find complete clarity to his thoughts and a direction to go in. For now, unless he could retreat, his mind was a jumble sale.

Tom, on the other hand, couldn't bide his time any more. His philosophy had always been one of targeting. "You can't hit what you can't see" had been an abiding principle for years, but now he had embraced the belief that it's very hard to hit a moving target. If Barry couldn't come up with a plan in the next twenty-four hours, he'd jettison him as dead weight and tear off alone. "Makes for a smaller target, anyway," Tom smiled inwardly and muttered to himself.

Chapter Eleven -

The Universe Develops a Hitch in its' Gitalong

It was apparent to everyone but Angel himself that he'd missed a sure bet by not becoming a priest. He liked rules, order and ritual. He also was the primary ear to bend with problems, concerns and confessions. The largest gulf between the bartender and any soultender however, was in matters of advice and absolution. Angel had no weighty tome to consult; he only had his own observations and experience. They were good, but far from perfect or universal in scope. Still, he recognized his limitations and tried to make sure anyone seeking his input saw his failings as well.

Of course, when it came to the issue of advice, Angel had one card up his sleeve. People rarely, if ever, in his experience, wanted his advice. What they came to him for was validation for a decision they'd already come to. Angel was an excellent nodder.

It seemed like the last two weeks of August, he'd done a lot of nodding. Everyone had something they needed to pass in front of him. First, it was Irene. She needed validation that Rick was a heartless jerk.

She told him all about the things that occurred in Telluride. Angel was distracted by the thought of meeting genuine celebrities and was hard pressed not to interrupt her with questions about the famous people she'd met. In his younger and less sagacious days, he would have. Now, he just let her pour out all her frustrations and anger. In a couple of weeks, he could feel her out on the matter of movie stars. For now, he just nodded.

By the time her anger and hurt were winding down, she seemed to genuinely be seeking some direction. There were innumerable phrases that made Angel cringe and "what should I do", made the top ten on a regular basis. However, this time it seemed to be a sincere request. He moved his bar rag in figure eights on the countertop; it was his tell that he was seriously pondering.

"Sweetie," he began finally, "unless you alter your location, you'll be back to Rick in a week. You two have been running around for I don't know how long and no matter what the guy does, you eventually come back." Angel paused, waiting for her protest and was surprised when none was forthcoming. He said nothing and neither did she. The space was filled by the hum of the refrigeration unit he kept the bottled beer in. Irene finally broke the impasse with a softly spoken, "I know".

Angel suggested that a change of scenery would do her a world of good. "It's not like you're leaving anything important. Mesa Azul will still be here whenever you get back and probably more welcome once you've got that guy flushed out of your system." They discussed options for a bit, eventually deciding that Irene should visit her sister Janice in San Antonio. Angel talked up the border town until he'd actually got Irene looking forward to it. By the time she left to head home and start sorting what she ought to take, the club owner was feeling almost saint-like. He decided to pour out four fingers for Saint Amandus tomorrow morning.

Carl and Troy came in a day or so later, full of concern over Doctor Pepper and their perceived failure in looking after the guy. Angel's own opinion was that the old fellow would have been mooching around Huernafano County as happy and healthy as ever if those two college kids hadn't become his tertiary shadows, but like any good priest, he kept it to himself. Angel was the sort of man that took everything at face value and didn't look for deeper currents to things. He was the kind of guy that accepts a miracle in the same vein as everyday events. If they happened, they happened. So the Doc suddenly could do all sorts of mystical things, big whoop. Angel had read a bunch of articles over the years about seemingly average people who suddenly developed extraordinary abilities. Who knew why?

At least the boys concern gave them a good thirst. They ordered a number of Coronas, which Angel was grateful for. The Coors distributor had talked him into a six-month contract and he found little market for the swill. Most folks that craved a cervesa wanted something with some bite to it, a Modello, for example. Corona had about as much kick to it as dishwater, so the counterman listened patiently to the boys maundering and happily watched them deplete his Corona stock. It was kind of funny though, the man they talked about didn't seem anything like the old Indian that Angel was familiar with. During all the time Angel had known him, Doctor Pepper was not only as bland as rice pudding but considerably less motivated. It seemed some very interesting things had occurred outside of Angel's sightline.

Troy and Carl seemed to desire a rational explanation for these things. If there was one piece of wisdom Angel could pass on it was that the universe wasn't quite as logical as people liked to suppose.

Angel never really understood why some folks felt everything needed an explanation. The boys' questions about the Doc, to a large measure, weren't any different than Irene's question about Rick. Irene wanted the bartender to tell her why Rick treated her so badly and these two college kids wanted to know why the Doc could burn wood with his hands and why he wandered off and fell into a coma. Angel wasn't Rick and he wasn't Doctor Pepper so all he could do was shrug and say, "why ask why?"

"Don't you wonder about those sorts of things?" Carl asked.

"I wonder about a lot of things," Angel said, "that I can do something about or that have a certain pattern to them. Other stuff? Hell, no. Life's too short and I got too much to do."

Troy accused him of being complacent and Carl said he was blasé. Being as Angel was a little unsure of what either term meant, he happily agreed. As far as he was concerned, Angel felt that he merely was accepting of the quirks of the universe. He'd witnessed inexplicable events throughout his life and took them as just happenstances he was lucky enough to witness.

"Let me ask you something," he said by way of an explanation, "have either of you seen a car crash as it actually happened?" Carl had been in a car crash, his own fault, when he was seventeen, but Troy stated flatly that he'd never witnessed cars smacking together in front of him. "I've seen crashes on television, though."

"Yeah," Angel agreed, "so have I. Along with monsters and giants and aliens and anything else those creative types can think up. But, I've never seen a car wreck as it happened. I've seen them after they happened, you know, smashed cars and glass all over. You see all that stuff and you presume to know what happened, right?" Both boys agreed and wondered where he was going with it.

"The trouble is," he went on, "you don't know for certain. You see this evidence or that and you accept it, mostly because it goes on all the time and you get the same explanation for it over and over again. It's life as you know it."

One thing Angel knew from personal experience, was that "life as you know it" varied from place to place. He had an uncle and a whole batch of cousins that lived up around Fort Garland by the Rio Grande in southern Colorado. When he was a young man in his twenties, before he inherited the Bay Club, he'd gone up for the summer to work on a construction crew building Forbes Ranch and hunker down in his uncle's place. During his residence the San Luis valley had a summer packed full of flying saucers and cattle mutilations.

His first personal experience with the phenomenon had happened just a week or so after he started work. He and a bunch of the work crew had gone to Fort Garland on a Friday night to drink away the aches of the week. Around midnight, they'd emerged from the Elk's Club bar and were happily were staggering towards their vehicles when a light as intense as the midday sun suddenly enveloped them. After freezing in their tracks from the shock, the light just as suddenly disappeared and Angel tried in vain, due to light dazzled eyes, to find the source of it. One of the crew, known as Easy Eddie, later said it was probably a helicopter with a halogen spotlight. "I got hit with one of those in Denver once," he said, "it was a freaky deal."

A freakier deal occurred just a few days later. Angel, Eddie and two other guys from the crew who were living in San Luis would share Eddie's truck to and from the Forbes Ranch. They were pouring foundation cement that day and had to run into some serious overtime, so that night they were headed down La Vida Pass well after ten in the evening. The guy sitting next to Angel, Little Pete, was the first one to notice anything odd. Off the slope of the road, down in one of the valleys below them, was a light. At first, it had a fiery orange tint to it and Little Pete assumed it was the beginnings of a brush fire. Angel, unlike these city boys had seen brush, prairie and forest fires and since there was not a lick of smoke, he knew there was no fire. As he was explaining that, the color of the glow down below the trees changed, running through the spectrum to a cool blue green. Eddie was so absorbed that he nearly ran off the road. La Vida Pass is not a good place to run off of though. The imminent demise of all and sundry inside Eddie's '66 Chevy distracted them from the curious glow. By the time their heartbeats had resumed a normal pace; the light was gone.

Before the weekend was out, Angel saw lights again. This time, he was at his Uncle's house, brushing his teeth just before bed when his periphery caught pulsing lights through the bathroom window. He dashed outside with his toothbrush still in his mouth and to the southeast, over the bed of the Rio Grande, he saw a series of colored lights, low in the sky. At first, they radiated out from a central hub like the spokes on a wheel then they changed into a series of concentric rings. As he stood in the field behind the house, dripping toothpaste onto his slippers, the odd lightshow went on, leisurely changing colors, shapes, patterns and intensity. Angel's Uncle Emilio wandered out and joined him. "What is that?" Angel asked.

"Las luces en el cielo," his Uncle replied matter of factly.

"¿Qué?," Angel said, dumfounded.

His uncle explained that the lights always showed up in the summer. "Las luces matan las vacas," he said and promised that they would go out to where the lights were the next day.

Whether it was due to the lights he saw in the sky or something else, there was definitely a dead cow near where they'd seen the lights the night before. On a dry stone shingle near the river lay a Hereford carcass. At first, it looked like it had just fallen there. From the angle they approached, someone might have thought it had drowned in the river upstream and been deposited on the gravel bar. On closer inspection, there were several puzzling features about it. Not only had it been killed, but also parts of it were missing. Its' eyes and lower jaw, part of the belly and its' genitalia were gone, seemingly excised in a neat, tidy and bloodless manner. The areas around the removed organs were smoothly beaded edges of flesh and tissue, like the bubbles left on steel worked over with a cutting torch. Everything below the point of excision had become a pink, con-

concave bowl, smoothly finished off. There was no blood to be seen anywhere and Angel's Uncle assured him that the carcass could lie there for a year and never decompose. "When the first one of these was found long ago, they buried it. Ten years later, a man plowing his field dug it up and he swore it looked like it had been put in the ground only the day before. Now we burn them."

Everyone who ever lived in the valley for more than a year had seen the lights and most people had come across dead cattle. According to Emilio, this was the way the summers always were, ever since the first settlers came to the San Luis. "Los Indios probably saw them too. Maybe they found dead deer or buffalo." The locals just looked at it as part of the cost of running livestock and the lights in and of themselves, were quite pretty to look at on a summer night.

"Now," Angel told the boys, "at first, it seemed like a crazy thing and I got pretty jumpy. But by the end of the summer, it wasn't any different than seeing a double rainbow or a doughnut cloud. It's just part of life in San Luis."

"So," Troy said in a puzzled tone, "you don't think there's anything extraordinary in life?"

"I see extraordinary stuff all the time," John said. He'd come in while Angel was spinning his yarn. "Hell," he continued, "I make it."

John knew where Angel was going with his philosophy and to a certain extent agreed with it. The human mind had an interesting way of processing what it perceived as reality. Based on specious input, you couldn't ever guarantee that the reality you experienced was really real. He mentioned that he'd had a motorcycle accident once that knocked him cold for nine hours. "For a month afterward, I smelled bread baking wherever I went. That, and sauerkraut. I was worried at first but a neurologist explained that I'd just fucked up the way my brain processed information. Pretty soon it would straighten itself out and sure enough, after a while it did."

The conversation soon went off track, at least from the line that Carl and Troy had originally set it on. John and Angel, swapping shaggy dog stories were soon joined by Corky Gonzales who had his own anecdotes to toss in. "Sure, Jefe," he said, "when I'm working on cars, my perception gets messed with all the time. Sometimes it seems like my hands are operating independently of me. I can see them, you know? But I can't associate them with being part of me."

"You're all nuts!" Troy exclaimed and left the bar in a huff, trailing Carl behind him.

Angel was sucking on a toothpick and he pulled it out of his mouth and studied it for an instant. "They've been here for what? Couple of weeks?" He slid the toothpick back in his mouth. "And they just now figured that out?"

Ted had a miserable summer. It seemed that all he'd done since returning from Mesa Azul was to meet with people. He hated meetings. In his opinion, all meetings should be held in hallways and shouldn't last more than ten minutes. Anything that couldn't be discussed standing up on your way to the coffee machine either wasn't worth discussing or wasn't ready to be discussed yet. There was another aspect of formal meetings he disliked. Certain words came up at them; loaded words such as ramifications and consequences and study and committee and round table. These words reminded him that ByteStream really wasn't his company anymore. Usually, he got what he wanted, thanks to his controlling vote on the board, as well as his prestige within the company, but he still had to justify his position.

He'd made a lot of people rich and to his mind, that was all the justification he needed. Inside ByteStream, there were very few visionaries of the same caliber as Ted and none with the same combination of luck and determination. Unfortunately, his company had slowly been infiltrated over the decades by bean counters and MBA types who sucked the creative spark right out the doors. Sometimes he felt if he heard the term "bottom line" one more time, he'd smash something over someone's head.

To Ted, money was the byproduct of the creative process. The point of Bytestream was to be innovative. Purchasing the license for John Elkfoot's compression technology was an example. It was revolutionary and would put his company back on the fine, razor polished edge of development. Using it as the core for a new development platform, ByteStream could completely reinvent communications on a global scale. Yes, it would fatten their coffers again, but the real reward for Ted would be the new shift in thinking the world would experience.

Unfortunately, in order to get the company where he needed it to be, he had to have meetings.

The proposal and development meetings were tolerable, but the meetings regarding his new development center were agony. They consisted of nothing but attorneys and accountants. Rather than rubber-stamping his plans, they looked for the angle, the hook that it was based on. Saying that he just felt in his gut that something there stimulated his creative processes wasn't a bankable argument. He thought back to his youth when ByteStream was just Marty Evans and he. All he would have had to say to Marty was, "it's a cool place, let's go!" It was exactly the conversation they had which led to their relocation to Seattle.

Now, even Marty was against him. Marty was just a few billion behind Ted in aggregate wealth, he certainly didn't need any more money, but he seemed very protective of the "bottom line". "You got to think how this will be perceived on the street, buddy," Marty said to Ted over and over again. "When we roll out the communications stuff, our stock's going to go through the roof. You can't kybosh that with this goofy move to the back of beyond."

"Why the heck not?" was all Ted had to say.

Ted finally let all his frustration boil over. "Doggone it, why can't I? It's my company, no matter what the prospectus says. If I wanted to make everyone shave their heads and wear purple tennis shoes, I ought to be able to. People buy our stuff because it works! Not because of how we run the company!"

"Ted," Marty said as soothingly as possible, "you got to look at this thing from my standpoint. We need Wall Street. We need all those brokers and buyers and stockholders to keep us going."

"Why? Between you and me we have more money than most of Wall Street does!"

"Where, Ted?" Marty said. "Show me the stacks of money. We have fortunes in principal. We got stock. When our stock performs, we're rich. When it's not, well, we've got enough certificates to wallpaper a couple hundred rec rooms and not much else."

Ted popped and fizzed for a bit longer and then settled back into getting his agenda pushed through. It was like wading through mud. Every day there was a new argument and everyday he had to grind away at it. The only thing that revitalized him was his weekly pilgrimage to the architect's office.

Weston and Morley had done something magnificent; something that was a balm to Ted. They had built a scale model of the Huernafano valley. There was Mesa Azul and the pueblo and the Blue Mesa, along with the roads and the slopes of the Sangre di Cristos, even the cottonwoods along the banks of the creek. He could pick out the Marguerita Bay Club and Corky's Garage. Even Barry's trailer inside its' copper mesh was there, at 1/36th scale. And just north of the pueblo, there was his vision, his dream. A collection of pristine, angular forms in brilliant white that would be his development campus. Every time he looked at it, he found the strength to go back and fight some more.

"It's not going to be a fight," Dan Bucknuts told Bob's Big Boy, "it's gonna be a fucking massacre." Ever since they'd met at the Inter-tribal Pow Wow, Dan had put every other case he had on hold and started working on his unfair employment practices case against ByteStream. It was the civil suit of a lifetime, possibly of all time. Every day, Dan came across something that bolstered his confidence. He had the perfect target with ByteStream and the perfect villain in Ted Marquis.

While he already knew that Ted wasn't a very well liked person, the depth of dislike the general populace, the press, even government itself had for the man was nearly overwhelming. Ted Marquis was possibly the most hated American since John D. Rockefeller.

"He seemed okay to me," Bob's Big Boy said.

"Fuck that noise," Dan snapped. The only liability he carried on this was his client. The Shantis as a whole were too bland, too nice, too contented. He'd told the tribal leaders down there they needed to figure out a way to look a lot more downtrodden. He was shocked at the appearance of the Pueblo the first time he went to Mesa Azul to meet with them.

"What the hell is wrong with you people?" were almost the first words out of his mouth. Pride of place, self sufficiency and a sense of community leeched out from every whitewashed stone, from each meticulously maintained adobe wall and even from the raked and smoothed gravel walkways. It looked more like an eccentric housing development for retired seniors than the last refuge of an oppressed people. To top it off, everyone was smiling all the time.

"I can't work like this," he told the tribal leaders. "I need you folks to help me out here. Where's the poverty? Where's the oppression? Where are the downtrodden and bitter faces I need to break a jury's heart?"

Unfortunately for Dan, those materials weren't at hand, and no one in the council felt like supplying him with any. Every suggestion he made, such as getting rid of the cable to the satellite feed, or letting the place get a little run down, was met with horror.

"Young man," Mrs. Fields said at one point, "just because we're poor doesn't mean we have to be slovenly!"

Dan made a mental note that this woman would never get on the witness stand. The more he looked around the Shantis pueblo, the more he realized this case should never go to court. There was nothing to tug at the heartstrings of the jury. If anything, people looking at Shantis pueblo might become a little jealous. It was an immaculate set of adobes in a beautiful setting. After two days there, he realized he'd have to change his strategy.

"What we need to do," he told the tribal council his last night there, "is to show ByteStream that the worst thing they could do is try to take this thing to court. We need to have a public showdown with Ted Marquis on television where we hand him a subpoena, paint him as black as possible for the nightly news and then wait for them to shove out a juicy settlement."

"I don't know," Bob's Big Boy told Dan as he was driving him to the airport in Santa Fe. "We're not looking for a big chunk of money, just a fair shot at the work ByteStream is bringing here." He went on to talk about the annual exodus of Shantis kids out of Mesa Azul. The valley held few opportunities for the young and most of them wanted the sort of life they saw on television every night. "You ever watch that show 'Cribs"?" Bob asked in reference to a television show that profiled the homes of celebrities, "that's what our kids want. They want the high-rise condo and the bright lights. They can't get that here. They damned sure won't get it working in the cafeteria of ByteStream."

Dan found the statement puzzling. "Buddy, they won't get that in Mesa Azul no matter what happens."

"I know, but if they had a shot at something better, they might learn that life is a compromise between what you want and what you can get. We just want them to be able to get a better deal than they have now."

"You folks are entirely too logical."

"Well, we try to see all sides of things."

"Yeah," Dan sulked, "which is why you guys need me."

"Barry!" Irene called out across the crowded Riverwalk in San Antonio. She saw Barry freeze and then turn around, scanning the crowd. Irene stood up from the sidewalk table she was sharing with her sister Janice and Bob, Janice's husband and waved to him. Rather than joining them, he quickly ran into a nearby bar.

The second he heard his name, Barry felt as though someone had dumped a pitcher of ice water on his heart. He thought he had an impervious disguise, although Irene could have told him he had a characteristic walk that gave him away as clearly as if he had a huge neon sign towering over his head that flashed "BARRY" in 5,000 candlefoot lights. Another thing that gnawed at him as he wound his way through the bar, which held a typical Saturday night crowd of Texas blues aficionados was the fact that Irene Naha of all people had recognized him. Many times since his exodus from Mesa Azul he'd mulled over who the spook in town could be. Irene never even made the list. She was too goofy, too flighty and too Irene-like for covert work. Then it dawned on him that she had the perfect cover. She'd never have been made if she hadn't slipped up just then.

He soon found his way through the kitchen of the bar and out the alley door. Sticking to the shadows and continuously scanning every side street and doorway, he soon made his way back to the motel he and Tom were staying in. Tom greeted him, as always with a .44 Desert Eagle pointing him in the face. Calhoun's mental conditioning had deteriorated significantly since they'd had to leave Amarillo and every time Barry left the motel room for even a minute, he ran the risk of having his face shot off every time he returned.

It made Barry nervous, but at the same time, he realized he had the human equivalent of a weapon of mass destruction. If the crunch came, he had no doubt that Tom would go berserk and the carnage following the initial explosion would likely give Barry a chance at a clean escape on his own. Calhoun seemed to have decided he was fated to be a martyr in the struggle to save humanity from the grip of alien overlords. He relaxed these days by composing, amending and revising his epitaph.

Barry had learned to treat Tom as an unstable element. It took him half an hour to tell his partner that he'd been recognized, slowly working his way into it and accentuating how careful he'd been. For a moment or two, it was a near thing. Barry kept his eye on Tom's gun hand as he talked and nervously watched as the knuckles whitened. Later on, he wondered just how close to being killed he came.

After Barry had finished his story, Calhoun stared blankly at him for a few moments. Barry stared back and witnessed the glow of enlightenment spread over his partner's countenance. Calhoun wasn't normally an idea man, that was Barry's purview, and Barry inwardly cringed at what Tom's revelation would be.

"You know why we have to run?" Tom started out. "Why we have to hide? Because we aren't on an even footing with the Estes boys."

Barry had to agree that this was true. The Estes Foundation's reach and resources were boundless, whereas he and Tom were nearly played out. After reaching San Antonio, they'd discussed their options and opted for figuring a way to hop the border unnoticed and then slowly work their way through Mexico until they got to either Brazil or Argentina, where Anglos didn't stand out like a nun in a whorehouse and try to live the rest of their lives in anonymity. They didn't have any other ideas since their network had been compromised and their identities known.

Tom had developed a new habit since he'd shaved his hair off, which was to absentmindedly stroke the top of his head when he was concentrating on something. "Even though you fucked up," he said, stroking, "you've handed us the first real leverage we've ever had against these bastards." Naturally, Barry expressed his puzzlement and then inwardly collapsed as Tom went on.

"You found someone we know that's on the inside. Someone accessible. Someone we can grab and sweat what we need out of."

"Who?" Barrry said incredulously, "Irene?"

"Exactly." Calhoun fished around under his bed and pulled out a sixteen inch K-bar knife. He slid it out of the scabbard and studied the edge. "All we need to do is grab her. You can lure her out, I'll take care of the rest." He ran his thumb over the finely ground edge of the knife. "I don't care if she's a human agent or some weird hybrid. Everything feels pain," he paused and smiled blissfully at his partner, "and pain is an excellent cathartic."

Coyote had finally reached the Doc. Not only physically, but down in the inky void the old man had drifted into. After his last conversation with John, the ancient spirit had gone south to Santa Fe and surrounded the shaman like a nimbus. As delicately as if he were feeling his way through a dark house with blinders on, Coyote tunneled his way into the Doc's consciousness. At first, Coyote had the same experience he'd gone through when the Doc was collapsed inside his house of sticks, the unending corridors of blackness, where the old soul wandered lost and unseeing.

Coyote pulled his old tricks, creating points of illumination that should have attracted Doctor Pepper's essential self, but like his previous attempts, the Doc slipped by each and every one of them, burrowing deeper into the void he'd created for himself. In frustration, Coyote thought to himself, "I don't know what else to do."

"Neither do I," Doctor Pepper replied.

Coyote was flabbergasted. In all of his experience, John had been the only human being, nearly the only entity in a hundred millennia who could actually have a dialogue with Coyote. But it was no mistake; the shaman had responded to his thoughts.

"So," Coyote said, "you haven't completely surrendered to whatever the hell you're going through?"

"Who are you?"

Coyote chuckled. No one had ever asked him that before. John merely accepted him as whatever he was and defined him in whatever terms he felt comfortable using. For himself, Coyote had never given the matter much thought.

"Does it matter?" he finally replied.

"I like to know whom I'm talking to," the Doc said courteously.

"Well," Coyote mulled it over for a second or three, "John calls me Coyote."

Since the Doc's brain activity hadn't ever reflected the comatose state his body existed in from the moment they attached monitoring electrodes, anyone looking at the devices he was hooked up to would have no idea that something had changed. It would be awhile before the Doc drifted out of the state he was in, but he was coming back, in slow stages. Coyote inadvertently was leading him back up into life as humanity defined it.

In the meantime, each of these two entities was having a unique experience. Doctor Pepper, having been lost within himself for such a long time, had forgotten his lifelong desire to commune with the spirits, so he appreciated the conversation with Coyote on the same level anyone having a beer with a new acquaintance would. Coyote, asked direct and seemingly naïve questions about his own being and state of existence by the Doc was being forced into introspection. It was all virgin territory.

The Doc, lost within his consciousness had achieved a state similar to Coyote's normal existence. He was cut off from sensory input; he had no definition of himself as a physical being and subsided within the narrow confines of malleable thought. He had memories of his physical state but they were far removed and nearly abstract. The disparity between what was and his current mode of being made him assume that his memories where merely a dream state. "I'm a thought that dreamed it was a man," he said to Coyote at one point.

"Trust me, Doc. You're real enough," the ancient entity told him in what he thought was a reassuring tone.

The Doc seemed to be a bit argumentative on that point. "Yes, I'm real in the sense that I exist. You're just as real as I am. The thing is though, I've broken through a plane of some sort or dividing line into something that's probably closer to the real reality of things and you're just being stubborn about it."

"What are you," Doctor Pepper went on, "other than essentially a thought?"

"Okay," Coyote acquiesced. "I'll agree I don't have the same sort of physical manifestation that you do. If I need a corporeal self, I manufacture it from random atomic particles. It's like that guy that bends spoons. An exercise of will."

"Me too," the Doc replied.

"No," Coyote said. "You've got a physical being, a bunch of stuff that you exist inside of."

"Nope. I'm just what you are."

In the course of trying to convince the Doc that he was a human being, the two of them ventured into the realm of philosophy. Coyote had always found the human predisposition for metaphysics interesting, but he'd never pursued it himself. To him, it ranked right up there with mankind's constant question of why. Suddenly, he found that the roles had switched. He was arguing why to a human being who was predisposed to accept his state of being without question. The Doc had somehow convinced himself that all his memories were a sham, and that he now had a clear understanding of what he was and what he'd always been.

"The way I see it," the old man patiently explained, "is that until this point in my life, I wasn't able to handle the true reality of my essential self and had to come up with a bunch of malarkey to keep from going nuts."

Coyote had to admit that the Doc was a tenacious character. Once he had an idea in his head, he gripped it like a Gila monster. The archaic spirit hoped he wouldn't have to cut the Doc's head off to get him to let loose. It did give him an idea though.

"Doc, let me ask you something. Where do you think we are at this moment?"

"Does it matter?"

Metaphorically, this response knocked Coyote back on his heels. This was his tacit response to almost every "why?" question humanity thrust out into the void. Shaken, the spirit responded, "Yes, in this instance it actually does."

"We're existing in your consciousness," he went on to explain. "This thing, this void we're in, is you."

"Maybe not," the Doc said. "Maybe you just believe this is my consciousness. For all you know, I could be in your consciousness."

Coyote explained that he had gone looking for Doctor Pepper. That he'd found him in a comatose state and that he'd entered into the Doc's essential being.

"Nonsense."

"Huh?" Coyote was nonplussed.

"I've decided something," the old man thought happily. "You're just an extension of me that I haven't gotten under control."

"You're nuts!"

"Exactly!" the Doc replied. "The part of me that has created you is the last nutty part of me. 'Coyote' is just that last part of me that refuses to accept what I am. Once I don't respond to you anymore, then I'll have completely accepted what I am."

The arguments went on like that for days. Since the Doc seemed to have no need to slip into an unconscious state, they were unending. Coyote found himself trapped inside the Doc's consciousness, endlessly arguing and desperately desiring release. He needed some alone time.

"Can't you just shut up?" he asked at one point.

"As far as I can tell, I'm not saying anything," Doctor Pepper responded. "I'm just mulling stuff around."

"Yeah," Coyote said, "but you're using me to mull it with!"

All at once there was a little shift, a tiny wrinkle in the fabric of being. Both entities felt it and for the first time, Coyote knew what men meant when they talked about fear. Coyote felt himself unraveling. He anxiously hoped the Doc wouldn't perceive anything else. It was another new reaction for the spirit. Hope. Something else that only existed within the human construct.

"You know what?" the Doc said with a sense of absolute clarity. Coyote tried not to think, to exist; to even be. He could feel the old shaman's thoughts probe into him. He could feel things changing rapidly. He couldn't do it though. Coyote was overwhelmed with sensation.

The last thing he heard the Doc say was, "You're the man and I'm the spirit. We had it all ass backwards!"

Coyote screamed and heard his voice through his ears. Light flooded in and as he sat up in bed, a nurse rushed up and said, "calm down! Let me get a doctor."

Chapter Twelve -

The Wonders of Modern Communication.

As much as Angel enjoyed being in the thick of things, there were occasions when he felt overwhelmed by his position as town crier. Today was one of them. He'd been awoken by his phone ringing, which had happened only once before during the miracle of the bridges.

A long time ago, when there were only a handful of people in the valley, some unknown engineer had constructed a bridge of sorts over the Huernafano creek. Made of wood and rope, it served its' purpose, as long as the person crossing it could keep their balance and wasn't easily nauseated. Repairs to it were haphazard, done in the depths of winter when there was no water in the creek and a handyman could set up a ladder in the creek bed to inspect the ropes and wood without being washed away. It sufficed fine for pedestrians, but cars and cattle either had to ford the creek or stay on whatever side of the river they started from.

The town council had discussed over and over again coming up with the funds necessary to build a proper bridge; one with stone pilings and a reinforced concrete span, but nothing ever came of it. Certified engineers would come out and bid on the project and the town would reel in shock at the ticket price, then forget about it until the next time someone complained about their limited access to the rest of the county.

Fifteen years ago, Huernafano County experienced one of the warmest and wettest springs anyone could remember. Even in March, the temperatures began to reach the seventies and Huernafano creek soon became a raging, muddy torrent, fed from an incredibly strong snow melt. Its' capacity was soon swollen by a week's worth of rain, until the center section of their rope bridge was completely submerged by the river. Angel, Corky, Freddy and Randall took hourly pilgrimages down to the water's edge to study the situation. It became apparent that the bridge would wash over before the water would subside and before long, bets were being taken on what time the bridge would go.

The bridge went, but not in the manner anyone had expected it to. Angel was woken by a phone call from Freddy Apodakus at three in the morning.

"Angel!" Freddy shouted as soon as the bartender picked up the phone, "you've got to get down to the bridge!"

"Why? If it's gone, I can see it in the morning. If it's going, it'll be gone before I get there."

"Not the old bridge," Freddy said, "the new one!"

It struck Angel that Freddy's exclamations made no sense at all. He couldn't be blamed, really, since the situation, in a rational world, didn't make much sense either.

It turned out that the rains had been playing hob with a few other bridges. Further upstream, where the Huernafano branched off the Arkansas River in Colorado, a very nice girder bridge had been torn loose from its' moorings and wound up traveling ninety-seven miles south until it came to the sandstone that made up Huernafano canyon. This neat little girder bridge hit Mesa Azul's crappy old rope bridge and took it right out, then traveled nine feet further where it got neatly jammed into the sandstone outcroppings on either side of the river. The more the force of the water pushed against it, the more firmly its' end spans were driven into the soft rock. By the time the floodwaters had receded, the town had a very well placed and solidly set bridge. No one ever came looking for it either. They named it "Roamer".

This morning's first call came at closer to a decent hour, at least. Just before six AM, Herbie Steinman, a subsistence truck farmer that was the closest thing to a neighbor that Barry Moss had, if proximity, rather than familiarity was the measure of neighborliness, let him know that a strange little caravan was rolling down the main drag of town, heading towards the pueblo. The lead vehicle was a white panel truck from the State Department of Health, behind it was a government issue tan minivan with EPA emblazoned on the sides and running drag was a car from the Center for Disease Control. "Are we in trouble?" was Herbie's question.

"Are they stopping at your place?" was the first thing that popped into Angel's mind.

"No," Herbie informed him, "they just rolled past."

Angel secretly hoped that someone had finally gotten wind of Herbie's specialty garden. After eking an existence merely raising miserable vegetables that, while completely organic, were so bug ridden he couldn't sell them to anyone, Herbie eventually discovered that he had a facility for growing exotic crops such as star fruit, jicama and bitter melon. While markets in Santa Fe, Taos and Sedona clamored for the stuff, Herbie was always trying to get Angel to expand his menu and include some of these regional specialties.

"No one in their right mind wants to eat this crap," Angel told him as gently as he could. After sampling a slice of bitter melon and having to gargle with Mescal to kill the taste, Angel was certain it was toxic and if the CDC had arrived in town to burn the crop, he'd supply them with matches.

Fifteen minutes later, Corky called with the same information. By the time Angel got to the bar, rumors were flying up and down the valley, speculating on everything from West Nile to the Ebola virus. Angel wondered why all the really scary diseases seemed to come from Africa. His ruminations on the matter where interrupted by a phone call from Jerry Moss of all people. Angel had seen Jerry twice the entire summer. Jerry liked to be on the road as much as possible in warm weather.

"Hey cholo," Jerry finally said, after the requisite gab about health and local conditions, "I got a nutty call from my brother last night."

"Gee," Angel said in mock surprise, "imagine Barry saying anything nutty."

Jerry laughed. "I know, he's a twink, but he keeps me in pickles and beer. Anyway, he wanted to know if Irene's around."

"No, she's visiting her sister in San Antonio. I hope he's not looking to get into a thing with Irene. She'd eat him for lunch."

"Tell me about it," Jerry agreed. "The little goof never has had a girlfriend that I've ever known about."

"You think he's gay?" Angel speculated.

"No," Jerry said. "I think aliens stole his cojones years ago. Anyway, you know Irene's sister's name by any chance? Or how to get a hold of her? Barry's real insistent."

Angel passed on what he knew and then wrapped things up when Corky and Freddy came into the club.

Over coffee and sugared fry bread, the three men discussed what might be happening up at the pueblo. Corky had already gone up to talk to their visitors and had been shut out completely. "Goddamned government jerks," he fumed. "They trotted out the old 'not of your concern' routine. I'll tell you what, if we've got some plague running around in our valley, you better bet it's some of my concern."

Freddy speculated that Corky was probably a little more belligerent than the situation called for.

"You saying I came on too strong?" Corky was aghast. "Fuck you, pendejo!"

"That's just what I mean!" Freddy protested.

"I was laughing when I said it, Loc."

Angel suggested that they get Randall and Julie Modesto, and then visit the government agents as a group.

Just as that decision had been made, Bob's Big Boy came in with the news that Doctor Pepper had come out of his coma, started screaming like a loon, then while the nurse who'd been attending him went to fetch one of the physicians on call, climbed into his clothes and jumped out a window.

"Shocked everyone," Bob's Big Boy went on. "According to the doctors looking after him, he should have been too weak to walk."

"Huh," Angel said while pulling disparate events together in his mind. "You don't suppose that whatever the Doc come down with is why all those government boys are here, do you?"

The big Indian just shrugged his shoulders. "Beats me." He snagged some fry bread and contentedly ate. "Whatever it is," he said between bites, "obviously isn't fatal."

Freddy said to no one in particular, "it seems like the whole county is going nuts this morning."

Bob's Big Boy grinned. "Going?"

In between moments of panic, Coyote found himself admiring just how tough human beings were. While he had been able to create the illusion of having a corporeal presence, he'd never had to actually function as one before. The sheer mechanics of a body were amazing and the abuse it had to suffer just by existing was almost more than the poor old spirit could bear.

Everything seemed to be imbued with sensation. Standing up, he felt the fluid in his inner ears wash over the sensory hairs that defined what was supposed to be level and it made him nauseous. His first step nearly overwhelmed him with the amount of miniscule actions and decisions it took to do it. He felt the muscles in his stomach, hips, thighs and calves adjust, as well as his arms acting as a counterbalance and his toes gripping. The pull of gravity frightened him and the shock that traveled up his leg as his heel came down was unbelievable. Absolutely everything he had to do required such concentration that he couldn't help wondering how humanity had been able to survive, let alone create all the things they did.

Hovering over all this like a dark angel, was the fear that he'd somehow devolved into the body of Doctor Pepper and that there was no way he could recapture what he'd been. He suddenly understood the endless prayers for help that rang from the center of human hearts up into the unresponsive cosmos. He could use a little help himself. All this thoughts focused on John Elkfoot, although Coyote would have been hard pressed to say why.

Coyote fled the hospital in search of a phone. He figured, correctly, that the medical staff wouldn't allow him the use of one, as he was supposed to be a critical patient, hanging on to life by just a fingertip, or possibly two. Those types of people aren't allowed to call friends and explain how they'd swapped existences with someone else. Those sorts of calls are best made from a pay phone.

Coyote felt a huge flood of relief when he accurately recalled John's number;

was able to figure out the operation of a phone and heard John accept the charges.

"This is a new one," John said after being told by the operator that he had a reverse toll call from Coyote, "you miss a light particle or something and can't get back here to bug me in person?"

"John," Coyote said breathlessly, "something horrible has happened!'

"Doc?" While John was perplexed, he was overjoyed to the old shaman's voice. "What's the deal with calling yourself Coyote? Where are you calling from?"

"John, shut up a second!" Then Coyote rapidly tried to explain what happened without sounding as terrified as he felt.

John, for his part, felt that the Doc had slipped the trolley. As he listened, he imagined that meddlesome spirit had gone mind diving in the old man's consciousness and somehow gotten everything into an even bigger mess than it was before. He squeezed his eyes shut and tried to tamp down the anger he felt at Coyote. Then he said in a calm voice, "okay, Doc. Everything's going to be fine. Tell me where you are and I'll call the hospital. Just stay put and they'll get you."

His instructions were interrupted by another outburst from Coyote, insisting that he couldn't go back to the hospital, he had to find the Doc and he needed John's help.

John leaned his head against the cool tile that edged the wall in the kitchen where he'd picked up the phone. He wasn't a psychiatrist and wasn't prepared to deal with this level of dementia. It was apparent to him, however that if the Doc didn't see him show up to deal with things, he'd probably go running again. Finally, he said, "Look, Doc, er Coyote. I promise I'll get to wherever you are and we'll get everything straightened away."

Ten minutes later John was flying down the trail from the mesa, in route to Santa Fe.

Steve Abrams hung up the phone after one of the sweetest calls of his life. All the planning and deal brokering he'd spent his summer on was going to pay off. He'd gotten a call from the legal department of ByteStream. They were interested in some property he'd recently purchased in Huernafano County.

He'd owned that property for all of a week. To say that ByteStreams real estate division was disturbed at the co-incidence would be a bit of an understatement. The attorney that he'd talked with sounded shell shocked over the phone. The titles for the land hadn't even been filed in the county registry yet and the only way Ted's acquisitions people had found him was by calling the previous owner. Steve grinned when he thought of how that guy must have felt.

August had been a sweet month. He'd truly enjoyed the agonies Rick Arnold went through watching the deal of his life slip through his hands. By the time Rick showed up at the title company to close the deal, he looked as though he'd aged thirty years. Arnold had lost weight, neglected his appearance and looked as though he hadn't slept in a month. It was a balm to Steve's soul. Steve had a few nervous moments when he withdrew everything he had, sold his Jaguar and cashed in his 401K to finance the purchase. He'd hoped he'd only have to come to the table with ten percent, but there wasn't a property appraiser in the state, nor a financial institution with a lick of sense that was willing to mortgage the purchase. He had to come up with the jack on his lonesome. He even had to put the bite on his old man for the final fifty grand. His father grudgingly advanced him the money, all the while informing Steve of the hardship it was putting him in.

Still, the nonplussed attorney's voices on the conference call he just had reassured him that he'd read the winds fine. Their offer of six hundred and forty seven thousand was plainly pulled out of someone's ass. His suggestion of adding another comma to the figure and a zero caused a momentary silence to descend, but the pause was so short lived, he was certain Ted Marquis was somewhere in the room. They said they'd get back to him in a couple of days. Steve rarely drank before noon, but a blue martini sounded wonderful just now.

Shantis pueblo was in an uproar. The government men were full of questions but weren't answering anyone else's queries. They were also getting their fingers into everything. The first thing they wanted to know was were the Doc lived, then they swooped down on his kiva and quickly bagged, tagged and carted away everything. Once that chore was dealt with, they went from home to home and snagged whatever they felt like. At Reddi Kilowatt's they took samples of the water and then rummaged through his refrigerator. They seemed disappointed that Reddi existed off of beer and microwave dinners. "Do you cook anything?" one guy asked him.

"Me?" Reddi said, "you've got to be kidding!"

Mrs. Butterworth had almost her entire freezer cleaned out. She was a big believer in the value of home cooked meals. They also scraped paint off of some of her hand-thrown pots, cut little chunks of abode off the walls of her home and seemed to vacuum the air with an odd device. The health official's constant statements of her having "nothing to worry about" did little to reassure her.

The tribal council had called Angel to find out if he was getting a quorum of the town council together. They decided to confront the government guys as a group and before long all the out of town officials found themselves surrounded by glowering natives. A few thoughts about General George Armstrong Custer flitted through more than one mind at that point.

"You give 'em beads," one of the CDC workers whispered to another. "It makes 'em friendly."

By general consensus, Angel usually acted as spokesperson for the community. After identifying most of the assembly as either town or tribal council members, he politely asked for an explanation.

A very tall and weather-beaten man stepped out from amidst the government investigators and identified himself as Doctor Pete Honneferan, lead environmental forensics investigator for the state. He motioned to Angel to follow him and the two men passed through the locals and out of earshot.

"We've got just a couple more things to do," Honneferan explained to Angel, "and then we'll be out of your hair. It's best if we can work uninterrupted. If you can get everyone to just go about their business and leave us alone, we'll stop by your office on our way out of town and give you a preliminary report on what we're looking at. You can put everyone's mind at ease. No one is in any imminent danger."

"See," Angel pointed out, "even using a word like 'danger' in a sentence doesn't reassure me at all."

Honneferan sighed. He'd argued to his boss the day before that having a single investigator from one agency would have been the way to play this out. Unfortunately, the doctors treating the old man who'd showed up comatose in Santa Fe a few weeks ago got jumpy and called everyone they could think of. Since then, Honneferan had been caught up in a jurisdictional pissing match where no agency wanted to give up ground. On the one hand, he could understand that everyone's budget was under scrutiny these days, and the best way to make sure your department didn't get trimmed in the next legislative calendar was to have something worth headlines to pass in front of the politicians. At the same time, having a bunch of health workers descend on a community was as useful as hitting a hornet's nest with a stick.

"It's routine," he told Angel. "Bureaucratic busy work. Honestly, it means nothing. I do this all the time."

Angel watched the man's face. The slight lilt of frustration in his voice, coupled with the bland placidity of his features reassured him. He agreed to get everyone to go home and the doctor trotted out a weary smile.

"State bullshit," Angel hollered out. "Probably a new strain of pollen or something." He went on in that vein for a minute or so until people began to disperse. Honneferan thanked him and got directions to the Marguerita Bay

Club. "One o'clock," Honneferan said as he walked back to his associates, "better have the Mayor there too. I don't like having to tell the same story twice."

Angel shrugged and then wandered off to find the Mayor.

Doctor Pepper was in awe. He felt as though he were everything and nothing. At the moment the transfer between himself and the thing that called itself Coyote occurred, he felt things expand and collapse simultaneously. Existence rushed in on him, replacing the void he'd been wandering around in with something that he couldn't quite grasp. It was the world and yet not the world. He seemed to be able to see everything at once. There was no point of reference that he was used to. Front and back, up and down or right and left held no meaning anymore. He was deprived of a contextual sense of himself as well. There were no defined boundaries to him. He seemed to have no beginning and no end. He was a point of being and all things radiated out from that point.

It was disorientating. Unlike Coyote though, he felt no panic, merely curiosity. "This will take some getting used to," he thought. "Heck, it's going to take a lot of getting used to. I have no idea about anything."

"Six million dollars?" Ted Marquis was incredulous. "Who does this guy think he is?"

Kurt Sorensen, ByteStream's lead negotiator for land leasing and realty purchases squirmed uncomfortably. "Well, he's our lead corporate sales guy in New Mexico, western Texas and Southern Colorado."

"What? Do I know this guy?"

"Yeah," Kurt said, "he's the fellow that took you down to meet with Blue Mesa CGI on the compression deal."

Ted thought back. That funny kid Carl kept popping into his mind, as did John and Angel and assorted townspeople and Indians. Even the helicopter pilot who'd flown him down was easy to picture, but he couldn't get a handle on anyone else.

"What's his name again?" Steve Abrams. Slowly a picture began to form in Ted's mind. Half the sales people for ByteStream could have fit the profile. His partner Marty had set up the standard for the type of sales rep ByteStream needed. They looked for aggressive, smooth and self assured people. Too bad loyalty or ethics didn't fit into the situation.

Ted had Kurt put a call into Steve's office. Steve's assistant, Sharon Marks informed them that Mister Abrams hadn't been in all day. As a matter of fact, she confided, he hadn't been in much for the past couple of weeks. She'd been fielding increasing impatient calls from customers he was supposed to be servicing. Kurt got Steve's home number from Sharon. After two rings, a very contented voice on the speakerphone said, "Yello?"

"Steve?" Ted said, "Steve Abrams?"

"One and the same. And you are?"

Ted identified himself and was cut off by a blast of raucous laughter. "Oh baby! What a day! I get a call from the Big Kahuna himself! Lemme guess, Teddy boy, you're less than happy with me right now."

"I really don't understand what you're doing," Ted said as calmly as could manage under the circumstances. "You know that land is nearly worthless."

"To everyone but you, buddy boy. Remember, I was there. I saw you. I know how much you need it."

"I could walk away," Ted said and felt his body temperature drop twenty degrees.

"No," Steve mused happily, "you couldn't. What's six million to you anyway? Chump change." Ted protested that no matter what people thought he was worth, he had to observe a certain level of fiscal responsibility to the company.

Steve laughed until his sides hurt. "Uh, yeah, right. That's why you want to spend God knows what building a campus in Crapville, Nowhere." This was a sweet as life gets. A lifetime of frustration was being rewarded. Steve thought that just having the Big Kahuna trying to weasel out from under his thumb was almost reward enough. Still, the money was nice.

"Listen, Teddy boy," he went on, "your Marketing VP, Irv Rollins stuck me out here to fuckin' die. I should have been an executive five fuckin' years ago. I've eaten more shit and kissed more ass than anyone has a right to expect from a fuckin' dog! Well, this dog has the bone you want and I'm gonna suck all the marrow I can out of it before I give it to you."

"You're fired," Ted said blankly. Steve's laughter echoed out of the speaker until Kurt reached over and turned it off.

"Janice Rael," Barry told Tom Calhoun as he flipped through the San Antonio phone book.

"Fucking border towns," Calhoun said. "Rael runs to four pages. I got two J Rael's but no Janice."

"Try Bernabé Rael," Barry suggested.

Barry had a few misgivings about what they were doing, but the longer he'd been away from Mesa Azul, the more his feeling of persecution and anger had grown. He wasn't sure if it was his association with Tom Calhoun or just his exposure to the world he'd hidden away from for so long, but he found himself quicker to boil and slower to cool. Insomnia had plagued him recently, something he hadn't experienced in years and almost everything he encountered irritated him.

The more he thought about Irene, the more furious he became. How someone could slip under his radar said less about his observational skills than it did her guile and chicanery. Barry snuffed out another unbidden flicker of sympathy and decided she would more than deserve whatever she got at the hands of Calhoun.

Bernabé was the right name and that night Barry and Calhoun watched the thermal signatures of Irene and her sister's family go through the mundane motions of an evening as glowing figures against the cool blue of the outside walls of the house. Calhoun, like a lot of survivalists, had an interest in military technology. Barry hadn't ever looked through a heat scope and found it fascinating.

The Rael household didn't seem to be a late night sort of place, Irene's profile moved around the longest, but even she seemed to have drifted off to sleep well before midnight. The house was in a suburb of San Antonio where the backyards seemed to peter out into the great wide open that led on down to the border. Calhoun parked his four by four thirty yards from the back of the house and the two men got out and crept forward.

Irene was awoken when something was crammed in her mouth. Whatever it was, it was fuzzy; she could feel that much with her tongue, and dry. It immediately sucked all the moisture out of her mouth. She would have screamed if something wasn't pressing painfully hard against her esophagus. She couldn't move either. Something weighty and at the same time slightly yielding was lying on top of her. She heard a raspy whisper next to her ear, "try to scream and I'll break your windpipe." She was completely disoriented.

Barry was a conflict of emotions. He was in awe of Calhoun's efficiency and at the same time, the moment he saw Irene helpless, his doubt as to what they were doing rose again in waves. Tom had worked fast, slicing through the screen on the open bedroom window, lifting himself into Irene's room as silently as moonlight and then quickly immobilizing and silencing her. Before they'd moved out, Tom had instructed Barry on exactly what to do. He'd given him a roll of packaging tape and a number of zip cords.

"As soon as I stuff this tennis ball in her mouth, you wrap the tape around her head. I'll make sure she co-operates and then you zip cord her thumbs and big toes together. I want to be in and out of there in less than a minute."

Now, observing Calhoun on top of Irene and her panicky expression, Barry paused. Tom glared at him, not saying anything but effectively communicating his anger at Barry's hesitation. Stifling his misgivings, he quickly wrapped packing tape around Irene's head to hold the ball in place, then flipped back the bed sheets and grabbed her legs. Irene began to kick and Calhoun hissed at her, pressing his thumb harder against her throat. She laid still and allowed Barry to pull her legs together, then loop a zip cord around both big toes and pull it tight. Tom rolled off her then and flipped her over effortlessly. Irene was wearing an oversized t-shirt as nightwear. When Tom grabbed her arms and pulled them up behind her, Barry felt a momentary embarrassment by what was revealed when her shirt rode up. Calhoun pulled her thumbs together and whispered to Barry, "zip 'em, asshole."

The instant he'd finished looping the second nylon band around her thumbs, Calhoun nudged Barry out of the way, threw Irene over his shoulder and moved quickly back to the window and out. Barry looked around for a second before following. The house was still and the only things out of place were the cut screen and the sheets on the floor.

In the four hours it took John to get to Santa Fe, Coyote had become completely familiar with the body he inhabited, and he hated it. Whether it was just the Doc's body, or humanity's general state of existence, the constant sensory bombardment, both internally and externally had become a gigantic, enveloping ball of pain. John found him crouched down next to the pay phone he'd used, terrified to move and nearly inarticulate with fear.

"I can't stand it, John," Coyote said as Elkfoot helped him into the Jeep. John muttered all sorts of calming words to the old Indian, while secretly shocked at the level of dementia the old soul had sunken to. Once he got the Doc settled in, he jumped into the driver's seat and headed back towards the University hospital. Almost immediately, he slammed on the brakes when the Doc started to howl.

"I can't do this," Coyote wept. "All this, this, stuff going on around me. The air was thundering my ears as soon as we started to move. I could feel it moving over every inch of me."

"Uh, yeah, Doc," John said. "That's pretty much what air does." John listened to his passenger's complaints for a little bit longer, then got out and flipped up the ragtop and buttoned in the isinglass side windows. "No more air," he told him as they took off again.

It was a long drive to the hospital. Every bump, turn, acceleration or braking elicited a new howl of agony from the old man. When he wasn't wailing in panic, the Doc kept up an unending monologue of how he and Coyote had switched existences. It was clear that whatever that idiotic old spirit had done was just the thing to push Doctor Pepper into some sort of schizophrenic state. The question that preyed on John's mind was whether they could ever pull him out of it.

Once they got to the hospital, John said, "you need a rest, old fellow. I think the folks here can help you get some sleep. A little peace and quiet and you'll right as rain."

By now, Coyote was willing to try anything that would just give him a few hours respite from this constant sensory bombardment. Even if he could only retreat into his own consciousness for a few hours, maybe he could gain some insights or clarity to the situation. "Anything," Coyote said. "I'll try anything. Just don't leave me. You're my only hope."

The Doc's physicians were in a slight quandary. Sedating a patient that had only been out of a coma for a couple of hours seemed risky. Still, given the state of agitation and incoherence he was in, it was clearly a necessity. They started off with a Valium, just to get him settled down enough to put him in a bed and get monitoring devices attached. His blood pressure, pulse, heart rate and brain activity convinced them to put him in a twilight sleep. Unfortunately, the patient at that point seemed to have receded back into a coma.

While all this was going on, Doctor Honneferan arrived back from his excursion. After getting a brief summary from the Doc's attendants, we walked down to the waiting room and introduced himself to John Elkfoot.

"What in the world is going on in that town of yours?" Honneferan asked.

"Until recently," John replied, "not much."

"You don't think it's odd that you have Indians named after cereals and sodas? You don't find it peculiar that all your roads are called Oak Street?"

"Hey," John shrugged, "every small town has its' quirks."

"I thought so too," Honneferan said, "until I met with the Mayor."

John couldn't hold back a grin at that. He ducked his head a little and looked up at the irate physician. "Oh," he chuckled, "You met Buckeye. How did that go?"

"How the hell do you think it went?" the investigator raged. "He's a damned dog!"

Irene couldn't believe what was happening to her. The initial assault and kidnapping was bad enough, but now she found herself tied to a bed in some seedy motel room with a knife wielding maniac and Barry Moss, of all people.

Every inch of her ached from being manhandled and the constant state of tension her muscles had been in since she awoke. Her head was pounding and she desperately wanted the thing removed from her mouth. She was having a difficult time breathing and her throat was so parched, she thought it was beginning to stick together.

Barry was a little discomfited himself. It seemed as though he'd crossed some line, somewhere back in the Texas panhandle and lost his sense of moral logic. Barry had always believed that there were certain tenets of life that defined humanity. Compassion, fairness and knowledge seemed to be key ingredients of the thing that separated human beings from everything else on the planet. Now he had cut himself off from the last vestiges of those things. He and Calhoun hadn't really thought anything out. They hadn't made considerations for circumstance and they seemed to have acted on impulse when they snatched Irene.

The girl's current state of helplessness and vulnerability seemed to have completely opposite effects on the two men. Barry wanted to cut her loose, explain the bizarre state of mind that led him to such an act and beg her for forgiveness. Calhoun, on the other hand, seemed delighted.

"Can't we at least cover her with a sheet?" Barry asked, out of the blue.

"Shut the hell up," Tom growled. Irene's pleading eyes clicked back and forth between the two men, finally resting on Barry in supplication. That didn't pass unnoticed by Calhoun, who grinned wolfishly at his partner.

"You're distracting her from what's important, pal," he said while turning his K-bar knife so that the light from the overhead fixture glinted off the edge. "I think you ought to take a walk." Tom looked at his watch. "Come back at two in the morning on the nose and I think we'll have some things to talk about."

A muffled squeak came out from behind Irene's tennis ball gag. Barry was drenched in sweat and he stammered at bit. His mind seemed overwhelmed by a hundred courses of action and what would be the right choice. Irene and Calhoun almost swam together in his vision because his eyes shifted so rapidly from one to another. He could hear Tom's teeth grind together.

"Walk, partner," Calhoun hissed. "If you think I wouldn't gut you like a fish in a second, your intellect is slipping."

Finally, Barry whispered, whether to himself or to Irene he wasn't sure, "I'm sorry," and slipped out the door.

Coyote gratefully slid into the darkness. While it wasn't his normal state of being, it was at least an existence he was used to. The deep recesses of the subconscious were old territory to him. He couldn't feel the Doc's body enveloping him in here and he now could concentrate on the task at hand.

He was baffled as to what had occurred. Existence, in his experience was irrefutable, but now it seemed the state of existence was a matter of belief. Somehow, Coyote rationalized, Doctor Pepper's belief that the two beings were misinterpreting what they were had caused this shift of planes.

Metaphysics wasn't Coyote's long suit. He embraced physical principles wholeheartedly, and inside that belief, he felt he was missing something. Everything had a cause and an effect to it. He was living with the effect and somehow he had to define the cause. Of course, he thought to himself, he couldn't do much about it until he located the Doc.

He drifted deeper into the darkness and allowed his thoughts to fly outward.

Chapter Thirteen -

The Cosmos Collapses into Meza Azul and the Marguerita Bay Club is Standing Room Only.

Ted was tired. He was tired of having every little thing in his life turn into a Gordian knot. Something as simple as buying a hunk of ground was now an economic and public relations hot potato. He ran his fingers through his hair for the umpteenth time, took off his glasses and massaged his temples.

Since he'd discovered that snake Steve Abrams had bought the land in New Mexico and was now holding it for ransom, other issues directly connected with it had come to pass. His legal team, the ones tasked with maintaining some sort of adherence to Federal job and hiring policies had been flooding him with memos in regards to a possible class action suit to be filed by the Shantis Indians. Ted was baffled. What Indians? After being given the particulars by his attorneys, he vaguely remembered the big guy that drove the bus down to Albuquerque. He'd seen that hungry look in the man's eyes and trotted out his usual "jobs for everyone" spiel. Normally it did a fine job of mollifying folks, but this time, it had stirred up a hornet's nest.

"Christ, Ted," Oscar Dunkin, his chief council for Labor Relations moaned, "a bunch of friggin' Indians are going to sue us for unfair labor practices? What's next? What else they got down there? This is New Mexico, right? La Raza is gonna be hot on their heels!"

"What do you want me to do?" Ted had asked blandly. "Everyone wants a piece of ByteStream. We come up with a new product; we're accused of trade restraint because everyone wants the operating system and our core architecture is going to default to our applications. We cut a deal with a hardware company and we're charged with a monopoly. It's insane."

The past few years had been rough ones for ByteStream, at least as far as the public perception of the company in general and Ted Marquis in particular went. It all began when a group of his competitors had approached a couple of congressmen with charges that ByteStream had a virtual stranglehold on the industry. They in turn, opened hearings that Ted refused to go to, making him seem aloof and indifferent to the government of the United States. Eventually, the congressional committee turned their report over to the Justice Department, who filed a suit against ByteStream. Naturally, ByteStream lost the first go round, being ordered to break the corporation up into smaller companies, but won on appeal.

Unfortunately, that opened the floodgates. Currently, twelve countries, fifteen states and forty-seven municipalities had suits filed against his company and Ted constantly saw or heard references about himself in every media outlet imaginable. Very few had anything good to say about him.

The most popular t-shirt in Seattle was a picture of a pair of buttocks with the ByteStream logo on it, emblazoned with the statement, "Hey Ted! Byte THIS!"

Curiously, even the socially conscience things he did had a habit of turning green and stinking up his image. Ever since he began to make a profit, Ted scrupulously laid aside forty percent of his after tax earnings for philanthropic and charitable donations. He'd never allowed his image handlers to broadcast what he donated and to whom, as he felt it was crass to make a fuss over largesse. His beneficence was well known inside the company, however and when the smear campaigns started, his public relations people began badgering him to surrender an accounting of his philanthropy so that they could put out press releases illustrating what a swell fellow he really was.

"Ted Marquis Squanders His Children's Birthright!" was typical of the headlines that ensued. Editors and pundits charged him with throwing his estate away in a cynical attempt to shore up his public image.

ByteStream had gone through a dozen Public Relations firms in the past year, leaving behind shattered and beaten hucksters who'd never regain the will to shill. At the same time, when the heat wasn't rising, it didn't bother Ted much. Since the original lawsuits were filed, ByteStream had bought four of the companies who'd charged him with unfair business practices. He just didn't like being in the center of the tornado.

Doctor Pepper was in the center of something; but he hadn't defined exactly what it was yet. He thought for a moment of the final scene in the movie "2001", where the star-child is hovering somewhere between the moon and the earth, overlooking all creation. The trouble was, that was the only context he could relate to; something solid, something tangible. He seemed to exist in between the solidity of the universe. It was as if the space between molecules had opened up and he inhabited that space. Distance, density; even matter itself was irrelevant to his world. "I wish I knew more about physics", he thought to himself. "Maybe then I'd understand what's going on."

If Doctor Pepper had any concerns at all, it was over this sudden shift in his worldview. He'd truly believed that there were mortals and spirits, each of whom were bound together by tenets of faith and understanding. Even though throughout his life the Spirits he had faith in remained inexplicably aloof; he knew they were there. Now he seemed to have somehow become a spirit and he was alone in the cosmos. It disturbed him as he had always looked outside of himself for the answer to any given mystery. Now he was in the heart of the greatest mystery and had to puzzle it out for himself.

"I'm a baby without parents," he said to himself. "Goo goo."

Barry had been shut out for three days. When he first left the motel and heard Calhoun slide the chain lock behind him, he'd been filled with remorse and concern over what was going to occur in his absence. He felt as though he'd thrown Irene to the lions. Or sacrificed her to one ravening beast, at any rate.

He'd wandered the streets of San Antonio all night, racked with guilt and wondering what he'd encounter when he returned. Visions of a room that resembled an abattoir, with little bits of Irene; fingers, toes, the odd chunk of flesh, scattered all over plagued him. His heart was trying to pound through his sternum when he arrived back at the motel door at eight o'clock the next morning. He paused before knocking, listening intently and heard nothing but silence. Debating with himself as to whether that was a good thing or a bad sign, he sniffed the air for the telltale copperish tang of blood. All he gathered in was the scent of desiccated leaves scattered among the white river rock that fronted the walkway of the motel. Finally he knocked. Getting no response, he rapped a bit harder and was greeted by the groggy, sleep-phlegmed voice of Tom, who tersely rumbled, "Go away."

"What's going on?" Barry hissed. He heard the bedsprings squeak and the heavy thump of Calhoun's feet hitting the floor. He heard a groan and a cough, shuffling across the carpet and then the door cracked open. All he could see was one of Calhoun's eyes peering through the crack. It was bloodshot and weary.

"Just leave until tonight," Tom told him. The door started to close and in a panic, Barry shoved against it. "What happened? Is Irene all right?"

Tom cursed and pushed on the door, slamming it shut and causing Barry to fly back a good two feet.

"Better than alright, pal," Tom said, nearly imperceptivity from the far side of the door. "She's fuckin' terrific."

And so it went. Barry was locked out. Over the course of the next few days, he came to the realization that he wasn't just barred from the motel room; he'd somehow become disconnected from life itself. While everyone else was able to bask in the sunlight, laugh along the River Walk and commune with one another, Barry was relegated to the shadows, a self contained pool of darkness, unable to reach out to anyone.

Even the bums down by the switchyards had some sort of camaraderie. Barry watched with a no small amount of wistful envy as four raggedy men walked among the rails, checking out the trains that were being made up and sharing an easy banter between themselves and the yardmen regarding what boxcar was going where. In the long shadows of late summer, Barry felt a chill of isolation as he watched the bums swing up and into a reefer and roll out. Even the outcasts of this world had something, while he had nothing but a knowledge so dangerous and terrifying that it sealed his mouth and glazed his eyes from the company of anyone except Calhoun and now even that seemed lost to him.

That night, after another closed-door dismissal, Barry found himself on a bridge over the Rio Grande, looking up at a fingernail moon. Just below and to the right, Venus flared brilliantly, nearly dispelling the notion of a cold and dispassionate universe. As Barry stared at it, it seemed to draw him in until he realized that the very sky was bending about him, growing blacker until what he'd mistaken for a planet was merely the reflection point of a giant compound eye. It stared at him, unblinking.

Bob's Big Boy loved the sound of a shaping iron and hammer against steel. Most of the other residents of the Pueblo, and Mesa Azul had no particular like or dislike of it until recently, and they'd grown to hate it. For some reason, the place where Bob's Big Boy was working carried the sound everywhere, with very little loss of resonance.

"You're driving everyone crazy!" Reddi shouted to Bob over the sound of a grinder. Bob was happily laboring away at Skunk Hollow Forge, an abandoned Quonset hut at the south edge of town that had been converted into a forge back in the nineteen seventies by a fellow who'd tried to make a living working wrought iron and what he liked to refer to as art for a few years before packing it in and being swallowed up by the country somewhere. Since then, the forge and everything in it had been viewed as community property. Corky Gonzales used it to mend radiators and reshape badly crumpled bodywork, but for the most part, it was the haunt of raccoons and fence lizards.

Bob's Big Boy was in pursuit of a vision, and it was all Reddi Kilowatt's fault. While Bob was looking after the tribal welfare at the last Pow-Wow, Reddi had wandered around the artisans stalls, looking at various Indian artifacts for sale in hope of coming up with some sort of inspiration that he could modify into a marketable image for the Shantis. In amongst the dream catchers and drums and painted cow skulls, he noticed some Kachinas that were particularly well done. His was stopped in his tracks by a White Mountain ogre whose geometric facial construction spoke to him on some primitive level and as a result, that evening he began to doodle.

Eventually, after numerous revisions, he came up with an iconographic figure that represented a man kneeling by a riverbank, his hands cupped, bringing water to his lips. Something about it appealed to everyone in the tribe. "I like it because it's not naughty," was Mrs. Fields' judgment and the elders agreed.

Bob's Big Boy was in a fever when they got back to Mesa Azul. Going up to John Elkfoot's place, they had the doodle scanned and cleaned up by John, who gave them back a file they could take to any printer and have press plates made from. Bob ran over to Taos and had a crateload of stickers made up, portraying the "drinking man" as everyone referred to it and the initials "S.I.P.", which stood for Shantis Indian Pueblo. Bob's Big Boy slapped them on everything, much to Mesa Azul's annoyance.

People would come out of their house in the morning and discover a "S.I.P." decal plastered on their mailbox. Leaving the Marguerita Bay Club, revelers would find one stuck to the rear window or bumper of their car. On a weekend jaunt down to Santa Fe, Bob barely avoided arrest after he'd decorated every car on Water Street. His plan was working, though. Residents throughout eastern New Mexico had come to know "Sippy" as they referred to the little figure, and they hated it.

Even the Pueblo began to grouse a little bit. "Bob," Moe Pep said to him one day, "you've got to slow down on your marketing campaign. Someone left this," Moe held out a peeled off Sippy sticker with a knife drawn in the back of the drinking man and the words, "Die, asshole" written on it, "in my mailbox this morning." Mrs. Butterworth pointed out that what Bob considered marketing, most of the world considered defacement of property.

Deflated, but not defeated, Bob's Big Boy holed up in his bedroom for a week, mulling over ideas that wouldn't be so controversial. One night, while he was asleep, it came to him. He saw a statue of the Drinking Man rising over Shantis Pueblo, all shining chrome and blinking lights. He woke in a fever.

For the rest of August, he roamed all over northeastern New Mexico, looking for material. At first, he thought he could build it out of any sort of steel and then have it chromed. However, after learning that chrome dipping was prohibitively expensive, he opted to go on a search for chrome bumpers.

Geography and local custom were a huge boon to Bob's pursuit. In the first place, people in the rural parts of New Mexico don't go off and buy the latest model car very often, the majority of vehicles on the road, referred to generically as "beaters", tended to have sprung from the era of Detroit steel, rather than the more modern trend of Japanese plastic and nylon. Secondly, these same New Mexicans drive with little to no regard for either speed limits or road conditions, resulting in a number of rusting hulks in deep culvert ditches. The Kit Carson National forest was particularly fertile ground for Bob to harvest from. It was narrow, twisting and prone to ice storms. By spring you could count on at least two dozen newly abandoned trucks decorating the ditches on either side of the two-lane blacktop.

Every morning, Bob headed out on the Blue Bus and every night he returned with at least five chrome bumpers. It was the minimum catch he'd set for himself. The week before Labor Day weekend, he had sixty bumpers and set to work. That's when the pounding began.

"You're going to love it," Bob told Reddi as he continued to shape a bumper. Bob turned off the grinder and pulled off his goggles. "Look at this," he said, walking over to a cardboard box. "I found all these while I was looking for bumpers." Reddi glanced at a huge conglomeration of taillights. "Yeah, Bob," he said in his 'what's wrong with you' voice, "terrific."

Bob beamed down at his friend. "Yeah, I think so." He picked up a taillight from a Nash Rambler, "I'm gonna decorate the statue with 'em. I can wire 'em up and turn 'em on at night. It'll be great!"

"Sure, Bob. But, uh, don't you think you could put in just a normal day's work? Your pounding and grinding and stuff keeps everyone awake all night."

"I can't, bro," Bob said. "I gotta have this done by Labor Day weekend." The Shantis attorney had started the wheels rolling on the big public showdown between ByteStream and the Pueblo. "They finally responded to the subpoena," Bob told Reddi confidentially, "and that Marquis fellow agreed to come down here on Labor Day to have a discussion on the matter with Dan and the Elders. Dan's gonna make sure that all the national news outlets are here with cameras. If I can get this done by then, Bammo!! Our new image gets exposure on every national news show."

Coyote had never appreciated emptiness before. His entire existence had been one of complete suffusion into the textures, rhythms and essence of being. It occurred to him, for the first time in eternity that there was a consciousness to the universe. He'd been a conduit of it. John would have said it was as if Coyote was a synapse in some sort of all encompassing brain, or a processing chip. Like a synapse, there were certain impulses Coyote had responded to and those that he hadn't. Still, he'd been aware of them all.

Now, rather than being a part of the process, he'd been removed from it all. Trapped in the being that had formerly been Doctor Pepper, he'd had no choice in what he could and couldn't react to. Falling back into a comatose state was as close to his old existence as he could get. Like a roaring fire that had banked down to a single glowing ember, Coyote had reduced himself that far. He'd become a tiny, beseeching thought, flying outward into the darkness; searching for Doctor Pepper.

The Doc, blissfully drifting into and out of the various permutations of existence that were now available to him, felt a tug. It was a curious phenomenon, magnetic in its' attraction. He'd been examining a light particle, slowly discovering that he had the ability to change the rate at which it vibrated. It had come zipping by as a wide band oscillation; pure white in being and he found he could zip along with it. He was surprised to discover that it had a structure. In his experience, light seemed the most ephemeral of things; you could pass in and out of it without feeling anything. And yet, as he hurled along with it, he could examine it in minute detail. It was almost like an engine; various polarities, pushing and pulling at the core, causing the vibration of it. By focusing on one polarity, he could lessen or increase its' attraction, changing the rate of vibration, thus changing the hue of the light itself. He'd surrounded himself in a nice violet fog when he felt the insistent tug. "Huh," the Doc thought, "I wonder what this means?" and he let himself be pulled along.

In an instant, he was drawn into a tunnel. At least, that's how he perceived it; that was made up of space, matter and time itself. All he knew was that it was very pretty and didn't hang around as long as he'd have liked. Before that thought had even passed, he found himself in a white room, with a railed bed and an ancient and still figure lying there.

"I don't belong here." Something reverberated in the Doc's consciousness.

"Where's here?" the newly created spirit replied.

"In you."

This was puzzling. "Oh well," the Doc thought to himself, "anything is possible."

"Yes," this presence or thought continued, "anything IS possible."

"Look," the thought said, "you really don't know what you're doing, do you?"

"No, I'm just making it up as I go along."

"I'm having a hard time connecting with you," the consciousness impressed on the Doc. "Can you see me?"

The Doc described the room and the old man that was in it.

"Go inside."

"Inside what?"

Coyote was discovering the frustration of trying to explain something that is instinctual. The Doc seemed to have a slight resistance to completely surrendering to thought. He'd hit a barrier and wouldn't enter Coyote's consciousness. The more Coyote tried to explain it, the more confused the Doc became.

"So," the Doc's essence mused, "you're saying that you're me? That I jumped outside myself somehow?"

"The essential you did, yes."

"Who are you, then?"

"Okay," Coyote thought wearily to the Doc, "follow along with me. You are inhabiting what I used to be and I'm trapped in what you used to be."

"I don't think so. I still feel like me."

"You can't FEEL anything!" Coyote raged. "That's the problem. I feel EVERYTHING!"

The real problem, which Coyote was unable to articulate, was that neither being had a proper frame of reference from which to view their current situation. Until a few days ago, this would have all been an abstract argument regarding the meaning of existence. Now it was a reality that neither being had the tools or understanding to cope with.

Coyote tried to get the Doc to just surrender to his situation; to allow the pull of Coyote's consciousness to draw him in, but the Doc just wasn't getting it. He was stuck trying to deal with the predicament from the realm of solid tangibles.

"Are you trying to tell me that I'm supposed to get into your body? How do I do that? Go up your nose or in your ear or something?

"Forget the body," Coyote whimpered, "it's irrelevant!"

"I still don't understand what I'm supposed to do."

It was a burdensome task, similar to teaching someone how to breathe, or process nutrients. And the results were about as satisfying. Coyote had always been instinctively drawn to a sentient consciousness; he could will himself into the same undefined space as any thinking being. Trying to explain HOW to do it, he had no analogies or references. As Doc would later tell people, "it was like teaching a fish to tap-dance."

Whatever fate had caused this to happen, it was benevolent enough to have had it happen with Doc, who was generous and compassionate, eager to help the whatever it was who needed his assistance resolve its' problem. Unfortunately, that eagerness quickly complicated the situation.

"Here's my thought," the Doc said, "it's pretty much accepted that consciousness resides in the brain, right? I seem to be able to slip into and out of things by threading my way through the gaps in matter, so if I get into the brain that you're in, maybe I'll wind up where you are."

"No, no," Coyote said in a panic, "it's completely different! You can't ..."

But it was too late. The Doc had assimilated his essence into the gray matter of his former body. He found himself looking at a complex matrix of tissue, nerve endings, neurons, synapses and receptors. He'd arrived at the frontal lobe, so there wasn't much activity going on, the occasional synaptic flare which the Doc found quite pretty, but other than that, the comatose state the body was in left most of the frontal lobe dark and quiet.

Out of curiosity, the Doc enveloped a synapse. Something about the Doc caused it to suddenly fire and the body's right leg twitched.

"Oh, crap", he felt Coyote think.

John felt as thought he'd somehow offended the cosmos and fate had decided to draw and quarter him. Everyone seemed to be clamoring for his undivided attention. On a personal level, whatever was going on with Doctor Pepper and Huernafano County itself was worrisome enough, but on top of that, he was behind on his production schedule for next season's "Warriors of the Whirlwind" and his brother had developed an annoying habit of calling three times daily to inform John that his muffed deliveries were putting his head on the chopping block.

"I got the syndicate's convention out here in a week and you've sent me bupkis! I got nothing but a bunch of bad actors and a blue screen to show people! You're killing me!"

If that wasn't enough, between everything else, he'd been called repeatedly by the senior development team at ByteStream regarding their version of his compression code and the problems they were encountering making enhancements to it. There seemed to be an unspoken rule within the industry that if something worked well, it was your duty to add features to it so that it worked less well than the previous release. BtyeStream's development team had decided that it needed encryption enhancements. This unfortunately had led to severe crashes within the decompression codex. "My stuff worked fine," was John's habitual response, "whatever you did to it, it's your problem."

Now he had Ted Marquis on the line. He wanted to find out if he and his core development group could come down to Blue Mesa and hang out for a week. "We're close, John," Ted said, "and a really feel the environment down there would clear the cobwebs out of everyone and we can wrap this up before Labor Day."

John rolled his eyes. Ted had sent him a blizzard of emails regarding the future of ByteStream and Mesa Azul all summer long. John's insistence that Ted was falling victim to a self-created delusion only made Ted all the more ada-mant. "Sure," John said resignedly, "just don't blame me if the genie stays in the bottle. There's nothing magic here, Ted."

The second he hung up the phone, John regretted his invitation. He was backlogged with work and now he'd have geeks overrunning his studio in just a few days. He thought for a moment, calculated just how much work he could get done in the next 24 hours, put on a pot of coffee and pulled out the box of logged tapes he was supposed to be working on.

"At least it'll distract me from all the other nuttiness going on around here."

Irene was using the back of a happily bound Tom Calhoun as a footstool and thinking over the past 36 hours. Events and self-discovery had occurred so rapidly; she was having a hard time processing everything that happened and how it came about. The insistent knocking of Barry Moss interrupted her mus-ings.

Barry sounded as if he'd reached the end of his tether. To an extent, she couldn't blame him. He'd been having to scrounge for three days and left com-pletely out of her and Tom's life. Sighing, she swung her feet off Tom, reached down and snatched up the K-bar knife she'd left on the floor and cut the rope that pulled Calhoun's knees close to his elbows. Tom groaned through the ten-nis ball gag as he rolled over onto his side and stretched his cramped appendages.

"Did I say you could change position?" Irene harshly demanded.

Tom shook his head while looking adoringly at Irene.

"Roll over on your back," she barked and then proceeded to undo the rope around his ankles.

Barry was nonplussed hearing Irene's voice bark orders through the door, but that was nothing compared to his surprise at Tom's appearance when the door finally swung open. Naked except for some sort of rope harness or co-coon that seemed to swaddle him from neck to knees, Tom seemed as helpless as a baby, and just as tractable.

The shock was so intense that Barry stammered for a good thirty seconds before he finally was able to ask what on earth had happened in his absence.

"That's something I'm trying to figure out myself," Irene said. "Things just happened."

Barry sat down stunned in a chair and let his eyes flicker back and forth be-tween the two. It was if the world had tilted on its axis, or changed polarities. Nothing made sense anymore. Irene was floundering about for an explanation and Tom just kept his eyes to the floor.

Finally, Barry said, "can you at least put some pants on him?" nodding his head towards Tom. Calhoun's obvious state of excitement made Barry very uncomfortable. Irene laughed.

"I suppose," she chuckled. "Tom's been a naughty boy. Getting dressed might be a good punishment for him." To Barry's chagrin, untying Tom seemed to involve much more caressing, stroking and teasing than he could tolerate observing so he grabbed Calhoun's OD pants and rifled the pockets for Tom's wallet. "I'll meet you in the coffee shop," he said, pocketing some money and hurrying out the door.

A bit later, over waffles, Irene and Tom began to explain to Barry exactly what had occurred between them, but Barry quickly threw up his hands and said, "I really don't want to know."

It was just as well, Irene thought. She was still having difficulty grasping the dynamic that had occurred between her and her kidnapper. Initially terrified and disoriented, she soon began to feel a spark of anger, not only over the situation she found herself in, but regarding every single event in her life that involved men. By the time Barry had abandoned her to the tender mercies of Tom Calhoun, she was a boiling over with rage and frustration.

As he loomed over her, rather than seeing the menacing ogre he'd hoped to project into her psyche, all she could see was yet another in the seemingly endless line of bullies, manipulators and liars she'd known that wore pants. Without thinking, when he leaned towards her face to hiss dangerously at her, she threw her head forward and beaned him. He went bolt upright in shock, an angry knot already taking shape as a large red blot on his forehead. The expression on his face caused her to begin laughing behind her tennis ball gag.

"You don't want to do that," Calhoun said. There was a tremor of uncertainty to his voice, however, that made Irene laugh harder.

Tom had lost his edge. Never in his life had anyone reacted to him in that manner. From the time he was a little kid, the normal reaction he got from anyone at the outset was fear. He felt impotent and strangely stimulated at the same time. He got off the bed and stood back, watching his captive writhe in fury, her hands hooked into claws ineffectually trying to reach the restraining ropes and even her toes grasped at the air. He was torn between two desires. His original intent to terrify her into revealing everything she knew about the Estes Foundation and the people she worked for and a new contradictory curiosity regarding just how much of a hellcat this woman would be unrestrained.

He stood there, flipping his knife and thinking. Then, almost unconsciously, he cut the cord restraining her right leg.

Irene lashed out, the side of her foot hitting Tom's forearm. The heavy knife flew out of his hand and buried itself in the floorboard as he yelped in surprise.

She was like something possessed, twisting and flailing with her leg and when he tried to grab it, she connected again, breaking his middle finger. An electric jolt of pain ran up his arm and Tom stepped back a foot, tucking his hand under his armpit and waiting for that first wave of agony to subside.

Irene, in the meantime, placed her right foot underneath herself and leveraged upward, straining against the restraints with a manic energy. The headboard, bolted to the wall and used as the anchor for the ropes that held her arms, pulled loose and Irene rolled off the bed, dragging the headboard behind her.

Calhoun, shocked, stepped forward to take back a certain measure of control and was hit full in the face with the headboard Irene swung at him. Pain blossomed again as his nose was reshaped by the heavy particle board. Tom's eyes watered with tears from the sudden agony and the room rippled and dripped in his vision. While he shook his head to clear it, Irene found the dropped K-bar knife, pried it loose, and cut her left leg clear.

She was in an adrenalin rush. An entire lifetime of bottled frustration and anger popped its cork and she launched herself at the hulking figure, swinging the headboard from the ropes still attached to her wrists. The corner of it drove into Tom's side and deep in the recesses of Irene's consciousness, she felt a glow of satisfaction at the sound of a rib snapping. As her former assailant fell back, she swung the headboard again, overhand this time and it slammed hard onto the top of his head, driving him to his knees.

Tom was stunned in more ways than one. The suddenness of this little woman's attack and the sheer fury of it, coupled with the physical damage she was doing was one thing, but the way his mind was processing the events was something completely unexpected. From the moment she began to fight back, his reflexes had slowed and a heretofore hidden recess of his mind screamed a joyful "YES!" This wild hare grew in intensity, begging for this surrender of will, the loss of control and the need to be helpless in the grip of another. Bizarre visions that he'd kept buried since adolescence flooded his mind and he half-heartedly tried to tamp them down. He might have succeeded if Irene hadn't clonked him on the top of his noggin and the lights flashed out.

Irene was wrestling with some conflicts herself. The sensible thing to do, the moment she realized she knocked her kidnapper out would have been to either flee the motel room for the safety of the check in desk, or at the very least, grab the phone and call the police. Instead, she stood over the crumpled figure, projecting every hurt, humiliation and slight she'd ever suffered on to him and felt a desire rise up and wash over her. She wanted to exact payment for the wrongs in her life her own way and in her own time.

When Calhoun regained his senses, he found himself handily tied, ankle and wrist, and Irene sitting in a chair near him, with his heavy knife in her hands.

She asked him how he felt and while he fished in his mind for an answer, she crept over to him and began cutting his clothes off.

The psychosexual dynamic that was created in those moments was like a drug to the both of them and for the next thirty hours, they happily wallowed in it.

It lingered like a hangover while they had breakfast with Barry. For Calhoun, the Estes Foundation, alien overlords and the eventual domination of humanity was now a non-issue. Irene, still processing her new status in the world, dismissed Barry's concerns about her connection to all his fantastic delusions. All she wanted was to wrap this up and get Tom back into the motel room.

Barry wasn't buying her explanation of coincidence regarding their both being in San Antonio at the same time. It was clear to him, however that he'd never get to the truth of the matter. It was also obvious that he'd lost his ally in Tom Calhoun. God only knew what the Foundation had done to him, but somehow, they'd altered his personality or replaced him with a clone that slavishly followed Irene's lead. It was clear that the only reason they hadn't gotten him was because he'd kept on the move. Apparently, that was the single option Barry had left; to run and keep on running.

"I need to use the head," Barry informed his dining companions.

Casually sauntering to the Men's room, Barry slipped inside, gratefully saw a window he pried open and kicked the screen out of, then ran back to the motel room, found the keys to the jeep and quickly tore out of the parking lot.

Like ants on the rim of a sand lion pit, everything slowly and almost imperceptively began to slide towards Mesa Azul. From the northwest, a ByteStream corporate jet cleared the ever-present rain clouds of Seattle and turned towards the Sangre di Cristos. Dan Bucknuts climbed into his Lexus and maneuvered it onto I-25; a straight shot from Denver down to Huernafano County, eight hours away. Hard against the Mexican border, a World War Two vintage Willies Jeep was running along dusty two-lane blacktop up towards the panhandle, carrying Barry Moss back to the only sanctuary he'd ever known. He figured he'd slip in during the witching hour, scout around and if things looked clear, sneak into his trailer and access his safe. He had close to a hundred thousand dollars in small denominations tucked away, more than necessary to get to South America and set up a new bolthole.

In New York and Los Angeles, network news directors looked over the cut sheets on possible stories for the coming week. The press release from the Native American Legal Aid society looked interesting. The richest man in America confronts some of the poorest over the issue of jobs. It might be worth a thirty-second spot. Ted Marquis was always good for feeding the indignation of the nation, so calls were put out to local stringers in Santa Fe and Albuquerque. Three affiliates sent cameramen and one sent a stand up reporter. Labor Day weekend was usually pretty slow so it was worth packing the talent out.

At the center of the vortex, life went on as usual. John Elkfoot had hurriedly put together the special effects necessary for two segments of "Warriors of the Whirlwind", even though he was slightly dissatisfied with the work, his brother had approved them and John was setting his satellite uplink. A commotion echoed up from the town below and John paused in his work, meandered out to his patio and watched Bob's Big Boy, Reddi Killowatt and the Pep Boys try to operate Corky's chain hoist. "You're scratching it!" he heard Bob cry out. A chain rattle and a booming, hollow crash followed. "Ah, Geez," Bob moaned.

The Shantis were trying to get Bob's creation onto a sledge. The hulking Indian had worked nonstop for a week and fulfilled his vision, after a sort. It didn't really look like what he had in mind. Actually, it seemed to resemble a praying mantis that had lost its' abdomen and a pair of legs. Still, it was big and shiny, which was half the vision. It seemed pretty sturdy as well; this was the third time they'd dropped it and the welds didn't pop at all.

"So much for 'third time's a charm'," Manny Pep said to no one in particular. Reddi wondered aloud if they'd fed the chain incorrectly through the hoist.

Movement and dialogue were going on elsewhere as well. Coyote and Doc were locked in the still recesses of the shaman's physical being, still trying to coordinate their efforts to regain their former identities.

"You know what I think?" the Doc put forward. "Whatever caused this to happen had a reason. I think we should just sit back and wait to see what happens next."

"No," Coyote cringed. "I can't do that. Your whole way of existing is too brutal for belief. It'll destroy me."

"You'd be surprised," the Doc offered. "People can get used to a lot of things."

"The trouble is, I ain't people."

Chapter Fourteen -

The Town Gets Wired While Coyote and Doctor Pepper Play the Old Shell Game.

Barry's worst fears had been realized. Leaving San Antonio, he'd run across the endless llano of far west Texas and into a sudden rainstorm. Huge purple clouds came rolling down from the New Mexican border and as he approached, it looked as though the world had a neatly etched line between the blue and sunshine he was quickly running out of and the near surgically precise cut of shadow and rain he was heading for. The instant he dropped into the darkness of the thunder caps, water hit the windshield as though it had been thrown from a bucket. The world became distorted and indistinct, waving and running in his vision until he'd gone past the squall on the leading edge of the storm. Things settled down and it was actually soothing to hear rain hitting the canvas top of the jeep, the slapping of the wipers and the heady aroma of wet sage. Lightening ran under the clouds or burst inside the dark cover of the sky. He heard thunder roll away from him.

These things sat comfortably in his head, natural phenomena that at one time held a mystical power because men couldn't explain them. Once the working of lightening and thunder were understood, they seemed as unremarkable as the shape of a man's fingers. It occurred to Barry that maybe he'd been reading too much into the world for too long. Water sheeted the blacktop in front of him and he could see faint reflections of the world he lived in, only darker and slightly warped. "Maybe that's what I've been looking for," he said out loud, "some reflection of the real world." He resolved to look up rather than down from now on.

By the time he'd crossed over the state line, it was late on the Friday afternoon of Labor Day weekend and even on the state roads, traffic was picking up. The storm had played itself out and rolled eastward, leaving behind a million tiny suns, trapped inside the water drops hanging off the heads of the buffalo grass growing in the median and the deep green needles of the ponderosa pine growing hard by the highway. The sun was just beginning to drop behind the mountains and every car running with or away from him seemed to be tinged with gold and a rich crystalline blue and inside those golden chariots were simple, happy people off on a last spree before the working world shut summer down for another year. Barry saw them as just that, not dupes or clones or subversive agents of some force determined to overrun his world. He realized that he'd been so busy worrying about the loss of the world that he hadn't spent any time living in it. The aroma of wet pine had overrun the sage and he rolled down his window to enjoy the rushing air.

As he wound his way up and over Glorietta Pass and down into the valley of the Rio Grande, Barry savored every moment of the passing time. He was a danger to everyone else on the road since he was so busy looking around at the sky and the land being enveloped in night that the highway held little interest for him. By the time he was fifty miles north of Santa Fe, he had slipped into the canyon of sandstone the river had cut out and he was so wrapped up in the strange iridescent properties of the mineral varnish on the canyon walls, he missed his turnoff for the county road that runs down the side canyon of the Huernafano, straight into Mesa Azul. He didn't realize his mistake until he popped out of the canyon near Fort Garland. He decided to have dinner at the Dinner Bell Diner and then take the east fork back down to Taos, over Doloroso Pass and hit Mesa Azul from the north side.

The sight of the alien structure in front of the Pueblo chilled Barry to his bones and drove all the carefree hours he'd just spent into the enveloping dark. The first faint prickles of apprehension had occurred as he got his first glimpse of his little town from the heights of the mountain. About halfway down the track, the trees and the rocks fall away and you can get a bird's eye view of the Huernafano valley. It was a new moon so the only thing lighting the land below was starlight. Something glimmered, but it wasn't the shifting silver of the creek, or the steady glow of the few lights still on at that late hour. Barry slowed down and stopped. It was curious, almost like points of light had been shaped to form something. There were also three rings of red lights, which burned like coals. He got out Calhoun's starlight scope and zoomed in. He'd been wrong.

They were here.

Ted was in high gear and even higher spirits the second he jumped out of the Bell Ranger on top of Blue Mesa. He loved the view from up there, seeing everything spread out like a scale model 400 feet below him. Momentarily, he wondered what it would cost to buy John's property, and then quickly flushed the idea. Ted had always shown great restraint when it came to using his personal wealth to get his way. Besides, he thought to himself, John seemed weirdly attached to the town the way it was and in less than two years, it would be something completely different. John would probably beg him to buy him out by then.

Along with the four-man development team that John would be working with to resolve the glitches in the video streaming process, Ted had hauled Sol Friedman, the current shining knight of his public relations group along with him. Reviewing the last county census, they discovered that there were at best 300 hearts and minds in all of Huernafano County to win over before the town hall meeting. They had decided that they would try to pay a personal call on every household in the valley before Monday "If we can cover the town itself and the Indians today," Ted speculated aloud, "we ought to be in good shape for the morning when the rest of the team shows up."

The rest of the team was a crew of professional boosters Sol had hired. They would be armed with glossy brochures, income and job growth projections and a sunny vision of tomorrow that ought to go a long way towards ameliorating any hard feelings the locals might have about the future of this little valley.

John Elkfoot's look of irritation after quickly glancing at their brochure caused Sol to lean over and whisper to Ted, "We can scratch him off the list."

First on Ted's agenda was to get down to the Pueblo and find out exactly what he could do remove the nuisance of yet another lawsuit. Ted's legal team advised him against approaching the Shantis personally, "we can thrash this out in negotiations," he was told, but Ted was fed up with feeling as though he walked through life with a large bull's-eye taped to his back.

"I'm sure they can be reasoned with," Ted muttered. His battery of attorneys pointed out that reason had little no association with the practice of law.

"This is pretty sweet, Ese." Angel marveled at the brochure he'd been handed by Sol Friedman, who was busy wondering if he'd caused any permanent damage to himself with the fiery poblano he'd just bit into. Angel absentmindedly popped the top on a Modelo Negro and slid it down the bar to the choking publicist. "So, where's my place?" he asked, tapping the artist's rendition of what Mesa Azul would look like when ByteStream's visionaries were done with the town.

"I don't know," Sol gasped. After killing three fourths of a cerveza, which seemed to merely bank the fires a little, he said, "somewhere on Main Street, I'm sure."

"Hold the phone, pendejo. What 'Main Street'?"

"The main drag," Sol said, "whatever you call it."

Angel shrugged and fished under the counter for a toothpick. He liked gnawing on toothpicks while ruminating. "This is Oak, bolillo."

"It is?" the sign identifying Oak Street as a crossroads he'd passed on his way to the Bay Club perplexed Sol, so Angel explained the history of their curious system for street assignment. "Well, okay," the publicist stammered, "I'm glad you really put it to the Post Office but naturally that will have to change."

Now it was the bartender's turn to be perplexed. "How do you figure, Sonso?"

"You folks have lived here forever," Sol explained, "so you already know where everything is. ByteStream employees will need proper streets and signs to find their way around."

"Maybe," Angel said, looking at the brochure again. "The way you got things laid out here, with everything looking the same, it could get confusing." He leaned in to confide with his guest, "when all that norteno dough starts rolling in, I'm gonna put in a big neon sign. That'll help. It'll be like the reference point for everyone." He looked under the bar for the napkin he'd doodled his idea on and once he'd located it, showed his sketch of a towering pole with squiggly neon waves, a palm tree and a pelican surrounded by the name of his establishment to his visitor. "Like something out of Vegas, eh, ruca?"

Sol chuckled. He loved hicks ideas of class. "Well, it would stand out, but we're going to be encouraging business owners to get a facelift that falls in line with our vision of the community. Angel looked at Sol with a slightly puzzled expression. Sol went on to explain the concept of planned communities and visual harmony. The ramshackle collection of architectural styles, for want of a better term, was going to be a thing of the past. The new vision was some sort of yanqui fantasy of southwestern style. Sol opened up to the center spread of the brochure, which showed a line of abode fronts, all connected by a sidewalk shaded by verandas extending from the buildings. "You see, downtown will have a nice uniform appearance."

"You can't tell one thing from another," Angel said incredulously. Sol explained that they would all have small tasteful signs hanging in front of each store. The bartender pulled out more paper napkins and spread them over the counter. Each one showed a dream of Angel's; such as the mural he wanted painted on the outside of the Club showing bikini clad women on a beach with gigantic cocktails and palm trees and parrots interspersed liberally about the scene. Sol smiled indulgently and patted Angel on the shoulder.

"Don't worry, old timer," he said as he walked out the door, "you're going to love what we've got in store for this place. You won't miss all the run down junk and Quonset huts, believe me."

"Yeah?" Angel rumbled after the Gringo's departure, "we'll see, you pinche nalga." He turned around to the phone on the wall. "Te voy a dar en la madre," he muttered while dialing. "Hey, lok," he greeted Corky when the mechanic picked up on the other end, "a real tirile is coming to see you. Meet me and the rest of the town council here tonight. We got things to talk about."

Ted, in the meantime, found himself in a nearly deserted Pueblo. After a half an hour of perplexed wandering, he finally came across Larry Pep, who was nursing a damaged foot, received during the relocation of the Sippy statue. "You know how you're supposed to let go on the count of three?" he offered as an explanation to a question that Ted hadn't asked, "I'm the guy that never lets go on three." The Pep Boy told Ted that everyone was up in the piñon forest collecting pine nuts. Two hot and dusty hours later, he finally found the Shantis.

"Hi!" Bob's Big Boy shouted to the exhausted mogul. Bob was busy working a long pole, knocking pinecones off the upper reaches of the evergreens. Nut harvesting seemed somehow to have evolved a rigid hierarchy over the millennia. Men always knocked the cones down, kids scrambled about collecting the fallen cones and inspecting whether they were ripe or not and the women broke up the cones and harvested the nuts.

"Hello," Ted said wearily and sinking down on a rock in the shade of one of the piñon trees. Bob stopped working and sat down next to the mogul, offering him some Gatorade. While Ted drank, he watched the activities around him and wondered aloud if this same thing occurred a thousand years ago. "Probably," Bob agreed, "except for the Gatorade and the running shoes." A shout of alarm distracted both men and they watched a young Shantis boy being chased by a kiabab squirrel. Bob laughed. "Those squirrels get tougher every year. One of these days they're going to get organized and then we'll be in trouble."

"Speaking of organized," Ted jumped on the conveniently placed segue, "I'd like to talk to you about the lawsuit your tribe has filed against my company."

Bob grinned. "Yeah, ain't that something? We're all going to be on TV."

"So you already know about the town meeting broadcast?" Ted was puzzled about how word of his public relations move had gotten out already. Both men looked at each other as if they had onions sprouting from their ears. Bob filled Ted in on Counselor Bucknuts' idea.

Bob's Big Boy had never actually seen the color drain from someone's face before. Until that moment, he'd assumed it was a colorful device that writers used. Worried that the man might pass out, he splashed Gatorade in his face, bringing Ted sputtering back to life. "Why are you doing this?" Ted finally asked.

Bob picked up a twig from the ground and twirled it between his fingers. Like a lot of men, he was on of those people who rarely looked anyone in the face when talking seriously. His eyes roamed the evergreen hillside, taking in the activities of his people as well as all the motion of the forest. Two butterflies danced erratically about each other in a patch of sunlight and a squirrel with sooty tufts on the tips of his ears peered cautiously at the Shantis from the far side of a tree. Bob's eyes tracked the dip and rise flight of a magpie and then a blue gray Steller's jay as it swooped down on one of the buckets the harvested nuts were tossed into. Mrs. Fields flapped at it and it tore upwards, nearly in a straight vertical flight, then veered with a squawk away from a great horned owl that blended almost completely into the pattern of the tree it sat in. "Huh," Bob grunted, "You don't see many of them in the daytime."

While Ted peered myopically in the direction Bob had nodded in, the Indian tried to explain to Ted the reasons behind the lawsuit.

"Every year we go to the Pow-Wow in Denver," he explained, "and I see all these tribes that have a history; a past and a future. The Shantis don't really seem to have either one. All we ever had was this land," he spread out his arms as if he was presenting the world to Ted for the first time. "This forest and the river and the valley down there. I guess nobody but a couple religious nuts from Mexico ever saw much in this country. It gave us everything we needed and kept away anything that could hurt us."

"Then that damned TV came along." Bob tossed his pine twig down and then found a rock that his liked. "You can't want what you don't have if you don't know you don't have it." Ted nodded and Bob began tossing the rock up and down in his hand. He explained how seeing what the rest of the world was like, what it had and what the Shantis were missing changed things. "Now, everyone wants all that nice stuff," Bob sighed. "Hell, even I want some of it, and I couldn't even tell you why. It's not going to make my life better, I don't think. But, you see it, and pretty soon you want it."

It made people itchy, Bob said. It only got worse whenever they went to the intertribal get together in Denver. "Tribes with casino deals, or resort deals. Oil leases and government enterprise grants. We come across like poor cousins. You can feel everyone else looking down on us. Hell, we can't even gripe about our history of being oppressed." Bob glanced over at Ted, a slight sense of sadness turning down the corners of his eyes. "We've never even had enough notice to be oppressed. Just ignored."

"Then you come along. A rich guy with the future in his pocket. You gave me hope, man." Ted pointed out that he had made a genuine offer of solid employment to Bob's people.

"Saying we can get jobs as cooks and cleanup people doesn't amount to much of a future for our kids." Bob talked a bit more about his meetings with Dan Bucknuts and the attorney's combination of indignation and avarice at the mention of Ted Marquis.

"It's a reaction I'm slowly getting used to," Ted sighed. He looked at Bob's profile. "Seems like we get the same reaction from people even though we're on opposite ends of the teeter totter."

"Huh?"

"Respect," Ted went on. "You don't get any because you're too poor. I don't get any because I'm too rich."

"I don't think it comes down to money," Bob mused. "Everyone has something they're proud of. With most of the tribes at the Pow-Wow, they got these long traditions and ceremonies and shit. They're proud of it, I can understand that. But they bolster it by looking down on us." He finally looked Ted in the eye. "Maybe people feel good putting you down because it's the one shot they can take at a rich guy."

Ted and the big Indian continued to talk in the shadow of the evergreens as the day deepened and the first stars came out.

Something was tugging at Coyote and the Doc. The old shaman, in his new ephemeral being, kept seeing a tunnel open up like a gun sight to Mesa Azul. Unfortunately, he seemed inextricably bound up in what was once his cerebral cortex. Coyote, inhabiting the Doc's physical being, had unbidden memories of Doc's existence in the Pueblo.

"Stop doing that," Coyote complained.

"Doing what?"

"Showing me your life," Coyote thought irritably. The Doc explained that he had no idea what he could or couldn't do. "If I'm doing it, I don't know how I'm doing it and I don't know how to stop it."

"It's making me nutty," Coyote said. "Weren't you ever happy?"

"I never thought about it."

"Well," Coyote observed, "according to what I'm seeing, it's like you never thought about anything else."

The conversation went on in that vein until the medicine man suggested that they needed to return to Huernafano County. "That seems to be the common connection to what we're experiencing.

"I don't want to move. I don't want to experience all the shocks you people put your bodies through. I don't want to wake up," Coyote grumped. "I think I'll stay in this coma until your body runs down. Maybe I can get out of here then."

"Is that what happens when people die?" Doc asked. "They just leave the body and become whatever it is I am? Did you used to be a living thing?"

"I've always been," Coyote said. "Existing, anyway. Living and dying are your concepts, not mine."

The Doc pointed out that since Coyote now seemed to be part and parcel of a living body, it might be an issue he wanted to consider. "Have you ever seen the spirit of a person?"

"What?" Coyote snapped.

"You know, when a person dies, or at least when their body stops working, does their spirit become like you?"

"I've never encountered anything like me," Coyote said. "So my guess would be no."

"It's got to go somewhere, don't you think?"

"Maybe." Coyote said. "It's a good question as to where though. It's a big cosmos."

"Huh," the shaman mused. "Well, it'll be a big adventure for you, won't it?"

"I'm having a big enough adventure now, thank you. Besides, I've roamed everywhere. Everything else seems to be contained within something. Except for me, or, you now." Coyote wanted to howl in frustration.

Doctor Pepper went on about the concept of spirits or souls. He speculated on what existence really was. He went on to say that both he and Coyote seemed to have their pivotal point of existence in Mesa Azul. Coyote scoffed at the notion, although he had to admit after listening to the Doc ramble on about it that he had a nagging concern that if the body died, he'd cease to exist. "I have, er, had," he corrected himself, "the whole cosmos to roam around in."

"So, why do you always come back to Mesa Azul?" the Doc wondered.

"I, uh," Coyote was a little hesitant. The old man was going somewhere with this and he wasn't sure he liked where it was heading, "I like it there. I like the land and the sky and the people. I like your dreams and thoughts."

"Can you be in anyone's dreams? Or thoughts?"

"Sure, I got into yours here."

"And now you can't get out," Doc noted. "That never happened to you before, did it?"

"True," Coyote mused. Now that he really thought about it, outside of Mesa Azul, he'd only caught those thoughts that people projected outwards, into the infinite. Until he'd recklessly climbed into the Doc's consciousness here, he'd never tried that stunt outside of the little valley to the north. In the entire Universe, it was the only place where he could romp around inside people with impunity.

"I think we need to go home," Doctor Pepper projected.

Barry spent his first night back in Huernafano County high on Dolorosa Pass, watching as the lights slowly winked out. He'd pulled the jeep off the trail and hidden it in a snarl of currant and blackberry bushes then spent a little time looking for a place he could hide. By the time the sun had finally cleared Madre di Cristo, he'd constructed a blind between some granite boulders he masked with sagebrush that he'd cut away and placed so that they appeared to be growing in the space between the rocks. It gave him a masked but relatively clear view of both the trail and the southern end of the valley. He could see his trailer just past the ridge of the rocks and everything leading into Huernafano Canyon.

Barry was both exhausted and wired with tension. He wound up sleeping in tiny snippets, interspersed with long stretches of almost hallucinatory wakefulness.

Nobody felt like taking the hard road to Taos on Saturday, so he was as isolated as if he were on the dark side of the moon. The glimpses of activity he noticed were just as alien in character to him.

Before noon, a small convoy of SUVs had arrived and wound their way up to John Elkfoot's house atop the mesa. An hour later, a panel truck arrived and a team of workmen began pulling parts out of the truck, stacking them near John's satellite dish. Almost immediately after the truck had arrived, the SUVs and the people in them left the mesa, heading off in different directions across the valley floor. One stopped at the far south end of the main drag and four people got out with bundles under their arms and spread out among the scattering of homes, knocking on doors and talking to the residents. He watched the tiny figure of one person approach his trailer, rattle the gate on the chain link fence that surrounded his property and then finally deposit something in his mailbox.

Late in the afternoon, a van with the logo of an Albuquerque television station pulled emerged from the mouth of the canyon and traveled past his sightline. Curiosity overcoming caution, Barry wriggled his way through the undergrowth until he could see the entire town through his binoculars. The van had stopped dead center on the main drag and two men got out. One walked into the Marguerita Bay Club while the other seemed to be looking over the abandoned NORAD tracking station. A few minutes later both of them met up again near the van, drove back to the NORAD site and extended a large transmitting tower from the roof of their vehicle. After twenty minutes, they retracted the tower, then opened the back of the van and started uncoiling thick black cables. They worked their way through the gates of the station and then disappeared inside the main facility building.

Barry ran scenarios over in his mind. In all the years he'd lived down there, he'd never seen this level of abnormal activity. His eye kept being drawn back to the odd structure in front of the pueblo he'd seen the night before. In the daylight, it had become apparent that the Estes Foundation had finally decided to come out from the shadows to reveal their true nature. The weird, shiny structure was a public declaration that the overlords from space had thrown off their disguises and if the final solution for their dominion over the earth hadn't already begun, it was only moments away. This towering object gave Barry mute testimony of its purpose, reflecting the light of a million alien suns.

Strange things went on for the rest of the day and well into the night. A midnight blue Lexus pulled into Shantis pueblo late in the day and a man in a well-tailored suit and a thick braid of hair got out. Ten minutes later, the faint sounds of a shouting match drifted up to him. Just before the sun went down, a black helicopter flew in from the south, raising a cloud of dust on the top of John's mesa, where workmen had been assembling a strange squat conglomeration of girders, poles and a seemingly fragile assemblage of aluminum panels that opened and closed like a metallic flower. An inordinately high volume of traffic went into and out of Angel's joint well into the late hours of the night. It was an easy guess that the town council was having an impromptu session. Barry recognized the bulldog shape and truculent stride of Corky as he walked up the street to Angel's bar, as well as Freddy Apodokas' beat up Ford truck and Randy Webster's even more weathered International Harvester.

Barry had to get down to the valley and investigate. Around eleven that night, he began hiking down the jeep track, arriving at the last stand of trees around one in the morning. Straight ahead was the pueblo, silent and dark. Aside from Bob and Reddi, Shantis tended to retire early, even on weekends. They lived busy lives that started at sunrise. Barry sat down in the shadows of the stand of cottonwood and waited for the Bay Club's neon sign to wink out and Angel's departure for home. By two thirty that Sunday morning, everyone in the valley seemed to be asleep and Barry had silently moved through town, reaching his compound and plucking the pamphlet left by ByteStream's advance team from his mailbox. Carefully, he entered his trailer. His brother had been there a couple of times since Barry's disappearance. There was a stack of mail on the kitchen counter, a bag of pretzels that mice had gotten into and empty beer bottles all over the place. Barry placed his hand on the refrigerator and felt the hum of the motor. He was happy to see that Jerry had been paying the bills; he needed electricity. He dropped through the trapdoor and into his tunnel. Sealed off from the world at large, he flipped on the lights in the tunnel and looked over the brochure.

"THE FUTURE IS HERE!" screamed at him in red letters against a painting of the vision of tomorrow that the Estes Foundation and its' flunky company ByteStream presented. Horrified, Barry flipped through page after page of bland, rigid uniformity. Houses and stores, looking as though they were stamped out in some giant mill press; a huge "campus', which was patently an indoctrination center and a world populated by lobotomized smiling idiots were presented in lavish four color printing. Another piece of paper fell out of the pamphlet. It was a personalized request for the Mosses to attend a town meeting at eleven in the morning on Labor Day at the Marguerita Bay Club. "All your questions will be answered. Big barbeque to follow."

"So, everything starts on Labor Day," Barry thought to himself. He turned off the light and huddled in the darkness, wondering what he could do.

"You people are nuts!" Dan raged. "Do you know how much effort and time I've put into this?" The tribal council had just informed the attorney that they'd reached an agreement with Ted Marquis without his help. During the course of that long afternoon in the piñon grove, Bob's big Boy and Ted had come up with a funded education program that would allow Shantis children who showed the aptitude for it to become programmers and developers while interning at ByteStream.

Mrs. Fields calmly wondered why the Arapahoe councilor was so furious. "We got what we wanted," she pointed out, "actually, more. It's almost an entitlement program."

"What about the fuckin' money?" Dan almost sobbed. "You could have had both. And publicity. You just screwed yourself."

"I've seen camera guys all over town," Reddi chimed in. "There's at least four different outfits roaming around. Some of them took my picture." He beamed at Dan. "they said I'm 'colorful'."

"Great," Dan replied. "There's a hot scoop. Colorful Indian found in Flyspeck, New Mexico. I'm sure the networks will lead with it." Not only was Dan upset over the loss of his potentially enormous contingency fee, he pointed out that this turn of events would sap some of his credibility.

"My connections with the networks are based on me being able to supply some good footage. You think any of them give a shit about some bootstrap program? They want to see the little guy standing up to an ogre like Ted Marquis!"

"Maybe they'll take pictures of my statue," Bob mused. Dan nearly slammed in to the chrome monstrosity as he tore out of the Pueblo, wrapped in dark thoughts and a tinted windshield.

Doctor Honneferan's suspicions were confirmed just as the weekend was about to roll around. The environmental reports on the air, soil and water of the Huernafano valley were delivered to him on Friday afternoon and after a quick review of the test results, he decided to visit the old Indian at the hospital. Unfortunately, the patient had disappeared again. The duty nurse had checked in on him at two in the afternoon, but when Honneferan stopped by at six, the room was empty.

"That's the most active coma patient I ever heard of."

Normally, he was one of those individuals who could remove all thought of work once they arrived home. And so it would have stayed if he hadn't run into a reporter he knew on Saturday night at the Kachina Club on Water Street. Janet Rivera worked for the number two rated news program in Santa Fe. She'd interviewed the doctor several times in the course of her career and they had formed a loose friendship, although Honneferan suspected any inquires into "how's business" where really fishing trips. Fortunately, she merely asked how his long weekend was shaping up. He shared vague plans of boating and cooking out and then volleyed the question back in her direction.

"Not much," she said, "I have to go to some little burg up north on Monday, so it's a another working weekend for me."

As soon as she said Mesa Azul, his entire demeanor changed. "Mesa Azul?" he asked cautiously, "what on earth could be going on up there?"

"I'm surprised you ever heard of the place," Janet laughed. "I'm a native and it took me an hour to find it on a map."

"Yeah, well. My job takes me everywhere." As nonchalantly as possible, he asked what the story was.

"Originally it was supposed to be a protest by some local Indians against ByteStream Information Systems. Exclusionary job practices." She shrugged, "the usual minority noise. Usually this sort of thing is a complete nothing story, but the big geek himself is there so the network thought a good pot shot at Ted Marquis would be worth a thirty second slot. I need all the network exposure I can get, so I volunteered to go there for a stand-up."

"Originally? How did the story change?" Honneferan's radar was starting to go off. Janet explained that Ted and the locals had worked their differences out and now it would merely be a local story announcing ByteStream's purchase of a piece of property and their intent to build a development campus there.

"They're also doing some 'gee-whiz' product launch," she concluded. "According to the press release we received this morning, 'ByteStream announces a revolution in the communications and entertainment industry'. I love hyperbole, don't you?"

Doctor Honneferan scrambled for an excuse to leave, walked casually to the exit of the restaurant and then ran wildly to his car. He needed to get ahold of the county registrar into the records office. Suddenly, he had to do some more research.

The Mayor of Mesa Azul was casually loping down the main drag of his town at around three in the morning that Sunday night, when something caught his eye. This wasn't very unusual as Buckeye was easily distracted. Since his duties were largely ceremonial, he had plenty of time to be distracted and very little that required his immediate attention. Besides, he enjoyed being distracted; he was open-minded in the sense that there was very little floating around in his head and such things as an interesting aroma, an odd sound or a quick movement in his periphery usually led to entertainment.

He veered from the track he was on and drifted into the shadow of the Marguerita Bay Club. There was a very narrow space between the bar and Hodel's store next door. The air in there was thick with the scent of human endeavor and riding just above that, barely perceptible was an acrid tang. Some bulky crouched shadow was making a soft scraping noise as he approached. Buckeye paused, sampling the air a little bit more. Another whiff of the high acrid aroma caused him to sneeze and when he did, the scraping sound stopped and the crouched figure froze. Whatever it was and Buckeye both played statue for a long count, then the figure changed shape. It was carefully turning around. Buckeye kicked his ears forward and took a quiet, careful step forward, then another. His tail started a tentative wag. "Shoo", came out of the darkness and Buckeye increased his pace, his tail picking up tempo as well.

Then he gave a sharp yelp of surprise as a rock clipped his shoulder. He turned quickly and ran back out into the street, finally stopping when he reached the walk on the far side of the tarmac. He was used to having rocks and dirt clods hurled at him and he took it in stride. It just meant that he was disturbing someone when they didn't want to be disturbed and he rarely took it personally. He settled down on his haunches next to the town's only streetlight and watched the space between the buildings for a good half an hour. Then the wind shifted and the smell of the rotten carcass of something or other drifted by from down near the creek. He turned and loped off, anticipating a dead fish or some other enticing fragrance to roll in.

Chapter Fifteen -
Barry's Last Stand.

"Barry?" John said in a mixture of shock and surprise.

For the past few weeks, John had been suffering a number of side effects to the stress he'd been under. Aside from renewing his nicotine Jones, he also had developed a severe case of acid stomach. This morning, he'd been rudely waken by a burning tide that scorched his esophagus so severely that it caused his throat to swell up and he'd sat up in bed, gasping for air. He looked at the bedside alarm and noted that it was only 4:30 in the morning.

"So much for sleeping in on a holiday," he thought to himself as he rolled out of bed. John adjourned to the kitchen where he drank half a bottle of water in hopes that it would dilute the acid wreaking havoc to his innards and then sat at the breakfast table while he waited for the coffee to finish brewing. Outside, the first reflected bands of light were just beginning to lessen the darkness beyond the window. He got dressed and then poured a cup of coffee to have on the patio while watching the sun come up.

Someone was crouching down by the receiver/relay scrambler ByteStream had just finished putting together near his transmitter dish. At first, he thought that it was one of the technicians, making sure that everything was in working order for today's unveiling, so he cheerfully muttered a quiet "Good morning".

Barry nearly panicked when he heard John's voice. Setting things up at Angel's had taken just a little longer than he'd anticipated and he'd had the devil of a time carrying his equipment to the plateau of the Mesa, which resulted in him being about an hour behind his time table. John's voice had come from behind him, so there was no chance that he could have seen the alarm that flashed on Barry's face. Barry slipped his transmitter into his shirt pocket and then put his hand on the Mauser in his waistband before straightening up. "Hello, John," he said with a shaky attempt at friendliness as he turned around and John recognized him.

"Where the heck have you been?" John asked as Barry walked towards him. Until his brother Jerry had made a few inquires about town, no one had even known that Barry was gone. Since then, the subject came up every now and again and speculation as to where the little nut had gone quickly became one of those standard gambits of conversation, like mentioning the weather. John offered Barry a cup of coffee and when Barry declined, he remembered the Moss fellow's curious paranoia regarding residual fingerprints, DNA traces and other assorted lunacies. "Don't worry," he said to Barry lightheartedly, "that gizmo you're looking at isn't jacked into the CIA or anything."

Barry cracked a smile and followed John inside to the kitchen. John kept up a combination patter of events Barry had missed and questions regarding where Barry had been. Barry, relaxed a little bit and slid the gun further inside his pants, bloused his shirt to cover the handle and sat at the table while John made some chorizo and eggs. While he appeared to be happily chewing the fat, Barry was actually sweating under his clothes. He felt as though he was in the belly of the beast or the mother ship.

When John had first arrived in Mesa Azul, Barry had, just as he did with any stranger, assumed the worst. John's openness about his previous career positions and absolutely ordinary behavior over the years had caused Barry to write him off as just another computer technocrat who'd suffered a case of burn out and run away from responsibility. Now, his original concerns locked back into place. The Rand Corporation, NASA, DOD; all of it was one blood red flag he'd chosen to ignore. The guy was good, Barry reflected. Even now, half of him wanted to relax, but his actions in the past few hours overrode any soft sentiment and he cogitated on how to escape John's surveillance without setting off alarms.

John, in all earnestness, was barely cognizant of Barry's presence. His mind was filled with the inevitable loss of his discovered hometown. This morning, Ted would have his little booster festival and get the residents completely sold on his vision and within a short time, everything he loved about this place would be gone. As an addition, he'd received a call from the hospital Doctor Pepper was supposed to be in on Saturday night, asking if he'd heard from the old shaman. The latest disappearance of the Indian had prompted him to spend most of Sunday cruising the various routes into and out of Santa Fe, hoping he'd catch site of the wily nut. Unfortunately, it seems as though the geezer had vanished into thin air. In the back of his mind, John had a vision of the poor old soul, dead in a culvert along the highway, covered by duckweed and skunk cabbage.

Barry joined John for a plate of eggs and then said he needed to poke around a bit more, check in on his friends and look at all the changes that had gone on since his absence. "Well," John said morosely, "nothing's changed except for people's outlooks and values." He held that thought for a long count and then added, "Yet."

Ted, the technologists and Sol came into the kitchen an hour or so later, hungry and full of excitement over the day's coming events. "I wish you'd get on board with this," Ted said to John. "Heck, the spirit of this town is the major attraction to me," he went on, "I'll make it my personal mission to keep the charm of the place intact."

John said little, other than to ask if everyone was through with their breakfast, he had dishes to clean.

"You're really being unfair," Janet told the exhausted health official slumped in the passenger seat of her Viper, tearing up Route 46 that morning, Mesa Azul bound.

"Jan," Honneferan said wearily, "trust me, if there was a story of any sort that merited being broadcast, I'd tell you."

He'd researched the county records for Huernafano County Saturday night, started making calls on Sunday and ran down a paper trail that dead-ended with one Steve Abrams. His voice mail contained the information that he was unreachable until later on in the week. On a hunch, he'd called ByteStream's offices in Seattle late in the day and was met by various automated messaging and call routing machines that in the best case, eventually handed him off to personal assistants who were adamant about not connecting him to anyone he needed to talk to until Tuesday. In between, he'd checked in with the hospital, hoping that the old medicine man had been found, called the State's EPA and CDC offices, as well as a couple of State's attorneys. So far, the only agency that shared his concerns was the CDC. The Environment office was completely flummoxed by his concerns, "maybe," Carolyn McFee, the one EPA official he was able to have an in-depth discussion with said, "but it's a natural condition. That's not really our mandate. Unless there's a serious environmental issue being created by manufacturing, construction or other human interdiction going on, we have nothing to say about it."

Finding himself effectively road-blocked, Honneferan finally decided to see if he could catch a ride with Janet Rivera the next morning and hopefully buttonhole Ted Marquis himself.

Janet's instinct for a real story was in overdrive. Nothing about her friend was ringing true. Something was gnawing at him and she was burning to find out what it was. Until Rich had given her a ring this morning, she assumed she was off on another waste of time. Getting a lot of short stand up color piece in the business slot of the news was not the type of thing a reporter needed to get into the big leagues. Still, Ted Marquis had such a dislike of the press that if she could grab even a single question and response from the guy, it would be a nice feather in her cap. Now she was running north with a man acting like someone had dropped a hot coal down his shorts. There was something juicy in the works; she just had to find out what it was.

"If I ever have something go off on time, on target and without some little pischer gumming up the works," Sol thought to himself, "I'll drop dead from shock." It was 11:30, a half-hour behind schedule and it finally looked as though Ted was going to be able to make his presentation.

Sol and two of the communications crew from ByteStream had shown up at the Marguerita Bay Club at nine, only to be greeted by the bartender and a bunch of other surly locals. At first, Angel refused to unlock the doors as a protest to ByteStream's seemingly unyielding viewpoint as to what their town would or wouldn't be in the future. As if that wasn't bad enough, this sort of confrontation on the main drag in town was guaranteed to attract attention and Sol noticed that a camera crew was walking towards the little group, adjusting lenses and checking their tape stock and sound levels.

Sol did some fast patter about discussing this all in more amenable surroundings, praised the ambience of the Bay Club and softened Angel up enough for him to unlock the doors. Sol scooted everyone inside as rapidly as possible and then confronted the cameramen. "Sorry boys, nothing to shoot right now. We're just having a little discussion about the logistics for the meeting." Then he slammed and locked the door behind him.

Unbelievably, the local gentry he had to deal with were upset over the proposed "World of Tomorrow". These guys actually liked living in a ramshackle hodgepodge of junk. As Sol listened, it grew on him that they just wanted a higher class of junk. It was easy enough to mollycoddle through. Whatever he promised them today was meaningless. Once ByteStream employees made up the largest section of the voter polls, Mesa Azul would turn in to exactly what the majority wanted and these beaners would be out on their collective ear.

"Fellahs," he said magnanimously, "I hear your concerns and believe me, ByteStream doesn't want to rock the boat. The flavor of your town is part of the reason we decided to build here. We're talking about improving life, not destroying it. This can all be worked out so that we're one big happy family."

A few more platitudes like that and he had them settled down and looking forward to the coming meeting.

While dealing with the local la Raza, Sol also had several other headaches parceled out to him in the same time frame. From a corporate viewpoint, this "town meeting" was being viewed as a product rollout for "RealStream" as they were calling their version of John Elkfoot's compression technology. They would do a live computer feed from the Bay Club to the main auditorium of their headquarters in Seattle, where several hundred employees, stockholders and reporters would watch the world's first high definition, digital streaming video come across without a single glitch or lag. At least, that was what everyone had their fingers crossed for.

This meant that the ByteStream team had to set up the cameras and microphones that would be used at the meeting. They interrupted Sol's negotiations with the town council to let him know there wasn't a spare circuit available in the breaker box at the Club. "Someone did some wiring recently," the tech whispered to him. "Actually, the circuits are overloaded. We got to find another electrical box." Sol sighed and asked Angel if they could tap into the trunk coming into the building. "Whatever, Ese," Angel shrugged. "I don't know from electrical. Just remember that if your boys fry themselves, I ain't liable."

Because cell phones didn't work in the valley, Sol had given the phone number of the Club to his assistant in Seattle who was supposed to be coordinating the presentation details at headquarters. Angel's phone seemed to ring every ten minutes, invariably for Sol and always containing a new little problem. Some health official had made a nuisance of himself the day before and Sol's assistant passed that information on. "And this is my problem, how?" he replied before slamming down the phone. More calls regarding the time lost while getting a test feed signal, the quality of lox that that been delivered as part of the buffet spread, and more minutiae until Sol was ready to beat his assistant over the head with the handset.

At ten thirty, the locals started streaming in. Angel got busy doling out coffee, soft drinks and ice tea, along with donuts and bagels. "Hey Angel!" Reddi Kilowatt complained, "this donut's stale! It's hard as a rock!"

"That's a bagel, ya dummy," Angel informed him. "ByteStream brought 'em in special."

"Geez," Reddi said, "they can take 'em out special too. Gimme a real donut."

Sol, in the meantime was figuratively banging his head against the wall over a new wrinkle. The presentation material that would be flashed behind Ted during his speech was completely out of sequence. The media group in Seattle that was going to stream video to a DiamondVision screen set up behind Ted had their cues bollixed up. Sol actually was the first person to use RealStream by setting up a hasty video conference in Seattle with the media group. "You've got fifteen minutes to get your shit together or we'll all be looking for work in an hour," was his sign off.

Doctor Pepper and Coyote had finally figured out a working relationship. The mere act of climbing out of the hospital bed was near agony for Coyote and he told Doc that he was going to retreat back into a coma. "Wait," Doc said anxiously, "just take a couple of steps so I can see how this works." While Coyote torturously lumbered about the room, the Doc monitored the behavior of the brain, figuring out what needed to be triggered or stimulated in order to move various muscle groups. After ten minutes, he asked Coyote to retreat back into the body's subconscious.

The Doc found himself trying to manage a lurching, whirling, top-heavy mass of flesh and bone. While he never caused the body to fall, it was a near thing. There was such a host of stimuli to manage that it took him a good half an hour before he could figure out how to keep the body on a level course and in constant forward motion. It was so difficult, he decided to dispense with attempting to maneuver the body into clothes and eventually walked it out of the building undiscovered, dressed only in a hospital gown.

Coyote had receded back into the darkness; receptive to none of the stimulus the body was receiving. Occasionally, he felt the Doc querying him but other than that, he felt as though he'd found a void, a pit of nonexistence and that suited him just fine.

Doctor Pepper slowly gained facility in operating the body. By the time they'd reached the outskirts of Santa Fe, walking was nearly second nature. His only concern at that point was the amount of abuse he was putting the body through. He could sense that the heartbeat and breathing were very irregular and as the temperature throughout the night dropped, he wondered how the body's core temperature was doing. Before sunrise, he'd developed a methodology of taking ten steps, then flashing quickly throughout the various systems of the body to check on heart rate, pulse, nervous system, essential nutrient and chemical levels and the external package.

The body's feet and legs were his biggest concern. Walking on pavement wore out the cotton slippers in just a few hours and by mid day Sunday, the soles of the feet were ragged and bleeding. Since the last thing he wanted was to be discovered and returned to anywhere but Mesa Azul, the Doc stayed away from roads entirely, cutting through fields and dried up washes, forests and scrub brush. The lower half of the torso was a mass of cuts, welts and bruises. Late in the day, as the first signs of dehydration became apparent, the Doc found a stream and with exceeding difficulty figured out how to get the body to drink.

It took an hour for him to get it upright again. The Doc had a strange sense of urgency, as if he were under some sort of deadline. He felt that something wanted him back in Mesa Azul before noon of the next day. He saw a reflection of the body as he finally straightened up and thought to himself, "the way I'm treating my body; I'm not sure that I want to get back into it. I'm going to be in a lot of pain."

Right now, all he could do was look at his former self as a vehicle, a means to get back to his valley before time ran out.

"Sweet mother of God," Honneferan said in disbelief. Janet had taken the turnoff for Huernafano canyon at white-knuckle speed and hardly had they regained their equilibrium when he saw Doctor Pepper walking mechanically down the roadway. Janet tromped on the brakes and left a fifty-foot skid mark, then backed up to where the Indian plodded along obviously.

Honneferan leaped out of the car and ran to the old man. The figure kept walking until the health official grabbed hold of him and impeded further movement. Honneferan was shocked that the patient was even alive. Feet ravaged, half his body an oozing wound and apparently suffering from both hypothermia and dehydration; for all intents and purposes he seemed to be in some sort of fugue state, a walking coma for lack of a better term. He was at a loss as to what he ought to do. The eyes didn't respond to anything, and nothing the Doctor said elicited any sort of response.

"Rich," Janet said from the car, "what ever you're going to do, do it. I've got twenty minutes tops before I'm going to miss any shot at Marquis."

"Jesus, Janet, show a little compassion!" Honneferan frantically ran options through his head. Santa Fe was out. Taos was nearly an hour away as well. This man needed emergency attention as quickly as possible. Mesa Azul was his only viable choice. They had to have at least basic medical supplies there and then he could call from a landline for an evac helicopter.

"You're not going to put that wreck in here?" Janet protested after Honneferan picked up the Indian and carried him to the car. "This is Corinthian leather!"

"Shut up and drive."

Gil Mueller looked at his watch again. He hated on-air talent. When he saw his assignment slip on Saturday, he cringed. Janet Rivera was without a doubt the bottom of the barrel. Self-centered, bitchy and unprofessional, the biggest assets she brought to broadcast journalism was a nice set of legs and an uncanny ability to shift blame. Somehow, if she was late and they missed their feed, it would be his fault. He climbed out of the van for another look up and down the main street of Mesa Azul. The whole weekend had been a wash. Sent down early by the network in hopes that they could pick up a good protest and lots of shots of Ted Marquis squirming under pressure, that story had fallen apart and now he'd been cooling his heels in this burg just to give ByteStream some free air-time under the guise of journalism. Now it looked like that might even be a go-bye thanks to Ms. Rivera's inability to be anywhere on time.

He'd sent his soundman into the building where they were having the meeting, with word to let him know if anything interesting was happening. Del had popped out once to say that ByteStream was doing the usual song and dance about technology being the nation's greatest asset and assorted homilies along those lines. "You're not missing anything. It's as boring as everything else in this town."

While chewing this over and coming to a slow burn regarding Janet Rivera's tardiness, one of the few locals not attending the town hall meeting walked up to him.

"Hi," Barry said, "are you from the television network?"

"An affiliate, yeah," Gil said, pointing to the station's call letters on the van.

"So, you guys have cameras inside?"

Gil explained that this was strictly chicken feed, a stand-up wraparound worth 30 seconds on the national news, if their reporter showed up. "You know, 21st century comes to Smallville, USA."

Gil had been a shooter for 20 years and had gotten used to the inevitable lens hunger the sight of a camera or news truck created. He'd come to believe that the mere appearance of news people altered the story they were supposed to cover. When Barry told him that there might be more of a story than he thought, Gil shrugged it off. It was a common comment; everyone had a beef that they wanted the whole world to hear.

The sight of Barry's automatic pistol pointing at his gut convinced Gil to take this fellow's concerns a little more seriously. Barry instructed him to get his camera and head into the Club.

"What the hell?" said Kevin MacCleary, the engineer at Channel 2 in Santa Fe who was monitoring the feed signal from Mesa Azul. The feed finally started and he was surprised to see Gil doing some sort of cinema verité, walking camera bullshit. Where on earth Janet happened to be was another question entirely. He saw Gil's hand come into the shot and open the door of the Club. Kevin groaned. This was first year UCLA film school footage, totally useless. Things got worse the second they entered the hall where the meeting was being held. The white levels dropped and the picture went black, the audio was obviously coming from the microphone on the camera and the sound levels were all over the map. Thanks to the anomalies of the place they'd sent Gil and Janet to; he couldn't even tap Gil through his earpiece to find out what was up.

He could hear a back and forth between Gil and someone else. Gil got his light readings adjusted and the picture came back in. The camera was shaking a little, but focused on Ted Marquis at a podium with a projection screen behind him. The head of Bytestream had noticed the cameraman at the back of the room and said something about no questions from the press, and then some bald guy loomed in front of the lens and told Gil he needed to wait outside.

Kevin turned from the monitor and began sorting through the sticky notes he had plastered all over the engineering console. Somewhere he'd written down the phone number for the Marguerita Bay Club. He had just found it when something on the audio coming through the monitor speakers caused him to look back at the screen. Something about a bomb.

He quickly punched in the network's news desk and told them to get ready for a real story.

"Just sit still," Barry continued as he pulled the remote triggering device from his shirt pocket. He was impressed at just how well he could command the crowd. When he first announced that there was a bomb in the building, everyone parted like the Red Sea. He and the cameraman were blocking the door, so all anyone could do was try to run either towards the bar or into the Acapulco Room. The second he'd barked out his first command, it was as if he'd frozen time. Everyone had become petrified, locked in place and afraid to even blink.

Barry gauged everything in his peripheral vision. He didn't want to recognize his neighbors, for fear that the same misgivings he'd had over the kidnapping of Irene would somehow weaken his resolve. He kept repeating in the back of his mind that these were not his neighbors. They were agents or replicants; the first wave of domination he'd struggled so hard for so long against. His eyes stayed on the podium, where the lead technocrat stared back at him in disbelief.

"Move around and point that thing at me," he instructed the cameraman, "but don't block my view or I'm setting things off right now." He ran his thumb over the broadcast button of his remote for emphasis. Gil turned around and backed up down the aisle until he had Barry in a three-quarters shot, terrified townspeople filling the edges of his screen. He though to himself that it was a good shot, the network would be tossing wood if they were getting this. He regretted that he didn't have a second camera in there for reaction shots.

"Barry!" John Elkhorn's voice echoed across the room. Without looking for the source, keeping his eyes locked on Ted Marquis, Barry told John to keep still.

"Listen, Barry," John went on unheeding, "I don't know what you think you're doing but..."

"Shut up, Ese!" Angel interrupted, "you want to kill us all?"

John calmly said, "No one's going to die, Angel." Then he resumed talking to Barry. "Listen man, you know that any kind of broadcast signal just doesn't work down here. The waves get messed up."

"You want to take that chance, John?" Barry said casually.

"Yeah," John said as he began to move from the front of the room towards Barry, "I do." Gil, operating on instinct swung his camera around and located John just as Bob's Big Boy tackled him.

"Don't go nuts, Barry," Bob shouted in a panic. "Nobody's gonna do nothin'!"

Barry was pleased at the cooperation he was receiving. Now that John was pinned down, he felt reassured that no one else was in the mood for heroics. As he'd always suspected, the aliens were a devious and cowardly lot, operating in the shadows and afraid of confrontation. Well, Barry thought to himself, that all ends here and now.

"Turn that camera back on me," he said and then began to tell what was left of the unconquered world just what the Estes Foundation, ByteStream and the aliens on earth had in store for mankind.

"Fucking GOLD!" cried the news director for 24 Hour Cable News. "Jesus! Can you believe this stuff?"

Whatever else was going on in the world didn't matter. They had human drama of unbelievable proportions flooding the airwaves. All the networks and news outlets had picked up this feed and interrupted their regular broadcast to put it on the air. All over the country, stations were flooding the switchboard in Santa Fe and Albuquerque trying to get stringers and affiliates on the road to Mesa Azul.

"I just wish they had a second camera in there," the director moaned.

Something happened the instant Janet's Viper emerged from the shadows of the canyon. Doctor Pepper and Coyote felt eternity bend and warp around them. Coyote had his darkness invaded by a flash of brilliance so intense he felt as though he'd been hurled into a sun and then an instant later he sensed infinity reform around him. He hovered over a red sports car that blasted up a two-lane blacktop with three passengers crammed in it.

Doc had the same sensation but the result was much less envious. He found himself surfacing in a sea of pain. His heart hammered irregularly and breathing was a labored effort. Everything else was complete agony. Vaguely he heard someone saying, "hang on, old timer. Everything's going to be okay."

Honneferan was unsure whether he was relieved or not that the old man had regained consciousness. Without any medical equipment or diagnostic tools, all he could do until the reached Mesa Azul was monitor the shaman's condition by checking his pulse and breathing. The old guy didn't seem able to focus on him and kept muttering something about a coyote. He urged Janet to step on it.

Moments later they burst out of the canyon and flashed by the outskirts of Mesa Azul. It seemed like a ghost town, completely deserted. "Where the hell is everyone?" Honneferan wondered aloud. Janet, glancing at the clock on the dash console said, "probably at the Margie's Beach Club or whatever. The damned meeting started a half hour ago."

They pulled up next to the Channel Two news van. "Fuck!" the reporter hissed, "where the hell is Gil?"

"Never mind," Honneferan said while jumping out of the car, "I need to find a phone and an emergency kit. This man is dying." He ran across the road to Hodel's and discovered it was locked. Frantically, he started banging on the door.

Doctor Pepper's appeals to Coyote for help seemed to go unanswered for a moment. The spirit was still trying to reorient himself to what happened and where he was. He could feel the Doc's urgent pleading, almost as a pressure surrounding him and bearing him towards the old man's consciousness. "Help me walk," The Doc cried. "Give me strength."

Honneferan had moved down the street, away from Angel's club and Janet was tracing the cable lines from the van into the satellite tracking station in hopes of locating her wayward cameraman, so no one saw the broken down old Indian in a torn up hospital gown miraculously rise up and out of the car and begin crossing the street to the Marguerita Bay Club.

A million or more homes watched Barry's tirade about alien plots, automatons and replicants. People sat mesmerized, waiting in uncomfortable anticipation for the instant his finger pressed the trigger of his remote device, some cringing and some looking forward to the carnage that would be beamed right into their living rooms. News directors around the country sat on the ten-second kill switch, having an internal ethics argument regarding whether or not they were violating the final edge of the envelope between journalism and complete, heartless voyeurism. Most came to the conclusion that they'd wait and see how bad it was. "Hell," one news director told his station owner, "the cameraman will get blown up with everyone else. All we'll get to see is the flash. People can stomach that."

Inside the building itself, Barry's audience was too preoccupied with their own final panicky thoughts to really pay a lot of attention to what their executioner had to say. Angel, after mentally acknowledging that Barry had finally hopped the trolley, looked across the room at the old photograph of his brother, Ruby and himself and was filled with a strange nostalgia. He hoped his grandfather's view of eternity would prove to be true, it would be nice to see Ruby again.

Bob's Big Boy calculated that every single Shantis in existence, aside from Doctor Pepper was in that room, in a few moments, they would be nearly extinct. "Too bad the Doc isn't a younger man," he thought to himself.

John, pinned down by his assailant, still believed that Barry's remote wouldn't work. Barry had explained in painstaking detail how he'd buried plastic explosives all around the outside of the Club, then wired it all to the junction box, with a receiver waiting for one short signal from the garage door opener he held in his hand to set it off. He'd also mined the relay scrambler on top of the mesa. Sighing, he hoped Barry would finish his spiel shortly, push the button and then maybe Bob's Big Boy would get off him.

Everyone else in the room seemed occupied with their own thoughts of eternity. As Coyote entered the Club with the Doc, their pleas into the cosmos overwhelmed him. Never in all his existence had he felt such a collective terror envelope him. And never before had he felt such a deep and passionate empathy for these strange creatures, these brave and willful beings. They clung to their identities like it was a single strand of gossamer thread stretched over the yawning abyss of nothingness. Now that he knew what it was to be human, his objectivity had been eradicated.

He also knew John was wrong. The low frequency signal that Barry's garage door opener would send out couldn't be impeded, distorted or interrupted by the magnetic fields and iron deposits of the valley. Circuits would be completed and all these souls would become nothing but memories. He needed to get inside Barry's head and stop him.

Barry felt the probing of Coyote without knowing exactly what it was and fought against it. He suspected it was a last ditch effort on the part of the aliens to stop him, to sap his will and paralyze his actions. Coyote was shocked at this reaction to his gentle touch on the man's consciousness and quickly backed out into the air of the room. Taking in everything, including Barry's shriek of "Stop fucking with me!" the spirit fled into the collapsing body of the old shaman and plied his last trick.

As with anything else that has ever occurred in the course of human events, the details changed with the telling afterwards. In the end, the only objective record available to historians and researchers was the broadcast itself, and even then, a number of skeptics would say that some sort of digital effects were used. There seems to be an unspoken rule of thumb that for every ten believers, there must be one doubting Thomas.

That record of events was played incessantly for at least a week on every broadcast outlet that could get its hands on it and the numbing repetition of the footage quickly robbed it of it's power. At the time it happened however, it was mesmerizing.

Gil Mueller's camera had stayed focused on Barry until the door opened behind him. By reflex alone, Gil shifted focus past Barry to the ancient and damaged figure that came hobbling in. Weak, bloody and staggering, this bizarre apparition in a shredded hospital gown paused just behind Barry and then froze, as if it's final ember of life had fled. Barry's expression changed, Gil refocused on him long enough to catch the alarmed look that passed over his countenance and then his scream of outrage. As Barry's thumb began it's descent towards the button on the remote, the ravaged figure behind him flared with light, as if some sort of Saint Elmo's fire had enveloped him. It spiraled about him for an instant and then ran like liquid down his right arm, coalescing around his hand and forming a sizzling ball of pure energy. The hand then lashed out in a blinding fury, grabbing Barry's hand and the remote control. Light so brilliant it caused everyone to blink and television sets around the country to experience a millisecond of absolute, humming whiteness exploded from the old Indian's grasp and both he and Barry collapsed in the aisle.

Everyone nearby, frozen in disbelief and afraid to even approach the two still figures saw their hands fall away from each other, revealing a smoking, melted and twisted garage door opener.

Chapter Sixteen -

In Which Everything is Tidied Up and The Sun Sets After All.

Nearly stepping off a precipice only to have an unexpected gust of air blow one back onto safe ground has the residual effect of causing one to walk around in a glazed state for a while. Mesa Azul was no exception to this principle and for a couple of days after Barry Moss' near destruction of the residents of Huernafano county people were awfully quiet and introspective.

This was a huge disappointment to the hordes of reporters that flooded the place over the next week. While the video of Doctor Pepper's miraculous intercession was played over and over, journalists tried in vain to get some good sound bites out of the locals, winding up with things like "you got me" and "I have no idea". Two tabloid reporters, cooling their heels in the Marguerita Bay Club renamed the town Mesa Azombie, one of them declaring, "you'd think we could get at least the standard 'I'm shocked, he was such a quiet guy - kept to himself' response."

Before the week was out, publicists for ByteStream announced that while the company would go ahead with its minority intern incentive; it had cancelled plans to build a development center in the little town. When asked if the decision was based on the events of Labor Day, corporate spokesmen stated emphatically that their decision was based on environmental concerns, not the character of the town.

Exactly what environmental concerns these might be were never addressed. Once the crisis in Angel's bar was over and people were busy sorting themselves out, Ted Marquis was approached by Doctor Honneferan.

"Lithium?" Ted said in confusion.

"Yes," Honneferan said. "The levels of lithium in the water, ground and air increase dramatically near the springs north of the Pueblo. While the government has no 'standard' of acceptable levels and couldn't stop you from building in this area, I think you ought to be aware of the potential health hazards you're facing."

Honneferan explained the basic properties and behavior of lithium, along with its prevalence in the environment in Mesa Azul. "It's a naturally occurring metal that seems to have been leeched out by the spring up there. North of the Pueblo, it even exists in low levels in the air itself."

Ted, amazed, speculated, "you're telling me that this whole town is doped up?"

"That's a little harsh," Honneferan said, "but essentially, you're correct. This whole valley gets its' water from artesian wells. While the lithium levels drop the further from the springs one gets, there is still enough in the water for it to act as a chemical agent, reducing anxiety and mania."

"Great," Ted said, sadly. "I was going to spend millions of dollars just so I could get high." Honneferan reassured Ted that it was a fluke that they'd even discovered the presence of the drug. "The poor old Indian camped out next to the springs tipped us off."

That poor old Indian had been evacuated by Flight for Life back to his now overly familiar bed in Santa Fe. While he had passed out during the final moments of his encounter with Barry Moss, he never slipped back into a coma. His condition was brought on by extreme exhaustion, hypothermia, dehydration and blood loss. An injection of epinephrine directly into his chest moments after he arrived in the emergency room stabilized his heart, which was near collapse and he was put on a battery of IV drips. Before evening he was awake and alert.

The Doc turned out to be the real payout for the press, with the rest of the Shantis people coming in a close second. Completely naïve and without guile, he soon became a minor celebrity throughout the country and a major inspiration to various fuzzy thinking new age spiritualists. Soon Shantis pueblo became a point of pilgrimage for crystal gazers and aura fondlers from all over the world.

Along with the true believers came the hucksters. It's hard not to make money off of people's need for something to believe in and a number of new enterprises quickly sprang up around the events and principle characters involved in the Labor Day spectacle. A well-respected publisher talked Doctor Pepper into writing; actually, ghost-written, a book about his journey into the realms of the spirit. "Across the Universe" rocketed to the top of the non-fiction bestseller list and eventually was published in fourteen languages. "Shantism", founded by ex-New Mexico State University undergraduates Carl Lumley and Troy Derlinger, became one of the fastest growing new religions in the United States. Carl's book, "Acceptable Mysteries", was viewed as the sacred testament of this order.

The rest of Shantis Pueblo profited from the Doc's notoriety as well. Dan Bucknuts, seeing opportunity unfold on his 36-inch screen soon after arriving home in Denver, immediately grabbed his still unpacked bags and hightailed it back down I-25, arrived the day after the dust had settled. Even before all the reporters and stringers had arrived, he'd incorporated Shantis Pueblo as a business entity, with its primary subdivision, "Blue Bus Enterprises" handling all licensing issues. Reddi Kilowatt's iconographic effort "Sippy" was trademarked and copyrighted and the formerly noisome image found itself emblazoned on an ever-increasing number of products.

The most popular item that carried the S.I.P. hallmark was "Blue Mesa Spring Water". Tapped from an artesian well towards the south end of town, it had just enough lithium in it to soothe jangled nerves and became the number one mineral water in the United States. Before a year had passed, they'd built a bottling facility that employed forty people. Trucks began moving product out of the valley five days a week.

All this new activity and industry swelled local coffers. Angel changed his business strategy a bit, converting the Marguerita Bay Club into a hotel with the Club on the first floor. It had 60 rooms and usually ran to around 80% occupancy. Angel did get to indulge in his neon fetish as well as his penchant for murals, although rather than garish artistic impressions on the exterior of the building, he had each room personalized as a different tropical beach; the "Tiki Tavi Honeymoon Suite" being the most popular. While he may have made a mistake in hiring Camille Ryland-Bowles as his muralist, the profusion of obscene blossoms amidst sun drenched beaches and azure waters struck most guests as highly amusing.

Even the Mayor of Mesa Azul discovered notoriety. Every reporter that arrived in town to write or broadcast about the fantastic Labor Day event made more than a passing reference to Buckeye; he even appeared on the cover of Time magazine. In the ensuing interest, a number of people made offers to buy the dog, which were turned down not only because it would deprive the township of their chief executive, but also because no one owned him. Buckeye was just some mutt that showed up in town and stayed. Quit a few debates went on in Angel's bar over who slapped the moniker Buckeye on him in the first place. It happened so long ago, know one could quite recall. Buckeye's station in life improved even more after the first kidnap attempt. A fellow from Los Angeles, anxious to build a television series around the dog, after unsuccessfully trying to purchase the Mayor went ahead and snatched him. After that, Buckeye discovered he was being bedded down in various houses around town every night.

While Buckeye never went to Hollywood, the town itself, or at least a watered down simulacrum, did. A series called "Miracle Valley" was hurried into production and a number of the prominent Azulians got to watch their lives become warped by the clumsy efforts of "dramedy" writers for twelve episodes until the show was cancelled.

Everyone in the county seemed to be profiting from the groundswell of interest in their little corner of the world; everyone but Steve Abrams. The single largest property owner in Huernafano county, he also happened to own the areas with the highest concentration of lithium to be found. State health official Richard Honneferan contacted Steve Abrams the same day, actually hours after Steve had received a personal phone call from Ted Marquis informing him that ByteStream no longer had any interest in purchasing his property. "According to the State health office," Ted chuckled happily while picturing Abrams on the other end of the line bashing his head against the desk, "your property is possibly one of the most naturally toxic pieces of real estate on earth." Getting a phone call from the man responsible for Steve's downfall allowed Abrams to vent his spleen, unfortunately, Honneferan was not the type of person to allow himself to be abused at random. After listening politely to Steve's aspersions on his character, parentage and sexual proclivities, Honneferan wished him luck, hung up, and then dialed the county clerk's office.

"Gene," he said to an acquaintance of his in the title office, "I'm going to be sending you down an environment analysis of several adjoining properties you've got on record. I'd like to have it attached to the abstract, along with an explanation of what prolonged exposure to lithium levels above one point five milligrams per liter does. Can you make it part of the permanent abstract of each property?" He smiled at the response, "Great! We've done a great service for the public trust."

Within months, Steve Abrams filed for bankruptcy, was disowned by his father and eventually found work as an assistant manager of a Checker Auto Parts warehouse in Adobe Wells, Texas. He never realized promotion due to his bad customer relations skills.

Possibly the only person in the valley unaffected by these events was John Elkfoot. Relieved that Ted had abandoned his plans for the Huernafano area, he could accept the incremental changes that did occur. The town retained its character and while traffic, noise and the populace increased a bit, the eccentricity of the place was intact. Just about the only thing that made him sad was the Shantis' purchase of the Moss brothers property and the removal of Barry's compound. Jerry had no compulsion about selling out; Barry's nationally televised rant had increased interest in his pamphlets, tracts and books. Jerry relocated to Santa Fe and opened a mail order publishing house; the bedrock being his institutionalized brother's works, but adding on quite a selection of material regarding covert governments, aliens and UFOs, as well as survivalist manuals and paramilitary books.

"There sure a lot of nuts with disposable income," he told John on his last day in the valley. After government agents had scoured the compound for addition armaments and explosive devices, Jerry was free to pack up all the left over material. He had a trailer stuffed to capacity with his brother's investigative files.

"Did they even look at any of this stuff?" John asked.

"Not really," Jerry said, opening the cooler he'd been resting his feet on and fishing out a beer. "State's attorney showed up a couple of days after Barry popped his cork with a subpoena and wanted to bag and tag anything relevant to their prosecution. You should have seen her face when she got a gander at the amount of stuff he'd collected. Looked like she'd just sat on pepper. I felt bad for her and gave her a bunch of his pamphlets. I guess that was enough to convince a jury he was missing a few sandwiches from the lunchbucket."

Curiously, Barry never raised a peep during the State's sanity hearing. While he had initially been charged with kidnapping, public endangerment, reckless disregard for the public safety, attempted murder and even terrorism; the Justice Department quickly washed their hands of the whole thing and the State's prosecution was downgraded to a sanity hearing. The first day was carried on the Justice Channel, a cable network that put cameras in the courtrooms of sensational trails, but when it became apparent that Barry had no desire to use the witness stand as a bully pulpit for his colorful worldview, they dropped the rest of the coverage. He wound up being parked down at a state facility in Albuquerque until such time as the State's psychiatrists felt he no longer was a danger to himself or the public.

"You know," Larry said after his final gulp of beer, "he's happier down there than I've ever seen him. He's actually a pleasure to talk to. Funny thing though," he tossed the empty into the pile of refuse left over from packing and walked around to the cab of the truck, "when I saw him at the hospital right after they'd charged him, he was a different guy. The lights were all on upstairs, you know?"

John found it curious as well. He thought about it and figured that possibly with the act of annihilation Barry had assumed he'd completed, resigning himself to eternity and then discovering he was still knocking around the crust of this old earth, had blown all the demons out of him. "I guess," John said out loud, then shook Jerry's hand and watched him pull out and head off down the road towards Santa Fe.

The buffalo grass had grown as long as it was going to; the seed heads had become imbedded in the fur of passing critters and the stalks now turned silvery, dusted with frost in the chill mornings. The aspen groves up on the slopes of the Sangre di Cristos were blazing yellow ornaments among the deep green mantle of evergreens and silver meadows and the cottonwoods down by the creek were orange and gold. Most of the town had turned out to watch or lend a hand as the collective cattle herd was driven down from the summer high pastures to the valley and scattered to the private fenced grazing along the east side of the Huernafano. John ached from a long day in the saddle and happily settled in a deck chair on the patio. He half-heartedly contemplated what to make for dinner while watching the final rays of the sun outline the edges of Los Hermanos to the west.

"Yippee kye yo, cowboy," a familiar voice said.

John kept his eyes on the mountains and the sky. The clouds over the peaks seemed to have caught a fire deep within them; the luminance fading to a purple around the edges like dying coals. "Funny," John said to his surprise visitor, "I thought you'd gone for good."

"What a thing to say," Coyote tried to sound crestfallen, but failed miserably.

John was trying to think whether he'd drunk out of anyone else's canteen or water bottle that day. When word of the lithium content in the local water had been passed on to the residents of the valley, he'd had a micro filter water purification system put in at the pump head of his well. He scrupulously changed the filters every six weeks. Since installing the system, his life had been remarkably Coyote free.

Coyote, easily accessing John's thoughts, chuckled. "So, I'm an hallucination, eh?"

"An auditory one, anyway."

"Hey, all you have to do is turn around to get the full impact," Coyote suggested.

"I'll pass, thanks." The words had barely left John's lips when Coyote rematerialized in front of him. John groaned.

"Huh," Coyote grumped, "talk about being gracious. I bet if I showed up at Doctor Pepper's doorstep, he'd be doing back-flips."

John moved his hand expansively over the valley below, "Well, there you go. More gracious company awaits."

Coyote shook his head. "I'm afraid it doesn't work that way. In all of creation, you're the only person that can actually see me. Why do you think I keep coming back for more abuse?"

"I just figured you were a masochist." John got up and walked inside, the ancient spirit trailing behind him. "I wonder how I got so lucky?"

"Just the way things work out, pal," Coyote told him while trying to imitate a solid figure sitting on one of the kitchen chairs. He watched John poke around in the refrigerator for a moment or so. "Hey, want me to clue you in on a secret of the universe?"

"Only if there's a book in it." John had just met the guy assigned to ghost write the Doc's revelatory tome. Spirituality and the secrets of the cosmos were a profitable enterprise, it seems. He started peeling the dried outer husk of a yellow onion over the sink. He felt like some fresh pico di gallo to bank his hunger pangs for a little while.

"You know why those books sell?" Coyote asked. John shrugged while slicing the onion.

"Because people want answers to everything."

"Yeah, well," John agreed, "that's pretty obvious, don't you think?" Any further commentary by John was choked off at the sight of a fat slice of onion levitating up from the cutting board. It continued to rise until it was at John's eye level, then the rings separated and drifted apart from one another. A stack of expanding rings hung in the air just an arm's length from him.

"Here's the secret," Coyote's voice emanated from the vicinity of the possessed onion, "there are no real answers." One of the smaller rings slipped into the center of another ring and they began to slowly spin on different axes.

Before John could interrupt, Coyote went on. "You've decided that I'm merely an hallucination brought on by lithium, even though lithium doesn't create hallucinations. And, in spite of the fact that you've always had filters on your taps, so the only exposure you'd even have to lithium since you first moved here would be when you're taking a shower. Still, it's your answer for me and it makes you happy so you buy into it."

The onion rings' rotation had increased in speed so that they resembled a gyroscope hovering in the air. The other rings then began to orbit around the central core. Coyote triggered minute particles of water within them to separate into hydrogen and oxygen, and then caused the oxygen to ignite, creating tiny solar flares that erupted along the edges of the rings.

"It's essentially no different than the explanation I've come up with as to why you, alone among everything in the cosmos, can see me. The way I figure it," Coyote went on while manipulating other ions within the oxygen flare, changing the color of the flames, "you and I are alike. We both observe and come to conclusions. We don't throw out meaningless questions and wait for answers."

"You're the thing that's always been," John said, flailing blindly while looking for the right words to explain his sense of the archaic being. "You keep telling me you've been here since there even was a here; that you were present at the birth of creation."

The little universe of onion rings now began to tip on a larger central axis, every piece retaining it's own movement within the sphere of the larger unseen pole that maneuvered it all.

"An assumption on my part," Coyote glibly admitted. "I came into being at the same time the plane of existence I reside within was formed." He caused the onionverse to waggle a bit, accentuating his point.

"At the same time, I have no assurances that what is now has always been or will ever be." He shifted the axis of his aerial creation and reversed the rotation of all the rings. "We could easily be a layer around one point of creation and be surrounded by another."

"It's too late in the day for metaphysics," John finally replied, breaking his gaze from the onion built galaxy in front of him. He found a tomatillo and diced it up.

"That's what I've been saying forever!" Coyote happily agreed, collapsing the onion galaxy back on to the cutting board. John wrinkled his nose at the burnt and caramelized rings and scraped them off then board and into the sink. He began mincing some garlic. While he continued chopping and slicing, Coyote talked about his experiences inside the Doc, along with the curious sensation that he'd been used as a pawn for something much larger and more omnipotent than he was. By the time he finished his narrative, John had finished his dip and was scooping it up with tortilla chips.

"This leaves no impression on you whatsoever, does it?" Coyote huffed.

"What do you want me to say?" John asked between bites. "That the universe is random and meaningless? That Sartre was right?"

"Who?" Coyote asked.

John gave him a freshman overview of existentialism. Coyote laughed. "I bet he was a fun guy to hang around with."

"To me," Coyote said earnestly, "there is a pattern to things. I just can't make out what it is. I could be completely wrong though."

"You should write a book," John laughed. "'The Spirits Are Stupid'."

"Okay, wise guy, what do you think?"

John munched contemplatively and slowly walked back out onto the patio. The clouds to the west had lost much of their fire, only a little russet, like gold flakes scattered in the bottom of a mining pan. The sky was now deep velvet, drifting into blue and then turquoise just behind the mountains. A large moon sat to the east and shed cold light across the mesa.

He looked down on the twilight of Mesa Azul. Bob's Big Boy and a few other Shantis were walking up the road from the pueblo towards the Marguerita Bay Club. Angel had already started construction of his hotel over the old club and they had to wind their way sinuously between the clutters of scaffolding. Camilla Ryland-Bowles stood at her front gate, whistling for the Mayor and Corky Gonzales interrupted the calm of the fall evening with the rattling cacophony of his corrugated metal garage door as he closed up shop for the night. All across the valley floor, lights were glowing and chores and meals were attended to.

Finally, John addressed the question. "What I think doesn't really matter either," he said. "It's what I feel that counts. And what I feel like is a grilled steak."

"Funny," Coyote said contentedly, "you don't look like a steak."

John noticed that Coyote had taken on the shape of a gigantic T-bone.

The stars shone on and the earth continued to turn and the night would end with the morning.

And so we go from one point to another.

www.ingramcontent.com/pod-product-compliance
Lightning Source LLC
Chambersburg PA
CBHW050528260626
47157CB00004B/1512